THE DARKEST GATEWAY

D1566385

BOOKS BY JERI WESTERSON

Crispin Guest Medieval Noir Mystery Series

*Veil of Lies**

*Serpent in the Thorns**

*The Demon's Parchment**

*Troubled Bones**

*Blood Lance**

*Shadow of the Alchemist**

The Silence of Stones

A Maiden Weeping

Season of Blood

The Deepest Grave

Traitor's Codex

Cup of Blood, a prequel to *Veil of Lies*

Booke of the Hidden Series

Booke of the Hidden

Deadly Rising

*Shadows in the Mist**

*The Darkest Gateway**

Historical Fiction

Though Heaven Fall

Roses in the Tempest

Native Spirit, writing as Anne Castell

*available as a JABberwocky edition

THE DARKEST GATEWAY

BOOK FOUR IN
THE BOOKE OF THE HIDDEN SERIES

JERI WESTERSON

Published by JABberwocky Literary Agency, Inc.

The Darkest Gateway

Copyright © 2019 by Jeri Westerson

All rights reserved.

This paperback published in 2019 by JABberwocky Literary Agency, Inc.

Cover design by Mayhem Cover Creations

This is a work of fiction. All of the characters, organizations, and events portrayed in this novel are either products of the author's imagination or are used fictitiously.

Paperback ISBN: 978-1-625674-25-8

Ebook ISBN: 978-1-625674-23-4

For more, visit **BOOKEoftheHIDDEN.com**

For Craig, who always says, "Write the bestselling book!"
no matter how wacky the idea.

PART ONE

"You mortal men know nothing of, whose name we loathe to utter. You will need to dig down deep, so deep, to come on them. Who got us into this fix? You're to blame."

—*Faust*, Johann Wolfgang von Goethe

CHAPTER ONE

THE THING ABOUT the Booke of the Hidden was its vicious element of surprise. You never knew what would come out of it or when, and I think the Booke took pleasure in the chaos it created with maximum terror potential.

In other words, the Booke was a dick.

I'd never heard of it until I'd moved to Maine, to the little village of Moody Bog. When I tore into that wall in my eighteenth-century shop, I had no idea I'd find it. And what it meant to open it. And that I'd had a history here in Moody Bog that I hadn't remembered until the spell making me forget was broken. How screwed up was that?

But here I was. Proud owner of *Strange Herbs & Teas* and pretty sure that it was all for nothing because of this Booke literally hovering over everything I did. Demons, gods, creatures of the night causing terror and death—and *my* job to put it all to rights. There was no instruction manual for this.

At least I wasn't alone. There was the demon of the Booke, my coven, an ex-boyfriend now turned werewolf because of me, and a few other supporters, but that was it. We were on our own. And Halloween was coming.

I was told that it would all be worse on Halloween night. Awesome.

Yesterday we were fighting zombies and maybe getting Doug's biker gang a wee bit on our side. But all that excitement had faded. My hunger had not. I was aware by now that it wasn't natural, that it was related to whatever got released from the Booke of the Hidden, because nothing in my life was normal anymore. It *all* had to do with that stupid Booke…

And I was growing closer and closer to it, thinking its thoughts, having its feelings. It was weird. And weirdly comforting. Which was weird in itself, because I knew—intellectually—that this wasn't right either.

Erasmus the demon was my anchor. And he kept looking at me with concern. I wanted him to go with me to Ruth's, our local Mayflower queen. But I also wondered if it wouldn't make things worse.

I must have looked pretty nervous because out of the shadows I heard, "I will go with you."

He often stood in the shadows. I didn't know if it was a demon thing or an Erasmus thing. Maybe some from column A, some from column B.

"You don't have to," I said, sounding a bit unconvincing even to my own ears.

He moved forward and postured, chin up, hands behind his back. "I will."

Boy, when he looked at me like that…

* * *

WE DROVE. HE could have transported me with magic, but we needed the appearance of a car. When we got out, I looked up at her mansion and started up the flagstone walkway. Erasmus joined me on the porch. We were both aware of the protection mandala, a mosaic designed to keep evil away, hidden under the doormat. Erasmus couldn't cross it but he found ways around it.

Stella, Ruth's majordomo, answered the door. By the way she eyed me, I got the impression that Ruth told her everything. But when her eyes fell on Erasmus, she seemed to soften. He had that way with women, the devil.

"Please come in," she said reluctantly. "If you can wait in the foyer…"

Stella left and I walked in. But Erasmus stood on the porch and stared down at the mandala. And like the last time we were here, he side-stepped it and hugged the wall, inching by, making sure he didn't touch the mat or what was under it. When he was close enough to the door, he leapt over the threshold.

I half-expected Ruth would kick me out. I kind of hoped she would, then I wouldn't have to make up some half-assed apology that I didn't want to give—

"What do *you* want?"

Ruth, her inviting self in the flesh, stood in the doorway between her living room and foyer. She was wearing another smart dress and sweater suit combination *without* her ubiquitous gold locket…which *I* had stuffed in my jacket pocket. She pruned her mouth as she glared at me, arms tightly folded over her chest. She glanced at Erasmus without one bit of the fawning I'd come to expect from most women.

Before she could throw me out, I walked boldly into her living room, past Stella, who seemed poised to do the dirty work of tossing me out.

"Ruth, we need to have this out." I pivoted and faced her.

She seemed startled that I was standing where I was, and she dismissed Stella with a subtle nod of her head.

Ruth walked forward and squared with me. "I can't believe you have the nerve to come to my house after you called me a witch and accused me of murdering a man for—what was it? A *ritual?*"

"I don't know. But there is something you aren't telling me and I want to know what it is. No, I *need* to know what it is."

"What you need is a good doctor and possibly an institution."

"If I live that long. Look, Ruth. You've got to tell me the truth."

"I don't have to do anything. Get out of my house!"

I dug into my jacket and pulled out the clump of hand-kerchief balled up around the necklace. I still couldn't bring myself to touch it directly. More Booke of the Hidden bullshit, no doubt.

"Here!" I grabbed her hand and shoved the bundle into it.

She snatched her hand from my grip and stared at the hand-kerchief. When she unwrapped it and found her necklace, she made a little squeak.

"Yeah, we stole it. Just to examine it. You must know it's Babylonian."

Actually, this looked like news to her, if her surprised face was anything to go by.

"And it does open," I continued. "'*Within the hurasu gates, the enemies of man shall fast remain.*' That's what it says inside. What does it mean, Ruth?"

Now she stared at me, open-mouthed. So that's what it took to shut her up.

She examined it again, turning it. "I don't see…I can't see where it opens…"

"That's because it has to touch the Booke of the Hidden to open it."

She looked at me steadily with just the tiniest of twitches. Was that recognition in her eyes? Had she ever heard of the Booke? I wanted to shake her, make her tell me.

But she said nothing. She slid her gaze toward Erasmus. "I think you'd better leave."

"Come on, Ruth! I can see you know exactly what I'm talking about!"

"I don't." She turned away. "Please leave."

"Stop the killing, Ruth. I mean it."

Erasmus made some sort of grumbling noise before he stepped forward, pushing past her.

"Where do you think *you're* going?" she asked. He ignored her and headed for the stairs. Sputtering, she took off after him, race-walking to the stairway. "Come down from there! I'll call the police!"

Stella came running out from whatever cubbyhole she stashed herself. "Madam?"

"Stella, call the sheriff."

Stella pulled a cellphone from her frilly apron pocket.

"Don't bother calling the sheriff, Stella" I told her as I rushed by to follow after them. Erasmus was making a beeline for the double-doored master bedroom, with Ruth hot on his heels.

"Stop! Get away from there!"

Before he even got there, the doors slammed open for him. He took two steps inside and stopped.

Ruth came up behind nearly running into him and I took up the rear. He was staring at the portrait of Constance Howland, the last Chosen Host before me. And, incidentally, my distant cousin…as well as Ruth's.

Constance was painted from life in that flat, eighteenth century style. She appeared to be wearing a gold necklace, but whatever was on the chain was cut off by the painting's perimeter. Gee, I wondered what it could be.

He turned his head toward Ruth who was panting and clutching the locket in her hand. "She looks the same," he said quietly.

"The same…as what?" she asked.

"The same as I remember her." He looked vaguely around the room. "I smell nothing here." His gaze settled on her. When he walked forward, she took a step back. He leaned in and sniffed her. Even with that terrified look on her face, Erasmus didn't seem to notice. "No, nothing," he muttered before he turned on his heel and marched out.

Ruth looked from the portrait to him then back again to the painting.

I scrambled to follow Erasmus as he stomped down the stairs.

Ruth stood at the top of the stairs, glaring down on us.

"Both the sheriff and the deputy are on my side," I told her. "Whatever you've got planned won't work."

It was very satisfying turning my back on her and even more satisfying slamming the door closed.

* * *

I MANEUVERED THE Jeep back toward Lyndon Road and my shop. When we arrived, I just sat in the car, staring at my front door—with its axe marks and twisted hinge. "That achieved nothing."

He gazed at me mildly. "What did you want it to achieve?"

"I wanted her to acknowledge it all. To stop doing her black magic. To…help us."

"That was an unrealistic expectation."

"Thanks, Erasmus. I can always count on you to state the obvious."

"Oh. Did you *not* want me to state the obvious?"

"No. Yes. No. I don't know."

He sighed.

"You were literally sniffing around…"

"For charm pouches. None were present in the house or on her person."

"But that doesn't mean anything. We saw her get graveyard dirt from her husband's crypt and I could swear there was something in her eyes when I mentioned the Booke of the Hidden. Do you think she knows?"

"I am uncertain. The more I mingle with humans, the less I understand them."

He was looking directly at me when he said it. And I knew what he was referring to in his roundabout way. I looked away. "I wish you could read her mind or something."

"I am not capable of that."

We sat staring out the windshield. And I had no choice but to look at my ruined door again. This would be the third door in so many weeks. The first was destroyed by Doug's biker gang. This door was hacked at by zombie Vikings. What next?

"My poor door," I sighed. "I have to get that fixed again."

Erasmus gazed at the door with steady concentration and then waved his hand. Before my eyes through my car's windshield, the wood knit itself together. Each hack mark enmeshed with the grain, and missing pieces flew back into place, smoothing out the face of it until it was as if nothing had happened.

I stared at Erasmus. "I seem to have the power to repair it. I have many new powers I did not know I possessed. I suppose it has more to do with my…my being in love with you."

He said it again. More plainly this time.

"Oh," was all that managed to come out of my mouth. He slid his gaze away from me and got out of the car. Belatedly, I did the same and without looking at him, I unlocked the door.

Inside the shop, Erasmus said, "I've made you uncomfortable."

"No. I just… It was all so abstract before. And now…"

He toyed with a handful of honey sticks displayed in a small vase. "Yes. Well…" He shrugged and looked around the room as if inspecting it. As if he hadn't looked at it almost more times than I had.

"Look, Erasmus…"

"You need say nothing. I expect nothing."

"It's just that…it's not that simple."

"What a very *human* thing to say."

"There's no need for insults."

He strode forward and then seemed to change his mind, pivoting and heading for the door.

"You don't have to leave."

"I've made you uncomfortable."

"Mostly I'm just…hungry. What could it be that's making me so hungry?"

He stopped, his fingers paused on the door handle. "It could be any number of creatures. I don't know the entire inventory of the book."

"Well…maybe I should go hunt it." I raised my hand and the

chthonic crossbow sailed across the room and slapped itself into my waiting palm. "I could use your help."

He rolled his shoulders and stared at the door he'd only just repaired. With love magic. Because he loved me.

And even though I'd thought about it, laid awake even when he was beside me and turned it over in my mind, I still didn't quite know what to think.

"If I must," he said in his most put-upon voice.

We plunged into the woods, which made the cloudy day seem just a dream. In between the trees, the light was cut in half, and I blinked, trying to adjust my eyes. I kept the crossbow ready, though it hadn't yet armed itself.

"Tell me about the whole Samhain thing again, and the convergence of power at the Winter Solstice," I said quietly, trying to tip-toe over the crunchier parts of the forest.

He gazed at me mildly, making no sound as he walked. "I thought it was self-explanatory."

"Well hit me again."

"I beg your pardon?"

"I mean, *tell* me again. I don't know that I was listening all that closely the last time."

He sighed. "How very gratifying that the important information I impart is only so much noise to you."

"Erasmus…"

"Very well. The time of the solstices has great power, but that power fades away. Fall is the in between time. The Winter solstice is ahead but not close enough. That makes it dangerous for mages and beings of power, as their power wanes and the evil power rises. The exception is Samhain, which seems to concentrate the magic for the one day."

"Yeah, that last part. Concentrating the magic."

"I don't make this stuff up, you know."

"I know. But…it's hard to wrap my mind around."

"It's simple. The power fluctuates. It grows as the solstice gets closer, but Samhain—or what you quaintly refer to as

'Halloween'—grabs hold of this wayward power for just one night. It focuses the magic."

"Like a magnifying glass."

"Precisely. It is at its most powerful at midnight."

"But not for powerful magical people. The bad magic rises, the good magic fades. Is that it?"

"Essentially."

"What would that do to the Booke?"

He shrugged. "I dread to think what would be released on Samhain."

"You mean it could dump its whole, uh, inventory?"

"It's possible. I have never been awakened near Samhain before. The creatures grow stronger and mages grow weaker, Kylie. A very dangerous time."

"I'm not a mage."

"That remains to be seen."

The thought overwhelmed me *and* my stomach—even as hungry as I was. "We've got less than a week, then, to stop the Booke for good."

"Kylie, I have told you before that this is impossible."

"No, it isn't. You said there is only one being who can stop the Booke."

Erasmus halted, and I looked back to see if he'd caught sight or scent of the new creature. But instead, he looked pale and... frightened.

"Kylie, I told you we must never speak of that."

"He's the only one who has enough power. The only one who even the Powers That Be are afraid of. Isn't that what you said?"

"I also said that I am terrified of Him myself."

I lowered the crossbow. "Look, I know you said you're scared, but...I think if we go together—"

"Are you insane? I will not bring you into the presence of... of *Him*."

"Satan. It's a name I've said countless times."

"But you have no idea what you are saying."

"I do. I—" The snap of a twig out in the forest caught my attention, and a sudden wave of hunger roiled in my belly. I cocked my head and listened. There was definitely something walking out there. When I lifted the crossbow, it was armed with yet a different quarrel I had not used before.

My instinct was to get closer.

I moved with the crossbow at my shoulder height. Whatever was out there moved as well. I could see a shadow amongst the trees ahead. I began to stalk it.

Erasmus clamped his mouth shut and sniffed the wind.

When it cleared the trees, I could plainly see it, walking in a shaft of sunlight. It had a deer skull for a head with tall antlers branching out wide. Its body was emaciated and though it didn't walk on all fours, it was slumped so far over it might as well have. It seemed to be wearing ragged clothes made of something like transparent buckskin, and a necklace of what looked like children's skulls, bone white against its rather ruddy appearance. Every one of its bones, every rib, every joint, was evident through its translucent membrane, yet instead of lumbering, it walked gracefully on two unnaturally long, thin legs. Until it stopped. The skull seemed to sniff the air and slowly turned…toward me.

Why wasn't I used to this by now? Why didn't I just fire?

It looked me over and slowly approached.

"Fire, Kylie!" Erasmus hissed behind me.

But I didn't. A dark wave of sorrow, of regret, of shame, suddenly flooded me, all blending together in a bone-deep sense of pain. And the hunger. I couldn't escape it. I almost doubled over in agony. It was *so* hungry. And it was shamed by it, too.

There was no expression on a skull with its empty eye sockets, and yet it seemed to be pleading with me. It didn't want these feelings any more than I did. It seemed to be asking me, *Why?*

I was overcome with the need to comfort it, to say that it would be okay. At the same time, the confusing mesh of hunger and longing emanating from it repulsed me. My skin crawled even as I was drawn toward it.

And then fear took over, because I knew what it wanted. It seemed that its hunger would only be satisfied by one thing. For human flesh. For me.

It wanted to eat me. And I was torn… I wanted what it wanted. I wanted to give in, not only to eat human flesh myself, but to *let* it eat me, to give myself to the creature. The utter horror of it froze me to the spot. I couldn't lift the crossbow. I couldn't fire, even with the faint call of Erasmus behind me.

Its skeletal hands landed on my shoulders, every joint of each finger digging in. I couldn't stop picturing tearing the flesh off of a human arm with my teeth…and *liking* it. And then picturing the creature doing the same to me…and liking it just as much.

With a strength that came from god-knows-where, I cried out and flung my arms up, dislodging its hands from me. It stared at me with a grim sense of sadness, before dropping its mandible to its chest and screaming. It was the sound of a thousand regrets, of unimaginable desire.

The scream was so high-pitched and so jarring that I nearly dropped to my knees. If it weren't for Erasmus' strong hands holding me up, I would have folded to become that thing's dinner. Pulling myself together, I raised the crossbow, but with another unholy scream it bounded away, disappearing into the long shadows.

I stared into the woods where it had gone, shamed by the hunger that churned in me, that couldn't be quenched with normal food. A hunger for the forbidden.

CHAPTER TWO

I CRADLED MY head in my hands, sitting in my shop. Erasmus was talking but I barely heard him over the goddammed *hunger*.

"A wendigo. An Algonquin creature made from the ravages of famine, and from those who indulged in the eating of human flesh."

"I know. I know. Stop talking about it."

He stopped pacing and stood over me. "Kylie. Tell me. Do *you* feel a desire for—"

"Shut up!" I jumped to my feet. I absolutely could not be craving that.

"It's not you. It's the monster that is doing this to you. It's not you."

"It sure feels like me." I grabbed him and was filled with relief that he had no fear in his eyes. "I need a spell. A magical cure. Something to dull this. I might be dangerous if I don't get something."

"You're right of course. I shall get Doctor Boone." He vanished.

I sank back into the chair. I actually felt marginally better. Maybe it was because help was on the way. Or maybe…because there was no one there to tempt me.

Because—God help me—I wanted to…to…

This was what it must be for Erasmus every day, every hour. To not want to hurt the person you cared about and at the same time crave their very flesh, not to love, but to feast upon.

How fucked up was that?

It might have been ten minutes. Maybe more. But the air displacement made me raise my head and there was Doc. He seemed a little befuddled at the transport but nonetheless delighted. He had his doctor bag, books, and other things bundled in his arms, looking as if he were about to drop it all.

"Don't you worry, Kylie," he said in calming tones. But all I could think about was chomping down on that thick, beard-stubbled neck of his. I closed my eyes, hoping it might help. But I could smell him—a blend of spicy aftershave, sweat, and skin. In my agitated state, the skin smell was the strongest.

"Just hurry, Doc," I gasped out.

He took his things to the kitchen. I heard the clank of an iron cauldron, the distinct sound of herbs being chopped, liquid being poured, and then the sharp scent of some kind of oil. He came bustling in again. The fireplace whooshed and I opened my eyes to watch the flames. Doc put the cauldron over the fire, and I focused my eyes on that. Until my gaze slid toward him.

I didn't remember standing up. I only sort of awakened when Erasmus grabbed my arms and said my name, in that smoky way of his.

"Kylie."

"What? Oh my God." I sat again, covering my face with my hands.

After what seemed like an interminable time of Doc muttering over the cauldron in true warlock fashion, he grabbed the cauldron from the fire with an oven mitt and set it on the hearth. With a ladle, he poured the liquid into a cup made of steer horn. His hand shook when he stretched it toward me.

"What is it?" I said softly, not looking at the skin of his hand, the sprouts of white hair, the spots and freckles.

"Well, it's a mixture of chickweed, licorice root, green tea, and fennel…with a spell or two over it. That should keep you until you get rid of that creature."

I noticed he stepped way back by the hearth again.

I didn't bother smelling it. I tipped it back and drank down the whole thing. Keeping my eyes closed, I waited.

Something warred inside me. The stuff tasted awful, and at first, I thought I would be sick. But I soon realized that wasn't it. Something was trying to overtake the potion, a back and forth of forces fighting for dominance. But Doc's magic wouldn't seem to let the other win.

All at once, there was sweet, blessed relief. A bit of hunger still lingered in the back of my mind, but it was nothing like it had been before. Nothing like when I wanted to jump Doc and sink my teeth into his flesh and tear and rip. The appetite for people was gone and only a vague sense of hunger remained.

"Oh, thank God!" I let the tears flow. "Thank you, Doc. It's way better. You're safe."

He visibly relaxed. "Well now. That…is an interesting symptom."

I wiped my face. The relief was amazing. I inhaled and couldn't smell him! "It's only because we're getting closer to Halloween. The Booke is getting stronger. It's pulling power from the ley lines, from Halloween itself. It's dragging me in." I slumped back in my chair. "We have to stop the Booke for good. And you have to help me do it. The whole coven does."

"What can we do, Kylie? Mr. Dark here says that—"

"We can. We just have to convince Satan to destroy it."

Doc just stared at me. Then he looked at Erasmus, who was bubbling over with anger. "Did I, uh, hear you right?"

I rubbed my forehead. Reality was sort of getting away from me. "Yeah. There really is a Satan, and he's apparently the Netherworld's boss."

Doc turned to Erasmus. "Mr. Dark…"

"I *told* her this would be utter folly. That it would be outrageously dangerous."

We locked gazes. "But it's the only way."

"Is that true, Mr. Dark? Can he destroy the book for good?"

He clenched his teeth. "Yes. But as with all denizens of the Netherworld, there will be a price."

"What price?" I asked.

Erasmus flung himself to his knees before me. "Kylie, this is no mere thing you ask. He will know the cost of this to you, to his own plans. He will exact the highest price."

"My soul?"

"Yes."

How did Erasmus do it? How did he curb his cravings for my soul? Perhaps love *was* stronger than fate. And I'd had a bitter taste of the same, needing a potion to stop me.

I knew at that moment, that in the future, if the Booke were allowed to go on, there would be a point where I couldn't overcome whatever was coming for me. It was really only a matter of time. I might have lasted longer than all the other Chosen Hosts before me, but I was dancing on a razor's edge. I couldn't do it forever. I was *so* weary of fighting the Booke's pull, of the oblivion that was to come. What was a soul compared to that?

"Okay, then."

"*What?*" He grabbed me, his face only inches from mine. "Do you know what you're saying?"

"Erasmus, I'm tired. I already figured out a long time ago that I'm not…I mean, my coven and you, and Jeff and Ed…you've all kept me alive so far. But it's only a matter of time."

"Kylie." His strange choking voice stabbed me right in the heart. He pulled me in, embraced me tight, almost too tight, as if protecting me from an inevitability.

"Don't you see? It was never going to end well. Even though you decided not to take my soul, it was still forfeit all along."

"No," he whispered. His breathing was harsh in my ear and his coat began to smolder.

"It has to stop, Erasmus. No one else should go through this. It has to stop."

He held me for a long time, and I welcomed it. I closed my eyes and felt his arms, his warmth, smelled his smoky scent. Listened as the leather of his coat squeaked and strained.

Finally, he pulled back and looked at me, hands on my face, thumbs caressing my cheeks. "I can't let you."

"You have to." But it then washed over me. I didn't care what happened to me, but the end of the Booke meant the end of him too.

I drew back, eyes roving over those familiar features. "I forgot."

"It's not for me that I worry."

"Erasmus…what are we going to do?"

"Now," said Doc thoughtfully, "we might be able to find a way around all that, young lady."

I raised my head wearily, perhaps out of habit. "Why do you say that?"

"Because we have our coven, darn it. And so far, there hasn't been anything we can't do. I'm counting on that. Let's get them together and find a solution, like we always do."

I agreed, of course. But in the back of my mind, I didn't hold much hope.

CHAPTER THREE

WHEN DOC LEFT that evening, he seemed cheered. He had a few ideas to bring to the coven tomorrow. Protection spells against Satan. Enchantments to keep me strong. I had a feeling that nothing we tried would work, but I figured let's go through the motions anyway.

Erasmus returned after dropping off Doc. Now that things were decided, I was strangely calm. I suppose it was the suspense that was killing me.

"May I…stay tonight?" Erasmus seemed hesitant. Maybe he thought I wanted to be alone. But I turned a smile on him instead.

"I'd like that."

"Oh. Then…I've been wondering something." He walked slowly around the perimeter of the room. He was used to doing that. He liked staying in the shadows. But I could tell he was thinking deeply about something. "If…if I were a mortal, we would simply be a man and a woman."

"Yes?"

"And as I understand it, a man and woman…court. Or as you would quaintly put it…date."

It was my turn to look a little dumbfounded. "Uh…You

want to go on a date? With the world crumbling around us in a cannibalistic mess?"

"It might be our last chance."

That sobered me. Yes, he was right. It might very well be the last time I could.

"When I interrupted you and your constable," he went on, "you were dining."

Demon logic. What did they care if the world was ending? "Okay. Yeah. But *you* don't eat."

"And yet I can drink."

Eat, drink, and be merry for tomorrow we— "You know what? Sure. Why not? I mean, I can't sit around, right?" I looked at my watch. "I think we have just enough time to catch the last seating at the café. Let me just slip upstairs and change."

He had the look of a man who got what he wanted but suddenly didn't know what to do with it. I got up the stairs and threw open my wardrobe. A dress? It was a date, so why not? Something not too elegant. And a little jewelry to set off my…amulet.

I stared at it in the mirror. It wasn't exactly romantic, that demon face with its tongue sticking out, and those red jeweled eyes. My hand went to it. Warm, as always. Maybe it had essence of Erasmus in it. After all, a demon's amulet was a part of them. When I snatched it off his neck three weeks ago—God, it seemed like longer—he was sort of put in my power. I could summon him, and it would protect me from him. But now it was more than that. It was part of him in a fundamental way.

Shabiri's amulet must be the same, the one Doug wore with the green jewels to match her eyes and that streak of green she wore in her long, dark hair. She was a different sort of demon than Erasmus. She wasn't attached to anything, far as I could tell. Except her amulet.

The amulet wasn't what I would call pretty. It was ugly, in fact. But now that Erasmus and I were…involved…I kind of… liked it.

Should I put my hair up? I experimented, lifting my brown,

shoulder-length hair up behind my head. No. I didn't have it in me to go to that much trouble.

I added some dangly silver earrings, then remembered at the last minute that demons shied away from silver and exchanged them for gold earrings, and trotted downstairs.

He looked me over. "You're displaying your legs."

"It's a dress. Don't you like it?" I gave a little twirl.

"I have not seen you wear this sort of thing…except when you were with your constable."

"It's for special occasions."

He merely raised a brow, but I could tell he was pleased.

I drove him to the Moody Bog café, still checking the skies for flying Baphomets. We both hurried inside. I was still hungry, but at least it wasn't for human flesh. I'd have a little bite while Erasmus…wouldn't.

We were seated by the window, and once Erasmus sat, he looked around. "Are all these mortals similarly occupied?"

"You mean on dates? Maybe." I scanned the room. Older couples who were probably married, groups of friends my age, one or two who might be on a date.

"What is the purpose of dating?"

I looked up from my menu and moved my water glass closer. "Well, it's a ritualized way for contemporary couples to get to know each other."

"And then have sex?"

I nearly spit out my water. I coughed, clearing my throat and finally setting my water glass down. "Uh, sure, in some instances. But I think the majority are in it for developing a longer relationship, leading to marriage maybe, which is a legal bonding of two people."

"Why?"

"Because human beings are social animals and we like to pair up, live life together, have children."

"Ah. Procreation. But a marriage bond does not seem biologically necessary to this."

I scooted in closer and leaned toward him so that others couldn't hear. "It's a cultural thing, an agreement to support each other, both emotionally and financially. It's expensive having children."

"So when you were dating your constable, was that your intention?"

I took another sip of water, then toyed with the glass. "I don't know. I was only just getting to know him."

"When I interfered." His eyes were blazing coals. He was proud of that. It pissed me off for a second, before I saw his side of it.

"If I had been set on him, you couldn't have interfered."

That took the glow from his gaze. He sat back, somewhat diminished.

"Besides, I wasn't looking to settle down yet. I had just gotten over a bad relationship—Jeff, remember? And I'd just started this new business, new everything." Which might well be over before it'd begun, if I couldn't get out of this somehow. But instead of wallowing, I looked up at him and smiled. "So what does it tell you that I'm here with you instead of him?"

He thought about it, brows dug deep into his eyes. I saw the moment the light bulb went off and he offered a tentative smile. "You chose *me*?"

"Yeah, you big idiot."

His smile faded. "But…why? Why would you choose a demon over another human?"

"Who knows? Just crazy I guess. Let's order. I'm hungry."

I got us a bottle of wine, and I asked for the lobster roll. And then we were left to stare at each other. I eyed that duster jacket that he absolutely refused to take off (unless we were in bed). Leaning an elbow on the table, I rested my chin in my hand, and smiled. "Tell me about this get-up."

"Get-up?"

"This outfit. That jacket you're rocking. Surely you weren't dressed like this in Babylonian times."

He looked down at himself and fingered his lapels. "These clothes are only a reflection of the era. In Babylon, I wore a tunic like everyone else."

"So wait. Are you saying your clothes are like…mood clothes? They pop up with the times? Are they an extension of you? Literally?"

"Yes. I merely think them and they take form around me. I take it the same is not true of mortals."

"No. We have to clothe ourselves with woven material or, I guess, animal skins made to our shapes. You've seen me wear different things. I changed only a few minutes ago."

"What you wear to sleep *is* different from your day wear…"

"You mean you didn't notice before?"

"I noticed tonight."

"Yes, you did. Points for you."

A hint of smile formed at the corners of his mouth as he fidgeted with the napkin in his lap.

"I don't know what's going to happen when this is all over," I said, robbing him of that burgeoning smile, "but my plan is to save you too when the Booke is destroyed. I think I'd like to pick this up where we left off. *If* I survive, that is."

"I don't understand."

The waitress appeared with the wine and two glasses. She opened the bottle, let me try a sip, and then poured more for each of us. After she'd disappeared, I noticed that Erasmus was still staring at me.

"I mean, when the Booke is gone, and you're free, we could… continue this." I gestured between us.

"What makes you think any of that will happen?"

I picked up the glass by its stem and gazed at the jeweled light through the wine. "If it doesn't, then we should enjoy this time together now. While we can."

When he lifted his glass, I reached over the table to clink mine to his. He gave me one of those "Are you insane?" looks, which made me laugh. "People do that. They clink glasses to toast each other. To celebrate."

Cautiously, he clinked his glass to mine. "This seems foolish."

"Just drink your wine, Erasmus."

* * *

HE WASN'T MUCH of a conversationalist. I mostly asked him questions, but he wasn't very good at elaborating. Comparing him to Shabiri, who was all narcissism all the time, I'd say that demons were as unique as humans. I figured that maybe he wasn't elaborating because he only had the barest minimum of experiences. While Shabiri got to live her life as a demon 24/7, Erasmus was a prisoner of the Booke, only allowed out and about for a couple of weeks every hundred years or so. That would put a crimp in anyone's knowledge base.

As we drove home, I was a little buzzed from the wine and happy about the companion beside me. "Do you ever wish you were as free-wheeling as someone like Shabiri?"

He rolled his eyes. "I have no ambitions to be anything like her."

"I don't mean be like her. I wouldn't like that at all. But… freer. To come and go."

He mulled it over and sighed just as we pulled into the parking area in front of the shop. He spoke carefully, slowly. "I have never cared before. Now I do. As long as it involves you."

"Wow."

"Did I say something wrong?"

"No. No, you said exactly the right thing."

We left the car and when I reached for the door, it unlocked and swung open with a mere wave of Erasmus' hand. I moved first to go in when a strange prickling started at the back of my neck. And then a powerful hunger stabbed at me so deep that I stumbled, grabbing the door frame. It wasn't as bad as before but still very noticeable.

I twitched my hand and the chthonic crossbow came to me. Erasmus sniffed the air, on alert. I was ready to make for the woods when a car pulled up. I quickly hid the crossbow behind my back, and a good thing, too.

"I'm sorry for coming over so late, Kylie."

Reverend Howard of the First Congregational Church of Moody Bog got out of his car and stepped into the porch light, highlighting his white, wavy hair in a halo. His smile was as laid-back as Doc's. "I hoped you were a night owl— Oh. I seem to be interrupting a…date?" He got a strange look on his face, but that was because I had told him recently I was dating Sheriff Ed. Oops.

His expression switched gears—must be the parson part of him—and he put out his hand to shake anyway. "I remember you from Kylie's dinner party," he said politely. "Howard Cleveland. And you're Erasmus Dark, Kylie's friend from California."

Erasmus stood stiff as a board, hands behind his back, and stared at the offered hand. "I remember you," he said curtly down his nose.

Reverend Howard glanced down at his own hand and let it fall to his side. "Well…I just came by to… How do I put this? I've been worried about you, Kylie."

"Oh?" Surreptitiously, I maneuvered the crossbow behind my back to Erasmus' hand where I'm sure he promptly vanished it. "Where are my manners? Won't you come in out of the cold?"

"Thanks." We got out of his way. While I turned on some lights, Reverend Howard walked over the threshold and said, "You know, I just can't get over how nice and homey this shop is. Of course, you live here, too."

"Yes." I shed my coat and hung it up. "It's too bad there isn't room upstairs for more of a living quarters. Can't escape work this way, but I think it will do. Would you like some coffee? Tea? Erasmus can—"

"No, he can't," muttered Erasmus.

"No, thank you," said the pastor. He sat down and clasped his hands together. "I've been hearing some strange rumors."

"Really? About what?" Sitting opposite the reverend, I leaned in, straightening my skirt. Erasmus occupied himself by making slow circuits of the room, always in the shadows.

"Frankly, odd things. Your neighbors have been reporting strange sounds and lights over here."

"They've been reporting it to *you?*"

"Well, people are scared, what with what happened to the Warrens and some of our other townsfolk. It's putting them on edge. And, well, when something can't be explained, they tend to come to their pastors."

"I can assure you that we're fine over here. No, uh, strange stuff."

He rubbed the back of his neck. "They've been saying some pretty wild things, I have to tell you. Seeing zombies and flying beasts. I just don't know what's gotten into the water around here."

"Wow. That *is* weird. What do you suppose is behind it?"

"It's near Halloween. Some folks start to get a little religious fervor this time of year. They wonder about letting their children go Trick-or-Treating, as if it's some sort of devil-worshipping. I do my best to tell them it has nothing to do with that, but people will be people. I know there's also teens who get up to mischief, scaring people on purpose. The sheriff's got to have his hands full this time of year."

"That must be weird for you. Counseling people that it's their imagination."

"It is a little. I mean grown people having these fancies." He glanced over his shoulder toward Erasmus. "People saying they've seen demons. It's crazy, isn't it?"

"The very definition of insanity," said Erasmus smoothly.

"I suppose a lot of it has to do with the Wiccans. Folks think that…well. You can imagine."

"That we're having nightly rituals?" I fake-laughed as my gaze slid toward the faded chalk pentagram in front of my fireplace. It was covered with a rug now, since Doc had said that the spell had pretty much expired. But I knew that Reverend Howard had seen it when we first chalked it and had remarked none too politely about it, too.

"You know how people talk. I just wanted to make sure that you're okay."

"Yeah, I'm fine. Nothing weird going on here, right Erasmus?"

He fiddled with his fingers for a bit before he was able to form an "OK" sign with his hand. It was not reassuring.

Reverend Howard stared at him. "All right." He got up and stuffed his hands in his pockets. "You will let me know if there's a problem of any kind, won't you? Villages are funny places. It's tough to win some folks over. But I think you will. Eventually." He smiled and shook his head. "I felt pretty foolish coming over here, I have to say. But you've both been nice about it." When he looked at Erasmus, the demon tried to smile and it was just as bad as his "OK" sign.

"I've interrupted things enough. I'll go now."

"Oh, do you have to?"

Erasmus growled behind me but I ignored him.

"You're being too nice." He reached the door and opened it. "Have a good evening, you two."

I leaned on the doorjamb and watched him get into his car. When he started it up, I closed and locked the door.

I couldn't sense the wendigo's presence anymore. Dammit!

"It's gone, isn't it?" said Erasmus into my ear. I could feel his warmth at my back.

"Yes. Unfortunate timing of Reverend Howard."

"I don't like clergymen."

"Is it the holy water?"

"Some of it. And some is their need to interfere."

I peeked out the curtains to watch him drive away. "I bet they interfered plenty with Constance Howland."

"If she had not committed suicide, they would surely have hanged her."

I let the curtain fall and turned to face him. "Humans must seem strange to you."

He stood stiffly, hands behind his back. "They don't know what they want. In each age, they view themselves as sophisticated and enlightened. But in the end, superstition takes precedence and their violent natures always overwhelm their intellect."

"That's a pretty bald statement."

"It's true. I've seen it play out for thousands of years."

"Sadly, I believe you."

We stood looking at each other…until he moved first, slowly closing the distance between us. "We've dined," he said in a sultry tone. "We've talked. What else does one do on a date?"

"I think you know perfectly well."

"Do I?" His smile was feral for only a moment before it softened. He touched a tendril of my hair and twirled it gently around his fingers. "I must confess. I have been intrigued with that very large, very solid table in your kitchen."

I laughed. "You are a naughty demon, aren't you?"

He didn't waste any more time on talking, getting in close, and sliding his arms around me. When he kissed me, it was gentle at first. I could tell he was holding back. But the promise of that kitchen farm table was playing big in my imagination too, and so I returned his kisses just as his heated up.

We kissed and moved together, groping our way through the scant light to the kitchen. He could see perfectly well in the dark, but I fished around the wall for the light switch. He was worth looking at.

The light flicked on and he smiled. He pulled me in to cover my mouth again, running his hands up my back…and down to grab a handful of my backside. I wriggled, rubbing against him, gratified at the growl that rumbled up his throat. He kept holding me tight as I tried to release my arms to push his jacket off and get in a few good gropes myself. He ignored how his jacket was hanging low on his shoulders—it was as far as I could get it—and his hands found my bosom and began unbuttoning the front of the dress—before he stopped.

Someone was knocking urgently on the damned front door.

"Beelze's tail!" he swore. "These villagers!"

"I have to see what it is."

Erasmus let me go and slapped his hands on the table. He hung his head between his shoulders.

I straightened my clothes, fixed my hair, and opened the door.

"Ed?"

Sheriff Bradbury scowled, looking more morose than angry.

"Ed, what's happened?"

"A couple down the block. We were called about a domestic disturbance. Turned out…they were…"

He suddenly paled and it looked as if he might faint. I grabbed his arm, pulled him over to a chair, and pushed him in it. He dragged his Smokey Bear hat off his head and clutched it in his hands. "Jeezum, Kylie." His voice was uneven. "There was blood everywhere. They…they *ate* each other. I mean literally *ate* each other…like cannibals."

CHAPTER FOUR

"THE WENDIGO," I breathed.

"You know what it is?"

"Yeah. I almost went berserk myself. But I thought it was just me, the Chosen Host thing. I almost tried to eat Doc."

"Jesus."

"But he gave me a potion that's working really well." I looked up at Erasmus hovering in the doorway. "I wonder if Doc could somehow cast a spell over the whole town. Go find out."

His eyes were blazing. "*Now?*"

If he thought I'd still be up for some kitchen table sex, he was out of his mind. "Yes, Erasmus. Now!"

"Beelze's tail," he grumbled and promptly vanished.

"What does that even mean?" said Ed.

"Forget him. Do you want some water?"

"Stronger."

"Coming up."

I ran back to the kitchen and got down some bourbon from the cupboard. I sloshed some into a glass and ran back out.

Ed knocked it back. He stared at the empty glass. It looked small in his large hand. "I'm not supposed to drink while on duty, but screw that." He twitched his gaze toward me. "You almost…attacked Doc?"

I swallowed. The memory was still very fresh. "Yeah."

"What is this thing again? A wendigo? I think I've heard of that."

"It's an Algonquin thing. In a famine, you turn into one if you eat human flesh. I've seen it. I was face to skull with it. And then I was taken over with this overwhelming need for human meat. Before I could kill it, it got away."

"I'm sorry you didn't. Kill it, I mean."

"I could feel its emotions. It was so sad. And so ashamed. I almost felt sorry for it. But I could also tell it wanted to eat *me*." I rubbed my temple. "These things are getting stronger. It's because of Halloween."

"What do you mean?"

"Erasmus says that there's power in the world that most people can't connect to. But talented witches and, I guess, people like me can. This power gets strongest at the solstices. But Halloween sort of haywires or hijacks it. It's a dangerous time for people like me because creatures get stronger and mages get weaker. At least that's what I got out of it."

"So Halloween's bad?"

"Very bad. The closer we get the worse the Booke will be. So I really have to get it destroyed before Halloween."

"How are you going to do that?"

I turned to Ed and took his hands. "I've decided to travel to the Netherworld. There's a being there who's strong enough to destroy it."

"Do I want to know?"

"Uh…probably not. And…he'll want my soul in exchange."

"Kylie!" His hand tightened on mine.

"But that's why I haven't left yet. I'm trying to get the coven to figure out a way for me to do that and *not* leave my soul behind."

He let me go and fell back against the chair with a sigh. "Well…are they any closer to achieving that?"

"I just started Doc thinking about it. Erasmus and I…well." I gave a nervous laugh. "We went on a date."

Ed made a sound between a snort and a laugh. "With all this going on?" He threw up his hands. "Hell, why not? And how was that?"

"It was nice," I said defensively, not meeting his eyes.

"Wow," he said softly. "You are really into that guy. Did our time together mean nothing at all?"

I rested my hand on his shoulder. "Of course it did. I treasured our brief time together. And if it had been right, I would have pursued it. But there was always something about Erasmus…"

"I didn't have a chance, did I."

"If he hadn't come into my life, you would have. I'm sorry, Ed."

He slouched in the chair. "That's all right. I kind of see what you mean. Shabiri is kind of a bitch but… She has her moments."

I couldn't help but stare at him. I finally blurted out, "Seriously?"

"Yeah, seriously. I'm surprised you'd even say that to me."

"Yeah, sorry. Demons, huh? What are you gonna do?"

There was a pensive look on his face, sort of wistful. "There's a…sadness about her. It's hidden there beneath her sarcasm. I can tell a defense mechanism when I see one. We've had…talks."

"Talks. About what?"

"About being a demon. About what it means to her."

I would have liked to hear that conversation, but I suspected it was pretty personal. For Ed's ears only. He looked uncomfortable mentioning it, so I didn't pursue it.

Ed stared thoughtfully at the cold fireplace. "Halloween is less than a week away."

Change of subject. Okay. "I know. And Baphomet is still out there. Plus, Reverend Howard came over telling me people have started reporting strange goings-on, like flying beasties and zombies."

"Uh oh."

"I don't know how to prevent people from seeing that. I'm surprised more people aren't calling your station to complain."

"I did get a call or two about a possible UFO and a flying creature—which I'm sure was your favorite Goat Guy. And then there was the damage he inflicted." He frowned. "We were able to call it a gas line explosion. People are dead."

"I know. I gotta stop it, Ed. This Booke has got to be stopped for good."

"Look. When the coven meets again, will you invite me? I want to have a say in this. If you go to this Netherworld, then I want to go with you."

"That's sweet of you. But I get the impression humans aren't welcomed there."

"*You're* going."

"That's different."

"Why is it different? Because I'm not some demon?"

"You know why it's different. I'm…I don't know. Sort of… in between worlds. The Booke is drawing me in." I couldn't help but turn my head to gaze at it.

"Dammit, Kylie. I sure hate that this has happened to you."

"You and me both."

He slipped his arm around my shoulders and I leaned in against him. Of course it was at that moment that Erasmus returned with Doc.

"Am I interrupting something?" said Erasmus nastily.

"No," I said nastily right back. Then I ignored him and looked at Doc. "Doc, Ed just told me—"

"Yes, Mr. Dark explained. I think that we can spread the spell to encompass the village. It might have some adverse reactions—"

"But not as adverse as cannibalism, right?"

"You make a good point."

"And anyway," I said. I couldn't help but walk to the window and peer out again. "It's only temporary until I kill that thing."

"We'll have to make the potion to work as a fine mist…" He began thinking of the problem and started pacing.

I was imagining something like a crop-duster, but I didn't think we knew anyone with a small plane. "Maybe I should just send up the Bat Signal," I said. I got out my phone and clicked the first member of the coven.

* * *

ERASMUS PACED, AND I could've sworn he was scorching my floor. I tried once or twice to mention it but there didn't seem to be a point anymore.

The door burst open and Nick, our Goth-lite barista with dyed black hair and black fingernails, stood panting in the doorway. "What have I missed?"

I leaned against the counter. "All of you Wiccans have to come up with a protection spell so Erasmus and I can go to Hell."

His gaze flicked toward Erasmus, who was still pacing. "Uh… okay. Why?"

"Because he and I are going to the Netherworld to ask Satan to destroy the Booke of the Hidden for good."

He bit his lip and his brows moved upward. "S-Satan?"

"The one and only."

"Right." He reached for a chair behind him and sat. "Because this isn't freaky enough as it is." He glanced at Ed and did an automatic chin raise toward him.

"We, uh, also have to stop the cannibalism that might be going around," I said.

He wilted. "I spoke too soon."

Seraphina, our middle-aged boho witch, hit the open doorway next. "Nick? How did you get here? Your car isn't in the parking lot."

"Oh, I ran. I forgot. Jeez, I hope no one saw me. I think I was on all fours."

There were times that I forgot he was a werewolf. A black, Goth werewolf.

"And Doc? Did you also…run?"

"No, Mr. Dark brought me in a most unconventional way."

She took off her jacket, hung it by the door, and faced us with arms folded. "What's the emergency?"

I held a hand up to Doc. "I'll field this one. There's a wendigo on the loose and it made me feel a little cannibalistic, so Doc hurried here to give me a potion…before I tried to eat him."

Doc smiled and shrugged.

"Oh my goddess," she said.

"But after that, we came up with a plan to destroy the Booke."

"I am against it," put in Erasmus.

"So noted in the record. He and I are going to the Netherworld to ask Satan to destroy the Booke."

She cocked her head, her mouth open. She walked sedately to one of the wingbacks and sat, folding her hands on her thighs. "You're just going to ask him? And what does he get in return?"

I took a deep breath. "My soul."

"Kylie!" She was on her feet.

"Everyone, relax! I'm not going to give it to him."

"I fail to see how you will avoid it," growled Erasmus.

"By some clever maneuvers, spells, and…stuff. Right, Doc?"

"Right. We'll have to put our heads together and do some digging to find all the protections we can. And we have to find a way to disconnect Mr. Dark from the book before you go."

Nick stood. "Can we do that? *Should* we do that?"

"Yes!" I said sternly.

Doc walked over to Nick and rested his hands on his shoulders. "Son, we're going to have to. And we've got less than a week to do it."

"Of course," he said. "Why not? Everything has a deadline. But we're gonna need Jolene."

"She'll be here," I said. Jolene, our teen-aged computer geek. She was also my part time employee.

Jeff—my ex from California, who was also now a blond werewolf—walked upright and not the least bit wolfy through the door and looked around. "What's going on?"

"Kylie's going to the Netherworld to talk to the Devil," said Nick in a rush. "I just really had to say that out loud."

"What?"

Erasmus charged him, grabbing his arms. "You have been her lover. Talk some sense into her!"

"Who, me?" He shook Erasmus off him. "Kylie is her own person. You can't talk her out of anything."

Erasmus growled and bared his teeth. "I won't be a party to this!"

"Erasmus!" I grabbed his sleeve before he could tear away. "I'll be all right. You'll be there."

"Don't you understand? I can't protect you. He can wipe me away like a speck of dust."

That took the wind out of my sails. "He can, huh?"

"He is the most powerful being on that world. On nearly *every* world. That's why He has the power to destroy the book."

"Okay. Well…we'll take that into consideration."

Jeff folded his arms and made a disgusted sound. "What are we doing *really*?"

"Mr. Chase," said Doc, "we are doing as Kylie said. We are looking at finding spells and potions to keep her safe."

"From the *Devil*? Is that possible?"

Nick waved his hand. "That's what *I* was saying."

The door slammed opened, the bell above jangling wildly.

"Did I miss anything?" asked Jolene.

CHAPTER FIVE

I HAD NEVER seen my coven so concentrated and involved. Doc had Erasmus fetch books from his house, while Jolene and Doc argued over what spell they could use.

Jeff was, again, by himself in a corner, much like Erasmus was trying and failing to do. Jolene and Doc kept asking the demon questions, and Erasmus' long hair was getting messed up from all the wild head-shaking he was doing.

"So what is this, Kylie?" asked Jeff softly as he emerged from the shadows. "What are you playing at?"

"I thought you of all people would know that I'm not playing at anything."

"I mean…you can do all the spells you want, but it doesn't sound like Old Scratch is going to fall for it."

I tried not to meet his eyes but he wasn't fooled. We'd been together too long.

"Hey." He touched my arm and then his fingers curled around it. "You're just making them do busy work?" he whispered.

I did meet his eyes then. I hoped that he understood what I was trying to tell him, because I really didn't have the words.

He swallowed hard.

"Take care of my shop," I whispered back. Stepping back

from his hand, I turned and headed out the kitchen door for some air.

They could fiddle with all the spells they wanted, but I could see Erasmus bristle, could tell by the sharp posture of his shoulders that he thought it was all nonsense. That nothing could really protect me. I knew that. It was a suicide mission. It always was. Had been for every Chosen Host in every age. But staying and doing nothing was suicide too. So really, why not try? The Booke had to be stopped. It couldn't be allowed to go on. I'd get there and negotiate for Erasmus' life. It was the least I could do.

When I looked back through the window, Jeff hadn't moved. He wouldn't say anything. He had his own cosmic problems. He wouldn't tell them. They needed hope too.

* * *

IT WAS A long night. Jolene's parents called and Seraphina was obliged to take her home, much to her protests. Deputy George arrived after doing his rounds, meeting up with Ed quietly and solemnly. Jeff was conferring with Nick—probably discussing werewolf strategy, and once Seraphina returned, she worked closely with Doc.

"Attention everyone," said Doc after a long interval. "We've finished the potion, and tomorrow morning, early, all of us will have to do our part and travel throughout the village—even into the hills and down into the hollows—to spray the solution at every home, and I mean get right up to the front door. If people question you, say that we're spraying for maple beetles on the sheriff's orders."

"*Are* there such a thing as maple beetles?" asked Nick.

Doc smiled. "Not that I've ever heard of."

"Some of those folks in the hollow aren't exactly friendly," Nick continued. "They like to speak with their shotguns first."

"George and I will take those people," said Ed.

Doc nodded. "Good. Then we'll meet back here come sunup and get going. Everyone, bring every spray bottle and tank sprayer you've got. But before we disperse, I think we really need to discuss this trip to the Netherworld."

"I'm against it," said Nick. "Kylie has no idea what she's up against."

Before I could say anything, Doc held up his hand. "And that's the point of this discussion. Mr. Dark, could you tell us all you know about…about Satan?"

George shot to his feet, hands raised as if in surrender. "This is not right. You don't need spells and potions, Kylie. You need God. You need His help."

Nick got up and laid his hands onto George's arms. "My love, this has gone well beyond crosses and holy water."

"Nicky, I just…I just…"

"I know. Come back and sit down. Just listen to what Doc has to say."

It was hardest for George. He was the religious type. It wasn't as if he could leave it all behind just because of the appearance of a god or two. And with his boyfriend becoming a werewolf… Actually, I was surprised he had kept it together this long.

Doc patted his hand as he sat down on the chair next to him. "I know this is hard, George, but none of us have faced this sort of thing before. And I'm afraid the Bible, in all its wisdom and eloquence, cannot equip us as we need. So how about it, Mr. Dark? Can you tell us?"

Wisps of smoke began to feather off his jacket. "I do not wish to speak of Him."

"I beg your pardon, of course, but we have to know all we can about him if we are to find a way to protect Kylie. And I know you want to do that."

He stared daggers at Doc, his shoulders rising defensively. "You are putting me in an untenable position."

I leaned toward him. "They have to know, Erasmus."

He wasn't play-acting. He looked completely miserable. I'd known him only briefly, but this much I did know: he hated looking weak. And talking about Old Scratch, that made him weak.

His hands at his sides curled into fists.

"He is…all-powerful," he began. And then he couldn't stand still. He paced, smoke wafting off of him, hands flexing. "He…He can destroy simply with His mind. He knows who comes and who goes in the Netherworld."

"Have you ever had dealings with him?" Doc asked calmly, as if interviewing a patient to understand his ills.

"No, and I am eternally grateful for that."

"Then how do you know that all this is true?"

"I have heard the tales from others. They were not His direct minions. I have no reason to suspect that they lied to me. And the Powers That Be fear Him."

Doc rubbed his chin thoughtfully. "All we have to go on are the prevalent Judeo-Christian beliefs—"

"Forget all that you learned. It is much, much worse than that. He is the demon of demons, the *omnis terminus omnes*, the alpha and the omega. He is no fallen angel. He has no beginning, he has no end. He sits in solitude in the everlasting pit like a stone."

"Can he leave the Netherworld?"

Erasmus shook his head. "It is said that this is the only thing He may not do. He *is* a prisoner there."

"Imprisoned by whom?"

"By the Ancient Ones. Their names are unknowable. Their reasons lost to time. It is not even known if *they* still exist, but the power of merely mentioning them strikes fear in the hearts of those in the Netherworld."

"I see. What does Satan do with souls?"

He flicked his eyes toward me once and then fixed his gaze to Doc. "He consumes them…I imagine."

"But it is your understanding that he is a demon like you, only much more powerful?"

He thought a moment. "Yes. But more powerful than a god."

Doc nodded. "But a demon…we can comprehend."

"You're playing with fire. You cannot comprehend His like."

"Demons are of certain types with certain weaknesses. We can prey on those."

Erasmus seemed just as angry as before, except…something dawned in his eyes and he took a step closer to Doc, standing over him. "You are a man of wisdom and…imagination. I will help you however I can."

Chapter Six

THEY TALKED. NICK and Seraphina jabbed Erasmus with questions, and he answered each one in a more open fashion than I'd ever heard from him before. This traveling to the Netherworld had only been an idea before, but now it was shaping into a soon-to-be reality. Shit was getting real.

I saw Ed sitting with the coven, trying to follow, but he finally gave up and flopped down on the sofa next to me. "I have no idea what they're talking about." He stifled a yawn.

"Look, Ed. You've had a long day. There's nothing you can do here. Why don't you go home?"

He looked at his watch. "I guess so. I'll have to be up in less than three hours. I might as well sleep when I can." He rose, stretched, and waved his goodnights, though no one paid him any attention.

I laid my head back and closed my eyes. Until I could feel Erasmus presence hovering over me. "What?"

"Nothing. I have nothing to say."

I didn't bother opening my eyes. "Boy, your nothings are always pretty loud."

"I take exception to that."

"Are you telling me that you *aren't* jealous that Ed was hugging me while we consoled each other?"

I could see him in my mind's eye, grumbling, gritting his teeth, looking around suspiciously. He said nothing more, so I assumed he absorbed it.

When next I opened my eyes, everyone had gone. I didn't remember falling asleep. I sat up and surreptitiously wiped drool from the side of my mouth. Nice. "Did everyone leave?"

Erasmus' rich voice emerged from the shadows. "Yes. They all left an hour ago but will return in less than two hours."

"Why didn't you wake me?"

"Doctor Boone said not to."

"What time is it?" I glanced at the clock. Four-thirty. "I guess I should get to bed for what little time is left."

"I'll take you."

"I can do it—" But he'd already touched my arm and I found myself transported to the edge of my bed. "—myself. Dammit, Erasmus. You could at least ask first."

"I'm sorry. Should I take you back downstairs?"

"No. I'm already here." I yawned.

"Get into bed. I'll stand guard."

"You don't have to do that," I mumbled, stripping off my dress. So much for our romantic evening. I slipped off my bra and crawled into bed in my underwear and was surprised when the blankets were drawn up over me. Erasmus tucked the comforter up under my chin.

"I noticed you like it this way," he said, somewhat embarrassed.

"If you're supposed to be evil, you're really terrible at it," I murmured. I was smiling when I fell asleep. But when I woke about two hours later, I could already hear Doc and Seraphina downstairs. Erasmus must have let them in. Since I wasn't opening the shop, there was no need to spruce myself up. I dragged myself into the bathroom for a quick shower, put on a sweater and jeans, and went downstairs to see what the witches were brewing.

They had obviously been there a while, because they were busily filling all sorts of spray bottles and tanks. I dove in where needed. When Nick and George arrived, there were even more bottles to fill. I looked around at all the containers that we had begun to load up into boxes and wondered if we could ever have enough.

Erasmus handed me a cup of coffee and I smiled in thanks. He gave me his usual smoldering look and *boy*. All I wanted to do was crawl back into bed with him. I grabbed his arm before he could turn away and planted a kiss on his lips. He stared at me, shocked.

I rested a hand to his fuzzy cheek. "Good morning. Sorry our date was cut short."

He sidled closer, looked around to see if anyone was watching, and said very quietly, "I'm sorry too." He glanced at the kitchen table once, gave me a knowing look, and turned to get coffee for Jeff, who had just walked in.

"No time for that," said Seraphina, giving me an elbow and a wink.

"Wait a minute," I said. "Are you warming up to him?"

She glanced at him as he made his way around the perimeter of the room, glaring at everyone from under his brows. "It's not what I would have chosen for myself—or you, for that matter—but he seems…genuine. He loves you, that much is clear."

It still made my cheeks warm but I accepted it from her. I guessed we'd all had a change of heart in the last three weeks.

We gathered our sprayers. It was time to get out there and protect Moody Bog. We'd just closed the back hatch to Doc's Rambler wagon when he turned to me. "Kylie, I don't think you should come with us."

I was taken aback. "Why not?"

"Because I think your time would be better spent hunting this wendigo with Mr. Dark. We'll do what *we* can and you do what *you* can."

Seraphina clutched my hand. "He's right. Do your thing."

Everyone was looking at me, poised by their car doors. I stepped away from the Rambler. "Okay. Looks unanimous." I raised my arm and the crossbow sailed from the house to land neatly in my palm. "I'll see you guys later."

Like a switch turning on, they started moving again, starting their cars, and driving in opposite directions. The autumn sun on the rise peered between the trees.

Once they'd all driven away, I turned to Erasmus. "Let's do this."

I don't know if I'd ever been as anxious to get rid of a creature as I was with this one. These things were affecting everyone now, not just me. And it was only going to get worse. Who knew what the Booke would release next or if it already had?

I stomped into the woods but then realized that all this noise-making wasn't the way to do it. I slowed and walked carefully until the utterly silent Erasmus lightly touched my sleeve.

"Kylie," he said. I don't know what it was, but I always got a little shiver when he used my name. "You are attuned to the book as no other Chosen Host has ever been. You must listen to it now. It can help you find the creature. Stop and listen."

Okay. Made sense, if anything did. I stood in the dappled forest, surrounded by trees that shed their leaves like a fluttering waterfall of gold coins. But the forest was also a dense maze of tangled shadows and twigs and foliage. I couldn't even see or hear the road anymore. I took a deep breath, closed my eyes, and reached out to the Booke. I pictured the magical tendrils that tied me to it, and then I felt it like a soft caress, reminding me that it was there, waiting. It seemed to stretch toward the edges of the forest. My senses tingled with the sudden bombardment of awareness. All at once, I could tell exactly where a cricket was on a shiny leaf…or a bird clutching a high branch…or a salamander slipping into a damp bog. I couldn't believe how alive the forest was, and then Erasmus whispered in my ear.

"You feel it now, don't you? You see the forest as *I* see it."

I nodded slowly. I didn't want to open my eyes and have the sensations pass. Keeping my eyes closed brought everything into sharp focus as if I could "see" the whole thing spread out before me.

"Wendigo," I whispered, searching for it in the map in my mind. All of a sudden, I was rushing forward, past cattails and reeds, over squelching bogs and grassy rises, and then deep into the darkest hollows of the woods.

And there, standing in a glade, I saw it.

My eyes snapped open. I began running.

I just went with it. I didn't know how I knew. I didn't stop to be amazed by it. I just went with gut instinct, running through bracken and fern, casting aside tangling bushes, leaping over fallen logs. And Erasmus was right beside me, a bright glow of pride in his eyes when he looked toward me.

There was the bog with the cattails and farther on, the shadowed hollows. The trees parted and I was at the edge of the glade. The wendigo was there. Its waves of pain and sorrow reached me, swept over me, but it did not affect me as it had done before. Doc's spell held as I watched it pick its way over the grasses and ironweed in long, graceful strides, oblivious to me.

I drew the crossbow to my shoulder. It had already armed itself. Could it be this easy? I took careful aim and fired.

The bolt spiraled forward with a hissing sound and struck true. The wendigo reared up. I lowered the crossbow and saw the bolt stuck right in its chest, and that bright light began shooting through it.

The Booke arrived but instead of writing in it immediately, I watched the creature writhe and cry out. It looked at me with those saddened eyes even as light beams tore at its face. I wanted to see it die. I wanted it to go away. I snatched the quill from the air, jabbed at my other hand that was never going to heal, and began writing. *Die, you miserable cannibal!* I wrote. *Go back to where you came from with your misery and shame and take your insatiable hunger with you…*

I wrote in some other details, thinking that maybe a diatribe wouldn't be adequate, and soon enough it began to burn away like a filmstrip catching on fire. And when I dotted the last "i," it exploded in a shower of sparks and was no more.

I slammed the quill in the Booke, heaved it to the forest floor, and glared at it. I don't know why I was so suddenly angry. Maybe it was the cannibalism that it had foisted on me and the innocent couple Ed had told me about. Maybe it was because now my coven was wasting their time spraying that anti-cannibal charm everywhere. Or maybe it was because I was damned tired of cleaning up what the Ancient Ones thought was a great joke: inventing the damned Booke to begin with.

I got my breathing under control and glanced at Erasmus. He had an orgasmic look to his face. I guessed a Chosen Host in charge fired his engines. Lovely.

"Come on," I told him, holding the crossbow down at my thigh and marching back through the woods.

A weird screaming sound off in the distance sent a chill snaking down my spine.

"Already?" I whined.

"Yes. Something else from the book."

"This is turning out to be very crappy week."

He sniffed the air and turned in the direction of the eerie sound. "What is the expression? I think you said a mouthful."

Chapter Seven

THERE WAS NO point in *not* hunting it. Besides, I was running on adrenalin. Who knew how long that would last? So I followed it, letting the Booke guide me, keeping my eyes half-lidded and feeling its magic lead. Miraculously, I didn't trip, even only half-aware of everything around me.

We heard the shriek again.

I stopped and glanced at Erasmus. "What do you suppose that is?"

"I think...I think..."

A burst of leaves and twigs, and the thing flew at me. All I saw before I went down was a pale figure with red glowing eyes and rags fluttering off of it, making that horrible sound.

I flipped over on the ground to my stomach, my crossbow out before me, armed.

The creature disappeared into the shadows. I was up and running, dead leaves flying off of me.

"It's a banshee," said Erasmus, running beside me.

"And what does a banshee do besides scream?"

"That's mostly what it does. Its scream heralds the death of someone."

"Heralds or causes it?"

He shrugged. "Perhaps a little of both."

We continued running. Must have been my Chosen Host skills because I wasn't tiring like I used to. When we came around a bend, we saw it perched high on a rock.

It looked like some crazy old woman with white hair blowing in all directions. Her ragged dress hung on her like a mummy's bandages. She was wailing with her head thrown back—a truly horrible sound that jarred me right to my bones.

I raised the crossbow to my shoulder, wondering if I could get her from here when she turned and looked right at me. It didn't stop me from pulling the trigger.

The bolt flew and stuck her in the neck. She fell off the rock, or tried to, but the fiery death that the Booke meted out caught her in mid-air, and the holes burned through her. Jeez, she wailed so loudly they probably heard her in the next county. Her cries echoed off all the rock outcroppings.

The Booke showed up, quill at the ready. I noticed I was leaving a smear of blood on the crossbow—which it probably enjoyed, knowing these Netherworld things—so there was still blood in my palm to write out what little I could describe about her in the Booke.

She burned up soon enough and the wailing became just a memory as all fell silent again.

I looked at Erasmus as I lowered the crossbow. "Why is this so easy all of a sudden?"

His eyes tracked all around us. "I don't know."

Another scream behind me made me whip around. This was getting ridiculous. I exchanged a glance with Erasmus and plunged down the side of the hill into the forest again.

* * *

I MUST HAVE dispatched three more beasties before I called it quits and headed for home. I was hungry, and not in a cannibal way this time. It was after two in the afternoon, after all.

The Wiccans had gathered at my shop. I dropped into a chair, laying the bloodied crossbow across my lap.

"How did it go?" asked Nick, bringing me a beer.

I took a long drink from the bottle before balancing it on my thigh. "How many was that, Erasmus?"

"Five," he said proudly.

"Kylie!" said Doc coming to sit on the ottoman in front of me. "You dispatched *five* creatures?"

"Six. Accidentally got a squirrel. I didn't mean to."

Nick sat on the floor next to Doc. "Whoa. Isn't that, you know, a lot?"

"Yes. It is." I took another swig of beer. "A lot to show up and a lot for me to just take down like I'm at a shooting gallery. I don't get it."

"So wait," said Jolene, putting down her skull Hello Kitty backpack. "You just—bang, bang, bang—" She mimed shooting an invisible crossbow. "Like, all at once? That's more than has ever showed up before."

"Yup." Another swig of beer.

"You're being pretty matter-of-fact," said Jeff, leaning on the top of my wing chair.

"I don't know how else to take it. So all that spraying you guys did… The wendigo had been gone since daybreak."

"What?" Seraphina, usually the calmest of us all had a furious look on her face. "And you didn't call us? We went all over Hades to spray every inch of this village and then some."

I lowered the empty bottle to my thigh. "I-I'm sorry, guys. I was just suddenly really up to here with creatures."

"Well," she sighed, crossing her arms over her chest. "I guess I can't blame you."

"I'm really sorry," I said again. I looked at Jolene and then my eyes swept over the clock. "Hey, what are you doing here so early?"

"Oh, I just skipped school today."

"Jolene!"

"It was far more important that my friends didn't eat

each other. And don't sweat it. I'm like six months ahead on homework."

"Don't let your parents get wind of it or they won't let you come here anymore."

"Don't worry."

She had a handle on it. It probably involved hacking into the school computer, but it wasn't for me to say anything. This was more serious than running a shop or going to school.

The bell above the door jangled as Ed stomped through followed by Deputy George. "Well, we've got trouble."

"What now?" I threw my head back against the chair.

He was brandishing a flyer of some kind. "Says here a town meeting's been called to address all the mysterious deaths and happenings in town."

Nick rose to read it over Ed's shoulder. "Uh-oh. In every movie I've ever seen, that's when the villagers start getting their torches and pitchforks."

"No one's going to do that," I said. But then I saw Ed's worried face. "Are they?"

"I will not let these villagers attack you," said Erasmus, shoulders billowing puffs of smoke.

"Wait, wait!" I said, rising. "Erasmus…" I gestured to his smoky jacket and he turned off the fire. "No one knows what's going on. It's all just speculation. No matter what some people might have seen, no one's going to believe them, right?"

No one said anything. Erasmus looked the most skeptical. I suppose he'd seen his fair share of mobs turning ugly.

"Um…so Ed, when is this town meeting?"

"Tonight. This really ticks me off. Because I think you know who is behind it." He didn't even have to say it.

Good old Ruth Russell.

Doc gently took the paper from Ed and looked it over. "I think it's in our best interests to show up to this. All of us, if we can."

"Some of those protection spells you've been talking about wouldn't go amiss," I said.

He smiled congenially. "Those are for Satan. But for this, I suppose a few charm pouches might be a good idea."

"Speaking of Satan," said Jolene eagerly. She grabbed her tablet and did some swiping. "Remember a while ago when we worried about Mr. Dark, uh, eating your soul?"

Who didn't remember that? Erasmus raised his nose at Jolene. "You might remember I vowed not to do so."

"Well," she went on, ignoring him, "Mr. Dark said he wouldn't agree to get a tattoo that would prevent him from eating souls."

"Certainly not," he said indignantly.

"But that doesn't mean that Kylie can't have one that keeps soul-eating away. It blocks the ability of a demon to suck out her soul. Look here." She turned the tablet around and showed a little design that looked like some curly-cues with dots. "If we make the ink with some strong incantations, I think this will do the trick, you know, against Satan?"

Seraphina studied the tablet's image. "How do we get a tattoo artist to use our ink?"

"If we can't, then we do the work ourselves."

"Whoa. Hold on," I said. "Like some prison tats? Uh-uh."

"It's a simple design," said Doc. "Yes, we can do it, if necessary."

I shook my head vigorously. "Like I said…"

Erasmus looked it over skeptically. "Satan is no ordinary demon. But it *might* work."

"Am I supposed to get this tattooed on my chest like Erasmus?"

"No, silly," said Jolene. "On the inside of your wrist. At the pulse point. We can do the spell on the ink today. We have the ingredients to do it right now. Maybe even get the tattoo today."

I gnawed on my thumbnail. I wasn't into tattoos myself. Nothing against it. Well, maybe the needles. I grabbed Erasmus' arm and dragged him away from the others. They were watching me as I turned my back to them, talking quietly to the demon.

"If I get this tattoo, then what about you and me?"

"What do you mean?"

"Will you still be able to…you know."

"What? I won't be able to consume your soul…even though I already made a solemn vow not to."

"That's not what I mean. Will we still be able to…make love?"

The tense crease across his forehead relaxed and his eyes softened. "Never fear. I will still be able to touch you…as intimately as you desire."

God, he could read the phone book and it would still come out sexy, let alone *those* words. Despite my worries, I was feeling a little warm.

"Okay, then. I just wanted to make sure."

He chuckled deep in his chest. "Who's a naughty mortal now?"

He made me smile, which was better than being afraid. I turned back to my coven. "Okay. Let's start with the ink-making."

"And I'll call the tattoo guy," said Nick. "I think he'll do it. He's okay."

I started to wonder if Nick was sporting his own tattoos. I glanced toward Deputy George. He seemed to know what I was thinking and blushed before turning his head away.

* * *

JOLENE WAS EXCITED to help make the ink. They'd be using carbonized ashes from burned wood, along with vodka.

"Why vodka?" I asked, watching the wood burn in the fireplace.

She pushed her clear-framed glasses up her nose. "Because it's antiseptic and has no color. Since it's going into your skin, it's better than just using water. It's an ancient recipe for tattooing, really. Some used berries, but the kind of berries we would need are dormant now. This is the next best thing. How clean is your blender? Never mind. I'll throw some alcohol in it first."

"Okay," said Nick, clicking off his phone. "Wendell, the tattoo artist at Moody Bog Tattoos, said he'd be okay with it, as long as the ink is fresh. I told him it was as fresh as can be. He can squeeze you in at four o'clock."

Everything was rushing at me kind of quick. I glanced toward Erasmus for reassurance. He gave me a small nod, which was enough.

Nick and Jolene huddled together by the fire, holding the tablet in front of them. Doc and Seraphina took their places behind them. And then they all began to chant.

I caught some foreign words and some English phrases about protection and keeping the gates of my soul closed. Seraphina tossed in some herbs over the fire, which sparked in colors of green, then blue, then a deep purple as the chant continued.

They looked very much like a coven of witches with their black silhouettes bent over the jumping flames. All the while I rubbed at my wrist unconsciously.

After the fire died down and the wood wasn't red glowing coals anymore, Jolene and Nick took the burnt pieces to the kitchen. We all followed them there as they carefully scraped off the carbon onto a clean piece of linen with a silver knife. Nick sluiced my blender with alcohol several times and dumped it in the sink, and then Jolene measured in a couple of tablespoons of ash and added a little vodka. She replaced the lid and turned on the blender. The whirring mixture looked a lot like ink to me. She finessed it with a little more ash, a drop more of vodka, and voila! Soul-eater deterrent.

"There's one more blessing," said Jolene.

The coven chanted together:

> *"O ash of burning wood,*
> *where once you were Tree,*
> *in whose bark keeps safe all secrets,*
> *dance like the dust in the wind*
> *and keep thy strange mysteries.*
> *Deliver the one who bears your mark.*
> *Keep closed the sacred gates.*
> *No creature shall take thine soul as long as this mark touches thee."*

There was the slightest puff of wind and I could have sworn the ink in the blender sparkled just a little. They all stood back, satisfied.

"That's it?" I said, breaking the sudden silence.

"Yup," said Nick, carefully removing the blender jar from the base. "And it's about time we get over to the tattoo parlor."

We all headed for the door when I stopped. "How many are going?"

Doc chuckled. "Oh, well. I suppose we don't all need to go. Nick knows Wendell, so naturally he'll go, and Jolene found the sigil, so she'll go. You, Kylie, of course. And Mr. Dark I imagine will like to oversee the proceedings."

"Mr. Dark would," said Erasmus coldly.

We all piled in my Jeep where I followed Nick's directions to the little shack of a tattoo parlor at the other end of town. I was nervous. I'd never had a tattoo before and I didn't relish it now, but I was beginning to feel a little better about my Netherworld journey. Erasmus seemed to go along with it anyway.

We parked out front. The lot was mostly empty, just a motorcycle and another car parked next to us. Inside the tiny shop, the walls were covered in tattoo flash, samples of the different designs the artist could do. There was a wide variety from simple hearts and four-leaf clovers, to more elaborate 3D stuff.

Wendell was a very tattooed individual with silver earrings going up the shell of his ear and spiked leather cuffs on his wrist. He was bent over a chair, where a woman with quite a collection of her own tats and piercings sat, getting something inked on her knee.

Wendell looked up and nodded to Nick. "Be with you in a sec, Nick. Just finishing up here."

The woman looked at me and popped her gum. She never seemed to flinch.

Wendell wiped her knee with a cloth and looked it over. "*Finito*, Jean," he said. "You know the drill," he said, carefully taping a piece of gauze over it.

"Yeah," said Jean. She jumped up right away. "That was awesome, Wendell."

"Come back soon. We'll get the rest of that leg done."

She nodded, walked past me looking me up and down, and left through the glass door.

Wendell stripped off his rubber gloves, stuffed them in a stainless-steel pail, and donned more black latex. "So what have we got? That your homemade ink?" He nodded toward the blender.

"Yup," said Nick carefully placing it on his work table. "There's more than enough to do it. Did you get the design I texted you?"

"Yeah. Printed it out." He grabbed a piece of tissue paper from the table. "Who's the victim?"

I swallowed and edged forward, raising my hand. "Tattoo virgin here."

"Hey, no problem. Have a seat. This is going inside your left wrist?"

I looked back at Nick and Jolene for confirmation. They nodded.

He spotted my amulet. "Wicked cool necklace. Where'd you get that?"

"Got it off a dear friend." I flicked a glance at Erasmus. The demon couldn't help but come closer, standing on the other side of me protectively.

"So this is Kylie," said Nick, introducing us. "This is Jolene. And that's Erasmus…Kylie's boyfriend."

Erasmus shot him a deadly look.

My glare at Nick wasn't too far from Erasmus'.

"The, uh, specifications must be exact," said Nick after clearing his throat.

Wendell glanced up at the demon standing awfully close to my chair but didn't seem to mind. He turned my wrist over to examine it. "I got Nick's instructions. It's a pretty simple design."

Wendall swabbed my wrist with what I supposed was antiseptic. "Okay, Kylie. I'm going to put an imprint of the design on your wrist and you tell me if this is right."

He put some cold gel on my arm and stuck some tissue paper on my wrist with the design facing the right direction, as per Nick's instructions. The tissue paper had the design on one side and what looked like a carbon paper image on the other. When he peeled it off, the design remained on my arm in a blue outline. "Look good?"

"As long as it's filled in entirely with the ink," said Nick.

Wendall looked toward Erasmus, but he was stone-faced.

"All right. Let me get some of that ink in a cup, and we'll get this party started. Allergic, huh?"

"What?"

Nick leaned in. "I told him how you're allergic to a lot of these inks and that's why we had to make our own."

"Oh. Yeah."

"You should be fine with this, then," said Wendell. He put the ink cup on his work table, and poised toward me with his machine in hand.

I sat forward. "Aren't you going to use any anesthetic?"

He chuckled. "You know, Kylie, I've been doing this for like twenty years…" He didn't look that old to me, but maybe he had good skin. "And I'm not gonna lie. It'll hurt. Kind of stings. Lots of little needles jabbing in you at the same time. But it won't kill you. Do you have a low tolerance for pain?"

I shrugged. "I guess not."

"All right then. Lie back and think of rainbows and unicorns."

Erasmus snorted but I didn't look at him.

I rested my arm on the armrest, tipped my head back against the paper-covered lounger, and grasped Erasmus' hand.

The tattoo machine buzzed in Wendell's hand. As soon as he touched it to my skin, I jumped a little. Yeah, it did sting, but as Erasmus squeezed my hand harder, the pain just…went away. He was healing me. I looked up into his intense eyes with as much gratitude as I could muster. His gaze softened and he even smiled a little.

Before I knew it, it was done.

I looked at it. It was attractive in its way. The skin puffed pink around it, but it was small, no more than three inches long.

"No emersion in water," said Wendall, sticking a gauze pad over it, "No baths, and especially no pools or Jacuzzis for a week. Keep an eye on it and change the dressing tomorrow. It will feel a little tender for up to a week, depending."

"It feels fine," I said. "Doesn't hurt or anything."

"Oh yeah? Well, good. Now toss the rest of this ink. It won't be good tomorrow. If you want more work done, you'll have to make more."

"I think this is all I'll be doing."

"So, what's it mean?"

It looked like Erasmus was about to tell Wendell to mind his own business so I rushed in with, "It's a very special symbol to me."

Wendall seemed satisfied with that. Nick and Wendall exchanged a bro handshake and hug, paid the man, and then we were back in the Jeep again.

"I don't think I'll be getting any tattoos," said Jolene, looking a little green.

"So this will do the trick," I said, glancing now and again at the gauze on my arm.

"Perhaps," said Erasmus, "but I am not entirely convinced it will protect you one hundred percent."

I glared at him. "You approved!"

"I said it *might* help. But Satan is a very powerful demon."

"Well…we'll just have to see. When should we go?"

Nick grabbed the headrest in front of him and pulled himself forward. "Hold on, Kylie. We still have research to do and more protection spells to cast. And we've got to think about the book. You had to kill five creatures. What makes you think something else hasn't already come out?"

"We're running out of time, Nick. What happens if the Booke is still active on Halloween? It could be far more than even *I* can handle. And they could still kill me."

"I will never let that happen," rasped Erasmus.

"They could overtake you, too, you know."

"Let them try!"

"I don't want to let them try. I want to stop the Booke now."

Jolene said quietly, "We still have to research how to unbind Mr. Dark from the book."

That shut me down. If we couldn't release Erasmus, then there was no use in my going at all.

Erasmus brooded. He faced away from me and stared out the window. Everyone's good mood seemed to have flown.

I pulled in front of my shop. Doc and Seraphina emerged to greet us.

"Everything all right?" asked Doc, searching each of our faces in turn.

I lifted my bandaged arm. "Everything's peachy," I said.

"Yes," he muttered. "I can see that."

I pushed my way into the shop. I could tell that Doc and Seraphina hadn't been idle. A load of charm pouches were laid out on the kitchen table.

Erasmus walked through to the kitchen and stopped dead. He raised his arm to cover his face. "I'll wait outside," he coughed and vanished.

"Well," said Doc. "That's a good sign. Looks like these are powerful."

I should have been mad at Doc, but I couldn't summon up the emotion. I was glad, in fact, that they'd made these.

We each put our charm pouches on leather straps and hung them around our necks under our shirts. No need to advertise. Ed called and said that he and George would meet us at the town meeting. Now all we had to do was…wait it out.

Jolene was busy on her tablet consulting with Nick, who was on his laptop. They argued back and forth about possible unbinding spells, but nothing seemed quite to be what they were looking for.

I couldn't resist looking at my tattoo so I peeled back a corner of the gauze. All the red puffiness was gone. I suspected that

Erasmus had healed that too. I plucked the rest of the medical tape off and threw the gauze into the fireplace.

"Maybe Doc has a book or two," said Nick. "Should we go over to yours later, Doc? After the meeting? If we aren't burned at the stake, that is."

"No one's going to be burning anyone at the stake," he said wearily.

I snorted. "I'm sure they said that in Salem, too."

"Actually, no one from the Salem Witch Trials was burned at the stake," said Jolene. "They were all hanged."

"Oh. Well, that makes me feel much better."

I wandered around, doing a little dusting. When some cars slowed by the shop, I decided to unlock the door and put out the open sign. Those customers doubled back and parked out front. I was happy to have something to do as I rang up their purchases. It was nice to get the cash register working again.

I thought about stashing my crossbow in the car, but I got the sense that I could carry the Spear of Mortal Pain with me instead. That was some ancient Irish weapon called *Gáe Bulg* I'd stolen off of Doug. Shabiri had gotten it for him, but now it was mine. It was a handy size that I could fit in my coat, telescoping down. I went to where I had stashed it in my kitchen and snuck it through the shop into an inside pocket of my coat, like a magic wand. I felt better armed.

Sooner than I'd thought, it was time to head over to the town meeting. What was the saying? *Start every day with a smile and get it over with.*

CHAPTER EIGHT

BECAUSE OF THE charm pouches, I hadn't seen Erasmus since the tattooing. I was beginning to wonder if it wasn't a better idea to get rid of my pouch so he could be with me. I glanced quickly at Doc and while he wasn't looking, I took it off and stuffed it in a seat cushion. Almost immediately I felt that rush of wind as he appeared behind me.

"Thank the gods you finally got rid of that," he muttered.

"I'm sorry. I thought it was a good idea at the time."

"*I* can protect you from any villager attacks." He seemed insulted that I would use any other methods. I could see his point.

"I'm sorry." I looked again to see if anyone was paying attention to me before I reached up and gave him a soft kiss.

He seemed more than mollified. A little melty, if truth be told. Some big bad demon *he* turned out to be.

He vanished again when Doc turned our way. "Shall we all ride together?"

I thought of all of us crammed in Doc's Rambler. "I'll take my Jeep. You all go with Doc."

I could tell that Jolene wanted to protest, but Seraphina gave me a knowing eye and steered the teenager toward Doc's car. Good old Seraphina. She knew exactly what was up.

Once the Rambler had pulled away from the shop, I got in the Jeep and wasn't surprised when Erasmus appeared beside me. Before I could do or say anything he reached over and kissed me. When he sat back, he seemed a little proud of himself.

I started up the car. "No hocus pocus when we get there."

"I haven't the least idea what you are talking about."

"No magic tricks. Just let everyone have their say. They're naturally worried. I mean, this would be a really bad time for Baph—I mean, Goat Guy to show up."

He shook his head the way he always did when I used my nickname for the god Baphomet. But he was the one who'd told me not to use his name in case the god interpreted it as a summons.

I couldn't help but touch the amulet, feeling its familiar and somehow comforting warmth.

We pulled into the driveway of the church parking lot, crowded with cars from the village. "Hey," I said, turning to my companion. "The church hall is hallowed ground, isn't it? You won't be able to get into the building."

He scowled. "I hadn't thought of that. I will be near, however. And if you should need me, I'll…" But it didn't look like he knew *what* he could do.

"I'll be fine. Maybe you'd better disappear for now."

Frowning, he glared at the cars in the parking lot and vanished.

I pulled into a spot and wrapped my coat around me as I slammed the door. I supposed the church hall was the natural place to meet. A central location with perhaps the biggest auditorium in Moody Bog. It was stifling hot inside so I quickly slung my coat over my arm. Seraphina was waving at me. Jolene waved too, though she was sitting with her parents. Jan and Kevin Ayrs looked rumpled in their corduroy and patchwork sweaters. I gave them a nod when they looked my way. They ran the plant nursery in town, seemed like nice people.

I was able to slide my way through the crowd. It was standing room only now, but I managed to get next to Doc and the coven.

"I think everyone's here," said Nick, stretching his neck to look around. "There's Deputy Mustache," he said, pointing, and using the nickname *I* had used for George.

I grinned. "He looks good in a uniform."

"Don't I know it," he said proudly. I was glad to see that George was taking Nick out in public these days. It had to be better than sneaking around hotel rooms. Maybe becoming a werewolf had been good for Nick…in a strange way.

Nick pointed in the opposite direction. "And there's the sheriff. He looks pretty good in uniform, too. Though…I guess he's off the menu, huh?"

"Yeah." But I looked anyway. He did look good. I sighed. Even if all of the rest of it wasn't happening, I still would have chosen Erasmus. It made me feel better to realize that.

Besides. Wasn't Ed seeing Shabiri, the other demon in town? What had started off with my suggestion that he get in close to her for a little undercover work had turned into…well, *something*. I don't know if I really trusted Shabiri, but then again…I don't know that I trusted Erasmus not to lie to me either.

Demons, I thought. *Trouble all around.*

I saw Hezekiah Thompson, the council manager, make his way through the crowd. Maine didn't seem to have mayors but that's basically what he was. He was a big man with a reddened nose. Friendly and boisterous. He had come to my grand opening and seemed genuinely pleased that I had opened my business.

The council members had assembled at a long table at the front of the room, flanked by a Maine flag and an American flag. I recognized some of the people there from the Chamber of Commerce Get-Together at the beginning of the month: John Fairgood of the Fairgood Gun Shop, Sy Alexander who owned the Coffee Shack where Nick worked, Reverend Howard and, of course, good old Ruth Russell. Two other people I didn't know sat at the table beside them.

Hezekiah tapped a gavel. "I'd like to bring this town meeting to order," he said loudly. He didn't seem to need a mic. "If we'd all be quiet and settle down… There. We're here tonight because… well…because we've never had such horrific things happening in our town before."

The crowd murmured.

"Murders, some really quite…unspeakable. I wonder if we can have Sheriff Bradbury come up and talk to us, if he can, about what's been happening and how far he is in his investigations."

More murmuring. I turned and spotted Ed. He didn't look too happy about being called up, but I could see him putting on his sheriff's mask and striding forward. He was taller than most and I could easily follow him through the crowd. He made it to the front and stood to Hezekiah's side.

"Good evening," he said.

"Good evenings," echoed from the assembled crowd.

"I'm not going to lie. Deputy Miller and I have had our hands full. Because of the nature of some of the deaths, we have had the help of the staties. But we are only one town and they have a lot on their plate. Beginning in early October, there were the deaths of Karl Waters, the tourist Joseph Mayes, Bob Hitchins, Nicole Meunier, Dan Parker, the Warrens, more recently the Browns, and the, uh, desecration of several graves in Moody Bog Cemetery. There are several missing persons that we are presuming dead at this point."

He looked like you wanted your sheriff to look: determined, calm, statesmen-like.

"We have no leads at the moment," he went on, "but we are working closely with the state on a forensic level."

Hezekiah shook his head. "Do we have any idea if…well, if such a thing was done by a person or persons living here among us?"

"It's too early to tell," he said, keeping his steady gaze out over the crowd, "but it is my professional opinion that it is *not* someone local." What else could he say? He now knew exactly what it was but certainly could never admit it.

By the sounds the audience was making, they weren't buying that.

"How could it not?" cried a man in the middle of the crowd. "It's all so personal, these attacks. Have you looked at Hansen Mills?"

"Yeah!" said a woman from the back. "How about that motorcycle gang?"

The crowd seemed to be in agreement about the Ordo. Some well knew that Doug was Ed's younger brother.

Hezekiah raised his hands. "Now folks, we can't all speak at once. We've got to be orderly about this."

"I've seen some odd things here!" said a man from the far side of the audience. "Weird stuff."

"Me too!" said another man. "Flying monsters! That wasn't no exploding gas lines. I seen the beast!"

Uh-oh. I exchanged a glance with Doc. I suddenly felt naked without my charm pouch.

"Let's quit pussyfooting around," said a man with a deep voice near the front. "I know we're all thinking it. None of these things ever happened…until *she* came to town!" He swung his arm to point…right at me.

Well, shit.

Ed's voice rose above the angry murmuring. All eyes were aimed at me, and not many were being nice about it. "Now hold on! This isn't a witch hunt." I think he might have winced a little, because he knew that the next words would be—

"And those Wiccans, too!"

Doc's expression was furious, as if he would leap up at any second. Seraphina even put a hand on his arm to hold him back.

How could I blame any of them? Because for once, they were right. None of this would have happened if I hadn't come to Moody Bog.

Reverend Howard stood with hands raised to quiet the crowd. And there was Ruth, just sitting there, her mouth in a pruney frown, her arms crossed over her chest and that damned Babylonian locket around her neck.

"Now let's all quiet down," said the Reverend. He was wearing his clerical collar and I thought *that* more than anything else let him calm the crowd. "Are you listening to yourselves? You sound like the cast of some horror movie. That isn't a sane argument. Kylie Strange has only brought something beautiful to this town: a lovely shop and customers who are now patronizing your store and yours," he said, pointing out various retail owners. "I mean, are you really accusing Fred Boone who has been a solid citizen in this community for over sixty years?"

Some hung their heads, shuffling guiltily.

Reverend Howard stared them all down. "I'm ashamed of some of the things I've been hearing from otherwise intelligent people. There are logical explanations to what you think you've been seeing. And it has nothing to do with Kylie and Fred Boone's Wiccans."

Everyone was quiet for a moment, until… "You of all people, Reverend," said someone from the crowd. A man stepped forward wearing a work shirt with a name stitched onto it. "You're supposed to see the evil that's around us and protect us. But I think there *is* something evil here. Something…not of this world. I know what I saw. Other people saw it too. Something big flying over us and it wasn't no explosion from a gas line. It was some kind of beast. And I don't care if it don't sound sane or not. Nothing like that ever happened…until *she* came to town."

He turned to glare at me again. I had never seen such spitting hatred as I saw in his eyes.

The assembly burst into argument again, some siding with Work Shirt and some arguing against. I was thinking a hasty retreat might be in order.

Doc seemed about to throw up some sort of protection spell, but I put a hand on his arm and got in close. "That's all we need. Do you really want to show our hand? Do you really want to prove that guy right?"

"Dear goddess," he muttered. "You're right, of course. We are in a right pickle."

I suddenly wished Erasmus was here, but that would have created the same problem.

A woman stepped forward, wearing a stiff pea coat despite the warmth of the room. Her hair was done in ragged braids and she had one of those hard midwestern Depression-era faces. "If she's so new to town, how come she started in with them Wiccans right away? She's always hanging with them. And just what was it they was spraying on my front door? I watched them. They was doing it at the crack of dawn to everyone's houses. It's either poison or some sort of hypnosis or spell or something."

Ed stepped forward in front of the table. "They were helping the county," he said. "They were spraying for maple beetles—"

"There ain't no such thing as maple beetles," said Work Shirt. "I looked it up. I saw you and the deputy spraying that shit, too. You're in on it with them."

"Roger Farley!" cried Reverend Howard. "Lisa Smith!" he said, scowling at Depression Woman. "I can't believe I'm hearing this from you two! It's absurd. Are you listening to yourselves?"

"I saw them Wiccans spraying that stuff, too," said a farmer type. "And screw it. I'm not calling them *Wiccans* no more. They're *witches*, plain and simple. Back in Salem, they knew how to take care of their like."

I knew Salem would get dragged into it, I said in my head.

Hezekiah tried to bring order back by pounding the table with his gavel. "Now listen! Hush up, all of you! That's all just plain crazy talk. Doc and his Wiccans aren't doing any harm and you know it. And there are no such things as flying beasts!"

The ceiling exploded. Cracked plaster, acoustic tiles, and snapped trusses rained down on the screaming crowd. And then Baphomet landed right in the middle of the carnage, with his stupid goat face and his huge bat wings.

This was *not* helping!

People scattered, scrambling over one another to escape. Some just dropped to their knees and began praying.

I swept my glance toward Ed, who was aiming his gun

two-handed at Baphy. George had managed to get his hands on his rifle. Though his aim was shaky—I realized that this was his first encounter with Goat Guy—he kept a fairly steady bead on him.

Reverend Howard was open-mouthed and flat against the far wall. And Ruth…

Well, well. Ruth was standing at a doorway, looking up at Baphomet, her mouth in a firm line. She seemed a little too nonplussed. Had she called on him? Damn her!

The Wiccans fanned out around him. At Doc's signal, they all raised their hands and started chanting.

A hazy glow formed around Baphomet and he looked down at their spell with disdain.

The glow was getting stronger, pushing toward the god. He seemed to be getting a little bit nervous as it began to surround him. Then he bared his teeth, crossed his arms over his chest like he was gathering himself, and snapped them open. The glow shot back, knocking my Wiccans over. I was lucky to catch Doc before he fell and broke something.

By then all of the townsfolk had fled, emptying the hall. None of the board members remained. Even Ruth Russell was gone.

Doc wrestled out of my grip spitting mad. "That will not do!" he cried. He stood up and began a different incantation. There was suddenly a purple aura around him and when Seraphina joined him, the aura spread to her. Then Nick stood beside him, then Jolene.

They could do what *they* needed to do. And I could do what *I* could do. I whipped out the Spear of Mortal Pain from my jacket. Pushing the button, it telescoped out into a ten-foot long sharp weapon.

I grasped it in both hands and stalked up to Baphy. "*You* are pissing me off!" I yelled.

His weird goat eyes slid toward me. "Kylie Strange," he said in that odd voice, somewhere between a lowing bull and a male baritone. "You continue to be a thorn in my side. Give me the book."

"What is *with* you people and the Booke? You can't open it."

"Mortals cannot open it. I am an *immortal. I* can."

Oh. I didn't like that. "And I suppose you want it to open a gateway to let in flowers and unicorns?"

"No." He leaned his twelve-foot-tall body down until his face was close to mine. I could smell the muskiness of the black fur on his face and shoulders, the male sweat from his human-looking torso, and some other scents like sulfur and tar. "I want to open a Hell Gate and let my brother and sister gods in. Mortals turned their backs on us centuries ago. I want them to pay for that insult."

"Is that all? Why didn't you say so in the first place?" Before he could draw back—and before I could chicken out—I hauled back with the spear and rammed it right into his eye.

It slipped out of my hands as he reared up, the spear still sticking out of his eye like a cocktail pick in an olive. He howled like the late banshee, screaming and cursing in some strange outmoded language, before he grasped the spear in a taloned hand and yanked it out. He threw it to the floor and I surprised myself with the presence of mind to go get it.

I must have really got him good, because he continued to howl, to clutch at his eye where black goo trickled over his fingers. He staggered back and leaned against the wall, which crumbled beneath him. Then he staggered forward and I thought he might fall on *us*. But he righted himself, beat his wings, and lifted from the floor, the wind knocking us all back. With a powerful stroke, he shot into the sky and disappeared.

I hadn't killed him but that spear lived up to its name. "Good spear!" I said, shaking it.

"Kylie!" Jolene ran toward me. "Oh my God. You scared him off."

I mimed jabbing him. "Right in the eye."

"Good work!"

Nick slapped me on the shoulder. "That was wicked awesome!"

"He's only gone temporarily," said Seraphina. I noticed they were all still glowing purple.

"What's with the purple?" I asked.

Doc waved his hand impatiently and it disappeared. "A powerful protection spell we've been working on." He put his hands on his hips and looked up at the hole in the ceiling. "That was a poorly timed appearance."

"Yeah. Now what? The whole town knows."

"And thinks we're conjuring him," said Nick, running his hand through his hair.

Ed and Deputy George ran up to us. "You okay, Kylie?"

"Yeah. Did you see?" I jabbed the spear again. "Got him in the eye."

"Yeah," said Ed uncertainly. "I saw." He glanced back toward the ruined door.

But what had everyone else seen? Only Baphomet and me before they scattered. "Do they still think we're the bad guys?"

"I don't think they think we're the good guys."

"Well, that's not fair."

"Everyone's scared," said George breathlessly. He held his rifle down at his side. "So am I, truth be told."

"We can't have the town against us, too." I pressed the button to bring the spear back down to ruler size. "Did you see poor Reverend Howard?"

"Did you see Ruth Russell?" said Jolene.

I looked around. "Where are they now?"

Ed seemed concerned. "I don't know." He was right to be worried. Everything they just said about us turned out to be true. If they'd only stuck around, they would have seen me *fight* the god not *side* with him.

Jan and Kevin Ayrs pushed their way back through the carnage in the hall and ran up to Jolene. Her mother grabbed her and Kevin wrapped his arms around the both of them.

"Mom! Dad! Not in front of the coven!"

"Is this what you've been doing all this time, young lady?" her father gasped.

She struggled and got free of them. "We've been trying to *stop* him."

"I don't understand," said Jan tearfully. "I thought you were just doing some benign pagan things. Crystals and herbs."

"I have been. But…there's also been some supernatural stuff going on and we…" she gestured toward the other Wiccans, "have been trying to help. There's a lot of dangerous stuff happening."

"Fred!" said Kevin, stalking up to Doc. "I trusted you to keep my daughter safe."

"And I have, Kevin. But you must understand, we couldn't do half the things we've needed to do if it wasn't for Jolene. We need her. If you're thinking of forbidding her—"

"That's exactly what we're going to do!"

"Kev, I give you my word that I will keep her safe. But darn it, we need her. You've seen what we're up against."

"Against? Are you trying to tell me you didn't conjure that creature?"

"That's exactly what I'm telling you, Kev."

"Mr. Ayrs," offered Nick, "I've been looking after her like a big brother. But honest to God—or whatever—we just can't get along without her skills. We'd probably all be dead by now if it wasn't for her."

Kevin ran his hands over his argyle vest. His face contorted with indecision. He looked to his wife, who gazed sorrowfully at her daughter.

"Mom, Dad, believe them. We're doing important work. We have a job to do."

"Well…what did that…that *creature* mean about a book?"

Right on cue, the Booke of the Hidden popped into existence in front of me. Kevin and Jan leapt back, hands over their mouths.

I grabbed it out of the air and held it tight. "He meant this. Boy, what to say?" I looked pleadingly at Doc.

"You'd best tell them the whole thing."

"This," I began, showing them the Booke.

"'Booke of the Hidden'?" Kevin read the cover.

"Right. I found it in the wall of my shop. For reasons too complicated to explain, I opened it and it released all these creatures into the world. The creatures have been killing all the people in town. I've been killing the creatures and putting them back in the Booke, but it hasn't been easy. And Doc's coven has been helping. Jolene's found a lot of really important information for us. It's been keeping me alive. So…so if you can see your way to letting her continue, we'll all be looking out for her…as we've been doing."

"Does she even really work at your shop?"

"Oh, yeah! She's been great there too. Um…sorry for lying to you, but, as you can see…" I swept an arm over the chaos. The roof was caved in in the middle; the chairs and tables were overturned, and some were crushed; the double doors were knocked off their hinges from so many people scrambling to escape.

Everyone had high-tailed it out of there, including Reverend Howard and Ruth Russell. Had they all just gone home?

Wait a minute. In that split second of realization, my chest suddenly burst with fear. "My shop!"

I threw the Booke aside and ran.

CHAPTER NINE

I SLAMMED MY car into gear and peeled out of the parking lot. Some cars and trucks tried to bar my path when they noticed it was me, but I burst through a low fence, off-roaded it over the village green, and hit the street. Erasmus suddenly appeared by my side. He didn't have to say anything. I saw it all on his face.

"Get to my shop," I told him. "Make sure no one is making trouble."

He didn't say a word, just disappeared again.

It wouldn't take me long to get there, and I could already see a line of cars...and someone had something that looked like fire.

I punched it around the back way through the woods, shut off the engine at my back garden, and ran around to the front. Someone had some burning rags on a stick, ready to lob it at my place. I skidded to a stop and held up my hands. I was lit by all the headlights of the villagers parked in the street.

"What do you think you're doing?" I said in challenge.

He didn't look threatened. "I'm gonna burn down this witch house."

"Not while I'm here to stop you."

"Maybe you *aren't* gonna stop me." He cocked back his arm when suddenly the torch went out.

Erasmus appeared beside me with a big thunderclap…the drama queen. His voice was unnaturally amplified when he declared, "Stand aside!"

Some did draw back, but I noticed a lot of folks seemed to have gun racks in their trucks…and the racks were empty.

"Now look," I said, lowering my hands and trying for a reasonable tone. "I know what you think you saw, but I was trying to fight that guy."

"That was the Devil!" said one of the faces in the dark. "And he came when you called on him."

"No, he isn't and no, I didn't. That was…that was Baphomet and he's a…a sort of god. But not a very nice one. I've been trying to stop him."

"Where'd he come from, then?" said Torch Guy.

I could easily implicate Doug, but looking across at the angry mob, I just didn't have the heart to sic them on him.

"There's something you should know," I said instead. "There's this Booke…" On cue, it appeared again before me to more gasps and even a few screams. "*This* Booke. I found it here in this house. It's been around for centuries, thousands of years in one form or another. And when you open it, it opens a gateway where terrible creatures come out." My throat was hot. I swallowed through a lump as hot tears spilled down my face. I couldn't help it. I kept thinking of the litany of names Ed had read at the meeting. All those dead people. "And…and the creatures killed those people. *Your* people. I'm sorry. It was my fault for opening the Booke, but I didn't know." I wiped my face with my sleeve. "And Doc and his coven have been helping me. I don't know what else to do. So I guess you have every right to torch me and my place—"

"Kylie!" said Erasmus. There was fear on his face, not that he couldn't whisk me away, but perhaps that I might not let him. He'd probably seen his share of villagers rising up and killing the Chosen Host.

"But I hope you don't," I continued. "I hope you decide to help me. I'm really not working for evil."

"So who's this?" said Torch Guy, gesturing toward Erasmus.

"He's a demon. But he's okay!"

Megan, our waitress from Moody Bog Café spoke up. "I…I saw him with Kylie at the café the other night," she said cautiously. "He seemed…really polite."

"What about our children?" said a woman in the back. "How do we keep them safe?"

"I don't know. I mean, Doc can help you with some protection charms. If you want them."

"We're good Christians here," said another woman in a long parka. "We don't want your devil charms in our house."

"They aren't devil charms. They're keeping the baddies away."

"Wicca is a pagan faith," said Doc suddenly from the back of the crowd. He slowly moved forward, and the villagers stepped aside like they didn't want him touching them. Doc made his way to my side and put a hand gently on my shoulder. "But being a pagan doesn't mean we reject the faith of others. In fact, we embrace *all* faiths. I'm still a Christian, but I also understand there is more than even the Bible tells us. I only strive for truth, in all it's facets. And being a doctor, my calling has always been to heal, not destroy. Now, some of you have known me a long time, I daresay, all your lives."

As he spoke, Nick pushed through to stand beside him. And then Seraphina came from the other direction and stood beside Erasmus. Even Jolene, a parent on each hand, wended her way forward until the three of them stood with us.

"And you know I have never steered you wrong," Doc went on. "We're sorry for not telling you about the troubles we've encountered." It was hard to see the faces of the crowd, backlit as they were. But everyone seemed to be listening. "But…" He shook his head. "How the heck were we going to explain it? Well, now you've seen some of it for yourselves. Look. If you destroy this young lady's house and business, you will have accomplished nothing. And if you run us out of town, the wickedness won't stop. In fact, it's set to get a lot dicier by the end of the week. So you can either help us destroy evil, or you can stand in the way of our good work and do the exact opposite of what you want to accomplish. Yes, there's evil in our town, but it isn't anyone standing up here in front of you."

Erasmus stared at Doc, a rather astonished look on his face. I reached down and clutched his hand. He looked at me with the same expression.

I waited. No one said anything. They shuffled in the cold, but I could tell there was a lot of thinking going on. I saw a gleam as someone raised a rifle and I held my breath. But the man only positioned it on his shoulder. He stepped forward. "Nicole was my sweetheart," he said with a shaky voice. "Do you know what happened to her?"

I slowly nodded. "Yes, I think I do. And I'm sorry. But she's… she's gone."

"What kind of creature was it?" he asked, face a blank. "The one we saw?"

"Um…no. Something called a kelpie, a water spirit. It looked like a white pony." There were a few gasps out there from the women. Could be that they had seen it too. "But I killed it… with this." I raised my hand and the front door slammed open. The crossbow whooshed through and slapped into my hand. More gasps from the crowd, followed by louder murmuring. "Everyone, lots of creatures have been coming out of the Booke. I've killed a bunch but there are more. I have a plan to stop the Booke once and for all. Soon, you'll all be safe again. It might be a good idea for everyone to get out of town for a while. Doc can let you know when it's okay to come back."

"So wait." A young teen girl, maybe a little older than Jolene, shoved forward. "*You're* doing this? Killing all the bad creatures?"

I wiped my face again. "Yeah. It's my fault. And frankly, it's kind of up to me. I'm only just beginning to understand all that's happening."

"Did you bring all this with you to our town?"

"No! It all happened here, in Moody Bog." I choked up a bit. Seraphina touched my hand and continued for me.

"Kylie never knew any of this existed. It was when she found the Booke of the Hidden that it all began. But she has been tirelessly fighting for you all. She's been in danger herself more times than we can count, fearlessly taking on this task. It isn't her fault. Call it fate or whatever you'd like. But Kylie is a hero. One of the best, in fact. And she could use your help."

"What could *we* do?" asked the girl.

I didn't know. I looked to Doc.

"I'll tell you what you can do, folks. You can believe her, for one. For another, you can make sure you keep safe. If you have to leave your house, travel with a buddy. And report any strange things you see directly to Sheriff Ed."

The girl marched up to the front and stood beside Jolene. "I'm going to help them. I'm not leaving. This is *my* town. I want to protect it."

"You get away from them, Jessica Marie!" cried an adult from the crowd.

"No, Mom! I want to help."

There was more murmuring, more arguments. We waited.

Another teen walked forward, a boy this time. "I'm standing with the Wiccans," he said, his voice breaking.

A group of teenage boys that I assumed were his friends came forward to stand beside him.

I could see more cars arrive. When the people got out, I could tell they were expecting an inferno or at the very least a fight. Instead they asked what was going on with confused looks on their faces.

Flashing lights came down the road. Ed's interceptor pulled up and screeched to a stop as his siren wailed and then wound down. On the loudspeaker he called, "Disperse! Or I'll arrest all of you."

I cupped my hands on both sides of my mouth. "It's okay, Ed!"

His interior light come on as he opened the car door and stepped out, head above the crowd. "What?"

"It's okay. They're coming around."

He looked almost as shocked as Erasmus.

Some people did start to disperse, those who just couldn't get out from under their own fears and prejudices. But many more stayed, and the coven started talking to each of them, explaining. It was the strangest thing to ever happen to me…and that was saying something.

Erasmus pulled me aside. "I don't believe what I am seeing."

"Me neither. It's a miracle."

"These humans are siding with you. I…I have never seen such a thing."

"Believe me, neither have I."

"I was certain they would burn you."

"I was kind of getting the feeling they would too. Except I knew you would rescue me."

"Of course I would have!" He puffed up.

"I never doubted it." I looked at him tenderly and then leaned in and kissed him.

"Kylie," he said, casting a suspicious glance around. "You confessed to these people that I'm a demon. You can't be seen—"

"Kissing you? Too bad." I clamped my hand around his neck and pulled him in again. He fought for only a moment before he gave in.

"You're a foolish mortal," he said, lips grazing my temple before he let me go.

"I know. But look at all these other foolish mortals. Erasmus, do you know what this means?" I was suddenly feeling a little giddy. I might have even giggled. "It means…now we have an *army*."

Chapter Ten

ERASMUS PACED. SO many people were stuffed into my shop listening to Doc's lecture that I decided there was no room for me. So I stayed in my back garden on my glider, swinging back and forth…as Erasmus paced.

"What's wrong, Erasmus?"

He stopped and turned his head to look at me. "I'm worried. We must go to the Netherworld soon but I don't think we are adequately prepared. If we can't offer Satan your soul, what *can* we offer Him?"

"I don't know. Hey, is there something he's always prized that only a human can get?"

He stared at me, his brows furrowing so low I thought they'd never be able to come back up. "Something he prizes? I hadn't thought of that."

"See. I'm still good for something."

He stalked forward and stood over me. "I can think of many things." His shoulders smoldered almost as much as his eyes.

"Now, now," I admonished softly. I patted the seat beside me. "Come sit with me."

He eyed the glider suspiciously and gingerly sat on the wooden bench. I pushed off with my feet and he grabbed hold of the edge of the seat with both hands. I laughed. "Calm down. We're only swinging."

Cautiously, he let go, but I could tell he was still nervous. So I scooted over until I was right up against him, shoulder against shoulder, knee against knee. "Isn't this nicer than in there?"

His eyes followed the places we touched. "Decidedly," he murmured.

"We've got all this help now. It makes me feel so much better that we can actually prevent more killings. It really does. So I think we'd better go in the next day or so."

"I understand your urgency. I, too, am anxious to put the book to rest. As long as I don't disappear with it."

I slipped my arm in his and laid my head on his shoulder. He stiffened for a second then relaxed. Perhaps he didn't realize that he didn't need permission to touch me. "I won't let that happen. I'll ask for that too. I'm sure we can give Old Scratch something worthwhile. I think I'm going to need my soul for a long time… as long as I'll be hanging with you."

He turned to me. His eyes glittered in the dark. "Kylie?" he said softly. "*You*…want a life with *me*?"

"Yeah. Didn't I ever mention…that I'm in love with you?" I smiled up at him. I wasn't afraid to think it out loud anymore. I knew I'd held back. Maybe I had been a little frightened at the prospect of what it might mean. But it had always been there. Even when I was with Ed, I couldn't stop thinking about Erasmus.

I reached up and stroked his cheek. Smoke wisped off his shoulders.

"You love me?" Those dark brows furrowed again.

My fingers brushed his cheek. I raised my face up as I brought his down. "Yes. Didn't you know?" I kissed him. My lips were gentle on his, lingering. When I drew back, he still looked surprised. Maybe not just surprised. Awestruck.

"But you're human. How can you truly be in love with a demon?"

"Because...you're you. Oh, Erasmus, you irresistible devil. Don't you think you're worth it?"

"I never gave it any thought before."

"Well...think it. Because this is happening. I told you that if both parties feel the same way, being in love can be a wonderful thing."

He didn't say anything. He slipped his arm around me and squeezed. His look of awe turned into something more tender.

"I don't suppose it happens very often," I said. "A human falling in love with a demon...and vice versa."

"Not in my experience. But as you've taken pains to point out before, technically, I have very little experience as far as that is concerned, being awakened only briefly every few hundred years."

I snuggled against his shoulder again. "Then I guess we're lucky."

His fingers entwined with mine. "And yet...I'd be hard-pressed to characterize it that way."

"Why?"

"Because—"

A clap of thunder right in front of us hurled us away from each other. But it wasn't a storm. It was Shabiri.

"Oh, for goddess' sake!" she shrieked. "Can't you leave these animals alone for one minute?" She was yelling at Erasmus. Which meant that *I* was the—

"What do you want, Shabiri?" he grumbled.

She seemed agitated. Since she was usually oozing with confidence, something must've been up.

"There's a problem. I absolutely hate to say it, but Doug is going to need..." She took a deep breath. "Your help."

"What?" I couldn't stop myself from laughing, though I tried to hide it behind my hand. "That's a good one."

"Stop your cackling, meat girl. I knew it was a stupid idea coming here." She paced in a circle and even wrung her hands. "It's not as if I *like* doing this. But I don't have enough power by myself."

That made Erasmus sit up. "What are you talking about?"

"Doug and his stupid Ordo. They're in big trouble."

"Good," I said, drawing my knees up and wrapping my arms around them. "Now he's getting a taste of his own medicine."

"Yes, yes. Ha, ha. Revenge is jolly, isn't it. But it's just a teensy bit more than that. You see, Baphomet no longer wishes to play. I'm afraid he's turned on the Ordo, on all of Hansen Mills. Someone over here in Kylieland got him mad."

Uh oh. I let my legs flop down. "What's really going on, Shabiri?"

"Like I said, Lord Baphomet isn't playing around anymore."

"You're the one who helped Doug summon him. Aren't you two working together to get the Booke? Wasn't that the whole plot to begin with?"

I waited. Puffs of smoke feathered off her shoulders and she was trembling with rage. She flicked a glance at Erasmus and shook her head. Her face was a rolling parade of different emotions. I tried to decipher each one as they morphed and disappeared into the next one.

"Yes," she hissed. "It was the plan. It's still his plan. But…now I don't think…maybe it… Oh, Beelzebub! Can't a girl change her mind?"

"Uh, I guess. Are you saying that—"

"We're wasting time."

For once, I was convinced by her sincerity and confusion. I put my hand up for the crossbow. It came to me as I stalked into my garden to the gate. "Come on, Erasmus. I'm going to get my car."

"Shouldn't you just—" She gestured toward Erasmus.

"I'm not just appearing anywhere *you* say. I don't trust you *that* much. It might be a trap. I'm taking my Jeep."

She clenched her fists and muttered something like, "Dreadful *monkey*."

"Shall we meet you at Doug's, Shabiri?" I called over my shoulder.

"Yes. And *hurry!*" She vanished in a puff of green smoke. Nice touch.

I threw the crossbow into the back seat as Erasmus got in on the passenger side. "Be careful with my crossbow!" he cried.

"It's fine." I started up the Jeep and scattered the leaf duff as I pulled a j-turn and headed toward the back road.

There was no moon yet and it was *dark* out there. My headlights were the only thing keeping me from careening off the road, lighting just a little bit of each bend in the highway as I drove. And just as I rounded a curve, my headlights swept over a man on a black horse, rearing up in the middle of the street.

I cranked over the steering wheel and screamed as we bumped over the verge and down into a ditch. The airbags didn't deploy so it wasn't that much of a jolt but it sure felt like it. "Are you okay?" I said to Erasmus, heart pounding.

He looked at me like I was crazy.

"You saw that, didn't you?" I opened the door and stepped out...but had no idea that my door and the running board were poised over the deepest part of the ditch. Down I went.

"Kylie!" Erasmus yelled.

"I'm all right. Just bruised my...ego." Getting up and rubbing my backside, I glanced over the hood to the road. "Holy shit! Is that a... That's a headless horseman!"

Yup, there he was on a black horse, cradling his head under his arm. Instead of a sword, he was swinging around a glowing whip. Was this guy from a re-enactment of the *Legend of Sleepy Hollow*?

Nope, it was way too creepy for that. And he wasn't running away or coming to help me like a real person would have. He had to be from the Booke and one of the weirdest to date.

He cracked his whip a few times and it seemed to get longer the more he did it. There was something odd about that whip, too. Maybe odder than the head in the crook of his arm.

"Is that whip made out of a...*spine*?"

It elongated again as he cracked it almost over my head. The greenish face of the head under his arm was pulled into a hideous grin from one ear to the other. Much like Erasmus when he did that thing with too many shark teeth in his mouth. His eyes were glowing too but they never stopped looking around and rolling in the sockets. He opened his mouth and laughed like a crazy man.

"Oh, this is not good. Really not good." The crossbow flew out of the car and slipped into my hand, as if telling me, *You're gonna need this.* "What in the hell *is* that, Erasmus?"

"I believe that is the Dullahan. A headless rider with the spine of a corpse for a whip. He kills by calling out your name."

"Oh shit. And we both said each other's names. How do I stop *that*?"

He gave me that "you are so stupid" look again. "Use the damn crossbow."

Oh yeah. I put the crossbow up to my shoulder. As soon as I did, the spine-whip snapped at it, pulling it from my hand. The Dullahan laughed out of his moldy face again. The crossbow sailed into the darkness.

"I know you, Kylie Strange," he said in a creepy, high-pitched voice.

I stopped dead, fear clutching at my heart. It seemed to stutter…but nothing else happened. I felt all over my torso with my hands and looked up at Erasmus. "I'm not dead."

"No. You certainly don't appear to be."

The Dullahan looked pretty pissed about that. "Erasmus Dark!" he screeched.

Erasmus gave the creature a filthy look. "I'm a demon," he said. "I can't die."

I could have sworn that head mouthed, "Well, fuck!" before he reared his red-eyed horse again and plunged into the depths of the forest.

I glanced at Erasmus. "Why didn't I die?"

He walked toward me, took my left wrist, and turned it over, exposing the tattoo. "It seems this offers you some protection."

"Not just my soul, huh? That's handy."

"Yes. Extraordinary."

"You mean you didn't expect that?"

"I expected…something. I didn't *think* his calling your name would kill you."

"Why not?"

"It was just a theory. Now I'll never know if it's true."

"WHAT?"

"No need to shout. Your exposure to the Netherworld. To, er, me."

I stood blinking at him for some time. "You *infected* me?"

"Exposed you. It could be that. Or it could be the tattoo." He put a hand to his scruffy chin and stroked it. "Or it could be a combination of *both*. Clearly a question for your junior Wiccan."

I scrambled around the car and headed for the last place I figured the crossbow had landed. "Here, chthonic crossbow." I raised my hand for it, worried it might be broken, but it sailed toward me like a trained falcon. I looked it over. "Seems okay." It had unarmed itself. "Should we hunt it or go on to Doug's."

"I have never seen Shabiri so distressed. I am inclined to pursue her coven."

"But what about the harm the Dullahan could wreak?"

"Use your contraption to call your Wiccans. They're probably wondering what happened to you."

"I'll need a tow truck anyway to get my car out of this."

He shook his head at me as I got my phone out. The Jeep was suddenly glowing and rising from the ditch. It hovered over the marshy grasses and slowly backed toward the road where it was gently set down.

I stared at Erasmus. He looked a little proud of himself.

"That was awesome. I won't ever need triple A again with you around." I clicked on Doc's number and he picked it up right away.

"Kylie, where in blazes are you?"

"I got an emergency summons from Shabiri saying that Doug

was in trouble with Baphomet. There's something going on in Hansen Mills." I looked in the direction of the town and saw a tell-tale glow in the distance. "It doesn't look good. Erasmus and I are heading over there."

"Do you need back-up?"

"I don't know yet. You seem pretty busy with the townsfolk." I could hear the commotion in the background.

Doc turned to say something to someone, but it was muffled. Sounded like one of the teens that had come over to the Wiccan side. "I can't tell you how surprised and pleased I am by their willingness to help," he said, returning to the phone. "I am truly humbled."

"Well, while you've got them there, you'd better warn them about the latest Booke creature. It's a headless horseman with a spine for a whip."

Doc didn't speak for a moment. I looked down at the phone, wondering if I'd lost our connection when he suddenly said, "I'm sorry. I thought you said it was a headless horseman."

"I did. The Dullahan. Have Jolene look it up. But tell anyone who encounters it to get away immediately. If it calls your name, you're dead."

"They must cover their ears," said Erasmus, leaning toward the phone and talking loudly. "So that they cannot hear their names. That should suffice."

I turned toward him. "And thanks for telling *me*."

He shrugged. "I knew you couldn't be killed."

I got back on the phone. "Another thing for Jolene and Nick to look up. I'm…not. Dead, that is. And it called *my* name. Erasmus thinks it's either my new tattoo or…or, um, exposure to the, uh, Netherworld. Through him. Contact with him."

"Oh. I see. That's…interesting."

"So tell them to beware."

"Sounds like good old-fashioned ear plugs will do the trick. Nick is forming everyone into patrols, four at a time. They are very anxious to help. We've made charm pouches for all of them and taught them some simple protection spells. I think it's the book's influence making it possible for them to be able to perform simple craft."

"These Moody Boggers. I'm impressed. Listen, I have to go, but I want someone—maybe Ed or George—to find out what happened to Ruth. She didn't look the least bit scared when Baphomet showed up. I think it's time we lock her down."

"I am reluctant to do so, but I think you may be right. Good luck, Kylie."

"Same to you." I clicked off and stuffed my phone into my jacket pocket. I climbed back into the Jeep, all squared away and positioned correctly on the road, and started it up. Erasmus sat beside me, chuffed to the hilt.

"Thank you, Erasmus," I said and punched my foot on the gas. It squealed forward and we were on our way to Hansen Mills and Doug's place.

The sky lit up even more the closer we got. Hellfire, I supposed. But when I turned the corner, it was just plain old houses on fire. Damn that Baphomet. I could see the charred streaks on the highway where he'd shot his beams of power. Karl Water's little museum was ablaze. All those archives and documents were going up in smoke. I could kill Goat Guy for this.

Yup, that's exactly what I planned to do.

I burned rubber up the road but had to slow when a firetruck with siren wailing came up behind me. I pulled to the side to let it go when I saw another burst of a fireball above the trees.

"Holy shit!" I punched it once the firetruck zoomed by. I passed the charred remains of Mike's Roadhouse and hoped there had been no one in there. It looked like some triage was going on in the parking lot, with volunteers and paramedics.

It was all-out war.

I headed for Doug's mobile home. When I got to the driveway, I saw what Shabiri had been talking about. There were holes blown in the dirt road up to his place. The barn had been reduced to cinders. The mobile home was dark but seemed okay…until I pulled around to the other side. That half of it was gone.

I killed the motor, reached back for the crossbow, and jumped out, scanning the skies and letting my Spidey sense help me out. I stood out in the yard and thought it might be better just to yell.

"Doug! Dean! Bob! Charise! Anyone home?"

At first all was quiet. But then the front door whined open. I waited. A figure appeared on the porch. It stood against the rail. "Come to gloat?" said Doug.

I lowered the crossbow. "No. I came to help."

He laughed, but it was a sour one. "*You* came to help. That's a good one. Why the hell would you?"

"Because…we're fighting something bigger than all of us."

He stood slumped, face still in shadow, until he finally turned back toward his door, waving me through. I ran up to the porch, Erasmus close behind me.

When I got through the door, I didn't recognize the place. The kitchen end of the mobile home was completely torn away, as if a giant hand had cracked it open. Maybe it had. Maybe Baphomet had grown to horrible proportions, clamped his taloned hand over it, and snapped it off. None of the lights were on and I assumed there was no power, but a few camping lanterns around gave off an eerie glow. When Doug turned to me I could see that his eye and half of his face had been slashed by what looked like claws. Crusty blood had dried on the wounds.

Without thinking, I lurched toward him. "Doug…"

"Don't even bother." He turned toward the living room.

Charise was on the sofa, cradling Bob in her lap. There was blood spattered all over the wall. I put my hand to my mouth in shock.

"Where's Dean?" I asked.

Doug lifted his hand. "In there." He waved vaguely toward the bedrooms. "What's left of him, anyway."

"Oh no."

"Yeah. Looks like Lord Baphomet was pretty angry."

I swallowed past a hard lump. "I'm not taking the blame for something you summoned."

He nodded. "Yeah, I know. Baphomet's, uh, not with us anymore. I guess he never was. So you were right all along."

"I'm sorry, Doug."

He looked at me, flicked a glance at Erasmus, then dropped his gaze back to me. "I know you are, darlin'. I think…well, there's no other way to put it. I think we messed up."

"Look, Moody Bog found out in a big way about my coven and the Booke. Some have washed their hands of me. Probably still plotting how they're going to burn me down. But a whole lot more are now joining us. You should too. We're going to fight."

"You can't fight that."

"I think we can. If two strong covens join together, we'll have the power."

"It's too late for Dean." Charise's voice was hollow, not even whiney anymore. She seemed in shock. Her black mascara had run down her face in an Alice Cooper sort of vibe, but I didn't think the dark pouches under her eyes were from makeup. "I don't want to end up like him."

"You won't," I said. "Let's get you all in my car. We'll go to Moody Bog, to my shop and strategize. Doc will fix you up, okay?"

It flashed through my mind for a second that this might all be a ploy, that Shabiri had set it up and that they were playacting. But I smelled the blood on the wall and, probably, from the other room. And I didn't think Charise was that good an actor.

"Erasmus, could you help Bob?" I had meant if he could help him *up*. What I didn't expect was for him to lean over him, place his hand on his face, and heal him in a bright yellow glow.

Bob snapped up, eyes wide. "What? What did you do?"

"Oh." I hefted the crossbow over my shoulder. "Well…Erasmus can heal…"

Charise jumped to her feet. "How come Shabiri never did that, Doug?"

"I don't know. I guess I don't know as much about demons as I thought I did."

"I can heal because I am in love with Kylie," he said matter-of-factly.

Doug barked a laugh of surprise. Some of the old sparkle was back in his remaining eye. "Oh, is that all? I guess I should have cozied up to Shabiri then."

I gestured toward them. "Come on, Doug. Bring whatever stuff you'll need. Charm pouches, spell books. We should get out of here."

"We haven't got much. Charise, how about those spell books?"

"I'll get 'em," said a spry Bob. He gave Charise a tender gaze. I guess Charise finally figured it out, that it was Bob paying attention to her all along, not Doug.

Bob lumbered into the hallway to a bedroom, slowing and staring into another as he passed. It must have been where Dean was.

Erasmus made sure Doug and Charise were in the car and I escorted Bob when he came back with several books under his arm.

They all buckled themselves into the back as I started up the Jeep. I maneuvered around the blasted-out holes in the driveway and onto the main highway. No one said anything during the ride to my place. When I pulled in front, a lot of the cars had dispersed. Perhaps the deputy Wiccans were out patrolling.

I walked in with Doug and company in tow. Nick made a squeaky noise and pulled up short when he saw them.

"Dean's dead," I said, and set down the crossbow.

It was just Doc, Nick, Seraphina, Jeff, and Jolene. They stared at the remaining Ordo members until Seraphina drew forward, took Charise's hand, and led her to a chair. "How about a nice cup of tea, eh, Charise?"

Charise nodded, didn't say anything, just looked at the floor.

"C-coffee for you boys?" said Nick charitably.

Doug dropped into a chair. "Yeah. Thanks."

Doc came over to Doug with his doctor bag. "That looks nasty, Doug. Let me take a look."

"Why doesn't her demon just fix him?" said Charise in a small voice. Must have been that voice that had attracted Ed in another day. He sure had varying tastes.

Doc looked toward Erasmus. "I...didn't think to ask."

Erasmus, face a blank, strode toward him. He looked Doug over, narrowing his eyes, perhaps reminding Doug whom he had menaced and that he didn't deserve this help. But when he reached for him, Doug grabbed his wrist. "No. I'm through with magic. Besides, chicks like scars. Just fix me up, Doc, so I don't get infected."

"That eye looks mighty bad, Doug. You should probably get to a hospital. See a specialist..."

"There's worse happening in Hansen Mills right now. Just... fix me up."

Doc set to work. Seraphina brought tea in a cup and saucer for Charise, while Nick put on his best barista performance— helped by Bob of all people.

I took that moment to pull Jolene aside.

"Jolene," I said quietly. "I need you to research like you've never researched before. Forget about all those protection spells. We've got to find something that Satan wants other than souls. Is there something that only humans can get him?"

The light went on in her face. "Got it. I'm on it." She rushed behind the counter to her bag and grabbed her tablet.

"They're going to need a place to crash for a while," I said to no one in particular. "I guess they can use this room, maybe borrow some blankets..."

"Why don't they stay at Grandpa's place?" offered Jeff.

"Then what about you?"

"I'll be there. Patrolling."

Doug winced at the antiseptic Doc was dabbing at his wounds. "That's fine. We can take a werewolf or two after this. But Doc, I want to help. Put us to work. As a coven."

Jolene looked up. Seraphina turned to stare at Doug. And Nick stopped mid-pour.

"You want to work *with* us?" said Nick. He set down the coffee pot. "I don't know that I trust you."

"Nick," I began.

Doug held up his hands. Doc had taped some gauze over his eye, which made him look more like a pirate than he already did. "That's okay, Kylie. None of you have any reason to trust us. I get it. But my place was trashed, my barn destroyed, and Dean was… he was pulverized by Baphomet." He pointed to his face. "I got this little number from him too. I was one of the lucky ones. We ran for our lives from Mike's. It's gone. There were fires all over the town. It's like Kylie says. It's war now. I think we've learned our lesson. At least I have. I'm done. Except for this last thing."

"Two last things," I said. "We have to stop Baphomet, but my priority is stopping the Booke, and we have to do it before Halloween."

"Why Halloween?" He waved in the air in front of him. "Never mind. I guess I can figure that out. So okay. What do we have to do?"

We all hesitated. I knew what everyone was thinking. Should we tell him what we were planning? He was the one trying to get the Booke for Baphoment. In for a penny, in for a pound.

I straightened my stance. "I have to go to the Netherworld and make a trade with Satan to destroy the Booke."

Doug stared at me and huffed a silent laugh. "Sure. Why not? I love this plan!"

"I'm not kidding."

"Yeah, girl. I figured that. Better you than me. It's a book thing, right?"

"Right. Only I can go. And Erasmus."

Doug poked gingerly at the gauze Doc had taped to his face. "What about Shabiri?"

"Do you think she'll help us? I mean, she came and got me when you were in trouble."

He seemed surprised. "She did?" He glanced at his fellow Ordo. "I never asked her to."

"I surmise that she was frightened," said Erasmus.

"Shit," said Bob. "If *she* was frightened…"

"Gods and demons don't generally get along," Erasmus explained. "Whatever deal he struck with Shabiri…well. He never intended to keep it. I'm surprised she didn't realize that."

Doug gave a wincing smile. "It wouldn't be the first time a demon's plans got derailed…eh, loverboy?"

Erasmus sneered and stalked toward him. I grabbed Erasmus' arm and pulled him back. "Look, it's been a long night. How about some food?"

"If it's all the same to the group," said Bob, "I'd just rather turn in. Where are we going?"

"I'd better take you," said Jeff. "Doc, can I borrow your car?"

"Keys are on the dashboard," said Doc, thumbing through one of his books.

A car pulled up out front. Ed and George jumped out and came through the front door without knocking. The sheriff pulled up short when he saw the Ordo.

"What's going on?"

"A bit of trouble out in old Hansen Mills," said Doug. "Baphomet on the rampage."

Ed stared at Doug and took two steps closer. He gestured toward the gauze on his brother's face. "You all right?"

It was the first brotherly utterance I'd heard Ed express toward Doug. Doug shrugged. "I guess I'll live."

"What happened?"

"Baphomet came to town. He, uh, wasn't best pleased with us. You'll find what's left of Dean's body at my place in the spare bedroom."

"Jesus."

"Yeah. If you don't mind, we're going to take advantage of Kylie's kind invitation to camp out at her grandpa's house. My place isn't exactly five stars at the moment. And don't worry.

We've switched sides, so there's no need for any surveillance. Besides, Wolf Boy here said he'll keep an eye on us."

Ed looked at me for confirmation. "Well…if you need anything, you have my number," he said. "If you want, I can swing by Moody Bog Market and pick you up some stuff, toothbrushes and what-not."

"That's nice of you, bro. Come by later. Maybe, uh…it's time to talk."

"Okay."

"Come on, people." Jeff gestured toward the door.

Doug stood and they faced each other. Jeff, werewolf blood surging through him, wasn't afraid of the larger man anymore. In fact, all the bruises that Doug and his gang had given Jeff had disappeared when he'd turned wolf that first time.

Doug looked Jeff up and down, no doubt trying to see the wolf inside the man. "Hey, I'm, uh, sorry about the…you know."

Jeff, looking like the surfer I had known and been attracted to all those years ago with his floppy blond hair and lopsided grin, just gazed back at him. "Yeah, I know. Karma, dude." He walked out the door without looking back, expecting Doug to follow. Doug looked around the room, at what remained of his gang, at Jolene on her tablet, Nick clearing dishes, Seraphina lighting a stick of incense, Ed, and finally me. He gave me a small smile and a chin raise, and headed out the door.

Ed slid his hat off his head. "I didn't know. We never got any calls."

"I heard on the radio," said George, "but there was no point in bothering you. Paramedics and Fire were there."

Ed fell into a chair and just stared at the floor. "It's pretty crazy out there."

"We have a new one from the Booke," I told him. "A headless horseman with a spine whip. If you encounter him, just get out of there and stuff your fingers in your ears. If he says your name and you hear it, you die."

"Weird." And that was all the reaction he gave. I guessed he was full up with weird today.

"I suppose it's time we all get some rest," said Doc. "We all have jobs for early tomorrow. Nick's patrols are out there and they'll need relief by morning."

"It's all scheduled," said Nick. "And I alerted them already about Kylie's new headless dude."

"Looks like I'm temporarily without transportation," said Doc, pulling on his jacket.

Seraphina was already in her alpaca wrap. "I can take you all. Shall we? We'll be here bright and early, Kylie."

"I promise to get that research done," said Jolene, putting her stuff in her bag.

As they headed toward the door, Ed rose. "I guess that's my cue too."

"You look beat, Ed," I said in sympathy.

"We'll have to head to Doug's before we go home," he said to George. They were both in for a long night.

George nodded wearily and gave Nick a significant look. And suddenly everyone was gone. It was just me and Erasmus.

I wondered why Baphomet hadn't destroyed *my* place, but Doc and his crew must have stuffed the rafters with protective charms. And looky there. Up in said rafters, I could see lots of charm pouches.

I walked around the room shutting off lights. Scrubbing my hair, I heaved a sigh. "This has been a weird day. But I guess it's no weirder than the rest of this month."

"I have never been awake this long at a time. It's interesting."

"Interesting." I paused at the banister. "Is that high praise from a demon?"

"Possibly."

I yawned and started up the stairs.

He stood in the dark. "I suppose I'll patrol…"

"Don't be an idiot." I waved him up.

"I'll…come up the stairs then, shall I?"

I don't remember if I answered. Just trudged to my bedroom to start my nighttime routine. Brushing my teeth and looking at myself in the mirror, I realized I looked pretty beat myself. A little moisturizer on my face, a brush through my hair, and I came back out. Erasmus was standing in the middle of the room, waves of discomfort pouring off of him. I tried to break the ice. "It was quite a day, wasn't it?"

"Yes. But I am used to chaos."

I clicked off one light, started stripping, and got under the comforter *au natural.* "I guess you are. Things coming out of the Booke left and right, hardly any time for peace and quiet…" He was gazing at me with interest. "Is this really the longest that you've been awake?"

"Nearly a month? Yes. It's strange."

We looked at each other for a moment. "Are you just going to stand there?"

His eyes darted from one corner of the room to another. "I…"

"Aren't you going to come to bed? You're allowed to, you know."

Instead of taking off his duster, he paced in front of the window. Then he stopped and snapped toward me. "I am not a boy."

I must have blinked for a whole minute straight. "Oka-a-ay."

"Whilst you were getting your tattoo, Mr. Riley called me your *boy*-friend. And just now, the Ordo leader called me lover *boy*. I am not a boy."

I pulled the sheets to cover my chest and sat up. "Oh." I chuckled. "They didn't mean it that way. A 'boyfriend' is a politer way to say that you're my…you know. Lover. 'Loverboy' is sort of a variant. But essentially, it's telling people that we are in an exclusive relationship. Sort of warning men off that I'm involved and warning women off that *you're* involved."

He seemed to think about it before cracking a smile. "You're jealous that other men and women might wish to steal me away."

"No! I mean…no. It's just a way of establishing relationships so others understand it. So I'd be called your…girlfriend." I wrinkled my nose. "'Boyfriend' is not a good name for what you are, though. I can't see calling you that."

"*Girl* friend," he muttered, mulling the thought over. "It doesn't seem an adequate description."

"'Lover' just sounds like too much information."

"Hmm." He sat on the edge of the bed.

"Are you going to join me?"

I could tell he was going over everything. "I do not know the boundaries," he said quietly, maybe even embarrassed. "Or the finer points of these dynamics."

He was adorable when he was befuddled. "Don't worry. I'll coach you."

"For instance." Erasmus ruffled was also pretty cute. "I thought that we would come to your bed mutually."

"What do you mean?"

"Before, we always arrived together, and usually you were in my arms. This time, you simply disrobed and got in. There were no formal actions, no embraces, no introductory salutations—" He huffed at my giggling. "Why are you laughing at me?"

I did my best to stifle it, hiding it with a cough. "I'm not laughing at you. I just thought you would be comfortable enough with the situation by now. We don't need to be formal with each other. We're just…you know. Together. We don't need to make these declarations of love and come together in a theatrical embrace. Also, this way there isn't any burning away of my clothes. Which I need and aren't as easily replaced as yours."

"I see. And so if I wish to be affectionate…I am allowed to simply reach over and…" He leaned toward me and caressed my cheek with the backs of his fingers.

"Anytime you like," I said breathlessly. "We can even kiss in front of the others. No deep kisses but a little peck is okay. Anything more would be impolite. You can hold my hand, you can put your arm around me. All those are signals that we're together." And now I could picture him doing all that in front of Ed just to rub it in.

"Interesting," he said again. He stood awhile gazing at me with smoldering eyes then peeled off his coat. Slowly—the demon version of a striptease, I supposed—he divested himself of all of his clothes one lovely piece at a time, and me with a front row seat. When he was in all his glory, he pulled up the comforter and got in.

"This seems very civilized," he said, surprised.

"Yes, it does. Cozy even."

"And so I may…" He scooted closer and slid his hands over my skin around my waist to embrace me, pulling me close so that our lips were only inches apart. "I may hold you like this." His voice was little more than a low growl. "And I may take a kiss." He leaned in and did, lips gently touching, caressing mine.

He kissed me for a long while and deepened it, holding me even tighter. I slowly sank beneath him and felt one of his thighs at my hip. He finally pulled back and looked down at me, eyes searching all over my face, and lifted a hand to run a finger over my cheek, my nose, my lips. "This is fascinating."

"It's amazing how freedom makes you feel."

"Yes. It is freedom, isn't it."

I nodded. "Except that we're still…together. Exclusive. Not *that* much freedom."

He smiled a little and gently kissed the edge of my mouth. "So, no Constable Bradbury," he whispered.

"No. Just you."

His lips traveled up to my eyebrow and nibbled. "No Jeff Chase." His voice tickled a bit over my skin.

"Definitely not."

His nose touched my face and caressed down my cheek before he kissed my lips again. "No one…but *me*."

I draped my arms over his neck and licked my lips. "Just you."

It might have been my imagination, but it seemed that his eyes glowed for just a second. "Just me."

"You crazy demon." I pulled him down and kissed him as passionately as I could.

His warm lips met mine. His tongue, the low growls from deep in his throat, all sent shivers through me. His hands never stopped moving, teasing over my skin, dipping, squeezing. Soon enough I was wrapping my thighs around him, feeling his hardness against me. I inhaled him, the deep scent of burning embers, distant fires, and dense earth.

His hands closed over my calves and lifted my legs, raising my knees to his shoulders, and with a grin, he dipped down. I lost myself in sensation, in all that he gave. His tender ministrations made me writhe and arch. A warm hand teased down from my collarbone to my navel and lower, where he did such wicked things with his lips and tongue. His touch sent me on a euphoric rise until I could barely breathe, but it only made me want *him* all the more. I flopped down and he moved over me, but I sat up and pushed him back till he landed flat on the bed, head at the footboard. Confused for only a moment, a feral smile soon bloomed on his face. He lay back as I climbed up on him. With his hands on my hips, he guided me where he wanted me.

We rocked together as I cast my head back, feeling him, listening to his moans and soft murmurs. He reacted in so human a fashion, I wondered briefly if we really were that different.

His fingers were tight on my hips when he made an impatient sound, and I found myself suddenly flipped on *my* back. He kissed my neck as his hands explored my breasts. He settled in place again, all the while his hips pushing against me quicker. Eyes blazing, he stared at me as he moved. I could feel him, every blessed demony inch of him. His hands, his lips, his growl tingled over my skin. I reached up and touched him, too. He liked it when I raked my nails down his chest, and his eyes slipped closed, writhing over me and reveling in it, in the tiny streaks of pain. And then, suddenly, his eyes snapped open, he threw back his head, and roared out his completion.

He dropped to lay on top of me, burying his face into my neck under my hair, harsh breaths calming as he lay there. And then he chuckled. I could feel it shiver all the way down my body.

He raised up to look at me, kissed my forehead, then reached up and curled a tendril of hair on his finger. "I have lived four thousand years," he said softly, "but I never knew such…such… *joy*." He said the word so tentatively and with such awe. It gave me a lump in my throat and a sting at my eyes, mourning for the lonely creature he must have been for all those centuries.

I couldn't help it. I gathered him in my arms, pressing him close, and kissed his temple. "You don't have to be lonely anymore."

When he finally rolled away, he was smiling. He tucked his hands behind his head and stared up into my rafters. "It's strange having a…a companion."

I rolled in next to him, running my hand through his chest hair and over that damned tattoo. "The two of us. Against the world."

"*All* the worlds."

I looked up at that strong jaw. "Did you make a joke?"

His smile grew wider. "I might have."

I drew up and kissed him. He returned it languidly.

"I can't believe after all these centuries that no one snatched you up."

"I am hard to peg down."

"That's for sure. But really. You never found anyone—man or woman—as a companion before?"

His smile faded slightly. "There was never time. I was constantly busy with the book. And the Chosen Host, none of whom ever wanted my help or to be around me."

"I'm so sorry."

"Why?"

"Because. It seems like it was lonely for you."

"Lonely. It's the second time you've said it. I wasn't lonely. I didn't know what companionship was."

"And that's even worse."

"Why? I had no point of reference. How could I know what I was missing?"

"But that's just the point—"

He closed his mouth over mine, kissing with heat and tenderness, holding my face with gentle fingers. When he drew back, there was a dancing light in his eyes. I amused him. My human emotions of empathy amused the demon. I gave up.

"What am I going to do with you?" I sighed.

"I'm hoping for more of what you just did with me."

I giggled. I wanted to run my fingers over that perpetual scruff, to tease more smiles from him, because the vibrations of his laughter deep in his chest made me feel warm and glowy.

But the sound of weird barking stopped my hand.

I sat up, clutching the sheets to my chest. A dog had a definite sound to its bark, a familiar noise from behind a fence, or even an annoying yapping next door. But this sound coming from the woods... It was hollow and mournful with a hint of... something else.

Tossing the comforter aside, I slipped out of bed and padded over to the window. I gasped. It was looking up toward me.

And it wasn't a dog.

Chapter Eleven

THE CREATURE LOOKED like a snake, with a snake's eyes, head and neck, but it had a leopard's body…with hoofs, like a deer's. As if it had been pieced together on a computer from lots of different animals. But it was there, standing in my back garden and challenging me. And then it made that weird barking sound again, before whipping its tail and bounding into the darkness of the woods.

I hugged myself from the cold. Erasmus' arms came around me from behind. "The Beast *Glatisant*, or the Barking Beast," he said in my ear. "It simply kills. For food. For pleasure."

I leaned back into him. "I can't. I can't think about it right now. Just a moment of peace."

"Don't worry, Kylie. You *must* rest. *I* have no need to. I will be alert for you. Come back to bed."

"I don't know if I can."

"You're exhausted." He tugged my hand and led me back to the bed, pulling the covers aside. He got in and gently pulled me in with him. Tossing the comforter over the both of us, I settled in his arms. It was nice and safe that way. He petted my hair and his lips kissed my forehead from time to time as he murmured to me in a strange lulling language until I guessed I must have fallen asleep. When I awoke, he wasn't there and a cup of coffee was steaming on my side table.

I couldn't help but run to the window. Nothing except some villagers milling in my backyard. Oops. I ducked and hit the floor. Well, wasn't *that* an eyeful I offered to the citizens of Moody Bog. Welcome to my shop! I crawled to the bed and yanked my bathrobe over the side, putting it on while I sat on the cold floor out of sight of the window.

When covered, I stood and peeked past the curtain. Only one teenaged boy was standing and looking up transfixed. You're welcome, kid.

I hurried through my morning routine, showering, dressing for the hunt in jeans and heavy boots, and finally heading downstairs. The place was crowded with people all standing around politely. Some were ogling Erasmus, which I could tell made him agitated. Nick was writing on a portable whiteboard some sort of symbols when everyone suddenly noticed and turned toward me.

I stopped on the staircase and waved with just my fingers. "Hi, everyone. I see you're all settling in. Don't let me interrupt."

They gathered in klatches. I was a little shocked to see Charise helping Seraphina organize charitable work, getting lists of the people who were hurt and injured and whose property had been damaged, and coordinating with others to donate this or that.

When I walked by Doc, he was teaching a class on protection charms.

Even Jeff was there. Looked like he was demonstrating some self-defense with brooms and pitchforks, anything on hand, and Doug and Bob were right there with him.

I had my own little Hogwarts. Except that *I* was Harry Potter and kind of doing a crappy job of it.

"Kylie," said Erasmus, rushing desperately toward me. He kept glancing over his shoulder. A bunch of young women—and one guy I didn't recognize—seemed to be following him a few paces behind. "I can't seem to get away from these people."

"Oh dear. You have demon groupies."

"What, pray, is that?"

"Never mind. I'll get rid of them." I pushed him away (did he forget he could vanish?) and confronted his fans. "Uh, look. Erasmus has lots of important, um, demon things to do. You're kind of cramping his style."

They exchanged glances with each other and seemed to acknowledge it. "Oh, sorry," said one young woman with glasses. They turned their attention to gazing longingly at Nick instead. I wondered if they knew he was a werewolf. They'd be over the moon…so to speak.

"Thank you," said Erasmus, still glancing suspiciously over his shoulder. "I did not like the look in their eyes."

"They meant no harm. I think they were fascinated by you."

He seemed to puff a little at that. "They are?"

"Down, boy. Don't you have some studying to do with Jolene? We've still got to find something Satan wants besides my soul."

"Oh yes." He made a move toward Jolene before he stopped, took my hand, drew me in, and kissed me on the mouth. Nothing lingering but enough to warn off anyone watching. "I remembered," he said softly, grinning.

My silly demon.

With so many people in the shop, I barely noticed when Ed showed up.

"So what's going on here?"

"Apprenticing Wiccans, I guess."

He frowned. I supposed that looking at all the people you'd grown up with suddenly going for the kind of stuff you disapproved of, could put a person off. He certainly didn't look like he approved. And then Deputy George came up beside him, his mustache displaying the same condemnation.

"It has to be done," I said. "They have to learn how to protect themselves."

I waited for George's religious diatribe but none came. I noticed that even he was wearing a charm pouch around his neck. This place *was* suddenly looking a lot like Salem.

I saw the moment Ed caught sight of Doug. He stiffened but when he saw his brother was actually helping out Jeff, he seemed more confused than anything else. "He's got nowhere else to go," I said softly.

"I haven't seen him do anything useful since we were kids."

"Today is a different day." I watched Doug too, still wearing that gauze eye patch. "Adversity sometimes brings out the best in people."

Ed looked at me regretfully. "It does in you."

"I'm kind of stuck with it."

"But look at all these people. I know that some of them were against you. Now look at them."

George winced and gave me a meek expression. Yes, he'd been one of the naysayers.

"They're scared," I said. "They want to do something. Now they are."

Ed fitted his thumbs in his belt. "If we all get through this alive, you will have friends for life."

"Let's hope so. Which reminds me. There's another beastie out there," I said. I could tell I had Ed and George's full attention. "It's a sort of…" I made gestures with my hands but none were adequate. "It's a leopard with a snake head and deer legs. Erasmus called it the Beast *Glatisant* or Barking Beast. It likes to kill and has this weird kind of bark." I grabbed my coat from the hook by the door. "I'm going to go hunt it. And maybe get that headless guy if I can."

"I got a report about him up by Hansen Mills. They were smacked by Baphomet pretty badly. Not a lot of structures left. Some of the folks here might be from Hansen Mills."

I looked back at my full shop. I regretted for only a moment that they weren't simply shoppers.

"Ed, did you find out anything about Ruth Russell?"

He shook his head. "Couldn't find her. She's not at her house. I'm beginning to feel stupid that I defended her."

"Don't be. She fooled everyone. If I find her…"

"Kylie, she's still human. Don't do anything you'll regret."

"What makes you think I'll regret it," I said, perhaps a little more vehemently than I had meant to do. I calmed myself and gestured toward my many guests. "They're welcome to anything they need. Looks like Seraphina and Charise are organizing some community outreach. You should coordinate with them. But I've gotta go." I raised my hand for the crossbow without thinking it through. Several people had to duck…while others gasped. "Sorry! Sorry about that!" I cringed, slipping out the door with it in my hand.

The air was crisp and clear. There was smoke in the air that would have been lovely and fragrant if it had been just people burning fall leaves. But I had the feeling it was Hansen Mills on the wind and I felt pretty bad about what people had lost.

Erasmus appeared beside me. "Are we hunting?"

"I thought I would go alone. You've got research to do."

"I'm not about to leave you on your own. Junior Wiccan can do the work."

"Her *name* is Jolene."

"Whatever."

We set out into the woods, fall leaves raining down all around us.

"It's different," said Erasmus, strangely conversational. "Just hunting the beast…and not the Chosen Host for a change of pace."

I glanced at him out of the corner of my eye. "I should hope so. I guess it must be weird for you. I mean, you probably were pretty hungry when you met me."

"With every intention of eating your soul," he said a little too glibly. "But then I got to know you. And fell in love."

I got a little squirm in my belly over the tender look he was giving me. "I guess I lucked out all around. What if—"

But I clamped my lips shut when I heard the barking in the distance. Not a dog. I stopped, closed my eyes, and did as I'd done before to reach out to the Booke. I felt its magic seize me.

In my mind, I was rushing forward between the trees, zooming faster than I could ever run. I went over a rise and down into a gully past a trickling brook. In the darkest part of a gathering of trees, it was there, face red with blood, tearing into…oh God. Was that a person?

My eyes snapped open. "We have to hurry." I broke into a run. I followed the path the Booke had shown me, skirting the dense growth of trees, heading down to the brook, and splashing through it. I didn't want to think about that person down on the ground, being eaten. Maybe they weren't alive. But maybe they were. *Don't think about it, just run!*

I slid down another embankment, sprinted up the other side and saw the dark grove ahead. I slowed only marginally while I swung the crossbow up to my shoulder. I ran while aiming it because I wasn't planning on waiting to shoot. When I came to the trees and spotted the creature, I fired. I got it in the chest but wasn't satisfied. I grabbed another quarrel from the stock, wrestled it out even as the crossbow fought me, and slapped it in the flight groove. I shot again. The creature thrashed and wailed in its strange barking call.

I stalked up to it, even though it had started to shoot out beams of light. Taking the crossbow like a club, I slammed it in the head and kept slamming till chunks of it started flying up at me. Still the light emanated from it as I beat it to a pulp. Erasmus grabbed my arms and swung me around. "You have to write in the book!"

I threw down the crossbow, stomped up to the Booke that had appeared, and took up the quill. I wiped bits of the Barking Beast off my face and used its blood to write how pissed off I was that it killed and how I wish I had hunted it last night and a few more details that seemed to satisfy. I felt the creature burst apart in a hail of sparks behind me. The Booke slammed closed and dropped. I left it there.

Erasmus suddenly wrapped his arms and warmth around me. "It's all right," he kept murmuring. "It's all right. Calm down."

"I just want to…I just want to kill them *all*!"

"I know. It's all right."

I took a shaky breath. "The person. Are they—"

"He's dead. Don't look."

I felt I should, but I couldn't. I just clung to Erasmus. "Is it anyone we know?"

"No."

I pulled myself together enough to drag out my phone. I swallowed a few times, from nausea, from dread. "Ed? There's a body. One of the Booke's beasts killed him."

"Where are you, Kylie?"

I lifted my eyes to the trees, the hills beyond. "I don't know. Erasmus?"

He took the phone and it was strange seeing him talk into it. "We are a quarter mile off the main highway and past the brook. A dense clump of trees, approximately west-southwest from Kylie's shop."

"Leave the phone open. I can follow its coordinates. Keep Kylie safe. And…thanks, Erasmus."

That sort of broke me out of it. I didn't think I'd ever heard Ed use his name. Erasmus was still holding me tight but walking me away some distance. "Sit here, Kylie."

"Shouldn't a Chosen Host be made of sterner stuff?" I said weakly.

"You are made of very stern stuff. But you are still human and you have a weakness for the deaths of your own kind. There's no need for you to see it."

"Okay." I dropped my face into my hands. "I kind of lost it there. I didn't mean to beat that thing."

"I have never been so proud."

"Ha. I don't think that was anything to be proud of. I lost it. I lost control."

"Under the circumstances, I don't think it was out of character."

"Erasmus—"

He dropped to a knee in front of me and took my hands in his. "You are just the same in my eyes. You, a human, have been stretched to the breaking point, yet you still show unparalleled courage. I have never admired a mortal as much as I admire and love you."

"Yeah?"

"Yes." He gazed at me a moment before drawing closer and offering a gentle kiss. "Humans are best at showing courage. That's why those in the Netherworld envy your kind so much."

"If only I could give *that* to Satan, this would all be over."

He rose and kept a hold of my hands.

A siren wailed in the distance. It wasn't long until I heard Ed calling my name.

"Your constable is here," said Erasmus, but the words held no jealous streak.

"Kylie!"

"I'm over here!"

He came crashing through the woods holding his rifle, followed by Deputy George, equally armed. Ed measured the both of us. "You all right?" he asked me.

I nodded and pointed back to the shadows. Ed turned and signaled to George. They both approached and stood over the victim.

"Jesus," Ed muttered. "Let's get the stretcher."

They worked while I sat. It didn't seem quite fair. But after a while, Ed came back to me. "I spoke to Doc about this, about encountering more book victims. The Wiccans decided it would be best not to call the coroner when we find bodies. We can get Doc to sign off on these cases. We're just sending them to the mortuary. When I asked, most of the town decided to keep it to ourselves. And those remaining from Hansen Mills who joined us seem to agree. There are some folks in town who aren't happy about this. Some have left. Others think we should call in the staties. I've been taking a lot of time to talk them down from that. Last thing we need is more people involved. They just don't get that there isn't anything they can do. Of course, there are some in that crowd that want me to arrest *you*."

"And that would be even worse."

"I tried to tell them that. Anyway, Doc's got enchantments on them so they can't leave or call out. Even covered the internet. But I don't mind saying that we need to bring this thing to a close and soon."

"I know. That Halloween deadline is looming." I rose.

"Will you be all right? We've got to transport the victim to the mortuary and he's taken up all of the backseat."

"No, we're fine. Any clue as to…to who that was?"

"Someone from Hansen Mills. I used to run him in from time to time for poaching. Maybe it's poetic justice."

"Don't joke."

"I'm sorry, Kylie." He turned to Erasmus. "Take care of her."

"With my life."

Ed gave him a quick once over, seemed satisfied, and headed back to his SUV parked just beyond the trees.

I picked up the crossbow, worried I had hurt it. But it was made of sterner stuff too.

We began trudging back to the shop. But I was feeling odd. Not quite myself. Yeah, I had just beaten that creature to a bloody pulp without provocation, but it wasn't that exactly. I felt…weak. And out of it. "There are only a few days left before Halloween, Erasmus. Is it my imagination, or am I feeling kind of weird?"

"It's the power, the ley lines. Remember that the power fluctuates this time of year. There's a place I wish to take you. May I?"

"Right now?"

"Yes." He offered me his hand. I took it. He pulled me into an embrace and the cold and dark suddenly surrounded us. When I could breathe again, we were on the highway somewhere.

"Where are we?"

"Hansen Mills."

"Why are we here?" I started scanning the skies for you-know-who.

"Because the ley lines cross here. And that is a most powerful place."

"Wait. I thought they crossed at my grandpa's house."

"And they do. But they also cross here. Many, many more of them."

"And that's a good thing?"

"I think you will see that it is a *very* good thing."

He walked ahead and I followed. Soon he turned off the road and headed up a verge. At least it was daytime and for once I could see where I was going, but it was still hiking over logs and rock outcroppings. We came to the edge of a fairly steep drop and he finally stopped…on the most precarious part of it.

"Here," he said.

"Here what?"

He sighed impatiently. "Where the ley lines cross. There's eight of them."

"Maybe this was why I was supposed to stay out of Hansen Mills."

"Your grandfather didn't trust the lines. It's good for some things, not for others. But for now, I think it will strengthen you. The magic converges here. Come. Stand here where I am."

"There's not enough room."

"Do you think I will let you fall now?" He reached out a hand to me.

For a split second, I felt the littlest bit of trepidation. If he had been lying to me all this time, it was the perfect place to dispose of me where no one would know. Well, it was too late for that. I was too much in love with him to care. If he killed me now, there was no fighting it. And with a shake of my head, I released the thought. No, he wasn't acting. He did love me. Everything he did and said showed that.

I took his hand and let him pull me up beside him.

He smiled down at me. "Do you feel it?"

And then I did. Wow. Surges of power. It lifted my hair. At least I think it did. A sort of electricity running down my arms to my fingertips. I tingled all over and more importantly, felt renewed, refreshed and suddenly full of energy.

Abruptly, Erasmus swept me up, enfolded me in his arms, and kissed me hard. I kissed him too, reveling in the power that seemed to pulse back and forth between us. He held me tight, kissing my lips, my face. And when he drew back to look at me, there was a kind of glow around him. It was a bright green and fluctuating. "What is that?" I said dreamily.

"What is what?"

"There's a green glow around you."

He looked at me hard. "You can *see* that?"

"Yes. What is it?"

"My life force."

"Really? What does mine look like?"

"Orange. And beautiful. Like you."

I kissed him again, because he was lovely when he let go like that. "Thanks, Erasmus. This was like…Chosen Host cocaine. I feel suddenly…really, really good."

"I suspected that you were feeling drained. Emotionally as well as physically, and it was because the magic was ebbing. Yet, still tied to the book as you are, it was forcing you to expend greater amounts of magical energy."

"That doesn't seem like a very logical system."

"That's what happens when too many Ancient Ones stir the pot."

"What a laugh riot those Ancient Ones must have been."

He said nothing to that and carefully guided me away from the edge of the cliff. I bet Constance Howland and all the other Chosen Hosts would have given their eye teeth for that kind of concern from Erasmus. Best not to think about that, either.

"I feel better. Thanks for that."

"It was my pleasure."

"How did you know this was here?"

"I have been here before, you know."

"Three hundred years ago, you mean."

"Ley lines do not change."

"Did you help Constance Howland like that?" *Way to go, Kylie. You just couldn't resist asking, could you?*

He paused. "I helped her with the creatures from the book. That is my purpose."

And then took her soul. I guessed it was on my mind lately. I wished that wasn't his thing.

"I know what you're thinking," he said cautiously.

"Do you?"

"Yes." He kept his head facing straight ahead as we walked. "You're thinking about how I ate her soul."

"No, I wasn't."

"Yes, you were."

"Okay, so I was. Soul-eating seems to be of great concern these days."

"I know. We *will* find something to trade with Satan. Your junior Wiccan is very good at what she does."

"Can't you just call her Jolene?"

He stopped and grabbed my hand. "I will not allow you to put yourself in danger. If nothing can be found, I will not allow you to give up your soul."

"How are you going to stop me?"

His whole demeanor changed. I could tell he was thinking hard and that he didn't know. "I…I will simply…"

"You don't control me. I control you." I fished out the amulet and looked at it again. "It's kind of an ugly thing."

"It is part of me."

"Erasmus, if we don't do this, the Booke will plague me all our days. And it's killed so many people. And what about Baphomet? How do I get rid of him?" I shook my head. Sometimes it was hard to believe this was my life. "I don't know how much longer I can do this. You see what I did back there. I beat that thing with the crossbow. That is not normal behavior for me. And you yourself said that no Chosen Host has lived this long… thanks to you."

He stiffened at that.

"It's true! You can be as nice to me as you want and I know you love me, but that is a fact, Erasmus. And it isn't something I can just dismiss."

"It is my past."

"But how long can you go without eating? You'll have to at some point."

"That's not for you to worry over."

"Yes! It is! We're talking about someone's soul."

"This is not the time to speak of this." He was getting more irritated and began walking faster.

"Erasmus! Slow down. Are we *walking* back to Moody Bog?"

He stopped again. "I will take you back, then."

"Wait. Wait." I just stood there for a moment, thinking. "What if…what if Jolene can't find anything."

"She will."

"What if she can't?"

He was huffing breaths in short bursts, smoke lingering at his shoulders. "We will find a way."

"What if we can't? Erasmus, you have to promise me something."

"What?" he asked suspiciously.

"You have to promise me…that you will help me close the Booke."

"I am already doing that."

"No. I mean…you *have* to let me go to Satan and bargain. With whatever I've got."

"No."

"You have to!"

"NO!"

"Erasmus, if you can't let me do that, then you might as well eat my soul right now."

He blinked at me and swept forward. "Kylie, no. I won't. I can't."

"I can't keep doing this forever."

There was real pain on his face. Maybe he'd just never understood humans before but he was getting the full lesson now. We were vulnerable, expendable, and we tired easily. He did the only thing he could think of; he enclosed me in his arms and held me tight. "I won't let you die," he whispered.

But I didn't see how he would be able to prevent it.

Chapter Twelve

BACK IN MY shop, I walked around greeting the villagers. They were mostly young people—high school age, college age—all with eager faces and earnest dispositions. But there were some older folks, too: housewives, a few retirees, some shopkeepers… like Jolene's parents. They had brought a box of old clothes and dishes and were handing things out. Some people had lost everything.

My villagers were learning magic left and right. I wondered if they'd still be able to perform it when the Booke was gone. And then I wondered…if I'd be around to see it.

Erasmus was bugging Jolene as she worked. She stopped to talk to him from time to time, no doubt asking questions. He seemed to be trying to hurry her up. But I knew she had to take whatever time it took.

Jeff was entertaining some kids by making his ears and snout grow. This was going to be one weird town when we got done with it.

Jeff glanced at me then from across the room and winked.

Nick came up behind me. He stood with me and watched Jeff change from a long pointed-eared semi-werewolf to a human again.

"I was never popular," said Nick. "Never one of the cool kids. Yeah, I did the whole Goth thing, but just for the look, not because I was emo and didn't belong. You'd think I used to be bullied for being gay, but no one seemed to care. Now look at us." He chuckled. "It's weird, no question."

"How's your paranormal patrol going?"

"We need a hipper name than that. But it seems to be fine. They've spotted Headless a few times, but everyone knew enough to give him a wide berth. How is the mission to Hell working out?"

"I don't know. Slow. And we're running out of time."

"I hear you got the Barking Beast."

"Oh, I got it all right."

"Yeah. I heard that, too."

I passed a hand through my hair. "Nick, it's getting to me."

He rested his arm on my shoulder. "I know, dude. But you've got to hold on. We'll come through for you."

"I hope so. This place is ready to pop."

Someone had brought in a police scanner, which suddenly crackled to life. "This is Sheriff Bradbury. Baphomet was spotted heading your way. Northeast. Get ready."

I panicked. Some Chosen Host *I* was. "Get ready? What can we do?"

Nick smiled. "Just you watch. Okay, everyone. This is not a drill. Positions!"

Suddenly, everyone mobilized. Even Bob and Charise were falling into assigned groups. Everyone grabbed paper bags that were set in a row against the front wall near the door.

There were scouts crouching near the windows sketching symbols on them with wax, while an old air raid siren went off somewhere in town, notifying everyone to take cover.

I grabbed the crossbow and the Spear and crouched next to the people at the window. There was a shudder like an earthquake and then a shadow passed over the road. A fireball suddenly erupted in the street. Despite trying to be ready, people screamed. I might have been one of them.

The roof and rafters creaked but nothing happened. Another fireball split a tree across Lyndon Road and part of it fell onto the street. And then a black shadow landed with a rumble. Baphomet was tall again, twelve, fifteen feet, and he fluttered his bat wings as he strode toward my door. "Kylie Strange! I command you to come out."

I grasped tight to the Spear of Mortal Pain and started to rise, but several hands shoved me back down. What the—

We waited. I glanced around at the villagers but they were all concentrating on looking out through the symbol-scrawled windows. People were reaching into their bags, sharing with their neighbors. It looked like different colored powders clutched in their hands.

"Send out Kylie Strange, people of Moody Bog, and be spared. It's her and her book I want, not *your* lives."

He got no reply, getting angrier by the second.

I grabbed the Spear and hit the button, letting it extend. "Can I open this window?" I asked of the teen who had scrawled a symbol on it.

He looked to Nick for confirmation. "Yeah," said the guy who I think was named Brad. "Go ahead."

"Good." I stood up and lifted the sash. "Hey Baphy! How's your eye?"

He turned his head. Oooh. That eye was bad. Looked as bad as Doug's.

Baphomet's goat face sneered. "I will personally eat you alive," he said in that cow voice.

"I don't see that happening. I've got this spear and you've still got one good eye left. I'd like to correct that."

He roared. With both hands, he flung balls of power at my shop. I ducked, but they bounced off and dissipated in a shimmering wave. That was one pissed-off goat.

"Okay, Moody Bog," I said to the assembled villagers. "Show us what you've got."

Those crouching by the window rose. One by one they

opened the sashes, and on Nick's "Go!" they all tossed the colorful powder and chanted, "Wayward one, begone! Goddesses and angels protect this house. Wayward one, begone! Goddesses and angels protect this house." Over and over again they chanted and threw clumps of powder, creating a rainbow shower all around the shop.

At first, nothing happened. But as I watched, the piles of powder shimmered and bubbled and started to rise. They formed into something like multi-colored bats, which fluttered and rose higher, moving toward Baphomet. No sooner had one risen from the powder than the next one was clumping and flying upward. From all around my shop, colorful bats fluttered toward Baphy, almost looking like butterflies. He backed away from them, wary at first. Until they zoomed at him, self-destructing when they hit him in little explosions of color. I could tell they stung, because now he was seriously batting at them, backing away, grimacing when they hit. Because more were coming, and faster.

Baphy swung his arms wildly now. He tried to summon a fireball but the bats converged on his hands and started gnawing away. He screamed and whipped around. Finally, he rose into the air, pumping his huge wings, but the bats pursued him. Some of us ran outside, those not chanting, and watched him fly. He was spiraling out of control. He clipped the top of a few tall pines and landed hard on the village green, still struggling and bellowing. He rolled but couldn't seem to dislodge the bats. He pumped his wings again and soared higher until he was out of sight, still pursued by a rainbow of fluttering creatures.

Everyone cheered, including me. But it didn't take me long to sober. "Okay, guys," I said. "That was great. But that only scared him off for now. He'll be back."

"We knew it was only temporary," said a young girl whom I thought was called Emma. She was out of breath and flushed with shining eyes. "But it worked!"

People were high-fiving each other. I had a whole town of witches and warlocks now. But I worried about those that weren't with us and what they would do. There were a lot of firearms in a rural town like this. I didn't know how we could protect ourselves from that.

"Has anyone talked to Reverend Howard?" I asked of those near me.

Nick popped up, dusting colored powder from his hands. "He's holed up in the church with some of the more conservative people in town. At least that's what I've heard. What happened to all that liberalism he was spouting?"

"Yeah. I wonder that too."

"Now don't go and cast aspersions," warned Doc, coming up behind me. "He was trying to talk them down from violence. I talked to him on the phone just a few hours ago. He knows what we're doing and he says to keep on doing it."

That was a relief. We needed people with a voice on our side. "Any more word on Ruth Russell?" I asked him quietly.

"Not a peep. Frankly, I'm worried about her."

"You're worried about *her*? Don't you think this is all *about* her?"

"Kylie, I've known her a long time. I just can't get up the ruffles to be suspicious of her."

"Well, it's time to wake up, Doc. There's no time for second guessing."

"I caution patience. There's always time to second guess. Wasn't it first impressions that got you on the wrong side of a few of our conservative townsfolk? Like George?"

I glanced toward Nick. It was true that George had been dead-set against the Wiccans at first, even though he'd been secretly dating Nick. And now he was a full-fledged member. But Ruth was a whole other story. She had never wanted to welcome me. Every bone in her body seemed against me and mine. And I was worried that she might be conspiring to pull another ritual like she did when murdering Dan Parker. Doc's homespun cracker barrel attitude was never going to convince me that she'd never been a part of that!

Erasmus suddenly appeared next to me. He had a gleam in his eye. "I have a whole new appreciation for humans," he muttered.

"We can kick ass when we need to."

"So I see. Twenty-first century, eh? It's turning out to be the most interesting century to date."

The police siren sounded in the distance. Poor Ed and George. They'd never been so busy in their lives. Just keeping their own heads was probably wearing them down. The air raid siren called the all clear and everyone seemed to relax for a bit. Seraphina and Charise were passing out tea and coffee, while Marge from Moody Bog Market sliced pecan loaf.

Doug was leaning against the wall, arms crossed over his chest and scanning the room. I sidled up to him. "Thanks for coming to the side of the light."

He glanced at me with his one good eye and smiled. "When the god you summoned turns on you, it's time to make a change."

"I'm sorry about Dean."

The smile faded. "Yeah. He got it trying to defend me. He was a good guy. Despite following me."

I didn't say anything. Doug knew how I felt.

"And hey. Thanks for getting Goat Face in the eye." He tapped the gauze covering his own injured eye. "A little eye for an eye. I like your biblical view."

"Yeah, well. He pissed me off."

"Remind me never to piss you off again."

I elbowed him good-naturedly. "This would probably be a good time to patch things up with Ed. If you can catch him in between runs."

"Probably. Anything's possible. He never came by the other night, by the way. Too busy, I guess. And you know what? I'm kinda sorry you aren't gonna be part of the family now."

"Oh really?"

"Yeah. He needs someone to get him in line. But…" He stretched his neck to glance at Erasmus, who was trying to lose his groupies again. "You're set on him, huh?"

I followed his gaze and smiled. Erasmus was being his grumpy self, trying to stare down the groupies, which only seemed to encourage them. It was pretty adorable. "I am. Don't ask me why."

He got in close. "Have you ever considered that it's that book?"

I didn't say anything, because I had thought of that. Lots of times. That maybe once the Booke was gone I wouldn't feel that way about Erasmus, or he about me. But I just as quickly rejected it. Wouldn't Erasmus have known if that were a symptom of the Booke? And it'd started happening to me almost the moment I met him. I was pretty sure Constance Howland never had any twinkle in her eye about him.

I gave Doug a smile as an answer and moved along.

Charise and I made eye contact but she looked away pretty quick. I didn't think there would be any heart-to-hearts with her anytime soon.

But when Seraphina had a moment, I sat next to her. "These guys have done an amazing job," I said. "I guess I should say that all of the coven has done an amazing job organizing them."

"Well, it's always better when people want to help. And it looks like we might have far more in the coven when all this is over."

"Seraphina, what do you think is going to happen to the magic when the Booke is gone for good?"

"I think you know the answer to that. It will fade and we'll all go back to the way we were."

"Will you be satisfied with that? I mean, once you've done real magic—"

"Oh my dear. We've always done *real* magic. It just manifests itself differently. I think that a lot of people here today will be pleased with what we can do afterwards."

I was still a bit skeptical about the others, but I was convinced she and Doc would be okay. Jolene would continue her research, and Nick…well. Nick was a werewolf and that wasn't going to go away.

It made me think of Jeff. I searched around, looking for him. Kids always seemed to gravitate toward him. Women, too. Especially good-looking ones. And sure enough, he was surrounded by admirers, both kids and ladies with stars in their eyes.

"Hey, Jeff."

"Hey, Kylie. How's the Chosen Hosting going?"

"Well, you know."

"We'll see you later, Jeff," said one curvaceous brunette, waggling her fingers at him. His eyes followed her as she went into the kitchen.

"Hey, you've got to be careful now that you're a…you know. What if you accidentally bit someone in the throes of passion?"

He glared at me. "Did I ever do that with you?"

"No. But you weren't on wolfsbane then. You *are* taking your wolfsbane, right?"

"God! Nag, nag, nag. Of *course,* I am!"

"Well, you've got to be careful."

"Believe me, I think about it 24/7," he said sourly. "There isn't a moment when I don't."

"I'm sorry."

"Don't keep apologizing. It isn't your fault." He crossed his arms and closed up. I hated seeing that. Jeff was always so gregarious. I shouldn't have spoiled it for him when he was getting a bit of his old self back. But maybe it was time to drop some of the habits of his youth.

I clutched at the amulet. It suddenly struck me what I was doing. I was saying good-bye to everyone. Trying to find out if they'd be all right. Because I didn't think I'd be around to see that they were. My heart pounded. It all scared me…for a moment. But then the Booke sent an undulating wave of calm toward me. When I turned, it was skimming in the air coming toward me. People fell silent and moved out of its way. When it hovered in front of me, its magic pulsed, engulfing me, soothing me. It wanted to be one with me…and I wanted it too.

I grabbed my coat to sit outside away from prying eyes. The Booke followed me. As soon as I was alone, I reached out and cradled it against my chest. And I realized that *I* was soothing *it.* "No one's going to get you," I told it. I meant Baphomet.

But did I? Was that all I meant?

It knew my plans. Oh yes it did. And it didn't want to be destroyed. It wanted to flourish. It wanted new life. It wanted *me.*

I was *becoming* the Booke and the Booke was becoming me. And it was too close to Halloween to ignore it. I felt it whisper that there was still a creature out there. Headless.

"*Let me tell you where it is,*" the Booke whispered, and I closed my eyes and listened.

"Kylie."

I ignored Erasmus.

"Kylie."

It was like my mother trying to wake me for school. I was dead to the world and just wanted to sleep.

"Kylie!"

I kept my eyes shut, trying to listen. "What *is* it, Erasmus?"

"Open your eyes. See where you are."

"What do you mean?" But when I opened my eyes, we were deep in the forest. "Why did you transport me here?"

He gazed at me steadily. "*I* didn't do it." He stared at the Booke meaningfully.

CHAPTER THIRTEEN

I WHIPPED MY head around, seeing only dense forest and shadows. "Oh shit."

"You are drawing ever closer to the book. *It* transported you here."

I was afraid to hold it and afraid to let it go. "It was talking to me. It wanted to show me where Headless was."

"And it took you there."

"Erasmus, I'm scared."

Gently, he pried the Booke from my fingers and held it for a moment, studying its cover. He must have looked at it countless times over the centuries, including when it was just a scroll. He must have been surprised when books were invented with pages and covers. Maybe he loved the thing. Maybe he hated it. It was his prison and his curse. But it was also the only life he'd ever known. I had the feeling that he wouldn't be sorry to see it go, even if he had to go with it. But I couldn't let that happen. It was unthinkable having a world without Erasmus.

He pushed the Booke away. It glided a few feet, as if it were floating on the surface of a lake. But I felt its pull and it turned and headed toward me again.

Erasmus grabbed it, shook it. "Begone!" he cried, and it vanished in a huff.

"It's getting stronger," I said.

"I know."

"It transported me."

"It is a gateway."

He meant it as an explanation on how it got me there, but I began to think. "It *is* a gateway. And a key."

"So it would seem."

"Maybe there's a way to use it to lock Baphomet away."

He shook his head. "We must concentrate on destroying it."

"I won't. Not until I can release you from it."

"Kylie…" He sighed. "It may not be possible. You must prepare yourself for—"

"No! I won't be responsible for killing you. I refuse."

"If you wait much longer, you may not be able to refuse the book anything."

He was right. Even now, when the Booke was far away and I knew exactly *where* it was, I was drawn to it. Wanted to do its bidding. "What am I going to do, Erasmus?"

"For now, you must hunt the Dullahan."

A spike of fear stabbed at my chest. "I don't have the crossbow. Wait." I reached inside my jacket. The Spear of Mortal Pain was still there. I yanked it out and pressed the button. It clicked to its full length, point glistening.

Erasmus took a step away. I didn't blame him. After all, he'd been stabbed with it once and said it lived up to its name.

It wasn't as safe as the crossbow since I'd have to get right up to the creatures to get them, but it would do in a pinch.

"Listen," I said, pointing a finger at him. "I'll do this now, but tonight we are going to do our research and then after, we are going to break that bed making love. Do you understand me?"

He had a shocked look on his face for only a moment before his whole demeanor changed and a wicked smile curled his lips. "Anything you say."

"All right then." *Grab life while you've got it, Kylie. But for now…* I clutched the spear in both hands and stalked forward into the darkening woods. I figured Headless wouldn't be where the trees were close together. He probably needed to be by a road, the better to encounter people. So I followed that tingle in the back of my head that was probably the Booke and headed downward to where the highway was.

I walked along the edge of the asphalt. A light sprinkling of rain had begun. I reached back and tugged my hood over my head. Cars moved along the road. I saw the people in them follow me with widening eyes, a hooded woman holding a spear, a man in a long duster following her. Yeah, that didn't happen every day. *Stick around here and you'll see plenty*, I yelled in my head.

My phone rang. I dug it out of my pocket and answered. "Hi, Doc."

"Kylie, some of the folks here seemed to think you, uh, well vanished. I tried to reassure them that it was just Mr. Dark—"

"No, it was me. Or, more accurately, the Booke. It's getting stronger. Tonight, we really have to concentrate on finding a way to deal with Satan. Grab some of your oldest books and come back to the shop. Right now, I'm hunting Headless."

He was trying to say something, but I didn't want to talk anymore so I clicked it off. I stuffed my phone back in my pocket and curled my fingers around the spear shaft again. I didn't want to do the Booke trick where I closed my eyes and went as one with it. We were getting too darned close as it was. If I used logic, I thought I would be just as successful.

Erasmus said nothing as we trudged up the slick road in the rain. I kept my ears pricked for any unusual sounds. I figured Erasmus would have my back and scan the skies for me in case Baphy showed, though I doubted he would. He was probably off somewhere licking his wounds. I wondered if there was something we could bribe *him* with, but it seemed all he wanted was worshippers. Maybe Satan wanted that too. I hoped Jolene could find the answer. I was itching to leave for the Netherworld and dreading it at the same time, but I was sure that whatever happened, I would beg for Erasmus' life. Not much else mattered besides destroying the Booke.

I stopped. Were those hoofbeats?

I moved to the very edge of the road and waited.

The sound grew louder. It couldn't be anything except hoofbeats. They clopped, not in a gallop but in a leisurely canter. And soon, there was the Dullahan coming around the curve. His head looked even greener and slimier under his arm than it had before, if that were possible.

His weirdly roving eyes spotted me easily. He kicked his red-eyed horse's sides and hurried toward us. All the while, he swung that spine whip. With each revolution around his headless neck, the weapon grew longer and longer.

I kept the spear close to my side. I didn't want that whip to catch it the way it had gotten the crossbow the last time.

He was almost upon me when he shrieked, "Kylie Strange!"

"That doesn't work on me, you idiot!" I yelled.

The face frowned under his arm. It cast its googly eyes toward Erasmus and opened its mouth to yell *his* name.

"He's a demon, remember? We've been through this before. Boy, you sure have a short memory. Must be because your brain is decaying faster than the rest of you. Looks like a bad case of melting Roquefort you got there."

His dead face either grimaced or it really *was* melting. "Then I don't need to say your name," he said in a high screechy voice.

He spun the whip. Before I could get out of the way, it came at me and wrapped around my body, trapping my arms at my sides. I barely got out a yell before I was yanked off my feet.

The horse started galloping and I was flung out behind it almost parallel to the road. I couldn't bring the spear up. I was whipping around in the air and getting a little seasick, but it was better than being dragged behind on the asphalt. There wouldn't have been much left of me after that.

The bones of the spine were digging sharply into my skin. I tried wriggling free. If Headless decided to fling me off a cliff, there wasn't much I could do about it. I knew Erasmus must be around somewhere, but this was up to me to figure out…if I could.

The Dullahan galloped around a sharp curve and I was thrown and dragged through the limbs of pine trees shouldering the road.

"Dammit!" I yelled, spitting out pine needles. "I am so going to kill you!"

He lifted his head up with his other arm. It swiveled and glared at me. "Not if I kill you first, Mistress Strange."

"No need to be so formal," I grunted, struggling. I slammed into some holly bushes and *ow*!

The face cackled and turned away, tucked back under his arm again. Then I looked up and saw what he was cackling about. The next curve of the road didn't have any nice prickly holly bushes or spikey pine boughs. It was just granite all the way up the rock face. "Shit!"

I started rolling from side to side. I used my solid weight like a rock to propel me far right and left, throwing the horse off balance. It whinnied worriedly, its gait stuttering. No longer were we at a full gallop, but an insecure clopping all over the road.

The head appeared over his headless shoulder again, assessing what I was doing. I managed to swing wide, but now that the horse was slowing down, I managed to get my legs under me and started running like some cartoon animal who'd suddenly found itself over a cliff. My shoes hit the road. I stumbled but managed to right myself and keep running. It was tempting to just stop and pull on that spine whip, but the horse was far stronger than I was.

Headless urged the horse to gallop again, but it was spooked (yeah, *it* was spooked) and wouldn't run. It headed for the grassy verge and slowed to a trot. I was able to get to a tree and run around it, making sure the spine whip was wrapped twice around the trunk and then I braced my feet against it.

Just as I'd hoped, the whip tore from Headless' hands. I pushed the loose spine down past my hips and stepped out of it, before running to another tree. Hiding behind it, I clutched the spear in my hands.

Headless shrieked his anger. He yanked on the reins to pull the horse around. There was no way I could throw the spear and hope to hit him. He could easily bat it out of the way. No, I'd have to get in close, which seemed like an incredibly bad idea.

I could hear him dismount and root around in the grasses and dead leaves, searching for his whip. I held my breath to be as quiet as possible. Carefully peeking around the side of the tree, I saw his back was to me and his head was in the crook of his arm, just sitting there. I quickly rounded the tree and kicked out with my foot, sending the head arcing into the bushes like a soccer ball.

The body turned. It reached for me but I feinted one way and plunged into the woods in the opposite direction. Just as I thought. The headless body without the head had no idea where I was. When I looked back, it was groping around trying to find its way.

"I'm here!" cried the head to its body. The body lurched and stumbled, trying to get to the head.

It was all so surreal.

The head had helpfully told me where it was. I followed the sound and soon found it among a patch of fern. It whipped around to glare at me. "You will soon die, Mistress Strange."

"Really? Not from where I'm standing." I hefted up the spear and aimed the pointy end toward the head.

Its eyes widened. It tried to roll away in a pathetic attempt at escape. It was just sad, really. Still, I hesitated. It was a human face, after all. Sort of. Kind of a squishy one. *Think of it as head cheese, Kylie*, I told myself, and brought the spear down hard through the top of its skull.

Beams of light shot out as it screamed bloody murder. I pulled out the spear with a disgusting squelching sound and jabbed it again. More screaming, more beams of light. I checked the body over my shoulder. It had frozen with arms bent and fingers curled in agony, beams of light spearing through it. Even the black horse on the road was neighing, rearing, and dissolving into shards of light.

The Booke appeared and I dropped the spear to write in it, all the descriptions of my horrific ride that I could think of, until all three pieces of the creature snapped into a flurry of sparks and disappeared. That disembodied head's screams echoed into the hills before quieting at last.

The Booke slammed shut and fell. I picked up the spear, hit the button to reduce its size, and stuffed it back into my jacket just as Erasmus appeared in front of me and grabbed me into his arms. "You were magnificent! I have never seen such a Chosen Host, such a *human* before!" He silenced anything I might have said with a kiss so feral I was almost ready to find a soft spot in the foliage. Almost.

I gently pushed him back and caught my breath. His eyes were shining and his smile was wide, but not weirdly wide and with the right number of teeth. "Um, thanks, Erasmus. I was just trying to stay alive."

"Indeed you were." He shook his head at it. "It was magnificent."

"Okay, all right. Let me just…sit here for a minute."

His jubilance turned to concern. "Are you hurt?"

"No, just a little winded is all. The adrenalin is still pumping." I looked at my hands. They were shaking.

He knelt in front of me and enclosed my hands in his. "I'm sorry. I have little understanding of human feelings. Were you not proud of your achievement?"

I blew a strand of hair off my face. "I don't know. I mean, it just had to be done, you know? I was just working on instinct."

"Your instincts are truly awe-inspiring."

"Jeez, Erasmus. It's like you've never met humans before."

"I have met Minoan warriors as heroic as you. And they were just as passionate."

That put an interesting picture in my mind. "Okay," I said diplomatically.

He released my hands to push a stubborn tendril of my hair away from my forehead. "But none quite like you," he said softly.

I kissed him because he was wearing that adoring look on his face that meant the world to me. And because I needed to feel him. But then I pushed myself away. "We'd better get back. Can you take us the Erasmus way?"

"Of course." He kept hold of me and glued his gaze to mine. We were encased by the dark and cold for mere seconds before the familiar shelves and stock of my shop appeared around us.

My coven jumped to their feet with surprised gasps and chatter. I gestured for calm as I took out the Spear of Mortal Pain and slipped off my coat. "I'm done for the day," I said. "I could sure use some pizza."

"I'm on it," said Nick, whipping out his phone.

It looked like everyone else had gone. Nope, scratch that. Everyone but the Ordo. Bob and Charise were talking together and sitting very close in a corner, while Doug and Jeff were at opposite ends of the shop, exchanging silent glares. Ed and George were absent. Of course, they'd be patrolling. Things were still dangerous out there with Baphomet and whatever the Booke might be spitting out even now. I hoped they were getting some sleep. This is what it must be like to be a soldier. To be on and in full danger mode for an hour or two and then nothing the next. Yeah, it was nerve-wracking.

Jeff emerged from the shadows long enough to greet me. "How about a beer, Kylie?"

"I'd love one."

Doug piped up with, "How about one for me?"

"Get it yourself, goat boy."

Doug looked at me and thumbed back toward Jeff. "Not too polite."

"Well, you did beat him up."

"Oh yeah. I keep forgetting."

"As a werewolf, he's not afraid of much anymore."

"So I noticed." He sat in the sofa near me and leaned close. "I hear he bit the little guy, the Goth dude, and made him a werewolf. Is that what happened?"

"It was an accident."

"Are those two safe?"

Jeff walked back in and handed me a bottle. "Totally safe," he said. "And with really good wolf hearing."

"Hey," said Doug, lightly touching the gauze over his eye. "I just asked."

Jeff sat with his own beer and sighed before taking a slug. "I take a wolfsbane potion and I don't have the urge *to kill*." He said the last with a bit of emphasis and looked steadily at Doug.

"Dude, I'm totally reformed. I've got no interest in hurting you and yours. I've turned a new leaf."

"That's good," said Jeff, drinking and toying with the bottle in his hand. "Because if anything should happen to these people, I wouldn't like it very much. And there wouldn't be enough wolfsbane in the world to stop me from taking matters into my own hands. Or paws."

I held up my hand between them. "Okay, boys. Dial it down. We've got enough baddies out there to fight without picking fights in here."

"Yeah," said Doug, sitting back again. "You should listen to your ex. She's a smart lady. And fierce."

"She is a warrior," said Erasmus, standing over me. He hadn't lost that glimmer in his eyes. Boy, a lady with a spear sure seemed to turn him on.

Nick stuffed his phone back into his black jeans and sat between Jeff and Doug. "How are we all getting along, children?"

"Fine," said Doug. "Your sire here just gave me the standard warning about hurting your pack."

Nick scrunched his nose. "He's not my sire. That's a vampire thing. He's my...uh, alpha, I guess. But mostly he's just Jeff." Nick rolled his shoulders, clearly uncomfortable with the details.

"Sorry," said Doug. "I never did do any studying on the finer points of the supernatural. Guess I should have paid more attention."

"No one knows this stuff," I said. "Well, maybe Doc and Jolene."

"Shabiri wasn't exactly forthcoming," he said.

"By the way." I took another drink. "Where *is* Shabiri? I haven't seen her since she begged us to rescue you." Yeah, I had to rub it in a little.

He shrugged. "I haven't seen her. And I certainly didn't call her."

"Maybe you should, just to see what she's up to."

"I don't give a shit what she's up to."

"Well, I do. I don't trust her. She might be helping Ruth Russell. And speaking of, how did you know how to summon Shabiri?"

He looked at me steadily. "Can't a guy read a book for once in his life?"

"Really? A book that told you exactly how to summon the right kind of demon and how to steal a demon's amulet to have power over them?"

The silence stretched. He cleared his throat and moved around on the seat cushion. "Okay, okay. There was this…this note. In the mail. With some cash."

CHAPTER FOURTEEN

I STARED AT him. "A note? A freakin' *note*? From whom?"

"So…yeah," said Doug, embarrassment reddening his cheeks. "Someone helped us, all right? And we never knew who it was."

"Do you still have that note?"

"Strict instructions to destroy it. And I did. Someone sends me unsolicited cash, I do what they say."

Excited at finally getting some concrete information, I faced him eagerly. "And they gave you detailed instructions on what to do?"

He nervously ran his hand through his hair. "Yup. Couldn't believe when it happened. It was the first time anything like that worked. At first, we thought there was a mage in town, but then later found out it was that fancy book of yours."

"But there *was* a mage…who sent you instructions. Don't you get it?"

"I do now. And you think it's that Russell witch."

"Call Shabiri."

Doug blew out a breath and called out, "Shabiri!"

Was anyone surprised she didn't come?

But now Doug was pissed off. He grabbed his amulet around his neck in a tight fist. "SHABIRI!"

She popped up behind him. "No need to shout." She looked around, taking us all in. "My, my. What a cozy little coven you've become."

I put my beer down on a side table. "Yes, Shabiri. We've all decided to work together for the greater good."

"So I'm just in time to sing Kumbaya?"

"Cut the crap." Was I ever tired of her. "I want you tell me the truth."

"Oh, of course, darling. All you ever needed to do was ask."

If I rolled my eyes any more, they'd roll right out of my head. "Are you working with Ruth Russell?"

She smirked and lifted her hand in the Boy Scout salute. "I solemnly swear I am *not* working with Ruth Russell. Whoever the hell *that* is."

I turned to Erasmus, who seemed to be narrowing his eyes at her. "She's telling the truth," he said, rather reluctantly.

"Good!" she said. "Now that *that's* out of the way." She made a move to depart when Doug threw his leg in her way.

"Not so fast," he told her. "Then who *are* you working with?"

She leaned over and ran her hand under his chin and up to his cheek. "I'm working with you, Dougie."

He swatted her hand away. "Knock it off. Who else are you working with?"

"I haven't the least idea what you're talking about."

"You're the one who told us to summon Baphomet."

"You wanted power. He could give it to you. Turned out he was lying. Not my fault."

He shoved the amulet in her face. "Who in *town* are you working with?"

She reared back, scowling at him. "I'm telling you for the last time; I. AM. NOT. Have you got that through that thick skull of yours?"

We all turned to Erasmus. He grudgingly nodded.

"Fine! Can I go *now*?"

Doug kept a hold of her amulet. "Kylie says we're all here to do research."

"Research? On what?"

I had to tell her. I took a deep breath. "I'm going to go to the Netherworld to ask Satan to destroy the Booke."

Her expression seemed to freeze for a moment. Until she burst out laughing. "Now that *is* funny. Who knew you could be so amusing?"

"It's not a joke. I'm going to bargain with him to detach Erasmus from the Booke and destroy it. And we need to find something to trade with him other than my soul."

She stopped laughing. She looked more than appalled. She looked frightened. "You're serious?" She stomped up to Erasmus. "And you're *letting* her do this?"

"I don't have a choice."

"You're an idiot, is what you are!" She pranced in front of the whole assembly of Wiccans and Ordo and looked us over. "You pathetic little creatures. Do you have any idea, any *clue* what you are demanding?"

I was tired but I got up to face her anyway. "Yes, Shabiri. We do. So instead of screeching like a banshee, why don't you pick up one of these books that Doc was good enough to bring and help us research?"

"I don't have to look at any of those books. I can tell you right now it won't work. He'll never do it for anything but a soul. He wants nothing more than that."

"That may not be true," said Erasmus.

"And you! The dumbest of them all. You fell for these pathetic humans. You think this will help them?"

"I *want* to help them. For the first time in my life, I *want* to be free of the book."

"For Beelzebub's sake, *why?*"

He cast his arm forward and pointed at me. "Because I *love* her."

Shabiri staggered back as if stung. I don't think I'd ever seen anyone so completely shocked as she was. I knew she'd had an inkling before, but this was the first time he'd said it. She tried to speak, but couldn't, until she gathered herself and placed a hand to her stomach. "You love a human? Are you completely insane?"

"No." And then he looked at me with all the emotions he possessed written clearly on his face. So much so that I took a step toward him. "I love her," he whispered.

Shabiri's anger had returned. She punched her fists to her hips with a frown. "Of all the stupid things. Of all the stupid reasons. And you!" She cast a vicious glance at me. "You did this to him. You and your stupid witchcraft and Chosen Host flim-flam."

"I didn't do any of that—"

"Don't think I haven't seen men and women throw themselves at him over the centuries. Oh, the mortal race can be very appealing and very deceptive if it gets them what they want."

I began to consider Ed. Was she playing games with him too? He seemed to think she was being honest with him, vulnerable. But was that just a lie?

Demons lie. Of course. Poor Ed.

"Erasmus knows how I feel. I'm going to free him from the Booke and then it's going to get destroyed so it can't pull this bullshit on anyone else."

"You are monumentally stupid to believe that."

"Yeah, well. That's us mortals, all right. We always believe we can make things better."

Shabiri stomped up to Erasmus. "You're not falling for this, are you?"

Somewhere in between all the yelling and accusations, the pizza guy must have arrived, because Nick was setting the pizza boxes on my coffee table, walking around the ranting demon.

"We must find something other than a soul with which to bargain with Satan," said Erasmus. "You can help us or not. But in either instance, stay out of the way." He shoved her aside and moved toward Doc's many ancient tomes, piled on a table. He selected one, opened it with purpose, and dropped his gaze into it to ignore her.

She looked at all of us incredulously. "I don't want any part of this idiocy."

"But you'll stay and help if I tell you to," said Doug, mouth full of pizza.

"I think you're overstepping your bounds, *Dougie*."

He dangled the amulet he wore in front of her. "Not with this, I'm not. If you aren't going to help, then sit down and shut up."

She closed her mouth with an audible click and sat hard on the nearest surface, which was Nick's laptop on an ottoman.

"Oh, um…" Nick reached, thought better of it and drew back his hand. "Could you…I mean, you're sitting on my…"

"Dear gods!" She snapped up and gave him all the disdain she had. "Take your blasted toy."

He snatched it quick and held it to his chest. "Okay. Thanks." He set his laptop down behind the counter, then grabbed a slice of pizza and chomped on the cheesy point.

"Okay," said Jolene, eyes on her computer screen and one hand on a pizza slice. "As for Satan, in the original Hebrew it seems to be a general term for 'accuser' or 'adversary,' but also seems to mean 'to obstruct or oppose.' Someone called '*the* Satan' also shows up in early Hebrew texts as a celestial prosecutor of sorts. He kind of gets mixed up with the angel Mastema, who *persecutes* evil. Anyway, Satan is supposed to carry out punishments in the name of God, and it's also his job to tempt humans in order to test their faith. There is a huge mishmash of ideas about him. By the way, he was never actually mentioned by name as the snake in Eden, and it took till about the 1600s for him to take on the whole ruler of Hell thing. And different from Lucifer, by the way, who was a fallen angel—the first to disagree with God about Man. So he may be none of these things…or, I guess, just as easily *all* of these things. But Mr. Dark says that for those in the Netherworld, Satan's sort of an absent dictator. Though not everyone has heard or seen him."

"Have you?" I asked Shabiri around my own pizza slice.

She looked around and then pressed her hand to her chest. "Oh? Am I allowed to talk now?"

Doug got to his feet, hands knotting into fists. "I really want to slug her."

"So do I," I said.

"Hey!" She put her hands to her hips again. "Is that any way to treat a denizen of the Netherworld?"

Erasmus heaved a sigh. "Just answer the question, Shabiri."

She stared Doug down before he sat again. She straightened her catsuit and shifted back against the sofa. "I've only seen Him once. That was many centuries ago and I *don't* want to do it again."

"Why?" I asked. "What was he like?"

"He is…" She wriggled uncomfortably in her seat. "He is very old. And very large. He knows every little thing that is going on around Him, who everyone is, and where they are. He sits in a burning pit and simply seems to…to brood, I suppose. And when He was approached by other demons, He seemed reasonable at first, until one of them made Him angry. And then He flew into a flurry and grew very, *very* large and very dangerous. He killed the demon with a mere thought in a very unpleasant way. We were all frightened, and I was able to slip away unseen."

"Wow." I hugged myself unconsciously. "So…don't get him mad. Good note."

"I don't know what you can find to bargain with," she went on, rubbing her arms. "He's consumed with souls. He obsesses over them. Nothing is as sweet or as satisfying." There was the merest twinkle in her eye. "Only Erasmus would know what I mean. Not all of us demons eat souls, my dear."

I couldn't help but turn to him, but he was studiously *not* looking at me.

"But this proves the point," said Doc. "He might be all-powerful, but he is still a demon and not a god. He can be dealt with as a demon is dealt with."

"You're a fool," she hissed.

"Shabiri," Doc continued, ignoring her, "does he, too, have an amulet?"

Her jaw hung open. "You've *got* to be joking! No, He doesn't, and even if He did, He'd know what you're planning. He knows what everyone is thinking."

"According to the *Necronomicon*," said Jolene, "he can only tell what *demons* are thinking."

"That's all I care about, you stupid girl," huffed Shabiri.

"Okay!" I said, cutting into what was shaping up to be a slap fight. "Can we just focus here? We need to research. The best way might be to partner up. How about Charise with Seraphina…" They both seemed amenable to that. "Nick and Jolene. Bob and Doug—"

"Oh, Christ," hissed Doug.

"And Doc and Erasmus."

"Yoo-hoo!" said Jeff. "What about me?"

"I think maybe you should work on what herb combinations I could use for protection."

Jeff seemed less than thrilled with that, knowing full well it was busy work. "And what are *you* gonna do?"

I looked over to where the Booke was hovering. I'd known it was there. It was nudging my mind, after all. "I'll be communing with the Booke. It has some secrets it wants to tell me and others it doesn't. I'm going to climb in and see what I can find out."

Erasmus stepped forward. "I don't advise that."

"Sweetheart, we've gone well beyond what's advisable."

He had a weird look on his face. "What…did you call me?"

"Oh, for Beelzebub's sake!" railed Shabiri.

Erasmus snapped out of it. His cheeks became ruddy, as if he were suddenly embarrassed. It was pretty adorable.

Everyone went to their tasks. Nick and Jolene talked to each other over the tops of their respective computers. Doc and Erasmus bent their heads over worn leather volumes that were probably at least as old as the Booke, while Jeff rummaged in my buffet drawers and took out handfuls of herbs to place in a stone mortar. He knew his business as well as I did. In fact, I'd bet he was making his own wolfsbane by now.

Bob hesitantly approached Doug, but soon they were reading and conferring with each other.

Shabiri just glared at me.

I took up the Booke, went to a quiet corner, and settled in. Closing my eyes, I immediately sank into the weird dream world of the Booke of the Hidden. It showed me landscapes well beyond Moody Bog. I wasn't even sure if they existed. And while it was calming and all encompassing, I had to drag myself back and get real with the Booke. *Now look here, I want to stop all this nonsense that you've been doing. Are you listening to me, Booke?*

Kylie…Kylie…don't you want to play in my garden?

No! I've got better things to do—

But it's a lovely garden. See the trees glittering in the sunshine? Watch the stream as it trickles along. Don't you want to follow it?

It does look pretty… Hey! Stop that! We're going to talk. What can I offer besides my soul? I need to give Satan something other than my soul? What else is there that humans have?

I know nothing about that. Come play!

No! Your kind of playing involves creatures who kill and then I have to kill them. It's not fair. It's not nice.

If you won't play…then I'll have to show you the darkness.

The what now?

The sun-dappled meadow with the sweet burbling water shifted. Everything suddenly went hazy. The sky darkened and sounds came out of the forest that didn't belong. Sounds that suddenly terrified me. I looked up; the sun was a black disc against a white aura and the shadows stretched and creeped toward me. The reeds and ferns looked rotted, dripping with something dark.

I don't like this.

This is the dark. This is what you said you wanted. Not the meadow.

I don't like this!

I snapped open my eyes and looked around. I was suddenly back in my shop. Things were going on around me just as they had been. I took several deep breaths to calm myself and get that nightmare out of my mind, when I glanced over at Erasmus. His nose was nearly pressed into the book he was reading. He was so concentrated on what he was studying that he hadn't noticed my staring. Looking at him calmed me—his handsome features, the twist of his lips, his narrowed eyes. Suddenly he jerked back, startled.

"Find something, Erasmus?" I asked, hopeful.

The way he looked at me made my heart give a lurch. What had he read? I was rising to go over there when he gave a half-hearted laugh. "It's nothing."

"Nothing?"

"Nothing." And then he clammed up.

I sat back down. It sure didn't look like nothing. But if he didn't want to tell me, I'd never get it out of him. His eye twitched as he read, but he was all in. I decided to leave him to it.

I stared at my own Booke and scanned the cover, its worn leather, the weird lock that only I seemed to be able to open. But when I glanced up at Erasmus again, he was talking quietly and fervently to Doc.

"Doctor Boone," he said softly, "I wonder if I may speak to you. Alone."

"Certainly, Mr. Dark."

The two of them disappeared into the kitchen.

What was all that about? I started rising to follow them when Emma, auxiliary Wiccan, asked me a question. I did my best to answer her, trying to look like the sage Chosen Host I'd never be. She left satisfied, though I was darned if I remember what I said to her.

Raised voices chimed in from the kitchen, though I couldn't make out the words. Nick glanced at me and shrugged.

After a while, Doc came back into the main room and surreptitiously grabbed a candle and some herbs from my buffet.

He noticed me watching and gave me a wink and a salute before disappearing back into the kitchen.

I looked at the clock. It was getting late. It would be two days until Halloween tomorrow. And we weren't getting very far. I decided to stretch my legs and see what everyone else had come up with.

Raised voices were arguing in the kitchen again. Doc and Erasmus obviously had a difference of opinion about something, but the thick plaster muffled their voices. There was a popping sound, which probably meant Erasmus was ticked off and left in a huff. I exchanged another "What are you gonna do?" look with Nick. He shrugged again.

I stretched, letting all my vertebrae click into place—but that only reminded me of the Dullahan's whip. I flexed up my arms and something metallic clattered to the floor. When I looked down, it didn't make any sense. I knelt to pick it up.

My amulet. Erasmus' amulet. I'd worn it since the moment we knew he was a demon and I'd snatched it from his neck, making me sort of in charge of him. It had a demon face with horns and extended tongue. With ruby eyes.

Except the rubies were now black crystals and where the metal had always been warm to the touch, it was now stone cold.

Chapter Fifteen

"DOC!" I SCREAMED. What was wrong with the amulet? "Erasmus!"

Doc came tearing through from the kitchen with a horrific look on his face. I held out the amulet to him, but he didn't seem to need to look at it.

"What's happened? Erasmus! *Erasmus!* Isn't he with you?"

But Erasmus didn't come.

"Doc? This just fell off my neck. What's going on? Where's Erasmus?"

"Oh my goddess." He sank to a chair. He seemed pale and older than he had ever looked before. Running his hand over his face, he winced when he looked up at me. "Kylie, I'm so very sorry."

Something clutched at my heart and squeezed, tearing the breath from my lungs. "What? Why are you sorry? What have you done?"

I could feel everyone's eyes on us. Everyone had stopped whatever it was they were doing. "Now Kylie, you must understand. This was his choice."

"WHAT HAVE YOU DONE?"

He fidgeted. He never fidgeted. He was always sure-handed Doctor Boone, wise warlock and kindly country doctor. But now he wouldn't even look at me.

"It had become obvious that we couldn't find anything for you to bargain with. Nothing. And Mr. Dark knew you would go regardless. Darn it, Kylie, we all knew. But Mr. Dark found another way, another solution in one of my older books. He found a spell to turn him…well, it would turn him human. And he insisted I help him with it. I…I refused at first. I didn't think it was a good idea."

"Turn him human?" My mind whirled. I had no idea that such things were possible. Why would he do that?

"Yes. He said he would go back to the Netherworld, invoke the spell by breaking an enchanted wax seal, and become… human. It's a very rare and ancient spell. Irreversible." He looked away from me, fiddling with a knot on the upholstery of my chair. "He explained that as a human he wouldn't have been able to get into the Netherworld…well, never mind about that. But once he was human he could—"

"He could offer *his* soul." *Oh my God.* I couldn't breathe. I grabbed the chair behind me to steady myself and tried to inhale. My face was suddenly wet and my eyes burned. "No. No. He's not allowed to do that. I was going to free him. He would have been free."

"He didn't want you to die. I looked into his eyes, Kylie. And for the first time, I believed him. I believed that he loved you enough to sacrifice himself."

"But he can't do that. He can't *do* that!"

"He…he begged me to help him."

"But why would you? Why didn't you ask me?"

"Because we both knew what your answer would have been."

I wiped at my tears impatiently as they continued to flow. "What right did you have? Why is my life worth more than his?"

Doc looked away. I knew the answer to that, too. Because he was a demon and I wasn't. But that made no sense. We'd gotten to know him, to understand him. His life was just as valuable as mine. And now he was human too.

"You've got to change him back."

"I can't, Kylie. I don't know how."

I shook the amulet at him. "You *have* to!"

"I can't." He dropped his head into his hands. "Goddess forgive me. I knew it was a mistake the moment I did it."

I whipped around, searching all the faces around me. "I'm going to go get him. And stop him."

Seraphina stepped forward. "And how are you going to do that, Kylie? Do you want his sacrifice to mean nothing?"

"I don't care! I want him to live."

Nick looked torn. He'd never liked Erasmus, never trusted him. All with good reason. "But how are you going to get into the Netherworld without him?" he said.

I grabbed the hovering Booke. "With this. It's a key to a gateway."

"You'll never find him," said the voice from the back of the room.

We all turned. Shabiri wore a grim expression. "The book might get you into the Netherworld, but how will you navigate your way through? There are no helpful street signs. No GPS. And your very life force will alert any and all demons of your presence. You wouldn't get three feet without being devoured."

I staggered toward her. "Come with me!"

"Are you insane? No way."

"It's Erasmus. You know him. You've known him forever. Please help me."

"No. I'm captive. I'd be a target too."

Captive? Her amulet. Doug had snatched hers as I had taken Erasmus'. I looked toward Doug.

He cottoned on easily. His hand went to the amulet around his neck. "What if I gave it back?"

She stared at him with surprise, then her expression turned hungry. "Yes, give it back."

"I don't trust her," said Nick.

"Help me save him, Shabiri."

"Why should I do that?"

"I don't know. It would be your next big adventure. What can I give you to help me?"

"Kylie!" Doc shouted.

I held a hand up to him. "What can I give you?"

"Well, isn't this interesting?" She moved a bit like a cat, slinking around the far table. "What could it be that I'd want?" She tapped her chin with a sharp nail.

"Don't do it, Kylie," said Nick.

"Nick's right," said Jeff. "I'll go with you. I'm part demon now anyway. I can probably figure it out."

"Y-yeah," said Nick warily. "I c-can go too."

"No. Only me. And Shabiri. If she'll take me."

She smiled. "I think I *will* go. And I'll think about what I want from you. If Dougie gives me back my amulet."

"Talk about dealing with the Devil," said Doug, eyeing me with a rock steady gaze. "I'll give it to her if you say so."

There was no choice. I had to go rescue him, no two ways about it.

"I agree to your terms," I said.

"Done!" She clapped her hands and then turned to Doug. "Dougie?"

He yanked the chain from his neck. "I've been wanting to get rid of this thing anyway. Here you go, bitch. It's been a slice. I free you!"

Quick as lightning, she grabbed it back. She held it up to her neck, the chain fixing itself around her with a small pop. The green gem eyes glowed brightly and she sighed in relief. "Mine again. My life is mine again." Her own green eyes glowed a little too. "All right, meat girl. You've got the Booke. Let's open that gate."

Suddenly, she was right next to me. With a hellish smile with a mouth too wide and too full of sharp teeth, she grabbed my hand, and everything went black.

PART TWO

"Farewell happy fields where Joy for ever dwells:
hail horrors, hail Infernal world…"

—*Paradise Lost*, John Milton

Chapter Sixteen

AT FIRST, I didn't know where I was. But slowly, the world around me came into focus. We were in a dark forest near a road.

"Wait," I said, my memory sharpening. "I was just here. With Erasmus. This is near Hansen Mills."

"Of course," she said, hiking up the incline. "Where the ley lines cross. The more lines, the better. And the stronger the magic."

"I thought we'd be going to the caves where the rift is."

"The rift could take us to the wrong world. With the ley lines and the book, we'll be on target. Or don't you believe me?"

Uh-oh. I suddenly didn't. Was this all a trap? Would she leave me for dead in the forest to get her chance at the Booke at last?

"Wait."

She stopped with her back to me and sighed like a teenager. "What is it now?"

"Maybe I *don't* believe you." I lifted the Booke. "I get why Baphomet wants the Booke. He wants to open a permanent Hell Gate to let all his god pals through. But why did *you* want it?"

"You're wasting time."

"Why, Shabiri? Why do you want it?"

She didn't say anything, and her shoulders suddenly tensed.

"Erasmus is tied to it," I said. And then if fell into place because I'm an idiot. "How long have *you* been in love with him?"

She spun, her teeth grinding and her eyes narrowed. I cringed, thinking she was going to hurl a spell at me. But then all the twisted anger in her face, all the tense tightening of her body, suddenly dropped away. She looked off to the side and inhaled a shaky breath. "For far too many centuries," she said. Then she laughed humorlessly. "Had I only known that all it took was to be a helpless mortal…"

"Does he know?"

She glared at me, her eyes glowing ominously in the dark. "No. And you had better not tell him."

"I'm sorry. It's not something I—"

"Oh, just shut up, won't you?" She stood awkwardly, face turned away, one shoulder hitched up protectively.

"Enslaving him with the Booke wouldn't have endeared him to you."

"And she doesn't know how to shut up," she muttered.

"I never set out to fall in love with him, you know, or he with me. It just happened."

"Still not shutting up."

"I'll…I'll step aside for you. I will. It'll hurt, but I will. As long as you help me save him." I didn't mean for my voice to wobble. I was sorry it did because I wanted to sound firm with her, not weepy. But it actually seemed to have an effect on her.

She turned toward me, her eyes rising to mine. "You would?"

"I can give you that. If that's what you want."

Her green eyes glittered with hope for only a moment, before dulling to their normal green again. "Nice try. But he loves *you*. And there isn't a damn thing I can do about it."

"I'd give you my soul but I'll need it for Satan."

She studied me a long time. "You'd do that…for him?"

"I was all ready to. That's why he left…without even saying good-bye. He knew that's what I was going to do."

She gritted her teeth again, then took a finger and swabbed at her eye. Was she crying?

"Aren't the two of you a pair," she said in her old disdainful voice, turning away. "A regular O. Henry tale."

I waited, counting silently in my head. If she didn't decide by the time I reached ten, then it was the Booke and me on our own.

At eleven she turned halfway back. "Well? Are you coming or not?"

I stepped forward. Her discomfort was obvious in the tightness of her shoulders, in her stiff bearing. I don't think she had ever bothered to do something for someone else before. Except... she *had* fetched me to help Doug. I wondered why.

We reached the place where Erasmus had brought me. Where he had kissed me so passionately, held me so tightly. There was nothing like his kisses, because he meant them every time. He didn't mince words. He never lied about that.

"Shabiri, is he still...is he still alive?"

She frowned. "I don't know. He's not a demon anymore. I can't find him."

He wasn't a demon anymore. He was human. He broke the magical seal and made himself a human and was making his way alone in the Netherworld. He was vulnerable. He had no defenses. The idiot!

Shabiri had stopped to stand on the mound where the ley lines crossed. "Erasmus brought me here before. The magic gave me strength."

"Yes. But now you must use the book to open the gate for you. I can pass easily through to the Netherworld, but you cannot. Only the book will allow it."

"So...how do I do it?"

"Gods! You and your pathetic Wiccans know nothing! Concentrate. Talk to it."

"Okay. Concentrate." I closed my eyes and hugged the Booke close. *Open the gate. Let me pass through.*

That's not wise. Play in my garden instead.

Don't argue with me. Open the gate.

The gate is dangerous. The garden is better. I can take you to the top of a mountain. Would you like that? Or we can go to the whitest of sandy beaches, you and me.

Just open the goddammed gate!

The Booke said nothing more. But I felt funny. Something was happening. It wasn't like when Erasmus transported me. It wasn't like that dark and cold place. It was like a thousand tiny ants were biting me at the same time, like my very molecules were breaking apart. It was like every nerve in my nervous system was suddenly on fire.

I screamed…and then someone slapped my face.

When I flicked open my eyes, Shabiri was glaring at me. "Do you want to bring every creature in the Netherworld down on you?"

I absorbed her words, suddenly aware of my surroundings. I wasn't in a forest anymore. It wasn't dark. It was like a perpetual twilight, but the sky was wrong. It was red-orange and the edges were black. Were they clouds…or something else? And the smell. Sulfur and other toxic gases. I covered my nose. "What is that smell?"

"Desolation," she said.

Maybe she wasn't far wrong.

I saw shiny hills made up of obsidian or black glass, which rose in jagged points like fangs. And below that in their foot-hills were vast plains of molten lava, casting up curls of smoke. We were standing on something like a road or maybe a bridge between lakes of fire, and in the distance were more rocky out-croppings and dense, black forests of something that couldn't have been trees.

"*This* is the Netherworld?"

"Yes. How do you like it?" she sneered.

"It's horrible! It's like every dream of Hell anyone's ever imagined."

"We just call it home." She looked around, sniffing the acrid wind.

Why would such a place even exist? Who created it? Who were the creatures who lived here? No wonder they were always trying to break into our world…and cause destruction.

I had let the Booke go without even noticing, but it stayed close to me like a scared dog.

"Shabiri, will The Powers That Be know the Booke is here?"

She looked worried. "They might. We'd better get a move on."

"Do you know where we're going?"

"Yes. And the less talking, the better."

Fine. I didn't much feel like talking anyway. Everything around me, every sight, was a horrific vista. But I didn't see anyone or any*thing*. Except far in the distance, there were flying creatures. They had large bat wings and long tails. As long as they stayed over there by that volcano, I was all for it.

I flapped my coat. It was distinctly hotter here, and steamy. Finally, I just took the layer off, making sure I grabbed the Spear of Mortal Pain first. I stuffed it in my jeans pocket where it stuck out like a magic wand. I carried the coat for a while until I tapped Shabiri on the shoulder. "I don't think I'll need this here. Unless there's a part with a frozen tundra. Is there?"

"Not where we'll be going. But if you must rid yourself of it, throw it in the lava so that no one will find it. The absolute last thing we need is someone reporting the presence of a human."

"Okay." I wiped the sweat from my brow and walked to the edge of the land bridge. I looked down into the slow-moving lava, where rocks floated along and then casually upended themselves to sink beneath the surface. It was a bit mesmerizing—maybe the fumes were getting to me. But when I wound back to heave my coat, the stone under me gave way.

I screamed and tumbled down the embankment, cutting myself on one of the sharp lava rocks that littered the place like scree.

"Dammit," I hissed, looking at my scuffed palms. I wiped the blood off on the jacket and tossed it in the lava. It caught fire right away and sank below the surface.

I heard the scrambling of rocks and Shabiri was suddenly beside me. "Can you make more of a spectacle of yourself?"

"I'm sorry, I slipped!"

She grabbed my hands and turned them palm up. "You bled? Why don't you just get a bullhorn and yell to the hinterlands that a human is here?"

I snatched them back. "I didn't mean to get hurt."

"They can smell it. The blood. *Everyone* can smell it!"

"I'm sorry!" I wiped them on my shirt, but realized that was no good.

Suddenly she was looking up. "Uh oh."

I turned to see what she was looking at. Those flying things were heading straight for us.

"Way to be stealthy, meat girl."

"I couldn't help it." But I pulled out the spear and clicked the button, extending it.

She seemed impressed that I had brought weaponry. "Don't leave home without it," I said.

Those winged things had the look of small dragons. Not that I'd ever seen big dragons, or any dragons. Assuming there *were* dragons. They were black, their scaled skins sleek and shiny. Their long tails whipped out behind them like the strings of a kite. They had long necks and long snouts with…yup, a whole lot of sharp teeth.

I didn't stop to think. I ran.

Along the shore seemed like a good idea until the shore started to narrow. If I even got close to that lava, I'd go up in flames. I could certainly feel the heat.

Shabiri was right behind me. I could hear her harsh breathing.

"Give me the spear," she said.

"No."

"Give me the damned spear!"

I had to trust her. I had to. Like a tag team runner, I handed off the spear behind me. When her hand closed on it, I felt it slide out of my hand. And I hoped that it was the right thing to do.

I looked back. She had stopped. I slowed too and watched. She braced the spear against the ground and when the first flying thing came down at her, she jabbed upward. It flapped away, but soon came back, its long neck and snapping jaws reaching for her.

I couldn't just stand there. I scooped up some of those warm rocks and started shooting them at the beast. One hit its nose and it squealed and shook its head. That distracted it enough. Shabiri stabbed upward, catching it right in the underbelly. Spitted on the spear, it screamed and fought, flapping wildly. She gritted her teeth, maneuvering it downward on the end of the spear and then at the last minute shook it free to fall into the lava.

It screamed as it caught fire and soon sunk beneath the crimson waves.

Its companion had been making circles, watching the whole thing, but soon turned away and flew in the other direction.

"Now we've done it." Without even breaking a sweat, she walked toward me and handed the spear back. "Keep it ready."

"That was really good."

"Of course it was." She brushed back her long hair with its streak of green and started heading up the embankment. I followed her, using the spear to keep my balance.

"Did we give the game away?" I asked after a while.

"That creature's companion will be complaining to someone and we are a very curious lot in the Netherworld. Plus, the smell of your blood."

"Then I guess we'd better hurry."

The landscape changed and, mercifully, we veered away from the lava to where it was much cooler. We started up an inclined path that lead through a canyon of sharp outcroppings that thrust up through the red soil. It was like walking through the mouth of some enormous beast with large teeth all around us.

We hiked a long way and I was getting thirsty. I wondered if there were any pools of water anywhere that were safe to drink. "Shabiri, there wouldn't be a stream or anything around here, would there? I'm a little thirsty."

"Humans," she muttered. "None of them would be drinkable. Here." She conjured a canteen and handed it to me. When I unscrewed the lid, it was filled with cool, clear water. I drank down.

"Thanks, Shabiri." I raised the strap over my head and let it fall diagonally across my chest. "So…Erasmus was created to guard the Booke. What were you created to do?"

"I wasn't created with any particular purpose."

"Oh? Erasmus seemed to think—"

"Well, he doesn't know everything, does he? He's not awake all that often."

"You've been to my world a lot."

"As often as possible."

"That's why you know so much about cultural references."

"My, you are a talkative one, aren't you?"

"I just think it would be good to know something about you."

She stopped abruptly and got in my face. "Let's get one thing straight. We are not 'pals.' We aren't just 'the girls,'" she said, making air quotes. "As soon as we save that idiot Erasmus, we won't have anything more to do with each other. I've got my amulet back—" She shoved it in my face. "So I'm free. And I don't plan on getting enslaved ever again."

"Okay. I just thought… Forget it. You're so big and bad. I'm scared."

She heaved a put-upon sigh. "Look, I'm just your average, garden-variety demon, okay? We like to wreak havoc and cause trouble. And we especially like messing with mortals."

"Were you messing with Ed? Because I got the impression he kind of liked you."

She scowled and marched on. "I didn't do anything to your precious sheriff. His virtue is safe."

"Well, that's…kind of a shame."

She walked along saying nothing, until… "What's a shame?"

"Like I said. I think he really liked you."

"He's human."

"So?"

"So I don't get involved with humans."

"But it's all right to mess with us."

"For the love of…" She swung back to glare at me. "Do we really need to get into these philosophical discussions?"

"I was just passing the time. How far is it, anyway?"

She turned back toward the trail and looked up toward the high rock faces. "It's difficult to tell. It changes."

"What does?"

"The landscape. The points of reference."

"That would seem to make it difficult to get around."

"Yes, you'd think so."

"Do you know why it's designed this way?"

"I have no idea and I really couldn't care less."

"Are there cities and villages here?"

"No. Not as such. Demons don't gather with one another. We only know each other in passing."

"Then how did you meet Erasmus?"

She stopped again and hung her head. "Are we really doing this?"

"I just thought…maybe you'd like to get it off your chest."

She stood still so long that I slid up next to her and got a good look at her for once. Maybe I hadn't paid attention before because I disliked her so much, but she really was quite striking. Her luxurious hair was long, several inches past her shoulders and moved in gentle waves. It was dark except for a flourish of green down one side. Her eyes were a vivid green, much like the jewels in the eyes of her amulet. She had make-up on her lids, too, to make them more catlike and her lips were blood red. But close as we were, I noticed the tiniest of flaws on her skin and a freckle here and there. It was as if her makers didn't want her too perfect, too unreal.

Her black leather catsuit clung to her like a second skin. She didn't seem to have any flaws along those long legs, even as she hiked right along with me in inappropriately high heels. She certainly had a look going, and it seemed to suit her whole mischief-making vibe. It made me wonder about her story all the more. But I doubted she would ever tell me details.

She returned the scrutiny. "You're a strange human."

"Not really. I think most of us are nice people."

"You'd give him up to save him. Netherworld denizens would never do that. They'd never offer it. They'd never think of it." She stretched out her hand to show the vistas before us. "We are a land of narcissists. We only care about ourselves."

"Erasmus doesn't."

"Well, he's different. He might have lived a long time, but he isn't acclimatized as the rest of us are."

"I'm not sure I believe that of you, either."

"Oh, she's trying to flatter me now. You forget, I'm in it for my prize. You offered me something of my choosing. I'm still in it for myself."

"Whatever you say."

She scowled and continued on.

The colors of the sky were changing, now a sickly green at the horizon and black above. "Will it get dark?"

She didn't bother glancing at me. "No. It's like this all the time. Except that the color changes. I quite like this green."

I flicked my gaze at her long green lock of hair. "So when did you meet Erasmus?"

"I really want to stab you with something," she hissed.

"All right, already! Jeez."

We walked along. There were mountains of a sort in the distance. They formed a jagged skyline and looked thoroughly unpleasant and treacherous to traverse. Of course we were heading there.

"I met him sometime in Mesopotamia around 500 BC." Her voice was wistful, and she'd lost her snarky tone. "We were both fairly new then. I was just getting to know things, understanding where I was in the worlds. Erasmus already had his purpose. He followed your ancestor around before making himself known to her. First thing I did was tease him about it." She laughed softly. "He growled at me. He hates it when you make fun of him. He has so little sense of humor."

"I don't know. He seems to have a wry sense."

"Yes. I suppose he does. He helped her as much as necessary and then…well. You know."

"Yeah." I touched my neck, missing the familiar weight of the amulet. I stuffed my hand in my pocket. It was still there, still cold.

"And then he was gone. And it wasn't until a few hundred years later that I ran into him again. I just thought he was intriguing. So set on his mission. He enjoyed hunting the creatures with her, though each Chosen Host was afraid of him. They had every right to be." She looked at me then. "Until you came along. Were you ever afraid of him?"

I thought back four weeks ago when it had all started. "No. I don't think so."

"Maybe that was it. You were fearless in your own mission. That must have appealed to him. Whatever I did, whatever I tried never seemed to interest him enough." She laughed. "I suppose you thought we'd been lovers."

"I assumed."

"You were wrong. He treated me like a nuisance. And that intrigued me all the more. He never once looked at me like—" She cut herself off and scouted around to hide her face. I gave her room to do it. She swallowed. "If he had only looked at me as he looked at you…I might have lost interest. Instead, his continual brushings off only made me want him more. And so I hatched a plan to get the book. It was a stupid plan. But I had nothing else."

I said nothing. If I told her I was sorry one more time, I think she would have thrown a curse at me.

"And now here we are," she said softly. "The lover and the spurned one. It's all so ridiculous."

"I think it's very noble of you."

"Oh, do shut up."

I did. We continued getting infinitesimally closer to that mountain range. How long till we reached it, I wondered. I took another swig from the canteen. What was I going to do when we caught up to him? I guess since he was human now, he couldn't put up a fight when we got him out of here. That gave me courage. But then we still had the problem of Satan and the Booke. *No, Kylie, we don't. You know what you have to do.* Yeah, I did know. I'd get Shabiri to get him out of here and I'd…stay.

What would Satan be like? Would he do what I asked after I offered my soul? Could I trust him? I had to hope that I could. I hoped…that it would be fast.

I sighed and looked at the scenery before me. This landscape could never be considered beautiful. I had been to plenty of deserts in California and the southwest. Those were stunning in their stark beauty, their vast spaces and rocks and canyons carved by ancient waterways and wind. But there was nothing to recommend this. Every tree and shrub was blackened by some disaster. Or at least they looked that way but probably just grew like that. Twisted in agonizing silhouettes with short and stumpy shrubs near the ground. Even the grass—what clumps of it there were—were black and droopy. It was like the dark place the Booke had shown me. It had been trying to warn me.

I looked behind and there it was, floating along. I could feel it trying to pull me back, trying to get me to escape this place. It might only take a thought from me to do it, so I looked away, trying not to think of it at all.

Something caught the corner of my eye and I turned to look. I thought I had seen something moving. I shrugged. Just my imagination. These weird twisted trees sure gave you the notion you were seeing figures, like saguaro cactuses with their human-like arms.

But now there was something on the left, and when I turned, nothing.

"Shabiri," I whispered.

"I see them," she said out of the corner of her mouth. "They've been tracking us for some time."

"Why didn't you say anything?"

"They weren't as close before. There are about ten of them. Maybe more."

"What are they?"

"Imps. Small demons. More primitive than my kind."

"Are they…dangerous?"

"Of course."

"What can we do?"

"Let me handle it."

I adjusted my grip on the spear. I wished I had the crossbow too and all those handy charms and incantations the Wiccans had worked on to protect me. I didn't have any of that. So much for all our preparations.

"Why can't you just transport us out of here?"

"It's a handy trick. But it only works on your world. As do many other handy tricks."

"Erasmus can heal others there. Well, he could when he was a…" I hated the idea of him being as helpless as I was. I hoped he was okay. I hoped that he stayed a demon as long as he could to get through all this.

"A healing demon," she scoffed. "Must be because of all that sticky sweet love."

This time I was *sure* I saw something move. When I turned, it wasn't hiding anymore. It looked like a solid black figure no more than three feet high. It was almost a cartoon version of a demon you'd see in those old Walt Disney animations. Horns and pointy tail and all. And it wasn't alone.

They seemed flat and two-dimensional as they moved over the rocks like a shadow, probably an illusion because of their color. They were like little black holes, because no sickly green light slide over their surfaces. They were just…dark. Absences of light. Except for cat-like eyes that shone, blinking at us like animals stalking us would.

"Can they reason?" I asked.

"No. They are very basic creatures. They probably smelled your blood. They are the vultures of the Netherworld, cleaning up the carcasses of others."

"I have no intention of being a carcass."

"I don't know that it's really up to you at this point," she said between clenched teeth.

I could tell she was coiling to spring. Because the creatures were coming out of their hiding places and slithering over the rocks with their eyes fixed on us. Well, on *me*.

"What do we do?" I tightened my grip on the spear and lowered it to jabbing position.

"For one…I'd run."

"We should run?"

"No. *You* should run."

Chapter Seventeen

I TOOK OFF over the rocky plain and zig-zagged between the fangy outcroppings.

When I looked back, there was suddenly a swarm of those little black creatures. They completely skirted around Shabiri. Definitely after me. I thought about different strategies since I knew I would tire soon. I looked back again and saw them defying gravity, crawling upside down up a rocky fang and over the other side like ants.

That eliminated a few ideas.

I scrambled up into a canyon, the loose rocks under my feet making it all the harder. It was too late when I realized I was boxed in. "Shit," I muttered. I got to the wall and looked up. Even if I could scale that, those little devils were far more agile than I was. I turned to face them. They were coming toward me fast from the floor of the canyon and up the sides.

When they got close enough, I could see rows of little razor-sharp teeth. Great. Their spindly little arms reached for me with little talons for fingers.

And then my Chosen Host skills kicked in. It all happened in an instant. I steadied the spear on the ground and swung around it like a stripper pole, kicking out with my boots at their greedy little faces. Imps flung outward, tumbling in the air. It was entirely satisfying when boot met imp, like kicking a football. I ran along the cliff face and swung around again, kicking some more.

But then the footballs were coming quicker and in greater numbers. There was way more than ten of them. It was a swarm. I couldn't swing on the spear forever. And sure enough, something grabbed my hair. I was yanked backward, hitting my head against the stone wall.

They were on me. I tried to scream, but too many little mouths were biting, too many talons scratching and tearing at my clothes. I kicked out wildly with my hands and feet, shaking my head to loosen them but it didn't help. I was sinking into complete panic, all traces of civilization slipping away. I screamed. I flailed. There was nothing left to do but die.

Then, a fireball!

The creatures all stopped and looked. Tiny, dreadful hands were still on me, still yanking my hair taut, but they had all frozen to stare at the fireball coming at them. Some were engulfed in flames and screaming in high-pitched whines, while others burst into puffs of black smoke.

They dropped me and started running. Up the cliff face, under rocks. But it didn't save them. Wherever they were, they burst into flames and disappeared in puffs of smoke.

Soon I was alone, sprawled on the ground, my clothes in shreds, my hair all over my face and in tufts on the ground around me from where they had yanked it out. A figure walked forward through the hazy smoke. When it dissipated, she was standing there.

I cried from relief. "Thank you, Shabiri!"

She didn't offer to help me up. Just stood there in a superhero pose…or was it super villain with her in her black catsuit?

I got up shakily, brushed myself off. My jeans were now very stylish with their rips but my shirt could have looked better. It barely covered me.

She waved her hand and the shirt and jeans stitched them-selves back together. I watched in amazement as each tear repaired itself.

I smoothed out my hair as best I could and caught my breath. I was so happy to see her I almost hugged her but decided that would probably be a bad idea. "I don't suppose you could conjure a bazooka," I said unsteadily.

"Mortal weaponry? That's very crude, isn't it?"

"Not from where I'm standing."

"You have to fight magical creatures with magical means. A bazooka might be fun but it would hardly do the job."

"That's too bad."

She looked around. "Well, everyone knows you're here by now. The next several miles should be a lot of fun."

"I take it we have to climb these mountains."

"Ten points to the annoying human."

I followed her out of the canyon, checking to make sure I still had Erasmus' amulet. It was important to me and I just wanted to have it, to hold onto something of him. *Please still be alive*, I chanted in my head. I wiped impatiently at tears I didn't have time for.

"For the first time, I feel a little useless," I said as we set out again. "I was always the one doing the fighting and killing."

"Interesting. Not Erasmus?"

"No. He was always a little…standoffish. But he did get in the way of the kelpie now that I think about it."

"Well, this book business is up to you, after all."

"Yeah. And I guess I get to finish it."

She started slow-clapping. "Oh, very good seventies telly dia-log. Bra-*va*."

"Can you *be* more of an ass?"

She smiled. "I'm sure I can try."

I watched her walk away and contemplated what she'd just done. Not only had she saved my life—again—but she got me out of my funk by making me mad. She was so not fooling me anymore.

"Shabiri, why did you ask me to save Doug?"

"Simple self-preservation, darling. He had my amulet."

"Oh? And what would have happened to it if he'd died?"

She fell silent and simply hiked on.

Yup. Not fooling me.

* * *

WE HIKED FOR hours, steadily moving up the mountain. I leaned against a black tree and then was sorry I had when it left a tarry residue on my hand. "Shabiri! Look, I have to rest." I wiped the black gunk on my pants.

"You want to rest *now*? We have miles to go."

"I know." I sat on the ground and took a deep breath. "But I'm only human."

"But Erasmus—"

"Is only human now too. He'll also need to rest." I took out the amulet and held it in my hand, gazing at it. It sure was ugly. And I loved it.

She stood at the edge of the road, fidgeting. Maybe she thought "resting" meant mere seconds. When she realized it didn't, she plopped herself down and hugged her knees. "Being human has got to be the absolute worst."

I ignored her. I knew her game now. She was more like Erasmus than she wanted to admit. She didn't come to my world because she wanted to get away from the Netherworld. She *liked* my world, she liked the culture, and she liked humans. Maybe she even liked Ed but wouldn't let herself get involved. After all, she was in love with Erasmus. And, clueless as any guy, he'd never noticed.

I glanced over at her. She was combing bits of stuff out of her hair. It might have been pieces of imp.

"I wonder what the coven is up to back in Moody Bog."

"What a funny little town that is."

"Would you go back?"

"Why in the twelve worlds would I?"

"Because you like it there. You like Ed."

"I do not."

"I think you do."

"Oh really?" She got that spoiled look on her face that I was beginning to think was just an act. "Don't start projecting your sentimental crap onto me. That's not who I am."

"I'm just saying, Ed is a pretty nice guy." For some reason, I looked over my shoulder to make sure no one else was listening, even though that was an impossibility. "And he's real good in the sack."

She stared at me a long moment before she rocked back with laughter. She laughed and laughed, the sound rolling up and down the canyon. "Kylie Strange, could it be that I *might* be starting to like you?"

I smiled. I hadn't thought I was capable with all that was happening, but I was. We were comrades in arms and all that. "I think you do already. Even as you hate me for…you know."

"Yes, I do hate you. Erasmus should never have fallen in love with the likes of you. But…well." She flicked her hand. "*C'est la vie.*"

"You should have let him get to know you. You should…you should let him when this is over. He'll need you."

Her smile faded. "And you are still set on offering yourself to…*Him*?" Quick as lightning she crouched over me, grabbed my wrist, and shoved back the sleeve. "Except for this."

The tattoo. I'd forgotten about it. Erasmus didn't think it would really work. But would it?

"Oh shit. Can I burn this off?"

She let my wrist go and sat down in front of me. "Just how insane are you? You were going to walk in here and offer your soul when you had that on your wrist?" She shook her head. "I admire your chutzpah."

"Do you think it will work? Should I get rid of it?"

"Not until you're standing in front of…Him. Then he'll know you're serious."

"I am."

She rested her chin on her hand and gazed at me from under her lashes. "If you succeed and are dead, Erasmus will be stuck as a human."

"Yeah. He'll need lots of help. He'll…have to eat real food. He's probably wondering right now why his stomach hurts. I know *you* don't eat…"

"Yes, I do. I told you not all demons are of the soul-eating variety."

"Oh. Well, if he's stuck as a human then you can show him. I'll let him know you helped me."

"That will endear him."

"I mean…that you didn't try to sabotage me. That maybe you didn't know what I was going to do."

"He can tell when a demon lies, you know."

"Not as a human, he can't."

Her brows rose. No, she hadn't thought of that. Now there was a real chance in her mind. She'd help me, all right. *Step this way into Satan's mouth, young lady.*

When we looked at one another, we suddenly knew each other very well.

CHAPTER EIGHTEEN

ERASMUS AWOKE AND opened his eyes. Everything—his sight, his mind—was hazy, and for a moment, he couldn't quite remember anything. When he sat up and looked around him, it all flooded back.

The red sky, the smoky flavors in the air, the jagged mountains in the distance. He was in the Netherworld. He had traveled as far as he dared as a demon, past the lava fields and lakes of fire, over the mountain, and down into the desolate valleys, and once he had nearly come to the place where the Powers That Be would usually call him, before they could reach out with their minds and find him, he finally broke the wax seal and muttered the incantation. It had blown him on his arse and knocked him out.

His head hurt. He rubbed at it and then looked down at himself.

Nothing seemed to have changed. His clothes were the same. His hands were the same. But he certainly felt...different. Had it worked? Out of curiosity, he opened his shirt. He swallowed hard; the tattoo that had characterized who he was for all the eons of his life was...gone.

He slowly rose, standing unsteadily. He had encountered no

one, which was a blessing. Of course, as a demon, no one would have noticed him. But as a human, his time would be short.

He had tried to get himself as deep into the Netherworld as he could without the Powers That Be interfering, and he seemed to have done it. Now to make it the rest of the way.

He had been in such a hurry to leave Moody Bog before Kylie could discover what he was doing that he had failed to bring a weapon, forgetting he'd need one as a human. Of course, he'd had no idea what being a human would be like.

He rubbed at his naked chest. It was…strange. Or course, the word "strange" called to mind Kylie herself, and something else surged in him. A deep-seated longing rushed to the surface. That longing had already been there but now it seemed so overwhelming, so big inside him that it was tearing his heart apart.

He bent over from the pain of it. What was wrong? Is this how love was for humans? How horrible! He straightened, trying to get his emotions under control. For a moment he thought his love for her would weaken him and spoil all his plans, but the opposite appeared to be true. It gave him new strength, new purpose.

He narrowed his eyes at the road ahead. He didn't need to hide from the narrow passages on the right where his masters were. They wouldn't be able to find him as a human. He'd take the road to the left, the one he would have done anything to avoid before. He was heading toward Satan. He hoped the spell had given him a soul. He tried to discern if he could feel it or not. Was it that sense deep inside him that made him push on? Was it among the feelings of love he felt for Kylie? The love was so strong it overwhelmed everything else. But he didn't mind it. It was the same feeling he'd had as a demon, he was sure of it.

He could picture her in his mind, her dark hair framing her beautiful face, that smile, the wicked look she'd shoot him, her courage in the face of danger. He was proud of her for all she had done, how she had used her skills and intellect to survive.

"What a human," he said, amazed again at her feats of prowess.

But despite pleasant thoughts of her, there was an undercurrent running through his emotions that made his mouth dry and his hands shake. Stark terror. Was that the demon or the human? Death was never something he considered before. Not his, anyway. He feared the Powers. They'd threatened him often enough, but he never felt strictly in danger from them. They enjoyed his mission certainly more than he did.

This was no longer an intellectual exercise. He was now a human with a soul, and he could do this for her. The notion calmed him. This would save her, after all. Maybe her constable would console her. Maybe…when he was gone, she'd fall in love with him some day. He didn't like it, but he knew it must be. She'd be safe, and he would simply remain a tender memory.

He began to wonder what it would be like, losing this brand-new soul. If it was anything like he saw in the faces of the Chosen Hosts whose souls *he* had eaten, it would be painful. They screamed when their souls were ripped from them. Every last one of them had. But that pain and terror would only last for a moment. And then…oblivion. It would be just as if the Chosen Host had died and the book had closed, as it had done thousands of times before. Only this time he'd never awaken again. That didn't sound too bad.

He watched the dragon raptors in the distance, circling the black peaks. They obviously didn't smell him, but others might. He hurried.

As he descended into the valley he had never been to before, he cast a glance back to the Netherworld he knew so little about. After all, he seldom spent time here. Only when he was awakened when a new Chosen Host emerged and opened the book would he then be called by the Powers That Be. Still, it was familiar. Perhaps not as familiar as Kylie's world.

He let himself think of her again. Why not? He had little else to do as he walked, and he'd much rather think of her than of the fate that awaited. Of her silky limbs that wrapped about him, her willing mouth. No human had ever been as expressive in their delight with him, even those who hadn't known he was a demon. But *she* knew! From the very first moment, yet she had never held back. She was not afraid.

It had all seemed too brief a moment to experience, to be in love for the first time. He had scorned others for it. Now it was he who would be scorned. And falling for a human at that.

Look where it had brought him.

There was a flickering in the distance ahead. He knew it was fire. Satan must be close. He practiced in his mind what he was going to say. That he came as a former demon of the Booke of the Hidden and wished for it to be destroyed for all time. And in order to properly seal the bargain, he'd offer his new soul. That, at the very least, should intrigue Him. He did not think the offer would be turned down. An enticing proposal such as this was bound to capture Lord Satan's imagination. Erasmus hoped that would be the case. A human in the Netherworld would be intriguing enough on its own. He was certain the bargain would be sealed. He only hoped it would be done quickly.

"Erasmus?"

He jerked to a halt. How had anyone crept upon him without his knowing? *Beelze's tail!* He was human now. He had no senses to speak of.

When he turned, he looked into the reptilian eyes of an old acquaintance whose feathered wings swayed with a stinking breeze. "Focalor."

"It *is* Erasmus, is it not? You smell wrong. You smell…like a human."

"Alas, I have been turned into one."

"Oh, my dear friend! What horror has befallen you? Who has done this to you? I will help you to eviscerate him."

Focalor looked mostly like a man except for the scaly ridge over his eyes that stretched over his bald head to his ears. His nose was large, almost like a beak. He greatly resembled a griffin, especially with his wings arching high over his body. He was naked except for a long breechclout that hung almost to his taloned feet.

"The fault is mine alone. I fell in love with a human and I enchanted myself. I needed a soul with which to bargain...with Lord Satan."

Focalor threw a clawed hand over his mouth. And then he eyed Erasmus suspiciously. "You're joking."

"I'm not. You smell me for yourself."

"Yes, I do." He slowly shook his head. "I must say, old friend, it's a war of the senses. I am glad to see you, yet I would just as happily eat you."

"Please don't. I have a mission."

"But wait. You're going to sacrifice yourself...for a *human*? Why would you be so insane?"

He shrugged. "I am besotted."

"You poor devil. That's why I spend as little time on that world as possible. There are far better worlds to escape into than that one. See what mischief can befall you?"

"I had no choice, as you well know."

"Ah. The book."

"Yes."

"Then you must tell me, for I am curious. Who is this human creature that has stolen your heritage from you?"

He glanced back toward the road. He still had a long way to go, but his throat was getting parched and dry, and he wasn't sure what that meant. "She...she was the Chosen Host."

Focalor laughed. Erasmus expected it but it still angered him. "The Chosen Host! The Chosen Host of the Booke of the Hidden?"

"There is no other," he grumbled.

He slapped Erasmus on the back. The powerful thwack sent him forward. He only just barely stopped himself from planting his face on the stony ground.

"Oh. Sorry," said Focalor. "You're frail and weak now, aren't you?"

Erasmus straightened and brushed at his dusty jacket. "Not that frail," he said cautiously. Even to an old friend, he dare not look weak or he could easily be devoured.

"And yet you fell for the Chosen Host. My, my. So I take it you have not yet eaten her soul."

"I promised I wouldn't."

Focalor clapped and laughed again. "But this is too good. Even with the evidence of my eyes and nose, I can't believe you would have subjected yourself to this."

"You don't know her. She's…courageous. Stubborn."

The demon nodded sagely. Such traits were rare in the Netherworld and highly prized. Erasmus knew it would strike the right tone. But would it be enough? If he could convince Focalor to go with him and not eat him, he would be better off for the protection. But he realized he didn't know the demon all *that* well. It was anyone's guess as to what he might choose to do.

Focalor blew out a breath and ran a hand up over his bald scalp. "I tell you, Erasmus. Eating a human is a rare treat. As I said, I don't like going to that world." His eyes roved hungrily over Erasmus.

"I must do this thing, Focalor. It shall be my last act…of bravery."

Focalor blinked his yellow eyes, their vertical slits widening and narrowing. His nictitating membrane clicked a few times in succession, though each eye was not quite in sync with the other. "That is an interesting prospect. I've never actually seen bravery for myself. I've heard stories, mind. But never saw with my own eyes. That could be exciting."

"I could use your help. I need your protection, at any rate. I have nothing to give you in return except for the story you can tell. But I imagine it will be a fascinating one."

"Oh, it will." The demon considered. "You make a very interesting argument, Erasmus. You've always been most intriguing to me for what you were able to accomplish with so little time." He rubbed his chin, staring at the ground. Abruptly he jerked his head up then down. "Yes. I will go with you! I want to see this. I want to hear what Lord Satan has to say." He rubbed his hands together. "It will be a marvelous tale to tell."

"Thank you." His emotions seemed overwrought. He felt his eyes sting. It must be this human body. All its emotions were so close to the surface. How did creatures live like this?

* * *

ERASMUS WATCHED FOCALOR warily. Though they walked side by side and the demon had agreed to accompany and protect him, it wasn't an agreement etched in stone. Focalor might yet turn on him. He hoped he wouldn't. There would be no way to defend himself. And though he had arrogantly announced that he was no weakling, he *did* feel weak, weaker than he had ever felt in his life. This human body was too hot, too thirsty, he reasoned, too…vulnerable.

"I fear…I need to rest," he said after a long bout of wrestling with himself.

"Really?" Focalor shrugged. "If you must, I suppose here is as good as anywhere."

Erasmus plopped to the ground, spine bent, wrists resting loosely on his knees.

The demon sat gracefully opposite him. Erasmus felt his scrutiny before he looked up and locked gazes with him. "Is it strange being human? What's it like?"

"Miserable. There are aches and pains I never knew could be. My feet hurt. Why is that? Feet are designed to walk on. Why should they hurt when one walks?" He rubbed his belly. "And there is a hollowness, just here."

"You're hungry."

"I have been hungry for centuries."

"Not for souls, my friend. For food."

"Ugh! I tried eating food once."

"What by the twelve worlds for?"

"Because…" He'd tried it so that he wouldn't have to eat Kylie's soul. It had been extremely sentimental and monumentally stupid. He scowled. "Curiosity," he growled.

"I like eating," mused Focalor. "There are so many interesting things and people to eat."

"I suppose it doesn't matter. I'll soon be dead."

"I wonder what that's like."

"In another day, I would have been happy to show you."

A smile grew on Focalor's face and he ticked a finger. "Now, now. I'm doing you the courtesy of not eating *you*."

"And I am grateful for it."

Focalor settled on the ground and leaned in. "What's it like being in love?"

"Terrible. Wonderful. Worst and best thing to ever have happened to me."

"Hmm." He sat back on his hands, pondering. "You are selling your soul, one you enchanted for yourself. Love must be something spectacular."

"It is. What I wouldn't give to see her, touch her just one more time."

"Good gods, Erasmus. I would never have thought it of you. You always seemed so stoic, so above the mundane, so sensible. And yet here you are."

"Here I am," he said miserably.

"Well, if this is what it brings you to I'm glad I'll have none of it. Let me devastate a village or two, devour my prey, and bring terror to lesser demons around me, I say. That fulfills me just fine."

"Sometimes I wish I'd never met her. But then I hate that sentiment. For I am more than glad at the…the joy I have experienced."

Focalor leaned in again. "Joy? Hmm. I have found great satisfaction swooping over a village, watching it burn, the inhabitants running for their lives. But *joy*? I've never imagined it."

"This will be worth it. To know that she is safe, that she will live on. I…I am satisfied."

"I'm just shocked. But I do like learning new things. Thank you for that, Erasmus."

"Don't mention it."

"I think I will avoid falling in love just the same."

"That is probably a wise choice."

They sat for some time. Erasmus would have liked to rest longer, but he knew he must move on. He rose and took a deep breath, surprised at the gratification filling his lungs gave him. Maybe that's what being human was about, enjoying simple pleasures.

Otherwise it seemed thoroughly unpleasant.

They moved slowly along the trail. It led downward to stark terrain. What lay ahead looked like a slash in the mountainside, the open maw of a cavern. But light flickered from within. They were close now. They'd only have to descend a few feet to reach the wide portal. And it would have been just that easy to simply walk through…if it hadn't been for the harpies perched above, glaring at Erasmus with a hungry look in their narrowed eyes.

CHAPTER NINETEEN

I FELL ASLEEP. I couldn't believe I fell asleep. Shabiri kicked me awake. "Oh my God, how long was I out?" I scrambled to my feet.

"Only a few minutes. I knew if I didn't let you, you'd be no good to me. You were exhausted."

"We have to go."

"No kidding."

I wiped my eyes, threw my filthy hair off my face, and set out after her. It must have been my Chosen Host strength, because otherwise I doubt I would have been able to take another step. We'd already come a long way and there was still a long way to go. Sometimes it was steep, and sometimes it was just a long switchback of a trail, zig-zagging up the incline. We scrambled over scree, losing our footing a few times. I helped Shabiri but more often than not, and she offered me a hand. It was truly the strangest journey I'd ever been on, and that was saying something these days.

I stopped near the top of the mountain and looked back. We'd climbed several thousand feet. The valley below stretched as far as the eye could see. The sky was a sickly yellow now with black edges like paint splashed on a canvas by a lazy artist. I could see smoldering volcanoes in the far distance with a haze of smoke lingering just above their peaks. It reminded me of Erasmus' smoky shoulders whenever he was agitated...or turned on.

Another volcano just at the horizon was erupting, spewing glowing bits of rock and lava high into the air. The smoke churning from its funnel was black with lightning spearing out of it. Dante didn't know the half of it.

What was especially strange was the lack of people. Or demons like Shabiri, I supposed. It truly was desolation. The two kinds of creatures I had seen so far were without reason, just like animals. And though they were fearsome, I feared still more any intelligent beings that might be watching us. And I knew—with the Booke's knowledge tickling at my brain—that they were.

"How far now, Shabiri?"

"Down this mountain we'll come to a land bridge. In one direction is the lair of the Powers That Be. In the other lies... Him."

"Is it...is it far? How many days?"

"Days? There are no days here. One hour leads on to another. Time is very different in the Netherworld."

"What are you saying? Do you mean that an hour here is not an hour back home?"

"I'm saying Time has no meaning. Days might have passed in your world."

"What? No! It might be Halloween already? What is the Booke doing back there?"

"You're right to worry. Just because it's floating beside you doesn't mean it isn't releasing nasty beasties back home. Just consider it not your problem."

"But it *is* my problem!"

"My dear, there's not a thing you can do about it now."

I looked back once more. She was right. I was as far from home as I could possibly be. I had to believe that Doc and Seraphina and Nick and Jolene...and even Doug's gang were taking care of things. Jeff would see to my shop and all would have to carry on without me. For good.

I took a deep breath. "Let's go."

* * *

GETTING DOWN THE other side of the mountain was somehow not any easier than getting up it. The constant pressure on my knees as I walked in a crouching gait seemed to hurt my legs even more. And it was more dangerous trying not to slip downward facing that way.

The landscape hadn't changed. Except for a grayish river moving sluggishly below, snaking between the hills. I couldn't smell it, but it sure looked like it was made of something unpleasant. "Why is everything so awful here?"

"One man's awful is another man's... You're right, it is awful here. I have no idea why this world was created as it was. Perhaps it was beautiful once, and *He* decided to destroy it all in a fit of anger."

She didn't like saying his name. I guessed I didn't blame her. "He has that much control here?"

"No one really knows. We just assume. It could just as well have been the Ancient Ones."

"Do you consider it strange...or just normal?"

"I guess I never really thought much about it."

"You are a pretty strange creature yourself. You're just as intelligent as—" The look she gave me dared me to finish that sentence. "You're intelligent," I said, switching tracks, "so why would you put up with this? Maybe there are others who want a change."

She laughed. "Are you trying to form an insurrection of the Netherworld? Oh, *He's* going to love you."

"I wasn't. I just think if you don't like something, then people should band together to make a change. Or demons should. Whatever."

"What a unique view you have of life. Civilizations don't always work that way. They come and go. The Babylonians disappeared, absorbed by the other tribes and civilizations around them. Same with the Hittites and Jebusites. Change happens all the time."

"You're citing history and cultures on *my* world. What about *your* world?"

She didn't say anything. If all demons were narcissists like she said, then it was easier to flee than to stand up for something and maybe get cut down. It could have been that there *had been* an insurrection…and this place was the result. Looking around at the desolation, perhaps I didn't blame her or the others who lived here.

We came to a flat spot. I took the canteen from off my shoulder and tipped it up to my lips. But there was only a trickle left. I was about to lower it when a shower of water poured from the canteen, soaking me. I stoppered it, wiped my face, and glanced sidelong at Shabiri. "You think that's funny?"

"I do, actually." She was smiling and so was I, until her grin suddenly vanished. She froze. I was about to ask, but she shushed me with a flicking hand gesture.

And then I heard it too. A low growl from…somewhere. The echoes made it impossible to know from where it came.

We both searched, walking in a circle. "If that's what I think it is," she whispered, "we are in big trouble."

"What do you think it is?"

She merely stared at me, looking suddenly pale. Okay, now I didn't want to know.

"What should we do?"

"I don't know if there's anything we *can* do." She sniffed the wind like Erasmus used to do and grabbed my arm. "Let's keep going. Do you see that land bridge down there? We're heading to the left."

I knew she told me this in case she couldn't go with me. In case she was…

I was too scared to speak, so I just hurried down the trail.

I kept hearing the low growls. If it was something Shabiri wasn't prepared to deal with, then what chance did we have? I had the spear—and I clutched it tight—but would it do any good against…whatever was stalking us?

We hurried down the incline between shiny obsidian rock walls. When we were almost to that black marble land bridge, I saw a shadow cast against the glassy rock face. I turned and wished I hadn't.

It made no sense. "It has three heads," was the stupid nonsense that came out of my mouth.

"Very good, meat girl. Gold star for being able to count to three."

It was a very large black dog and it had three heads. Something tickled the back of my memory. Something from ancient mythology about a guardian of the underworld.

"Cerberus," I muttered.

Chapter Twenty

JEFF COULD FEEL, with his wolf senses, that the coven was as anxious and tense as could be. But of course, you didn't need wolf senses to know that.

Kylie had gone to the Netherworld with Shabiri two days ago, and he had used all the control he had not to shed his clothes, shift, and go bounding after her. Because this was it. Erasmus had gone to sacrifice himself for her and she was going to do the same thing for him. She was going to die and he didn't know if he was prepared for that, even after all the danger they'd all been through.

And now it was Halloween, D-day for the book to let all its beasties loose. As the sun got lower, Jeff alternated pacing and staring out the window. There was no trick-or-treating for Moody Bog kids this year. With all that had been going on, no kid wanted to go out at night, let alone masquerade as the very beasts that might just jump out of the darkness to devour them.

Porches stayed dark. Pumpkins remained un-carved. Some people had even taken down what Halloween decorations they'd had from their lawns. Ghosts were removed and witches were banned from windows. Moody Bog felt like it was on lockdown. The only beasties prowling the streets this night would be the real thing.

The Wiccans had been strategizing at Kylie's shop for hours. Even Doug and Bob were offering ideas. Immediately after Kylie had left, it was decided that no one should go after her. Jeff had strenuously argued against that idea. He'd almost left in a huff, thinking of going alone, but when he thought it through—yeah, something he wasn't used to doing—he realized the futility of it. She loved Erasmus. And he loved her. And only two people that connected would be willing to die for the other. It made him sick to his stomach, not just her sacrifice…but that he finally realized he had never been in love with her. Not like that.

He sat alone in a corner, growing his nails into claws and retracting them again. He cast a glance at Ed, who was looking completely miserable. First Kylie and then Shabiri. That guy sure knew how to pick them.

Finally, Jeff couldn't stand it anymore. He jumped to his feet. "Look, Doc." Everyone stopped talking and turned toward him. "It comes down to the basics. Can we use that crossbow?"

Doc, who had aged plenty in the last few days, pondered it. "I should think we could use it, wound the creatures. But without Kylie's abilities, we have no hope of defeating them completely."

"But we might slow them down," said Doug. "Bob," he said, turning to his fellow Ordo member, "do you want to see if you can find my flamethrower? It's in the shed at my place. And I think it's untouched."

"If I can borrow a car," he said, rising.

"I'll take you," said Nick, surprising Jeff for only a moment. He could tell that Nick was letting the wolf take over. The wolf had no fear. Jeff had been letting it do the thinking for him, too.

They left and Jeff paced again. "We're not on a rescue mission anymore," said Jeff. "I get it. We have to stop talking about spells and enchantments that won't do any good. We have to concentrate our efforts on *this* world. Because…" He took a breath. "Kylie and Erasmus…they aren't coming back."

"No!" said Jolene, jumping to her feet. "They are! Kylie will find a way."

"Look, kid, I wanted to have hope as much as you, but the reality is, she isn't coming back. She knew it all along. She told me as much days ago. Now it's up to us. I think we have to call our auxiliary coven back here to get our defenses up. It's Halloween and you know what that means. Just because the book isn't physically here anymore doesn't mean all hell won't break loose."

Very slowly, Doc stood. "Jeff is right. We must accept the sorry fact of it." He put a comforting arm around Jolene's shoulders and gave her a squeeze before he released her. "And I've been thinking too. We've been ignoring something very important. Remember what Kylie's grandpa said? He said we must 'close the door.' And he said the same thing in his writings. We've been thinking of the book all this time, and even if Kylie or Erasmus do end up destroying the book—and it will close in any case…" They all knew what he meant. "We've still got that rift on our hands."

"That's right," said Seraphina, tapping her purple lips. "The least we can do is close that rift. Who knows what might come through if Baphomet finds it."

Jolene was still standing in the middle of the room with old tear streaks on her face. She was really just a kid. Jeff thought it was horrible bringing her into these life or death decisions, but she was probably the smartest one there next to Doc, and they needed her.

"Jolene," he said as kindly as he could. He knew Human Jeff still had enough charisma to break through her defenses. It seemed to be working; she was looking at him with a little less confusion. "We need to start researching how to close the rift. That's our next important task."

Slowly, she nodded. "Okay. You're right." With new purpose, she sat and clutched her tablet like her life depended on it, then dove in.

Doc gave Jeff a grateful look. "I believe I have some books on the subject. I'll have to go back home for them."

"I'll take you," said Ed. God knew how long Ed had stayed awake. He looked exhausted, but there was no telling him to rest. He'd rest when he could.

That left only Seraphina, Doug, and Charise.

"We've got two things to do," said Jeff. He couldn't believe he was actually taking charge. It wasn't his thing. Not by a long shot. But desperate times, he guessed. "We've got to prepare for the next Baphomet attack. I don't think those colorful flutters are going to scare him away again. *And* we've got to be ready for the next things that come out of the book."

"I've been thinking about that," said Doug. "When Bob brings back my flamethrower, I think we can add a few new enchantments to it. Fire is a pure element so it's useful on these creatures. But enchanted fire is even better."

Charise tentatively raised her hand. They all looked at her. She had been pretty mouse-like since the Ordo had surrendered to the coven. "I had an idea. Jolene helped me research it," she said as meekly as Jeff had ever heard her. "Since we can't kill them without Kylie, maybe we can temporarily contain them with magic? You know, like a salt circle?"

Doug looked at her askance. "*You* thought of that?"

"Yeah. I mean, we should be able to. In something as simple as a ceramic jar. There are plenty of those here in the shop."

"Darlin', you're a genius!" Doug grabbed her and kissed her, but she shied away from it. She'd been trying to get his attention all this time, but she had finally discovered Bob. It had been a weird few days, Jeff decided.

"Let's do it!" said Doug. "What do we need, Charise?"

She glanced toward the buffet where Kylie used a lot of decorative glass jars, but she also had shelves filled with ginger jars. "We'll have to empty those."

"No problem," said Jeff and walked over behind the counter. Kylie had stepped it up from Jeff's shop and arranged the place just so, catering to a more upper-class clientele. Jeff's place was at the beach, only a few blocks up from the strand. He targeted a more down-to-earth customer. It was more head shop than tea, but it worked.

With a silent apology to Kylie, he grabbed the first jar, took off the lid, and dumped the contents into a large wooden bowl on the buffet. He set that jar aside and grabbed the next one.

Charise picked it up and looked inside. "We've got to put salt in these. Just enough to cover the bottom."

Doug was on it. Jeff had really hated those guys, but in the last few days they'd all become one happy coven. Comrades in arms. It, too, had been weird.

"And then," Charise went on, "Jolene printed out this incantation. We say it when we've got a creature cornered or wounded or whatever, and then we bring an open jar. Once it disappears, we snap on the lid. She said duct tape would be good to keep it closed so we don't accidentally knock it over." She looked to Jolene to confirm, but the teen was already immersed in research.

"I'm sure there's some duct tape in the kitchen," said Jeff, dumping more expensive herbs into the big bowl. It was too bad they hadn't thought of this idea before. It might have saved Kylie a lot of trouble. He couldn't stop the stinging in his eyes when he thought of her. He kept his head down and worked faster.

A car pulled up outside. Looked like Doc had returned alone in his Rambler. Nick and Bob pulled up, too, and then more cars began showing up. The cavalry had arrived.

The auxiliary coven came into the shop, two, three at a time, and as they crowded in, Doc had them settle where they could find a place. "We thank you all for coming when called. It's important to let you know that things have changed. Kylie... well, Kylie went on a dangerous mission to destroy the book for good and...and she..." He stopped, choked up, and covered his eyes with his hand.

Seraphina stepped up and put her arms around him. "Kylie's making a sacrifice. And if we don't want it to be in vain, we have to work extra hard and do what she would have done had she been able to stay."

The villagers exchanged worried looks with one another.

"Some of you will have to help us the next time Baphomet comes back," she went on. "But even though the Booke of the Hidden isn't here, it's going to cause trouble."

"That's why we're getting these jars ready," said Jeff. "We can't kill whatever creature comes out of the book like Kylie could've, but we can trap them in these jars. We'll teach you the incantations and give them to you for your patrols."

"And then the rest of us have to close a dangerous singularity," said Seraphina. "But we'll leave that to the original coven. I'm sure now that Doug has his flamethrower, he's anxious to get the book's creatures."

"You'd better believe it!" he crowed, strapping the thing on.

Jeff cringed, thinking he might set it off inside, but Doug wasn't that stupid. The Ordo leader waved some of the heartier souls to him. "Come on, boys. I'll give you a demo."

Some left to go outside with Doug, who sparked the flamethrower off. Still others followed Charise's instructions to fill the empty jars with a thin layer of salt. They stuffed them into *Strange Herbs & Teas* shopping bags, divided into their patrol groups, and took off into different directions.

Doug had taken several men with him to hunt. Jeff watched through the window as they disappeared into the woods. It was where all the trouble seemed to end up.

Inside, Doc and Jolene conferred over ancient books and modern tablet on how to close a rift.

Jeff leaned back against the buffet. With most of the coven and townsfolk working together, he had a moment to watch them all. He almost felt they could do it. There was the slimmest chance. But now that *both* demons were gone and Kylie too, he worried there wasn't enough supernatural help. Even though he was part demon, he didn't have the chops to understand the paranormal world. He could shift if necessary, but that was all he could do.

The police interceptor rolled in and George got out. Nick

rushed outside to greet him. There was no more hiding in the closet for the deputy, Jeff noted, since Nick had him in a full-on lip lock right outside in front of everyone. And no one had even noticed.

Nick dragged him inside the shop, talking rapidly about their plans. When George slid his gaze toward Jeff, they exchanged chin tilt greetings.

"So we have to go to that cave again?" George asked.

"That's where they're keeping the rift," said Jeff.

"But...before we had Erasmus to help us through the caverns. How will we get through it now?"

"I can do it," said Nick and Jeff at the same time.

"Jinx," said Nick with a smile. "Anyway, Jeff and I have wolf powers. We can get in and out, no problem."

"Oh." George looked worriedly toward Nick. "I suppose it's dangerous."

"It's *very* dangerous," said Jolene, eyes still glued to her tablet. "If we do it wrong, we run the risk of opening it wider. But I know we can do it."

Nick ran his hand up through his already messed-up hair. "Oh. Good."

Two by two, the coven patrols left on their book creature rounds, ginger jars under their arms. So far, there had only been one report of someone getting killed by a book creature. Those seemed like better odds than before, but then again, Kylie had still been there.

"What do you suppose—" Jeff began, but a flash outside interrupted him. They all ran to the window.

It was a giant snake with wings and two little arms. It glowed with a fluctuating light, its long tail-like body squirming and coiling in the air.

"That's a thing from the book, right?" said Jeff. He couldn't seem to take his eyes off of it.

"A lindworm," said Jolene. "Yeah, it's a fair bet it's from the book."

No one moved. Jeff felt his hairs stand up, like he wanted, *needed* to shift. "So now what?"

Jolene pressed her face to the glass. "Someone's still got to wound it, otherwise we can't get it into the jar."

Still, no one moved. Jeff turned to Nick. They were really the best choice. "Should I?" he said to Nick, even as he could see hair sprouting on the back of Nick's hands.

Something flashed forward. A glint of steel as a figure rushed toward the lindworm. A sword? *Sure, why not?* Jeff mused. Try as he might, he couldn't see their face under the hood, but it had to be a villager. The swordsman slashed at the lindworm, even as the beast snapped its jaws. It tried to coil around the figure, but the assailant swung the sword around on their wrist with a swoop like a Ninja and slashed down. Quick as lightning, part of the creature's tail spun away. The lindworm howled and coiled its injured tail inward. But now it looked angry. Its glow was a burnt red as it flicked its forked tongue and gathered itself to strike. The figure swung again, at the head this time, but only managed to nip off the tip of its nose.

The lindworm struck, jaws wide, fangs bared. But the figure wasn't there. They had managed to leap aside, and when the neck of the lindworm was extended to its fullest, the sword came down and cut through its spine like butter. The head rolled off, jaws still biting, as the rest of the body jerked into a tight loop of rope. Rays of light shot out in all directions from the beast. It slithered in its death agonies as more and more light shot out of it.

Jolene stepped forward and opened the door. "We've got to do it, just in case!" She raised her hands and cried, "*Ego te capere!*"

Nick stood ready beside her with a jar, his arm wrapped around it. The three pieces of lindworm squirmed, trying to get away. But even as it stretched in the opposite direction it began to elongate. Light burst forth from the ginger jar; the lindworm was sucked slowly toward it like a giant vacuum. All at once it snapped inside the jar and Nick slammed down the lid.

The jar jumped in his arm once and settled down. He looked around. "I…I think we got it!" He kept his hand firmly on the lid. "Someone get me the duct tape." Seraphina handed it over, but Nick urged her to do the honors. "What happens if we drop the jar and it breaks?"

Jolene shook her head solemnly. "Don't."

Jeff was slowly walking toward the door. "Who is that? *Kylie?*"

It was a woman, for sure. Her back was still to the windows. And she was still in the posture of having cut off the lindworm's head. Her legs in a lunge, elbows crooked, sword upward. She straightened and lowered the sword, black gunk dripping down the blade. She was wearing fatigue cargo pants and what looked like an army-issue olive sweater with a leather patch on one shoulder where one would rest a gun stock.

Carefully she turned and narrowed her eyes at everyone in the coven.

Doc opened his mouth in shock. "Ruth Russell?"

CHAPTER TWENTY-ONE

KYLIE, YOU SURE knew how to find trouble, I thought. Each set of the three-headed dog's eyes was on me. Each mouth was snarled open, revealing very sharp teeth. I looked at my now feeble weapon and knew that even with all the Chosen Host skills in the world, I couldn't defeat that creature with the Spear of Mortal Pain. He was too much animal for me to handle. Even with Shabiri's help, there was no chance we could do it.

I glanced back at her. "You should run."

She looked at me as if I were crazy.

"No. You know the way. Save Erasmus. I can't."

Her expression changed to one of astonishment. I had to turn away to keep an eye on Cerberus, who was stalking closer. "I don't think I can hold him off. And I have no powers. So you should get out of here while you can. It's after me, not you."

"In so much of a hurry to get rid of me?" she said uncertainly. But I could tell she was already retreating by where her voice was coming from.

"Yeah. You...stupid...demon...person."

"So convincing."

I had fought off so many creatures. I took down the wendigo, the kelpie, even Draugr. The crossbow had been great. I had even handled the Dullahan with the spear. Including Baphomet… Wait.

"Shabiri!"

"What?" Her voice came from quite a way down the road.

"I need you to take this spear. I have an idea."

She swore in a different language and cautiously returned. Once she was beside me, I handed the spear off to her and whipped around to snatch the Booke.

"This worked before." I held it up in front of me, hoping for another surge of power as it had done with Baphomet.

One of Cerberus' paws swiped toward me and struck. I went flying, gripping the Booke tight.

I lay on the ground, remarkably still clutching the Booke, and thought furiously. What went wrong? Baphomet was a god. He was also throwing balls of power at me. But Cerberus was just a creature. Maybe it wouldn't work the same way.

Something was itching in my mind. An idea I couldn't quite grasp. *Come on, Kylie. You can do this.* Definitely something to do with the Booke.

"Shabiri, what day is it?"

"*What?*" She was poking at the dog heads and keeping them at bay, but I knew it wouldn't work for long. "Why in the twelve worlds do you need to know *that?*"

"Just tell me!"

"It's…it's Samhain. For all the good it will do us. That means nothing here."

"I'm not so sure."

I staggered to my feet and held the Booke before me, thrust forward. *Listen, Booke. Now's the time. It's Samhain. You want to let loose. And for all I know, you're already doing it back on my world. But how's about a little Netherworld action? Let it loose. Let it loose on this damned dog!*

There was nothing. I couldn't hear the Booke, I couldn't feel it. Except…something was happening.

It trembled once in my grip. A few seconds passed before it did it again. I licked my parched lips, waiting. And then…

A light so bright I couldn't look at it burst forth from the Booke. Shabiri screamed beside me. I clenched my eyes shut, holding the Booke forward as steadily as I could.

When I was able to open my eyes again, things were flying all over the place. Lacy wings, some transparent like chiffon, all in black and dark purples. What *were* these things?

"The Sluagh," said Shabiri in wonder. She watched them fly around. They zipped and zoomed wildly in all directions in front of Cerberus. His three heads whined as he backed up, trying to nip at them, swat at them. But he couldn't. It was almost like that magic trick we pulled on Baphomet with those multi-colored bat things. But these winged creatures seemed to have a destination in mind and were angry at the three-headed dog for blocking their way. As if he were responsible for their troubles. For all I knew, he could've been.

Cerberus backed away, his snake tail between his legs. Like a naughty pooch disciplined by his owner, each head looked away, eyes downcast. He shook himself, black fur flying, before he bounded back up the trail into the foothills. Some of the winged creatures followed while others flew off toward parts unknown.

I supposed they were heading for my world. I didn't have time to worry about it. When the Booke was destroyed, they'd die. Or…if I died, the Booke would close. Either way, their time was short.

"The Sluagh," said Shabiri again. It sounded like she said 'slaw.' "Spirits of the restless dead. Welcomed neither in Heaven or Hell…so it is said."

"And that came from the Booke?"

"The book is a gateway to many places. Where do you think all of those creatures come from? They don't all come from here. Particularly on this night, they come from all over. You were lucky."

"No," I said, grabbing the Booke out of the air and looking at it again. "I can almost control it."

"Don't start getting ideas. It's only because of Samhain. You know darned well you *don't* have control of the book. Don't for one minute think that you do. It's only *fooling* you into thinking so."

It was very convincing. I knew Shabiri was probably right, but the Booke was telling me otherwise, that I had become a powerful mage and there was far more I could do. I was the longest living Chosen Host in history, it insisted. That proved it.

"What's it telling you?"

"Huh?"

She put a fist to her hip. "You've been standing there in a daze for quite a while. What is the book telling you? Is it contradicting what I'm saying?"

"N-no." I bit my lip. "Y-yes."

She made some gestures. "Why don't you…let that go for now, Kylie."

I didn't want to. But I knew in my heart of hearts that what the Booke was doing to me was bad. So I summoned up the courage to release it. It scooted a few feet from me and stayed there like a good little Booke.

I shook out my head. "I know what you're saying is true. But boy. The Booke is telling me all this stuff and I *want* to believe it."

"You are the oldest living Chosen Host ever," she said, a weird echo of the Booke itself. "It's got to be dicking with your mind something awful."

I put a hand to my forehead, massaging the conflicting bits of information away. "Yeah. A good way to put it." I rubbed some more. "I thought you didn't know much about the Booke. You led Doug to believe…"

"I was using him, you know. I wasn't quite sure what it would do to a human. Now I do."

"You took a chance."

"Why not? Look, now that Cerberus is busy elsewhere, do you feel up to continuing?"

"Oh. Yeah, sure."

"*Erasmus*, remember?"

"Yes. Oh God, yes." Boy, it really *was* dicking with my mind if it could make me forget *him*.

We were already close to the black marble land bridge and were ready to cross it. I looked down into the muck of whatever was in the slow-moving river below.

My stomach was tied up in knots, and I rubbed it to ease the roiling sensation. I'd been here two days in Moody Bog time and I wasn't hungry. I guess constant fear could do that. But I would soon see Erasmus again, and I planned on his face being the last thing I saw.

The thought of him made me hurry. He must be here already. He had to be. He knew his way around. God, I hoped he was still alive. I didn't know who to pray to anymore, but anyone who would listen and grant my wish was all right by me.

The Booke suddenly nudged me hard. I whipped around. "Stop that!" While I watched, it did it again. I was trying to go to the left, but it kept herding me to the right. I reached down and grabbed it, but it started bucking wildly. "What is wrong with you now, you stupid Booke?"

"Kylie Strange."

I stopped. That wasn't the Booke. "Shabiri. Do you hear that?"

She had stopped too and was clenching her fists.

"Kylie Strange," said the chorus of voices again, all speaking in the same tone.

I supposed there was no point in not answering.

"Um…yes? Wh-who is this?"

"We are the Powers That Be. Come forth and present yourself to us."

I glanced toward Shabiri. She was shaking her head furiously. I glared at the Booke. *Little snitch.*

"I'm a little busy right now," I said to the ether. "Can I talk to you later?"

In answer, the Booke yanked me to the right of the land

bridge, nearly tossing me over the side. I still didn't know what that sludge was down there but I didn't think it would be healthy for me to be in it. Still, the Booke pulled me along toward where Shabiri said I shouldn't go. It didn't seem as if I had a choice anymore.

I let the Booke go and it floated along, beckoning me. I looked back and Shabiri hadn't budged. I opened my hands to her, beseeching, but she wasn't going to help. Fine, then. I figured if I refused, the Powers would just send some other sort of hellish creature after me. Or maybe they'd be happy that the Booke was going to be destroyed. Yeah, and how was my luck so far?

I girded myself. If they killed me, the Booke would close, but Erasmus was human now, so he wasn't tied to it anymore. Maybe…just maybe he was my backup plan. He'd bargain with Satan and get it closed for good. Unfortunately, the both of us would be dead. There was no benefit from that. But maybe that was okay. Maybe, in some other world in some other form, we'd meet again. Why not? I could put my hope in that. Because the tears I was angrily wiping away wouldn't do me any good. I'd wanted to at least see him one last time, but that didn't seem possible anymore.

I stalked forward into the shadows and came to a huge arch of rock, where a hallway had been roughly hewn out of the stone walls. Torches were set in niches to either side of me. "Because this isn't creepy enough," I muttered. I followed the long corridor and finally came through another arch to open sky. Before me was an altar made out of black stone, which didn't reflect the flames behind me or the sky above. It seemed to absorb all light. "Because that's not creepy either."

I waited, listening to my panting breaths. The waiting was almost worse than anything I could possibly see. I didn't know what was supposed to happen now. These Netherworld creatures really seemed to enjoy my terror.

Something stirred on the altar. At first, I thought it might be my imagination, but a small green flame, no bigger than that of a candle, hovered right in the middle of the black stone. It began to grow until it was the size of a small bouquet. It just hovered inches above the surface of the altar, flickering, dancing. A green flame with no purpose. Until it talked.

The chorus of voices spoke in a measured, precise tone. "Kylie Strange. The Chosen Host."

So, no fooling these guys.

I made an awkward bow. "Um…greetings, Powers That Be."

A chuckle on the wind.

All of my neck hairs stood up. This was crazy dangerous, but not more so that meeting Satan himself, I guessed. This was just an appetizer…if I survived it.

"You have lived a long time, Kylie Strange. Longer than any other of your kind."

"I know. I've had help."

"No doubt. Where is Erasmus Dark?"

They didn't know? Maybe that was a good sign. "He's…on another mission. For me."

"We cannot sense him. Where did you send him?"

"It's, uh, a secret."

"We like secrets. Teeeelll ussssss."

"Look, I'm on my way somewhere important, and there's kind of a time crunch, so if you don't mind—"

A thunderclap sent me to my knees. Why did these guys always send a thunderclap?

I tried to rise but it felt like hands holding me down. I looked up but there was nothing there. Nothing that I could see, anyway.

"A human in the Netherworld," they said, voices like liquid velvet. "It is unheard of."

"What would you say if I told you I'm trying to destroy the Booke? It's plagued you for a long time and I'm going to get rid of it. Wouldn't that be a good thing?"

"What have you done with Erasmus Dark?"

"I didn't hurt him. I would never hurt him."

Their voices rushed all around me in a whirlwind. I felt and heard it all at the same time and I cringed away from it. The flame on the altar jumped and pulsed with their words. "WHAT HAVE YOU DONE WITH ERASMUS DARK?"

"I didn't do anything. I love him."

A furious whispering crescendoed around me and I covered my ears. "A human in love with a demon?"

"I can't believe this is so out of the ordinary. Surely there have been...enigmatic demons before."

"He has failed in his mission. For the first time in over four thousand years, he has failed."

Their voices sounded darker, more menacing.

"He's human now. Unbound from the Booke. You can't push him around anymore."

The sounds of their voices swirled around me. I decided to stay on my knees. Maybe it would endear me to them.

"Why is he human?"

"He did it to himself."

"Why is he human?"

"He...he needed a...a soul."

They paused. Only the rushing sound of wind blew over the top of my head. The wind whistled, then formed into the sound of voices. "Why did he need a soul?" they spoke at last.

"To bargain with. With...Satan."

The wind hissed, moaned, cried out. I had been hot the whole time I was in the Netherworld, but now I was suddenly cold. I hugged myself, staring at the altar and its green flame, even though their voices came from everywhere *but* that fire.

"He is beyond us now," said the voices. I felt a little relief for him. "He has failed but we can do nothing."

"Okay, then." I started to rise. Nothing seemed to be pushing me back now. "I'm trying to get to Satan too."

They seemed to have lost interest in me. The flame was getting smaller. I didn't wait. I turned to go.

And then their voices whirled around me again, rising and lowering in pitch and volume. I held myself tighter.

"The book. You have brought the book."

I spun toward the flames. "Yeah, I did." I glanced over my shoulder and there it was, just hovering. "And why the hell is it even a thing? You could have taken it to Satan yourselves at any time! Why did you have to create Erasmus and keep him a prisoner just so he could kill the next person who opened it? It's stupid. It's the dumbest thing I ever heard of, and it makes you sound weak! You're all weak!"

The floor began to rumble. Okay, maybe I had gone a bit too far, but honestly, I was so done with these guys.

"Oh, make an earthquake. So what? Send more creatures after me. Go ahead. It's still stupid. It will go down in history as the stupidest thing ever done. And you could have done something really great with your great collective minds, but *this* is all you could come up with? Well, I am the Chosen Host and I've been alive for a full month and I walked into the Netherworld myself and told you bitches off. Etch that in stone somewhere."

I stomped away even as the ground continued to tremble. The torches in their sconces wobbled and bits of stone rained down on me in that corridor, but I continued on adrenalin alone, marching through that hallway and out the arch that cracked as I walked under it, and made it out to that marble land bridge and looked back one more time. I gave them the finger as a final, "Fuck you!" and moved forward toward Shabiri, who was looking at me with astonishment.

I don't know why I survived that. Maybe they were all talk and really couldn't do anything to me. Maybe they never could've all along. Maybe they couldn't even have hurt Erasmus. I guessed I'd never know. And you know what? I didn't care.

"Let's go," I said to Shabiri, and took the leftward fork down toward Satan.

CHAPTER TWENTY-TWO

RUTH RUSSELL SHEATHED her sword in the scabbard on her belt.

Jeff's instincts were taking over. He could feel the wolf scratching to come out, felt his ears stretch to points, his hair grow, his nails turn to claws. He wanted to do her harm, maybe... maybe...tear out her throat.

But the wolfsbane thundered in his ears too, pulled him back against the doorframe, burned in his blood and made his ears shrink and his teeth retract. He listened to it and calmed himself, told his blood not to boil, not to want. His claws became nails again and dug deep into the door jamb.

"Ruth," said Doc in a voice so taut that Jeff could almost feel his anger bubbling below the surface. "I think it's long past time we put our cards on the table."

"You're right, Fred." She took the rest of the coven in with one glance and strode to the front door.

She passed Nick, who couldn't help but let out a low growl. She stopped and looked at him carefully. "Is he a werewolf?" She jerked her head toward Jeff. "I know *he* is."

"Hey, lady," said Nick, clutching the ginger jar and getting in her face. "How the hell do you know all this? Who do you think you are?"

"Mr. Riley, could you please stand aside. It's rude to get into someone's personal space."

She shouldered past him and squared on everyone from the middle of the room. Jolene sidled up to her, examining the sword. "Unless I'm mistaken in my legendary Irish swords, that's *Fragarach*, 'the Answerer,' isn't it?"

Ruth's lips moved into something like a curt smile. "You do know your mythology, don't you, Miss Ayrs."

"But…how did you get it?"

"Never mind that, Jolene," said Doc in a rush. "Ruth, darn it!" Doc wasn't having it. "You need to explain yourself. We've got the sheriff out looking for you as a suspect."

"A suspect of what? I don't think any of this is in the law books, do you?"

"Ruth!"

She made a conciliatory gesture and settled down. "I didn't know if I could trust any of you. Especially Miss Strange. There she was, creeping around my house looking into my personal files, stealing my necklace." She touched it over her sweater. "Telling all and sundry that we were related. But until she told me about her grandfather, Robert Strange, I hadn't remembered he existed. That must have been one powerful forget-me spell."

"You know about that?" asked Seraphina.

Ruth spared her a glance. "There have been some very odd things going on. Before I knew who she was, I didn't know if she was the cause of it."

"Well," said Doc, "technically, she was. With the Booke of the Hidden."

Ruth's eyes roved over the shelves and up to the rafters. "It was in this house, wasn't it? I always suspected it but was afraid to investigate. After all, I always assumed I would be the Chosen Host. But a lot of things have fallen into place in the last few weeks."

"You mean you've known all this time?"

"Yes. I discussed it at length with Robert Strange." She shook her head. "That man. He made me waste a lot of time. If I had only known who she was from the start…well. Where is she? It's time we talk."

Jeff kept his eyes on Doc. No one spoke a word. Doc gestured for Ruth to follow him as he shuffled toward the kitchen. The coven and the Ordo gathered around Kylie's kitchen table, where Doc eased himself into a chair. "I think I've aged ten years in the last few days alone. Sit down, Ruth. You need to hear this, since you're the last living relative of the Howlands…and the Stranges."

Ruth swept her scabbard out of the way and lowered to a chair, her back as straight as a rod. "What do you mean the last living relative?"

"Kylie was a very accepting and unique young lady. The short of it is, she fell in love with Erasmus, the demon of the book."

"She *what?*"

"I know this is mighty unusual…"

"That's saying something."

"But she felt it was her responsibility to halt the book for good. She didn't want anyone else saddled with these perils. And she discovered that the only creature capable of destroying the book was…Satan himself. So she was planning on journeying to the Netherworld and asking him to release the demon and destroy the book."

Ruth shook her head in disbelief. "But that's impossible. The only way to do that was to bargain with your… Oh no."

"We were all trying to figure out a way around that. Well, Erasmus—that is, the demon—did figure out a way. You see, he was just as in love with her as she was with him. He found a spell to make him human, so that *he* could bargain in her place."

"With a new soul." She placed her hand over her mouth. "And what happened?"

Doc raised his eyes to Jeff. "Well…we just don't know. The book is still active and…we just don't know."

"So it's possible that I *will* become Chosen Host…if I'm not already."

"No," said Jolene sternly. "I believe in Kylie. She'll figure out a way. Shabiri, the other demon, took her to the Netherworld."

"There's another demon?"

"The Ordo," said Doc, gesturing to Charise and an abashed Bob. "They had their own agenda, but...they're on our side now, seeing that Baphomet destroyed half of Hansen Mills because of them. They, uh, were the ones who summoned him in the first place."

Ruth sank her forehead to her hand. "So wait a minute," she said, raising her eyes to Bob and Charise. "You were a black coven?"

"One of their own was killed by Baphomet, so no," said Doc, "not anymore."

"Isn't Sheriff Bradbury's brother your leader..."

"Yeah?" said Bob. "So what? We changed sides. Is that so hard to understand? And who are you, lady? Someone with a lot of money helped us summon Shabiri and Baphomet. Maybe it was you."

"What are you talking about? The last thing I'd want is a god on the loose and for someone to summon demons."

"And yet here you are with some sob story about how you were supposed to be the Chosen whatsit. I think you're full of it," accused Bob.

"This is ridiculous," said Ruth. "I don't understand. I never summoned anything. And I killed the lindworm. It was going back to the book. Doesn't that make me the new Chosen Host?"

"We don't know that it was going back to the book," said Nick, still holding the ginger jar.

"But we do!" said Jolene, growing excited. "Don't you see? The book is still active. That means she's got to be alive! And Mrs. Russell, you can't be Chosen Host unless you open the book too."

"You all seem to know a great deal about it," said Ruth.

"She may not be a Wiccan," said Nick, "but Kylie's part of our coven just the same. We've been helping."

"She's made it a month? Alive?" Ruth shook her head in disbelief. "I can't believe she's survived this long."

"It's the coven," said Doc proudly. "She might just be the first one who has ever had help."

"And she's bound and determined to be the last one," said Seraphina, a tear glistening on her lashes.

Ruth heaved a deep sigh. "I see. An entire drama was being played out and I didn't know anything about it."

"It's your own fault, Ruth," said Doc. "If I'd only known, I would have invited you into the coven. And what in tarnation did you need to hide it for? Jeezum rice, Ruth. You and Gene have known me all your life!"

"I saw how the rest of the town treated you when you quit the church. I...have a place to uphold here."

Jeff stepped forward. "You could have helped. You could have told Kylie what she needed to know. Instead, you worried about your status in this little shit town? Who gives a fuck about that?"

"*I* do, Mr. Chase. I have to live here. My family has lived here since the founding of Moody Bog. You might say I *am* Moody Bog."

"Nobody *cares* about that shit!"

"Language, Jeff," Doc admonished. "Maybe where you come from it isn't as important, but folks put great stock in claims of heritage around here. It's a status symbol, yes, but it's also a point of pride. Folks from away don't quite understand it."

"You're damned right I don't. I mean." Jeff pushed his hair off his forehead. "Just what did she *think* was happening here?"

"Oh, I suspected," said Ruth. "But it made no sense to me. Because I always thought it was going to be me. I didn't remember about Kylie's family, if you recall. I've been training a long time. I had no intention of being caught off guard."

Everyone fell silent. Jeff made an exasperated noise and retreated into the shadowed corner again. No one spoke for quite some time until Ruth finally said, "What are we going to do about Baphomet?"

"You didn't seem surprised to see him," said Nick. "We saw you at the town hall meeting. Maybe you did send money and instructions to the Ordo."

"Oh, I was surprised. I just didn't know whom to blame."

Nick shifted the ginger jar to his other arm, until Jolene carefully extracted it from him and put it quietly in the buffet cupboard. "I don't think we can trust her," said Nick.

Ruth sat for a moment before she raised her left arm and pushed back her sleeve. She bore an identical tattoo to the one Kylie had just gotten.

"That only proves you want protection," Nick snarled.

"The fact that I know about it *and* the demon of the book should mean something."

"The fact that you know only means *you* could have killed Dan Parker in that ritual."

"So it comes back to that. Kylie accused me of the same thing. It wasn't me."

"Prove it."

Ruth laid her hand on her sword hilt. Jeff wondered if it was an unconscious gesture…or a threatening one. His neck hairs rose. "What about the Ordo?" she said. "They're the ones summoning demons and gods."

"We didn't have nothing to do with Dan Parker!" cried Bob.

"It wasn't them," said Nick sternly. "I'll ask again. Prove it wasn't you."

Doc raised his hands wearily. "Now settle down there, Nick. We—"

A siren wailed outside, seeming to pull up in front of the shop. Everyone scrambled from their seats and into the main shop to see Ed and Deputy George get out of their Interceptor. Doug came trotting up, too, flamethrower still strapped to his back.

"Somebody said they saw a dragon over here," said Doug, shrugging the pack from his back.

Ed glanced at him and then at the coven. "That's what I heard and we came— Ruth Russell?" His eyes traveled over her. "With a sword?"

"We've got to catch you up, Sheriff Bradbury," she said.

"Wait a minute." Doug stomped over to her. His gauze eye patch was making him look particularly piratey. "This is the old lady we've been looking for? She's the one summoning assassins and shit?"

"Look who's talking," said Nick.

Doug looked pretty intimidating, towering over Ruth, though she looked a little less little old lady-ish in her trooper outfit. Doug reached out to…well, Jeff didn't know what he'd planned. But Ruth moved quick, and before even Ed could shout, she had twisted his arm and had him kneeling on the floor, arm shoved up high against his back.

"It's not nice to point," she said.

"Let him go," said Ed, hand resting noticeably on his gun.

She did and stepped back, even helping him up.

He rolled his shoulder and rubbed his wrist. "That's a good grip you got there, granny."

Her familiar sneer was back. "Don't call me granny."

He put his hands up in surrender. "Whatever you say, lady."

"Ruth," said Ed. "We've been looking for you."

"Getting a pyre ready, no doubt. Why don't you sit down, sheriff, and I'll fill you in?"

"I'll fill him in," said Doc.

Ed seemed fit to burst. "Somebody say *something*!"

Doc put a hand to Ed's chest. "It's all right, Ed. Ruth here was just explaining to us how she'd been preparing all her life to be the Chosen Host. Because of the forget-me spell, she didn't remember Kylie's grandpa until very recently."

"You mean the ghost?"

Ruth pushed past Doc. "You saw Robert's ghost?"

"I didn't. The others told me about it."

She turned to each coven member. "Why aren't we talking to Robert's ghost?"

"We did!" said Jolene. "But he couldn't stay on this plane long."

Her glance this time to the coven was one of admiration. "Now I am sorry I didn't come forward sooner."

Ed still had his hand on his gun. "Are you all telling me that Ruth had nothing to do with Dan Parker's murder?"

"Heaven's no," said Doc. "I told you I would have had a hard time believing she'd done such a thing."

Jeff glanced at the others. Clearly, the rest of them weren't so certain about Ruth. Including Jeff.

"She's undoubtedly on our side," Doc went on. "She subdued that lindworm."

"Lindworm. You mean dragon?"

"Much the same thing."

Ed's hand fell away from the gun, and Jeff was surprised how tensed *he* had been. He relaxed but stayed alert. Nick kept exchanging glances with him, doing that alpha/beta thing, but Jeff was a bit clueless as to how it all worked. In truth, he didn't like to think about it.

"Our immediate problem seems to be the rift," said Doc.

"What about Baphomet?" asked Ruth.

"What about Kylie?" said Ed.

"What about her?" asked Doc kindly.

"Well…" He swept his Smokey Bear hat off his head and gripped the rim till it bent. "It's been two days with no word. Aren't we going to go after her?"

Doc stepped toward him and looked up to the taller man. "I know we'd all like to run in with guns blazing, Ed, but right now, this is Kylie's story, and she's already decided the ending."

"But we can't just let her—"

"You know very well that at this point, it's all been said. Either Kylie or Erasmus will walk away. Or…neither of them will."

He stood a moment before he slapped his hat to his thigh and turned away. "I *hate* this!"

Scowling, Jeff thought he'd spoken for all of them.

Her eyes still shining with tears, Seraphina said, "We have to concentrate on the rift."

"But Baphomet," said Ruth. "He's a danger we can't predict. We need a way to contain him or send him back."

"What about the ginger jar thing?" asked Nick.

Jolene shook her head. "He's a god, not a demon, remember?"

"Besides," said Doc, "It's got to be the rift. If Baphomet finds it, there's no telling what hell he'll bring us."

"I don't know what this rift is," said Ruth, "but by the sound of it, I agree that's your priority."

"It was caused by the book," said Doc. "At least we think so. It's keeping a gate open where creatures can get in—"

"From all the worlds," she said softly.

Jeff had been listening but not clearly understanding. "But won't it close when the book is closed?"

Jolene clutched her tablet tight to her chest. "Not necessarily. The book works in mysterious ways. It may not even need the rift. It might be independent from it now. No one has ever destroyed the book before. We just don't know."

"That's not the only danger," said Ed, his face blank as he presumably stowed away his emotions. "There's more talk in town of destroying the covens. They don't trust you guys, especially since you've been recruiting more people. They think it's all a conspiracy to—I don't know. Turn everyone in Moody Bog into Satanists."

"We aren't Satanists," said Jolene.

"You and I know that, but *they* don't. I don't know what they're planning but I know it's something bad. They're trying to enlist Reverend Howard to their side but he's still holding out. And they've started to suspect something about not being able to leave town or call outside."

"Nick," said Doc, "maybe you'd best call in your patrols. Tell them to hole up here."

"Okay." He took out his phone and began punching in numbers.

"There's more room at my house," said Ruth.

Everyone turned to look at her.

Doc smiled kindly. "That's generous, Ruth. For now, we've got to protect *this* house as well as the people in it. And it is more isolated than your place in case Baphomet comes to call."

"If you change your mind…" She made as if to leave when Doc stopped her. "Ruth, it might be best if you stayed here, too. Maybe there are some secrets here you can help us with."

She glared up at the rafters. "I went over this place with a fine-tooth comb before I decided to sell it. I checked every stick of furniture, every inch of the walls, and the plumbing."

"And you still managed to miss it. So maybe there are things we have yet to learn."

"Has anyone found anything in the basement?"

"Basement?" said Jeff. "I don't think even Kylie ever talked about a basement. Maybe she never knew there was one."

"Oh for heaven's sake!" She shoved the settee aside and kicked the rug away, then dug her finger into what looked like a knot on the plank floor and lifted. What had appeared to be a seamless floor was obviously a trapdoor.

"No one knew this was here?" She shook her head and held out her hand. "Flashlight?"

Five flashlight apps suddenly shone down on her and the dark rectangle below. She smiled and climbed down the steps. Everyone followed her.

The place looked covered in centuries-old cobwebs and dust. Thick wooden posts held up the beams and floor joists. There were the remnants of shelves and broken jars seem to litter the place. Old root cellar storage, Jeff supposed.

"This was the only thing I ever found," said Ruth, pointing to strange letters carved into the posts, "but I could never translate them."

"That's Enochian," said Jolene with awe in her voice.

Ruth looked at her surprised. "You can read Enochian?"

"A little. Mr. Dark was teaching me."

"The *demon* was teaching you?"

"Yeah. He's a pretty cool demon…as demon's go, I guess."

Ruth seemed to absorb this. "Then…what does it say?"

Jolene scampered from post to post, while the rest of the coven shone their lights on the scrawled letters. "I can't be sure," she said, going back to the first post and squinting at it through her glasses, which kept sliding down her nose. "But it seems to be saying, 'Beware the book. Beware the gods. The gates shall close.'"

"What does that mean?" asked Doug.

An explosion drowned out any response. Jeff led the charge back upstairs and stopped when he saw another tossed Molotov cocktail heading toward the shopfront.

"What the hell are they doing?" he shouted.

Some of the townsfolk had gathered out front. The kind that were happy to have pitchforks and torches. It seemed that the magical wards and charms were holding, but for how long?

"Dude," Jeff said to anyone. "We gotta do something."

Doc had a worried look on his face. "Our coven has to get to the caves. If we don't close that rift, it doesn't matter what this lot does."

"We can hold them off," said Doug. "Listen bro, you two with the badges. You've got to go outside and cool them down."

George touched his side arm. "And if we can't?"

Doug looked at the rest of the Ordo. "Then I think the rest of us know how to rock and roll."

CHAPTER TWENTY-THREE

ERASMUS SIZED UP the harpies. "Focalor, can you conjure me a weapon?"

Suddenly, a heavy club of wood formed in his hand, sharp spikes sprouting from all sides of the head.

Erasmus smiled and hefted it. "This will do."

The harpies—winged creatures with the faces of women—dropped from the ledge above and swooped low, baring their teeth and striking out with clawed feet.

Erasmus cocked back the weapon and swung, smacking one of the female-faced creatures full on. Broken and bloody, she fluttered to the ground, dead.

The other harpies screamed at the loss of their sister. They doubled their attack, going for Erasmus. Focalor bounded into the air and chased them with his own fangs bared. He could only chase one at a time so the three split off in all directions.

Erasmus felt the sting of claws raking along his head and was momentarily stunned by the pain. It wasn't like that as a demon, when he could withstand a great amount of punishment. As a weak human, he was nearly undone. He dropped the club and fell to his knees, gripping his head. Such agony! His flesh was rent and he realized with a pang of fear, that he couldn't heal like he had before. When he looked down at his hands, there was blood. Not the black blood of his demon self, but red like any other weak human. The hands he looked at trembled. *Get a hold of yourself!* he admonished. What did it matter? He wouldn't be alive long anyway. All he had to do was hold out long enough to bargain with Satan.

He gritted his teeth, clenched his fists, and looked up to where the harpies were circling overhead. Focalor had managed to capture one and was devouring it live while it struggled, bloody feathers cascading around him.

The last two screamed again and looked to be doubling their efforts to get at Erasmus. He waved his hands at his head to protect himself as he scrambled to the cudgel. He snatched it up and held it with both hands, waiting to strike them again. Blood from his scalp trickled down over his forehead, dribbling to his eyebrows. He blinked it away while the harpies split off and came at him from opposite sides.

When one got close enough, he swung, ducking the approach of the other. He missed.

"Focalor!"

"What?" the demon asked around a mouthful of harpy. Black blood was smeared all around his face, and his hand dripped with it too.

"A little help!"

"You're so needy now, Erasmus." He cast aside the remains of the corpse and wiped his mouth with his arm. "Now," he said, scanning the skies. "Where are those tasty creatures? Ah!" He lifted off, zooming toward one of them. Erasmus looked on with envy at Focalor's wings. Now, of course, he couldn't change at all.

Erasmus impatiently swiped at the blood in his eyes and adjusted his slippery grip on the club, eyes tracking the skies.

Shoulders! Pain! She had come from behind and dug her claws into his shoulders, dragging him forward. If she got him down on the ground, she'd sink her teeth into his neck, and he'd be dead in seconds.

With a yell and his muscles working with all their might, he snapped the club up behind his head and hoped for the best. It smashed something and the creature shrieked. When the claws let him go, he spun. The harpy was flopping around on the ground, moaning and flapping with a deep injury to its face.

He smiled, stalked up to it, and raised the cudgel, bringing it down again and again. Bits of bone, feather, and black blood flicked up at him. When it was a flattened mass, he smiled, dropped the club, and turned.

Focalor was hanging in the air in the process of tearing the harpy apart, flinging a leg here and a wing there. He touched down beside Erasmus.

"You're bleeding. Human blood. Can I…can I taste it?"

He sighed. He had to give the demon something for his trouble. "Yes…but don't bite."

Focalor positioned himself in front of Erasmus, grasped his upper arms, and drew him in, first licking his forehead with a long, flat forked tongue and making moaning noises of pleasure. He ran his tongue along Erasmus' wounded scalp and over his bleeding shoulders, clearly enjoying himself. When Erasmus sensed Focalor was lingering too long, he shoved him back. "That's enough," he growled.

Focalor licked his lips. "You taste divine, my friend. It's too bad I agreed to help you…and not devour you instead."

"Yes," he said, backing away. "You promised. You will have an amazing story to tell. Something that will last far longer than a mere meal."

Focalor studied him with narrowed eyes. He took a step closer. "That is true. And I did promise…"

Erasmus took another step back. Now he wished he hadn't dropped the club, a tantalizing four feet away. "An amazing story to tell of the bravery of a demon."

Focalor stopped. The hungry look in his eye diminished. "You take the fun out of everything, Erasmus."

He breathed a relieved sigh. "So I've been told. But the end of my tale will come soon enough." Glancing up at the arched cavern and the glint of light within, he moved forward. He heard Focalor behind him, muttering to himself.

The cavern descended as he expected it would. They traveled down a long spiraling trail hewn out of the rock. Stalactites and stalagmites in gray stone marked their path. Huge cascades of dripping stone laid out like giant church organs held up the walls. For the first time, it was strangely cold in the Netherworld. Erasmus knew of worlds that were covered in ice, but the region on this world he was most familiar with was hot and humid. Not that he could have felt the difference before. The sensations his human body endured were that much stranger to his situation. Especially the pain of his head and shoulders. He was almost grateful that it all would be over soon.

There was flickering ahead. He knew it must be where the flames were, where...*He* was, and when they rounded a corner, they saw it.

Focalor stopped Erasmus' with a touch of the arm. His eyes were round and he didn't need to speak. Indeed, neither of them seemed capable at the sight before them.

Satan was as tall as a two-story house, and yet he was still only sitting. His skin was like black rock with a myriad of glowing red cracks spread over every inch, as if he himself were made of a crust of cooling rock with a core of lava. It might be so. He wore no clothing and his horns would have been the envy of Baphomet, for they speared upward well over his head in the graceful shape of a lyre. He was sitting as a man rests in a bath, with his knees up, his elbow on one knee, and his pointed chin resting on his hand. Except instead of water, flames crackled all around the pit in which he sat. He stared at nothing, pondering his thoughts, slowly blinking his red, glowing eyes over and over.

Above him in the rising cavern living gargoyles were perched, sitting like cats and following the visitors' progress with their yellow eyes.

Erasmus wondered if he should say something. Move forward

and grovel. Drop to his knees. Instead, he was trapped by fear and couldn't move at all. Why had he decided to do something as insane as this? In his terror, he suddenly couldn't remember, until an image flashed through his mind. Kylie. He saw her face, her smile, and he remembered.

"This…is very interesting," said the surprisingly soft voice of the demon of demons. He didn't turn his head but Satan's nostrils flared. "I smell…a human."

Finally, He turned his head, which was a feat of engineering from its size. Erasmus suddenly imagined gears of a waterwheel and pulleys turning the enormous visage. But when those eyes fixed on him, he had no choice but to fall to his knees. His legs wouldn't hold him up anymore.

"My Mighty Lord, I…I come to you as a recent human, for I was a demon before this. Erasmus Dark."

"Erasmus Dark?" Satan tapped his chin with a giant finger. "Created by the Powers That Be to guard some silly book? Is that you?"

"Y-yes, Mighty One."

"And you say you're human now? What in the twelve worlds possessed you to do that? Who was it? I'll eat him for you."

"No, my Great Lord." He couldn't believe how frightened he was. True, he had been frightened as a demon, but as a human, he had nothing, no way to protect himself. More trickles of blood streaked down his forehead. He dared not wipe at them or even glance away. "It was my idea."

"And so you come to me with…Focalor. Hello, Focalor!" He waggled his fingers toward the frozen demon, who had hung back and flattened himself against the cave wall. "But *he* is still a demon. Were you not happy with your lot, Erasmus?" His voice was that of a curious yeoman, wondering about the cattle foraging out in the pasture and the price of hay. This calm and easy voice was disconcerting.

"Focalor came to escort me. He has nothing to do with my decision."

Satan cocked his great head. The shadows of his horns moved across the uneven cavern walls, darkening several layers of gargoyles perched on each stone outcropping. "Are you…protecting him?"

"Yes. I would not have him punished for my sake. He traded devouring me for the chance to tell this tale he will witness."

"Well, now I *am* intrigued. A demon protecting another. And one keeping his promise not to devour. It does sound like a tale to tell. Tell me, Erasmus."

Erasmus licked his lips. The rocks beneath him were tearing into his knees, but it didn't matter at this point. Only a little while longer would do.

"I came to beg that you destroy the Booke of the Hidden."

"But…the Booke of the Hidden is all you know. It is your home, your protection. Why would you ask me to do that?"

"Because…because the Chosen Host…wishes it."

"The Chosen Host? A human? Why would you bring such a thing to me? Oh, no, no, no. I thought this would be more intriguing." He began to lift his arm, and Erasmus feared it was to destroy him.

He jumped to his feet. "Wait! Please! It was because of her that I became human…so that I would have something with which to bargain."

Satan froze, blinking at Erasmus for far too many heartbeats. Erasmus held his breath.

Satan slowly lowered his arm. "You did it for her? It sounds as if she yet lives."

"Yes. I did not…could not take her soul."

Satan stroked the length of his pointed chin. "A demon friend who would not devour you and a Soul-Eater who would not eat a soul. Focalor, you are right. This is starting to become a very interesting tale indeed."

Focalor shrunk further into the wall, tucking his wings in tight.

With his hands on his knees, Satan stretched and leaned

toward Erasmus. His great shadow raced across the floor. "And why, my dear eater of souls, did you defy your own creation to promise her this?"

His knees trembled, threatening to buckle under him again. He could not look away from that burning coal of a face. "Because…because I…love her."

Erasmus waited. He thought that Satan might laugh at him, believing it to be a feeble and mundane excuse. He thought Satan wouldn't hesitate to kill him. He waited and hoped…

"You love her," said Satan. "As a human, you loved her?"

"No, my Dread Lord. As a demon. I love her. I love her even now. And I am here to destroy the book and offer you my soul in return…before she did so herself."

Satan sat back so abruptly Erasmus thought his horns would scrape the ceiling, but the roof was much higher than he had originally thought. "By the Devil Myself, I don't believe it. This woman, this Chosen Host whom you have promised not to kill, had designs to come to me and offer her own soul to destroy that troublesome book? My, my. You know, Erasmus, I never gave the thing much thought. Oh, I wondered about it, who had made it, and why. But I never troubled myself to think about it. And now…well! Now I must. There is no question that I can destroy the book, but you are bound to it by—oh, I see. Now that you are human, you are not tied to it. Clever. But, of course, you'd be dead just the same. If I thought this new soul of yours was worthy, I might consider it. A new soul is fresh, after all, and not the best as with a well-worn soul."

"I know, my Great Lord."

"Indeed, you are a connoisseur yourself."

"Only of Chosen Hosts."

"Ah, yes. But tell me." Satan adjusted his seat in the pit and rested his long-fingered hands on each side of his face. "How did you fall in love? Were you toying with her?"

Erasmus stared at his feet. "She…she seduced me," he grumbled.

Satan rocked back and laughed, a roaring, booming sound. The gargoyles on the walls flapped their wings and took their time to resettle on their precarious ledges.

"Oh my dear Erasmus, this is very entertaining! It's certainly worth my time. I thought for a moment to destroy you and your Focalor, but now I don't want to. I want to hear more."

Erasmus risked a cautious glance back at Focalor. He was making his way stealthily back the way they had come. But a gargoyle spotted him and flew down lower with a warning glower not to leave.

"There is not much left to tell, my lord. She was searching for a way to avoid trading her soul and looking for a way to release me from the book at the same time. I had at first thought…well. She is working with a coven of very intelligent Wiccans. I had hoped that she could find a way and we…we could be together. But…alas."

"That's touching. Can you tell me, Erasmus, what is it like being in love? I have heard it is painful."

"It can be." He looked off to the side, trying to parse his thoughts. "It is like…a glorious revelation. A never-ending joy that grows and warms. To know that I am loved as I love her…" He shook his head. "I don't know how best to describe it."

"And…this love. It has brought you here. But you will ultimately be destroyed. Is that, too, love?"

"Yes. For in loving her, I would gladly sacrifice myself to keep her from harm."

"But you will never see her again, nor she you."

"I know. But…it somehow…seems…right."

Satan slowly shook his head. "It sounds like madness. Are you certain you aren't mad? This is something beyond my understanding, Erasmus. But I have heard similar tales of humans and those creatures on other worlds. This love that is so strong that it makes them fools."

Erasmus hung his head. "Yes. I am a fool. But I am not sorry for it."

"Erasmus," said Satan, "my dear, dear Erasmus, your story is very intriguing. One for the ages, really. But I—"

A commotion at the cavern's path turned Satan's head. Focalor looked up the trail and backed away, but then looked at Satan and instead pressed himself even tighter to the wall.

"Will you get out of my way?" someone shouted.

Satan's nostrils flared. "This is a banner day. I smell yet another human…in the Netherworld!"

"What?" Erasmus snapped his head toward the entrance and his heart gave a jolt at what he saw. *Kylie?*

CHAPTER TWENTY-FOUR

IT HAD BEEN decided that Ruth would come with them to the caves, which was a good thing, Jeff thought. But their cars were all in the front where the mob was. Ruth hadn't brought hers, but if they could get it... Jeff straightened. "Give me the key and I'll go get it and pick you all up," he said.

Ruth rested her fists on her hips. "How are you going to get there faster than the rest of us?"

Jeff smiled. He began peeling off his clothes and by the time his trousers fell away, he was all wolf.

She stared at him dumbfounded until Doc nudged her. "Your key?"

Mouth still open, she reached into a pocket of her cargo pants and handed it to Jeff, who took it delicately between his teeth. Doc leaned toward him. "Ruth lives at 421 Mill Pond Road. She drives a green Mercedes."

Of course, she does, Jeff thought, before he bounded off, skirting around the back way through the woods. He ran full pelt, ashamed to be reveling in it. But he realized if he went too many days without wolfing completely and tearing through the wilderness, he got jumpy and angered too easily. It was good to get out of his human skin sometimes. He wondered if it had always been that way. He got the same sort of thrill from surfing, getting a little agitated when he went too long without being on the waves. It could be that the original werewolf had looked for him, knowing his restlessness. Maybe it was some sort of fate. *Whatever*, he told himself. He hated it…but he kind of loved it, too.

He got to Mill Pond Road and figured what the hell. He ran down the middle of the road looking for 421 without worrying about anyone seeing him. Too late for that. There! With the shiny Mercedes in the front driveway, newly washed. Good thing, or it might have been in the garage. But once he got there, he realized that to get in the car, he'd have to shift back…and he didn't have any clothes.

One problem at a time, he mused and shifted. And without fur it was considerably colder. He fumbled with the key fob and clicked the button. He heard the door unlock and quickly got inside, cranking up the heat. In no time he was feeling better.

He hoped Ruth wouldn't mind his naked butt on her leather seats and chuckled to himself. *Kylie would have loved this.* But backing out of the driveway, his smile faded. Not past tense. She wasn't gone yet. He could cling to the hope that she'd somehow get out of it. If anyone could, it would be his babygirl…though not *his* anymore. That demon. Why had she fallen for *him*? There was no accounting for it, but she had. But more importantly, the demon had fallen for *her*. That's what had kept her alive so far.

Jeff took all the backroads he could think of to end up parked near Kylie's backyard. The coven seemed to just appear from behind the trees. Seraphina got in first and dropped his clothes on his lap.

"I thought you might be needing these," she said with a serene smile.

"Thanks, babe."

The rest of the coven crammed in. Ruth did wince when she noticed Jeff's undressed state on her smooth leather seats, but she didn't say anything.

"Where am I going again?" asked Jeff.

"Get to the highway," said Doc, "and I'll let you know when to turn."

Doc directed from the back seat and Jeff drove fast up the highway. He occasionally locked glances with Nick through the rearview mirror. He could tell Nick was ready to shift too, fingers drumming anxiously on his thigh.

Jeff maneuvered the car up Falcon's Point Road and parked at the trailhead. He slipped from the driver's seat just as he shifted, avoiding any embarrassment, though he hardly ever got embarrassed by it anymore, truthfully.

Nick started undressing. "You two can get us in and out of the cave, right?" asked Doc for the fifteenth time.

"Yeah, Doc, no sweat." Nick nearly jumped out of his shirt and trousers and stepped out of his shoes not with feet, but with paws. He glanced at Jeff, who just led the way up the trail.

They both ran side by side. Jeff lifted his muzzle and sniffed the air. No trace of Baphomet's scent of ash and tar. Nick kept stride and it was wonderful. Jeff tried not to think about the plans he'd made, the plans to go back home to California after all this was over. Nick was his pack and he didn't know if it would be possible to leave him. But he needed to do it, had to.

Nick glanced at him like he knew what he was thinking. Likely, he sort of did.

They kept going until they made it to the cave entrance. The sheriff had roped it off with police tape so no one would wander in and get sucked to another dimension, or at least that's how Jeff understood it.

He and Nick sat and waited, though he could tell that Nick wanted to nuzzle him. It was a pack thing but Jeff was uncomfortable with it. Not because Nick was gay, but because he liked keeping his humanity, even when he was a wolf. Maybe *especially* when he was a wolf.

It took about half an hour for the others to make it up the trail. Jeff hadn't been too sure about Ruth, but smelling her as a wolf, she seemed to be right with him. If there was something amiss, he was sure Nick would know, too.

They entered the caves and Jeff sniffed around. Yes, he knew the way. He could definitely find this scent again. He took the lead while Nick took the rear. It was getting darker and he could still see, but thank goodness for flashlights because he doubted even he could see in the pitch blackness with no light at all.

He saw the green glow before the others. He gave a yelp and they headed toward him.

It was a glowing crack in space slowly turning like some weird virtual reality game. But it really was just a crack. Did the book bring it? The coven seemed to think so. All Jeff knew was that it stunk. He hated the smell of it. He noticed Nick thought so, too, because he was wrinkling his nose at it and kept shaking his head, trying to get the smell out of his muzzle.

Right? Jeff was saying in his head. He let his tongue loll, trying to catch some other better scents to mask the terrible one.

Ruth walked around it, simply studying it. "I never would have guessed."

It was funny listening to people talk when he was a wolf. They sounded like they were talking into a cup, kind of hollow and muffled. He was just happy to be able to understand them. Without the wolfsbane, their voices sounded garbled. He supposed that being a werewolf made you forget your past self, forget those you loved even, just so you could kill. Yeah, the wolfsbane kept him just that much more human. He never missed a dose and was even getting proficient at making it himself, under the careful guidance of Seraphina.

"How do we start?" said Ruth.

Doc took out some things from a bag and Jolene took more supplies out of her backpack. Jeff never bothered with the details of what they were doing. He wasn't into Wicca. He knew plenty of people back home who were into it, from teenaged girls who just wanted to dabble to full-on witches with tattoos, braided purple-dyed hair, and serious piercings. He'd slept with one of the latter once. She was a bit too intense for him.

Soon, the coven had surrounded the rift and began chanting. Doc had a big leather-bound book that he was reading from as a sort of call and repeat. He didn't quite understand what they were up to, but the rift sure seemed to. It began pulsating. Jolene tossed some colorful powders into it and the rift sparked and bucked. The chanting got louder. There was a strange electricity in the air. He felt it crackle around him, and his fur started to rise.

All at once, something flashed and Jolene was yanked back, as if she'd been attached to a rope. She fell into the darkness beyond their flashlights and lanterns. Seraphina ran to her and lifted her head into her lap, cooing at her.

"Are you all right, Jolene?" she asked softly.

Nick wandered toward her, lay down beside her, and licked her face.

Jolene lay there and suddenly snapped open her eyes. They glowed red. Everyone jerked back, especially when she said in a deep voice not her own, "Weak mortals. You think to close the gate. The gate is open! It will remain so. The game is not done."

"Oh, it's done, buster," said Ruth. She had something like a willow wand in her hand. She pointed it at the rift and then slowly walked it closer.

"What are you doing?" said the voice. "Stop it, you fool!"

Ruth poked it right into the glowing crack. A boom and light burst in all directions, blinding everyone.

Jolene started to float off the floor. But her head was shaking violently and the voice was saying, "No, no, no, no, NO!"

Ruth held the wand in the rift. She shut her eyes against the blasts of wind and gritted her teeth. She held up her wand arm with her other hand to keep it steady. The rift was expanding. *Was it supposed to do that?*

The wolf's self-preservation was taking hold of Jeff. He backed away. Wanted to run. Had to run away. But the human side, the Jeff side, forced the wolf to stop. *You stay right there, wolfboy. Don't you dare leave them. They're your pack and they're in trouble.* That seemed to do it. He whined to Nick who looked like he was ready to bolt too. Nick whimpered and stood his ground, though his tail was between his legs.

Jolene suddenly turned her head Exorcist-style toward Ruth. "Get away from there, mortal. You don't know what you are doing. No one has ever interfered with the book!"

"Get used to it!" screamed Ruth.

"YOU'LL ALL DIE!"

"We've all got to die sometime," yelled Doc. He opened the book in his hand again and started reciting the strange words. Seraphina and Ruth repeated. They all talked louder and louder over the noise of the wind and the rumble coming from the crack. The cave's floor began to tremble, like an earthquake. Pebbles fell from the roof, but Jeff was worried bigger ones were on their way. He admonished himself again when his paws edged toward the exit.

There was a sudden and powerful boom that knocked all of them off their feet, throwing Ruth back. She landed on Nick, who gave out a yelp.

When everyone looked up, the rift was gone. They all turned toward Jolene. She was lying peacefully on the ground as if asleep.

Doc knelt beside her and opened her lids, looking at her eyes. "Wake up, Jolene. Wake up."

But she didn't stir.

"Get my bag," said Doc to no one in particular. Nick padded over, closed his mouth gently over the handle of the black doctor bag, and brought it forward. Doc dug inside and grabbed a little pill-looking thing, snapped it, and waved it under her nose.

Nick and Jeff shied back. Ammonia.

Still she didn't stir.

"She's not breathing," he said worriedly.

"Maybe you should start CPR," said Seraphina. Big tears rolled from her eyes.

Doc hesitated, as if he was arguing with himself. "Get me the book," he said at last. Seraphina raced to the book and put it into Doc's hands.

He flipped some pages and stopped, holding his whole hand over Jolene's face. He muttered some kind of incantation. It was a garbled sort of language, not demonic or else Jeff would have been able to understand it. Doc slowly lifted his hand away. A pale light hung in an arc between her face and his hand, like some kind of chalk smear. He seemed to hold it for a moment more before suddenly clenching his hand into a fist. The light went out and Jolene coughed.

Doc bent over her again. "Jolene?"

"Yeah, yeah I'm back." She wiped at her face and Doc helped her to sit up.

"Are you all right, young lady?"

"Yeah. Just a little woozy. Another possession. Not nice. He really didn't want to go, even though the rift closed."

"No, he didn't."

"He *is* gone, though. I can feel it. I can probably stand now."

"Are you sure?"

"Yeah, let me get up." Doc helped her and she stood, maybe a little wobbly at first but she got better quickly.

A few more rocks tumbled down from the ceiling and edges. The cave trembled. She looked up. "Maybe we'd better get out of here."

"By Godfrey, I think you're right!"

Seraphina and Doc each took her arm and ran out of the room with her. Ruth followed after and Nick ran following her.

Jeff looked back to the place the rift had been. No light remained. He sniffed and couldn't smell it. That was good enough for him.

He ran and caught up to Nick in the lead. The wolves trotted, often running back to make sure the humans were following. Dust and rocks kept falling. There was a great rumbling behind them. *Get moving!* cried Jeff, but all that came out were some barks.

The entrance was in sight but now some serious rocks were falling, and the dust was making the exit hard to see.

Nick and Jeff barked, urgently herding them toward the entrance.

With a mighty roar, the ceiling crumbled. Everyone leapt for the entrance, rolling past the police tape. It seemed as if the whole mountain was coming down. Dust and debris crashed, filling the entrance with rubble and collapsing part of the cave opening.

Jeff quickly assessed, pacing back and forth in front of the cave, and was satisfied that everyone had made it out.

Seraphina and Jolene helped Doc to his feet. He was a bit scraped up but no worse for wear. "That's one down," he said. "And a mighty big one at that. Good job, everyone. Now all we have to worry over is Baphomet."

"And an angry mob," said Jolene.

"We'd better get back," he agreed. They hurried as fast as they could up the trail.

CHAPTER TWENTY-FIVE

KYLIE, GIRL, THIS is it. I was actually going to walk into Satan's lair. If anyone had ever told me… Nope. Not any of this would have been believed.

We got to the cavern. It looked like dead birds were scattered by the entrance in all directions. Some looked beaten, some torn apart. Wild beasts? More demons? I shuddered at the black blood and feathers everywhere. I had to carefully pick my way over one to enter the cavern.

Shabiri followed me and then skittered in front of me. "Listen, I know I promised to take you here, but now I'm not so sure it's such a good idea."

"You can leave anytime, you know."

"Yes, I know." She stopped and watched as I stalked forward. But then she seemed to change her mind and ran after me again, her ridiculous high heels clacking over the stone. "But maybe it's not a good idea, talking to…*Him*. Did you ever consider that He might be angry at a human trying to tell Him what to do?"

"I'm not going to tell him. I'm going to beg him. On my knees if necessary. Shouldn't that please him?"

Yeah, I began to wonder what I was getting into. What Satan would be like. Would I be too terrified to speak? But at the moment, I was good. I was running on adrenalin and chutz-pah and moxie and anything else I could grab from my DNA. I mean, this was it. I could put everything I had into this because after it, there wouldn't be any more. Might as well.

Funny, but I wasn't as scared as when I'd started out.

Shabiri was still blocking me, even as the cavern grew cooler. It looked like the cave at Falcon's Point with stalactites and sta-lagmites. But unlike the caves there that got darker the more you dove into them, this one was becoming lighter due to all that fire. Okay, *that* was giving me pause. Satan, fire, hell….souls. *Too late now, Kylie. And anyway, this was for Erasmus.* I swallowed past a thick lump in my throat. "I know you're scared, Shabiri, but you don't want to see Erasmus die, do you?"

She didn't look like the confident bitch I had known. Her face was twisted in uncertainty. For one, she loved him. For another, demons apparently didn't do this kind of thing for each other. It was dog eat dog in the Netherworld. Acts of selflessness were alien to them.

"Shabiri, you got me here. You helped me. I'll tell him that before I die. You can wait outside. You don't have to go in there."

She looked like she was pondering it. She really wanted to leave, but she also might hate herself if she did. "What if…what if…"

"No more what ifs. I'm here. I'm going through with it."

She got in front of me again and held her arms out, blocking me.

"Will you get out of my way!" I shoved her, hard. She might even have fallen, but I didn't care. She didn't follow me. I stalked forward and suddenly found myself in a doorway to an enor-mous chamber. And then my breath stopped.

Satan was enormous. Huge. All out of proportion to what I'd expected. And he was in a pit of fire, just…sitting there. He looked like a walking lava flow but with red glowing eyes and towering horns.

And he was looking at *me*.

"*Kylie?*"

Erasmus' voice. Then I saw him. A choking cry wrenched from my throat. "Erasmus!" I ran. There was some sort of fluttering from the rock walls but I paid no attention to it. There was even some kind of demon looking like he was trying to *become* the wall, but I had no eyes for anyone but Erasmus. When I finally reached him, I flung myself into his arms. We held each other, gripping tight. "I thought I lost you!" I wailed into his shoulder.

"You can never lose me," he said. He brought my face up and kissed me.

I held on and kissed him back hard. But then…he tasted different. He smelled different. He felt different. I couldn't help but push him back to look at him. He wore the same face, the same physique, but something was off. His face. It seemed paler, the angles softer, the eyes more expressive and open.

He was human. I reached up with both hands and stroked his face and hair. "What have you done?"

"I'm human now. What…what do you think?"

"I think I don't want you to do this."

"But…I'm human. I thought you'd like that."

"I don't! You're Erasmus. A demon. I love *him*."

He looked stricken. "So…you don't love *me*? As I am now?"

"Of course I do, you idiot! I'd love you no matter what!"

"Excuse me," said a voice of rounded tones and controlled strength. When I looked, it was Satan, gesturing toward me with a delicate finger…that had a huge talon on it. "If I may cut in…"

"Oh!" I broke away from Erasmus but clasped tight to his hand. "I'm…I'm so sorry. I forgot for a minute…"

"A human forgetting the sight of—well, not be a braggart or anything—but look at me. I'm pretty impressive, no?"

"Oh yes! Yes, you are. And *frightening*. And…*big*. And great…"

Erasmus hissed out of the side of his mouth, "Stop talking."

I tried to smile but I don't think it came out very well. And then Satan leaned toward me. He was far bigger than Baphomet at his biggest, and he leaned *far*, getting his long, pointed nose close to mine. My whole view was taken up with those glowing red eyes. There were pupils within, but instead of being round, they were dark squiggles that widened and narrowed as he examined me.

"You are the human, the Chosen Host."

"Y-yes."

"And…you fell in love…with him." He moved that enormous finger and pointed it at Erasmus.

"Yes. I don't want him to die. I came because I want you to take *my* soul instead. But before you do, I was hoping you could destroy the Booke of the Hidden. For good. Because no one should have to go through what I've gone through ever again. And…well. You don't have to unbind Erasmus from it because he's human now and I imagine he isn't tied to it anymore, so…he saved you a step." I was rambling but I just couldn't stop.

He grinned. His teeth were sharp and glowy. "And yet, you would come to me…with this?"

Two fingers clasped my left arm and lifted me off the ground. I pumped my legs, terrified that he'd just drop me into his big mouth and chew.

He was looking at my left wrist, the one he was holding me by. The one with the tattoo!

Oops.

"I can explain that."

Satan still smiled. "I think you had better."

"I thought I could protect myself. I didn't know if it would work. But now I see what a stupid thing it was getting it. You can burn it off if you need to."

"Or simply pull off this arm."

My lip trembled. "O-or…that."

His fingers released me and I fell to the ground. Erasmus made a move toward me but seemed to be thwarted by a look from the Big Guy. "Did you really think a simple tattoo would stop me? I can easily bypass such pedestrian magic. That is for the simple demon, the Soul-Eater, like your beloved. Tell me, did you get this tattoo before or after this great love occurred?"

I rubbed my wrist and the knee I landed on. "After. And it wasn't to protect me from him. It was to protect me from…well, you. I'm sorry."

"Never mind," he said, waving his hand distractedly. "It doesn't matter, as I said. It's good to be cautious in my presence." He settled in again, the flames jumping around him like bubbles in a spa. "But now, mortal, tell me. *Why* should I do this thing for you?"

"I…I never came up with a why. I was just hoping you would. I'm…" Since I was already on the floor, I got up on my knees, grabbing hold of Erasmus' hand. "I'm begging you. Could you please, *please* destroy the Booke and take *my* soul?"

"No!" Erasmus cried. "Please! Take mine, not hers."

"No!" I leaped up and got in front of Erasmus. "You don't want his. He was a demon. Who knows if it's any good as a soul? Mine's probably much better."

Erasmus pushed me aside. "But *I* was a demon! Think of the rarity, the unique quality of such a soul. You've never had another like it."

"Wait, wait," said Satan, waving his hand. "We could do this all day. Ultimately, it's up to me to decide."

I couldn't stand it. *Someone make a choice!*

Suddenly Erasmus reached down and clasped me to him. He was my choice. I chose him. "I love you," I said urgently. "Why did you have to do this?"

"Because I love *you*, you silly human."

"You're human now too."

"Yes, and I've detested every moment of it."

I hugged him, pressing my face against his shoulder, getting tears all over his shirt. "It really doesn't suit you."

"No, it doesn't." He hugged me back, brushing my hair away from my face. I must have looked a fright; face and hair dirty, with bits of creature stuck to the strands. But he'd never looked more handsome, more appealing…except when he was a demon. And darn it, he smelled all wrong. None of the smoke was there anymore. Humanity really didn't suit him…

A thought shot through me, like electricity sparking every synapse, every nerve ending. Humanity didn't suit him *at all*. It was all wrong. He needed to be a demon again, but not just now. Only at the exact right time.

"I've thought it over," I said abruptly, pushing Erasmus away and facing Satan again. "And I think, all and all…you should take Erasmus' soul."

Erasmus shot a look at me. "*What?*"

"As long as you promise to first destroy the Booke. I mean, that's the deal…or there's…there's *no* deal."

Satan curled his hand under his chin, resting his elbow on his knee. "You know, technically, I don't have to give you anything in return. Because you're the ones who walked into *my* lair."

"I know," I said, giving Erasmus a determined look. He was staring back at me with astonishment. "But…it's got to be one of the most interesting things to have happened to you in a long time."

"Oh, a very, *very* long time." Satan cocked his head, measuring me. "So after all that professed love, you think it best to sacrifice your lover?"

"It's not *that*…" I gazed back at Erasmus, trying to let him know with only my eyes that it wasn't that at all. "It's just…I mean I'm never getting out of here, am I? The Netherworld is too dangerous for a human, and with the Booke destroyed—as it should be—I can't get out. And he's gone to the trouble to become human for me. It's the last gift I can give him."

"Well, that is certainly very true. Demons are not, as a class, brave, you see. Or selfless. I'm certain it will be a tale told for thousands of years."

"Exactly. I can't take that away from him. It's…the noble thing to do."

Erasmus was still looking at me as if I'd lost my mind, eyes flicking toward Satan and then back to me. I squeezed his hand again in reassurance but really, I wasn't sure either.

"But…it only makes sense," I said, "if you destroy the Booke first. Otherwise, it will just look like an afterthought."

"You think so?" said Satan.

"I mean, I don't know the Netherworld, but I've met a few of its denizens and…well…"

"Yes, I know. Not the brightest demons in the ether." His eye slid toward the demon with the feathered wings, trying to look like the wall. "Sometimes it's a bit disappointing. That's why they travel to other worlds, like yours, so often. They don't know how to…care."

"You could change it, of course. This would be a great story to tell to encourage them."

"Hmm. Perhaps. But then I'd have to be *inclined* to change it and, well…I'm not."

I stepped forward. "But will you? Will you destroy the Booke?"

"You drive a hard bargain, human. Well, let me see the thing."

The Booke had been hiding from me *and* Satan, but I called to it. It argued with me, but ultimately came floating forward from the shadows, trembling a bit. I grabbed it out of the air. *This is it*, I thought, looking over the worn leather cover, the tarnished brass at the corners, the strange lock that didn't need a key. I held it once to my chest—because I was feeling what the Booke was feeling and didn't want to surrender it. But all I had to do was look over at Erasmus—who was still staring at me with hurt bewilderment—and I was done.

I walked it over to Satan and stood at the rocky edge of his pit. Holding the Booke one last time, I offered it to him. He was so large that he took that big Booke with two fingers and looked it over.

I scrambled back to my place beside Erasmus. I knew I had to stay close. While Satan was busy examining the Booke, looking like someone studying a miniature from a dollhouse, I quickly kissed Erasmus' cheek. I hoped I was right. It was a chance. If I wasn't right and had made the ultimate mistake, I wouldn't be alive long enough to worry about it.

"This little thing," said Satan, tutting to himself. "It means nothing to me. But I have enjoyed how the Powers That Be have squirmed over it, pretending that they *had* any power. They lorded it over you, didn't they little Erasmus? Of course, they created you and so have *some* power, but not much. Only enough to keep track of this thing. But you say, little human, that it has caused chaos. That *is* the purpose of demons. It is our joy. Except the two of you have found a different joy. Ordinarily, I wouldn't like that. I don't like my demons going off on their own."

"But my world isn't your world…"

It was a mistake. I knew it the moment I said it. His eyes narrowed. "No, little human, it isn't. But it is my joy in creating havoc wherever I wish, on whatever *world* I wish."

"I apologize," I said, lowering my face. "I didn't mean to imply that you couldn't do whatever you want. You could—"

Erasmus urgently hissed, "Stop talking!"

I did. I shut my lips tight and I clutched his hand.

Satan eyed the two of us, then his gaze traveled up over the walls to the creatures above. I hadn't really noticed them much, but now I followed his gaze. They looked like gargoyles but alive. There were hundreds and hundreds of them. If he quirked a brow, they'd be on us. We couldn't hope to run fast enough.

"I think of them as my children," he said, sensing my sudden terror. "They consider themselves my guardians. But I don't need guardians. Do I, Erasmus?"

He bowed. "No, my lord."

"No. I have them here because it pleases me to do so. I do what I like when it pleases me. And…it pleases me now to agree to your bargain."

I swallowed my sob of relief. Tears flowed down my dirty cheeks. "Thank you, thank you."

He looked at the Booke, still trapped between his fingers.

The Booke was in a panic. It had never been in this state before and it sent out waves and waves of terror. Back home, it was probably releasing more monsters than it ever had before. And I was torn between dread that I had left my friends in danger of the Booke, and dread because I felt what the Booke felt and I wanted to help it, too.

Satan stared hard at it. "You are nothing," he said to it, breath like smoke.

Suddenly, a bright light burst forth from the Booke. Satan didn't seem bothered, didn't squint, merely looked at it curiously. I, however, *couldn't* look at it and was suddenly gripped by the searing pain and torment that the Booke experienced. I fell to my knees, gasping. That light shot beams as far as the eye could see, maybe as far as to my own world. The monsters and creatures that had used the Booke as a gateway screamed in one long wail in my head. I felt as if *I* were being ripped apart and I writhed on the ground, clutching my head, holding the bone and blood together with my hands and will alone. Vaguely, I sensed that Erasmus knelt over me, cradling me, but I could feel nothing but the Booke's agony as it slowly died.

Some pages suddenly flew out of it, soaring in all directions. The cavern rumbled, but it might only have been in my head and my twisting body. The roar of thousands of years and hundreds of Chosen Hosts swelled in my brain. And I screamed and screamed *with* them as their shadows passed over my eyes, hundreds of them, thousands, along with dark wings, curled claws, sharp teeth, black scales—all roiling in a mass like a fevered tornado, swirling skyward. The Booke flung open, the rest of its pages flipping madly and it screamed for itself with its own voice—so old a voice—until it all died away in a long, lingering echo, until even that was gone and the echoes faded to nothing.

More than nothing. Absence of nothing.

Satan let the book slip from between his fingers with only a raised brow. It slammed to the ground with a whoosh of dust, a hollow, empty shell.

The pain was gone. The screaming and roaring in my head were gone. Slowly, I rose. I felt nauseated, empty, and pretty wobbly. I swallowed down the taste of bile and gingerly shuffled toward the book, barely believing this was happening. Falling to my knees, I reached out and touched it. Nothing. I felt nothing. I used the tip of my finger to lift the cover, but it was just a leather cover and blank pages of parchment. And in my head, it was no longer a capital B-o-o-k-e…but a plain and ordinary *book*.

"You did it," I whispered hoarsely, my own throat torn from screaming. "You did it."

"Of course I did. It was nothing to me."

I looked up at him, so huge in his pit of flames. I swallowed. My throat felt like it was on fire. My body felt the residual pain of having something ripped away. As if the book had had a soul that had inhabited me and had been pulled out like a dagger ripping through my flesh. So vivid was this image that I put a hand to my chest, surprised to find no hole there.

I felt lost. Alone. I hadn't realized how much a part of me the book had become. I ran a hand over my ruined face, wet with tears and fear. I swallowed again and looked back at Erasmus. He was looking at me with terror. All he had ever known was the Booke of the Hidden, and it was now gone. How must *he* have felt?

I staggered toward him and he caught me in his arms. He held me fast but he was trembling. When he looked at me, he seemed as lost as I was.

"We must finish the bargain," said Satan, his mouth curling into a demon's smile, too wide with too many teeth.

I clutched desperately at Erasmus. Had I figured it wrong? Was I making a mistake? If I was wrong, then I'd lose him for good.

We locked gazes and he looked at me with such tenderness that it wrenched a sob from me. He leaned forward and kissed me gently. "Don't weep for me," he said, his own eyes glossy.

His hand gently moved my hair from my face and gazed at me with his human eyes. "Remember that I loved you. Remember that I still do." He bent to kiss me again and I returned the kiss desperately.

"I love you," I whispered, and he smiled. But then he suddenly stiffened and threw back his head, mouth opening in a silent scream.

I gripped him and looked back at Satan. "No!" I cried. I almost told him to take me instead. How I wanted to! But if this were to work, *if* it were, I *had* to keep my head. I held Erasmus tight and kept my gaze on him. He was in agony. Maybe I had only felt a small portion of what it would be like to have my soul ripped out when the book left me, because this looked far worse. I tried not to think about how many souls *he* had eaten and that he had once planned—like he had for every other Chosen Host—to take mine. Instead, I clutched at him, looking into his eyes. Would I be able to tell from his eyes? I couldn't be too soon, but God help me, I couldn't be too late either.

Carefully, I reached into my pocket. My fingers closed on the amulet that had belonged to Erasmus. It was cold where it was supposed to be warm, the eyes dead where they were supposed to glitter with the shine of gemstones. I grasped it in my hand and waited.

His eyes, so wide open, were almost the same as they were before, but softer, more human. But the light in them was fading. *Just a little longer*, I told myself, terrified I'd get it wrong. *Just a little bit longer*. He was weakening. His soul was leaving, almost all of it. His eyes…his eyes were becoming as dead as the amulet's eyes.

I couldn't stand to wait a moment more. I reached up and slammed the amulet to his neck. Immediately it glowed with life. "I release you!" I cried. I didn't even know if I needed to say the words, but it couldn't hurt.

The broken chain snaked around his neck on its own and mended, fastening tight. And the amulet's eyes! The eyes glowed bright and hot with the demon light, as if a switch had been turned on. I watched as Erasmus' face, so dull and ashen before, warmed not with human life, but with demon life. His skin was no longer pale, but tanned and firmed with a light touch of sun. His soft angular features sharpened again. His hair seemed suddenly more luxurious. And when he looked at me with those dark and bright demon eyes I knew he no longer doubted me. He understood what I had done. He knew that I had waited for Satan to take his human soul, as much of it as he could, and when it was mostly gone, to give him back his amulet—a part of his demon essence—to restore him back to his immortal state. I'd had to choose carefully. I couldn't risk that it would be too late and he would be dead, but I also couldn't choose too early because too much of his soul would remain.

He was mine again, and with a glisten of love in his eyes, I could tell that he forgave me because he knew exactly what I had done.

But so did Satan. And he wasn't happy.

CHAPTER TWENTY-SIX

"AREN'T YOU THE clever little human?" said Satan, politeness dripping from his words. He gritted his pointy teeth and his eye twitched. "Aren't you so amazingly clever?"

"You got your soul fair and square," I said, pushing Erasmus behind me, as if that would do any good.

"Did I? Did I get it 'fair and square'? Did I get every last drop of it?"

"I…I'm sorry. I wasn't sure it would work. I tried to give you enough."

Erasmus grabbed my arm. "What do you mean you weren't sure it was going to work?"

"I only guessed. I didn't know giving you back your amulet would do it. I only just thought of it."

"Beelze's tail! You were betting with my life!"

"Well…yes. You were going to sacrifice yourself anyway. And it worked!"

"If the two of you are done?" said Satan, his voice growing louder and tighter.

"Oh." I lowered my face, keeping hold of Erasmus' hand, which was hot now like it was supposed to be. "I'm sorry. But…the deal is done. You destroyed the book—thank you for that—and in return you got a soul. Most of a soul." I tried to smile.

"I tell you what I'll do," said the demon of demons. "Pick *that* up…" He gestured toward the now dead book. "It was intriguing, the whole thing. Your strange little love story. This quaint book. And for that reason alone, I'll be generous…and give you a head start…of five minutes."

"H-head start? What—"

Erasmus tugged on my hand. "He means run."

"Run? Oh shit."

I lurched forward, grabbed the book, and let Erasmus pull me up the path. When I looked back—why did I look back?—the gargoyles were fluttering down from their ledges. They were slowly trailing after us. Hundreds and hundreds of them. I clutched the book under one arm.

I hadn't quite thought that through. What had I expected? You trick the demon of demons and he's gonna be pissed. If we could just get out of the Netherworld…

"Focalor!" cried Erasmus, running past the weird lizard-faced demon trying to be the wall. He peeled himself away and ran with us.

When we got to the cavern entrance, Shabiri spun and stared, taking in Focalor and then Erasmus. "I'll be damned," she muttered. "You did it. You stupid, frail, little human. You did it."

"What is *she* doing here?" Erasmus growled.

"She helped me get here. She protected me, helped me find my way."

He stared at me with amazement as we ran and looked back at Shabiri running with us. "Why would you do that?" he said to her.

She shrugged as she ran. "She convinced Dougie to give back my amulet. I see you got yours back."

He reached for it with his other hand and then turned toward me. "You're a marvel, do you know that?"

"And…I'm…running…out of steam." I had already traveled

for days in the Netherworld on nothing but fear, adrenalin, and a little water, and it was catching up to me.

Before I knew what was happening, Erasmus swept me up in his arms and doubled his running speed. Focalor, the winged guy, zoomed passed us, scouting ahead. "The way is clear so far, Erasmus. But Satan is still angered. He will send his minions."

"I don't doubt it."

"We'll face whatever he's got," I said with more bravado than I felt.

Focalor looked back at me with admiration. "Oh, Erasmus! This is going to be a *great* tale! I'll be very popular."

"If we get out of it alive," I said.

Focalor looked at me with confusion. "It doesn't matter to the story whether you are alive or not. Farewell, Erasmus! I hope you live. But if you don't, I enjoyed this. Part of it, anyway."

"Wait!" I said. "Is he just flying off? Isn't he going to help us?"

Erasmus watched Focalor wing away but he didn't seem concerned. "He fulfilled our agreement. He owes us nothing more."

"Demons." I shook my head. "You guys are the damnedest."

"Aren't we just?" said Shabiri. "But it might behoove us to change shape. We'd move faster. I suggest something like a dragon raptor."

Without missing a step, Erasmus grew and stretched, all the while holding on to me. His jacket became wings. He looked more like a stingray than a flying beast, but he managed to fly just fine.

"That's a really neat trick," I mumbled, crossing my arms over his neck, pressing the book between us, and nuzzling into him. I hoped we could get out of this too, but for now, I had him back and my heart was full.

He shook his head slowly. "You had no idea it would work," he said.

"I didn't. But I hoped."

His voice roughened when he said, "You came for me."

"Of course, I did."

He was still smiling when he looked down at me. "Without a plan. You are the most remarkable human I have ever encountered."

"And the only one you'll ever be in love with, mister."

"I can't imagine loving another."

Shabiri flew next to us, sneering and rolling her eyes.

"Hey, wait a minute," I said, watching her elongated shoulder wings flap. "If you could have done this before, why did you make me walk all that way?"

She put a hand to her ear as if she couldn't hear me. "What's that, darling? It's very windy up here." Then she rolled over onto her back like a swimmer doing laps in a pool. She looked behind us. "Here they come. That was a fast five minutes."

I glanced over Erasmus' shoulder and saw that the greenish sky was speckled with little flying creatures, like a huge flock of birds. "The gargoyles."

"And they are pissed," she said. She seemed to be enjoying this. Maybe she was as delirious as I was that Erasmus was alive and a demon again. As long as she stayed with us to help, I didn't care. And I had a feeling she would.

"Can we outfly them?" I asked.

Shabiri squinted at them. "I don't think so. They're catching up fast."

"Did you encounter any trouble journeying through the Netherworld?" he asked.

"Jeesh, nothing *but* trouble."

He shook his head. "How one human can find so much misfortune…"

"I figured they smelled a human and came running, looking for a snack."

He sighed as his coat flapped. "I'm sorry for that. I'm afraid they must have smelled me first. When I was human."

"Did you like being human? Even a little?"

"No. It was dreadful. Aches and pains I never knew before. And that evacuating of fluids. It was disturbing."

"Can we cut the chit-chat," said Shabiri, back to her old snarky self, "and come up with some strategy? It's not as if the two of us can fight a legion of gargoyles on our own."

"I can help," I said. But actually, I was pretty exhausted. I was doing everything I could just to hold on to Erasmus.

"Like I said," she said with a sneer. "There's only two of us."

I stuck my tongue out at her. She wasn't fooling me.

"What do you suggest?" Erasmus' deep voice rumbled over my body. I was in heaven in his arms, listening to his voice again. I gave a girlish sigh.

"Splitting up won't help, they'll just go after you," she said. "Are there any canyons around here where we might be able to lose them?"

He stiffened and then changed directions, almost going back toward them. "I know of one place."

"What are you doing?" Shabiri complained. She made a scoffing noise and turned to follow. I couldn't tell exactly where we were, up above it all, but I had a vague sense of where we might have been. Down that way was the lake of fire. But now below was that sludgy river. And that was…yes, that was the marble bridge and that way was… I looked up at his face, as much of it as I could see while he was concentrating on flying. *Oh, Erasmus, you silly demon.*

And he *was* a demon again, with all the vengeance and pettiness I'd come to know and love.

We swooped down toward the narrow, obsidian passage where the Powers That Be lived and circled until we reached that open area with the black stone altar. We descended, Shabiri still shouting at him. "I'm not going down there!" Her voice echoed off the walls. She didn't land and stayed aloft, circling like some great manta ray/condor mash-up.

Erasmus set me gently down and I clutched the book to my chest. "You probably shouldn't do this," I said.

"Like hell I shouldn't." He stood before the altar, hands on his hips. "Show yourselves!"

A green flame jumped from the altar, hovering just above it. "Erasmus Dark," hissed the chorus of voices. "We see you are a demon again."

"But I'm not *your* demon. And I'm making that clear now. The book is dead."

"We created you. You will always be ours."

"I am tied to nothing. You cannot master me again. I am no one's slave."

The flame flickered but said nothing.

"I am…grateful to my creators for making me. But I am done with you and your altar."

"You are our creation. This will always be so."

"No. I am done with you. I declare it to the seven winds!"

And, strangely, winds began howling from several directions. I stepped behind him.

"I renounce you!" cried Erasmus. "What you have failed to do, Satan has accomplished. The book is dead."

"The Chosen Host stands behind you," they said.

"She is Chosen Host no more. She has survived the book. The first and the last to endure it. As I have."

"Erasmus!" called Shabiri from above. "They're almost here!"

A smile stole across his face. "You can command me no more. Show yourselves. I would look into the faces of those who had imprisoned me all these centuries."

The flame burst higher. "We do not need to show ourselves to you. You were our slave. Now you are nothing."

"Show yourselves, damn you! You've threatened me all my life and now I come to learn that your threats were useless, only breath in the wind."

The flame grew higher and wider. "We have might you know not of, Erasmus Dark, we who gave you that name."

"Then show yourselves. For if you do not, I will spread it far and wide that the Powers That Be are nothing but wind. They are weak and none should fear them."

A whirlwind swept through the enclosed space and voices

rode on that wind. Finally, three figures appeared as walking flames. And they were raising their "hands" in a threatening manner.

Erasmus grabbed my arm and ducked with me to the ground as a bolt of power shot from one of them and exploded on the obsidian walls behind us.

"We have more power than you can ever imagine!" cried the angry chorus.

Erasmus looked up to the sky. The corner of his mouth drew up in a smiling sneer. "Yes, my lords. I see that you do."

Suddenly, the sky above us darkened as a swarm of gargoyles blotted out the light. The flaming figures looked up. With his hand still closed over my upper arm, Erasmus sped us down the rock corridor in a streak of speed, just as the gargoyles flooded the open chamber. Power blasted in deep booms behind us, and the shrieks and cries of gargoyles disintegrating in splatters on the walls were filling the chamber, but we were already far from there. He scooped me up and, while running, he changed again into the flying manta ray and shot up into the sky.

When I looked back, a black funnel of gargoyles mindlessly followed the ones in front to their doom in the halls of the Powers That Be.

I glanced up at Erasmus, who was looking mighty proud of himself. "You planned that."

"I…only had a notion it might work."

I smiled back. "You stole that idea from me."

His gaze steadied on the distant horizon. "Maybe I did… maybe I didn't."

We soared onward.

* * *

I COULDN'T BELIEVE I could fall asleep in a demon's arms while he was transformed into a kite and flying. But I did.

I awoke with a start just as he lighted down. "It's a relief to

have the strength of a demon again," he said. "Being a human…
well. I know now how weak and frail you are."

I slammed him in the shoulder with the book. "Weak and
frail, huh?"

"Well," he said, rubbing his shoulder, "maybe not you."

"Where are we?"

Shabiri landed in front of me. "We are as far as we can go by
flying. We'll have to make it the rest of the way on foot."

"Why?"

She looked at me as if I were the stupidest creature alive.
"Because it's too dangerous."

"Why?"

"Because there are flying creatures much bigger than we are."

I was about to open my mouth when she interrupted. "So
help me if you ask 'why' again, I will feed you to the next beast
to come along."

"I wasn't going to ask why," I muttered. "I was just going to
ask if there was anything to eat. I'm starving."

Shabiri gave Erasmus a confidential look. "*She's* starving."

I pressed a hand over my mouth. "Oh my God, Erasmus, are
you still hungry? For…you know."

He opened his shirt and looked down. The tattoo was there.
He was looking at it as if he hadn't expected it. "It's back," he
said.

"You mean it was gone?"

He smiled apologetically. "As a human, yes. It was gone."

"And…you still want to eat souls?"

"Yes. But not Chosen Host souls, because there aren't any
more of them." He smiled.

It didn't make me feel any better.

"So how far is the place we need to exit? Wait. The book got
me through before." I hefted it. Somehow it felt lighter. "But it
can't now."

Erasmus took it from my hands and ran his hand over the
spine, then over the cover, fingers grazing the worn leather in a

caress. This had been his whole life. I laid my hand on his arm. "Are you all right?"

He looked at me, puzzled. "Yes. Why wouldn't I be?"

"Well…this." I gestured toward the book.

"Is a prisoner ever sorry when his prison is destroyed? No. I merely wished to examine it. Ah. It is as I thought." He handed it back to me. "While it is true it is no longer a gateway, it is still…a key."

"And I can open a lock with it? Oh, thank goodness. I thought I'd be stuck here."

"No. We are returning to the place—I presume—you went through; where the ley lines crossed. The place I showed you. The place that Shabiri likely brought you through."

Shabiri looked to be busy scouting around, and I sidled up to Erasmus and said quietly, "You should be nice to her, you know."

He scowled. "Why?"

"Because she helped me and she didn't have to."

"You convinced Doug to return her amulet."

"Believe me, he was ready to hand it over. No, she…she did something nice and not for anything back. You should…maybe you should thank her."

"That's absurd. I will not!"

"Come on, Erasmus."

"Honeymoon over already?" said Shabiri, glaring at us with arms folded.

"Just a little…disagreement," I said, giving Erasmus a sharp look.

God, he was such a child. He screwed up his face in a scowl and he would have stomped his foot if he'd thought of it. "Shabiri…" he began.

"Yes, darling?"

"Shabiri…" And then his face softened. Maybe he finally realized what her help had meant. "Shabiri…I want to thank you for helping Kylie. It was a dangerous enterprise, and I know she couldn't have done it without you. It was…very brave."

Shabiri stood visibly taller. "Oh. Well…I guess you're welcome. It was a fairly selfless act." She preened, picking nonexistent lint from her leather catsuit. "Just like yours. It's strange… isn't it? That we two should…should be so…selfless."

"Yes. It is strange. Maybe…maybe Moody Bog has some special quality to it. Perhaps you and I…aren't so different."

Boy, he struggled getting that last bit out, but I was proud of him, and behind Shabiri's back, I blew him a kiss. He seemed to redden and turn his head.

"Yes, Shabiri. I'd like to add my thanks to you," I said. "I really *couldn't* have done it without you."

Now she was fluffing her hair. "All this praise can turn a girl's head."

"Can it turn it into food?" I asked desperately. "I'm really hungry."

* * *

SINCE ERASMUS HAD no idea about food, Shabiri conjured me a cheese sandwich. It was the best thing I had ever eaten. When I'd wolfed it down, I wiped my hands on my trousers. "How far now?"

"Not far," said Erasmus, coming up beside me. "I'm having trouble believing what happened."

"Me, too, I guess. Looking back, it seemed a little too easy."

"Too easy?" said Shabiri with a hysterical note to her voice. "We were chased by dragon raptors, shadow imps, and gargoyles. What about this has been easy?"

"When you put it like that…"

Erasmus turned quickly toward me. "Are you all right?"

"I'm fine." I grasped his hand and walked with him. "I'm fine now."

He looked down at my hand in his. "This…was entirely unexpected. You. These emotions. This whole journey."

"Good grief," said Shabiri, making a face.

"You know," I said to her, "if you keep doing that, your face will get stuck that way."

"What?" She grabbed her face and felt around her cheeks and nose, before she dropped her hands away and sneered at me. "Oh, ha, ha."

Erasmus chuckled. "You shouldn't tease her."

I laughed. "Look who's talking. I recall the two of you having the cat fight of all cat fights."

"Well…" He glanced over at Shabiri and she fluffed her hair again. "I suppose I don't have any more ill will toward you, Shabiri. In fact, I might owe you."

"What's that, darling? You *owe* me?"

"Hey, you two. Wasn't it enough that we made it out okay with all our parts and pieces? No one owes anyone…*right*, Shabiri?"

She licked her lips and looked directly at me. "I seem to recall that *you* offered me something…of my choosing."

Erasmus' eyes darkened. "I thought you said she came with you without any payment."

"I might have forgotten about that bit. It's been a trying few days."

"What did you offer her?"

"I didn't have anything, so I told her to…choose… something…"

"Beelze's tail! Don't you know better than to grant a demon such an offer?"

"I thought I was going to be dead."

"She thought she was going to be dead," said Shabiri, *unhelpfully*.

Erasmus was about to open his mouth with a rejoinder… when he stopped and sniffed the air. He looked back and scowled. "You might yet get your wish," he said, walking faster. "Satan is not done with us. We're being followed."

CHAPTER TWENTY-SEVEN

SHIFTED AND DRESSED, Jeff drove the coven back up to the tea shop but skidded to a stop a few yards away. Sheriff Ed looked like he still had his hands full. They could hear a lot of yelling and other sounds of people spoiling for a fight. Seemed like they wanted a good old-fashioned witch burning for their Halloween.

Jeff's claws grew and he could feel his nose becoming a snout, but he left it at that and stalked forward.

"For the last time, she is *not* responsible for this," Sheriff Ed was saying, for probably the umpteenth time. "Now Ted, you take your group away from here or I am going to have to start arresting people. And I'm gonna start with you."

"You can't shoot all of us, Sheriff. And there's far more of us than of you and the deputy. Now we mean to burn this witch out and there aren't any god-fearing folk in this parish that'll argue against it."

"What about Reverend Howard?" said Ed. "He doesn't approve of any of this."

"That witch in there has turned our Christian townsfolk into more of her kind. I seen them out there doing their witchcraft—"

"Dammit, Ted! You know darned well they've been fighting all the things that are going on out there. And Kylie is no witch!"

"Is there some trouble here, sheriff?" said Jeff, flexing his claws.

The mob gasped.

"He's a monster!" cried one of them, pointing.

"I've just got a little bit of a werewolf problem, but it's under control. Except when my friends are threatened."

There was a glint of metal as someone in the crowd raised a rifle, aiming at Jeff. He wasn't *too* worried. He didn't figure that they'd had the time or inclination to fashion silver bullets, but he worried they'd miss and hit his friends. He postured forward.

Deputy George was faster. He had his gun out and was aiming it two-handed. "You'd better be stowing that rifle, Ron. I freaking mean it."

Nick was partially wolfed next to Jeff.

"He's a monster, too!" shouted someone else.

"I'm ready to defend my pack," he snarled.

"Everyone!" cried Doc, running forward in a stiff gait. "Just calm down."

"We're tired of listening to your lies, old man," said another with a Budweiser knit cap drawn down to his bushy eyebrows. "You're the one who ignored your Christian upbringing. You're the one denying Jesus."

"I deny no such thing. Honestly, Chuck. Have I ever harmed you or anyone in this town? Didn't I fix your broken arm last spring when you fell on the ice? And didn't I sew up your little Chrissy's eyebrow when she fell out of her highchair?" he said pointing to one of the few women there. "I see you back there, Leona. You going to overlook all the good I did for you and hundreds of others in this town? I've been a declared Wiccan for ten years, and that never stopped you from calling me in the dead of night when you had a sick baby or your kid got a burr in his foot. Now if you follow the good book like you profess, aren't you supposed to love your neighbor and welcome the alien among you? Kylie was a stranger here and she never deserved this treatment from any of you. She's put herself in danger and now she's in the worst possible peril. You should be saying prayers for her, not fixing to burn down her place."

Doug burst through the door, flamethrower on his back.

"Well, looky here. The gentle folk of Moody Bog have come to call. I hear you want to burn a witch. Well? Come on, boys. I'm a witch!" He flicked on the flamethrower and tossed a short jet of fire into the air. "Me and all my friends here," he began, gesturing toward Charise and Bob, who were armed with a fireplace poker and a bat respectively. "We're *all* witches. And I'm here to fight fire with fire. So you either get the hell off this land now or I'll start toasting you marshmallows." He shot off another flame, edging it closer toward the wary crowd.

That was enough for most of them. They backed away, yelling taunts.

Charise ran forward with her poker and twirled it over her head, giving out a feral call. Men stumbled to back away from her.

But before any of the people could get to their cars, the street burst with light. Suddenly the entire area was crawling with strange beasts, dragon-looking creatures like the lindworm, gauze-shrouded phantoms, things that looked like Orcs that carried war hammers and axes, tiny biting black creatures with long tails, monsters that looked like a combination of all the deadly animals fused into one, and even some with two heads.

"It's Halloween," said Jolene. "It's the book!"

It looked to Jeff like a Scooby-Doo episode gone crazy. Everywhere he looked, monsters were running after humans. And then some of them turned toward the coven.

"Get inside!" yelled Doc.

Jeff and the others ran for the tea shop. Once everyone was inside, Jeff grabbed the coat tree and braced it against the door. "Now what do we do?"

Seraphina looked wildly around. "Get as many jars as we can find."

Nick got the message and began gathering everything they hadn't already given away.

"But I think we have to attempt to kill them," said Ruth, "or they won't go toward the jars."

"And who's going to be crazy enough to go out there?" said Jolene.

Ruth laid a hand on the hilt of her sword. "I guess that means I'm up."

Doug lifted the nozzle of his flamethrower. "And me."

Sheriff Ed stepped forward, slipped off his gun belt, and held it forward. "Is there any way for you to enchant my bullets, my gun, and this magazine? I mean, even if I can't kill them, I can at least injure them enough to make them get into those jars."

Seraphina took the belt but obviously hadn't anticipated how heavy it was. She nearly dropped it. "Barring that these might be silver bullets…"

"They're not exactly standard issue."

"Then I think we can come up with a quick enchantment. Help me, Nick."

"George, give me yours," he said. George reluctantly handed over his belt, just as something slammed against the front door.

Everyone froze, looking to see if the wards held.

"Hurry up!" said Jeff, his back propped against the door.

Seraphina and Nick huddled over the guns and started to chant. They tossed salt over them and as they finished, the gun belts each glowed for a moment.

Seraphina handed Ed back his belt. "It will do some damage now."

"Thanks," he said with a grim expression.

George didn't seem happy about the whole exercise. The religious type. But he belted up, and the two of them readied to go out the door, along with Ruth and Doug.

"Have you got the crossbow?" Jeff said to anyone.

"Got it right here," said Doc.

"Good. Because as soon as I open this door, some of them are gonna want to come in. Aim for them, not for me."

"You got it, Jeff."

"Okay, on the count of three. One…two…three!" Jeff yanked open the door and the four rushed out. He slammed it shut. Nothing had tried to worm its way in.

As soon as Jeff looked through the window, he saw the problem. The monsters were scattering, heading toward unprotected dwellings, no doubt. Soon the coven wouldn't be able to find them before they struck.

Jeff was getting the feeling he should go out there too, because it had occurred to him that the patrols hadn't returned to base. "Nick, what are your patrols saying?"

"They were returning here when the monsters came out. I've been getting texts from everyone." He scanned his phone. "They're taking shelter wherever they can. But nothing is coming into the jars."

"Because they have to be wounded. Maybe we should go out there."

"I'm game. Doc?"

"You boys may have to. I'd hate to think that our patrols are getting into a fix."

Jeff was already pulling his shirt up over his head. "Okay. Nick, you take the east forest, I'll take the west."

They each left a pile of clothes as they shifted. Jolene ran to the door to man it. "Okay? Be careful, boys." She pulled it open and they both leapt out.

Blond wolf Jeff sprinted around behind Kylie's shop and dove into the woods. He didn't have to look to see where Nick went. The only thing he couldn't do was bring a jar, but if he could save the patrols, that was all that was needed.

He speared through the trees, keeping his nose up and smelling for any people or beasts. Something weird was ahead. He could definitely smell something dark. He headed in that direction until the sharp scent of people and fear touched his senses. He sped up, leaping over logs and boulders. When he got to a clearing, there were people up in the pine trees, barely holding on.

The creature was something straight out of Dungeons and Dragons. Stoop-shouldered, it was big, like a goblin, with a heavy spiked club over its shoulder. It was naked from the waist up with gnarled muscles and an animal pelt as a breechclout hanging from a wide, studded belt. Its jaw was heavy and tusked.

Jeff stood above it on a rock and assessed. If he could get it away from the patrol long enough and maybe wound it in some way, then—if they weren't too scared out of their minds, that is—they could still trap it in the jar. *Here goes.*

He lifted his head and howled. The sound rose above the treetops and rolled along the hillsides.

The hobgoblin turned and grunted, sniffing the air. Was wolf tastier than human? Nope, didn't look like it, because he turned back toward the people screaming in the tree.

The hobgoblin swung back and slammed his club against the pine. It shivered and one of the patrol members slipped off their branch, hanging now by their hands. He wasn't going to last long.

Jeff leapt. He landed just short of the hobgoblin's enormous shoulders, scratching down his back with his claws, and clamping down on the back of his arm.

The hobgoblin roared, shaking his arm to loosen Jeff, but Jeff bit down hard and wouldn't let go—even though it tasted awful.

Jeff tugged back using his strong shoulder muscles, but the hobgoblin was a big fellow. It was getting more annoyed than injured and kicked out at Jeff with his pelt covered foot.

With a whine, Jeff flew backward. *Damn, that hurts!* No time to lick wounds now. He shook out his head and drew forward, stalking low. He had to go for the neck. But if he couldn't do that, he'd have to tear out a hamstring. If he got the neck, he'd have to maneuver around to the front of the beast, but that could prove dangerous, especially with that club he was slamming into the tree again. That guy was hanging pretty precariously from that branch. Another good whack and he would be dinner.

Hamstring it is, he decided. When the hobgoblin lunged next, Jeff shot forward, opening his jaws on the back of the thigh.

Instead of just clamping on, he shook his head, trying to rip as much of it as he could. The hobgoblin started to spin in a circle, swinging his club back, but Jeff ripped with jaw and claws, leaving a black, bloody mess in his blond fur and on his face.

The hobbled hobgoblin went after him. Jeff growled and sneered, taunting the monster to come on. Grunting with pain and lifting his club, the creature limped toward him. Jeff backed away, growling all the while. He flicked his gaze toward the guy in the tree and he dropped down softly on the pile of pine needles. He motioned to the other one who tossed the ginger jar down to him.

The man opened the jar and yelled, "*Ego te capere!*"

Suddenly, the hobgoblin started to stretch. He glared down at himself in puzzlement but was compelled to slide toward the jar. He spun like a whirlwind, shot forward in a streak of color, and slipped into the jar's opening. The man slapped the lid on and laughed in relief.

"Is that…Jeff?" he said uncertainly, looking at the blond werewolf.

Jeff raised a paw and bounded further into the forest.

But after a while, he couldn't seem to smell anything except that hobgoblin muck covering his jaws, and he was damned if he was going to lick it off. He began searching for a stream and trotted down to where the shorter birches and cottonwoods grew. He padded over the stony shore of a stream-fed pond, and stepped into the icy water until it was deep enough—up to his chest—to dunk his head. He shoved it into the water, the cold taking his breath away, and was grateful that it seemed to be washing away the smell of the demon blood.

He pulled his head out and shook it. One more dunk should do it, he decided, and dunked again. Swishing his head in the water, he looked up…into the face of something that looked like a giant potato bug.

He sputtered and jumped back, fur dripping. Something emerged from the pond, slowly standing up. It had a wide, raw-looking head with no hair but a lot of teeth in its wide mouth. It seemed to have fins on the backs of its arms and legs. So, not from around here. More like from the book. Jeff shook out his fur and backed away, snarling.

It started to wade through the pond to the shore. There was no one with a jar around, but if he could wound it enough that it couldn't get away, he could always bring someone back to clap it up.

He stalked along the edge of the shore, head low between his shoulder blades, eyes glued to the creature. *What the hell are you?* he wondered. *If Jolene were here, she'd know.*

The beast was on the shore, its flipper feet flapping wetly on the stones. It seemed to gather itself for a moment, curling and uncurling its webbed hands, when suddenly it burst forward. Jeff ran to meet it, snarling and growling.

His jaws closed over something that smelled and tasted like day old fish. Clamping his jaws, he bit down and shook his head. He had managed to grab its neck at the shoulder. Not ideal but it still could be a mortal blow. He did his best to rip the flesh and bite down for more. In the back of his mind, he knew that if he were a werewolf without his wolfsbane, this could have been a person. With a silent shudder, he pulled out more flesh, covering his muzzle again with fishy black blood.

When it stopped moving, he drew back, sniffing, checking for vitals. It lay groaning, and parts of it were bursting into light, but he knew it would never disappear completely without Kylie writing in her book.

He left it there, washed off his face again, and trotted onward, lifting his nose to the breeze and hoping to catch the scent of more monsters.

* * *

FOR HOURS HE tracked creatures, brought them down or chased them away from the patrol. When he stopped to catch his breath, he stood on a promontory and looked out over the woods. The trees broke away in the distance, opening to a view of the dark Atlantic.

He hoped Nick was doing as well as he was. He felt that if the other wolf was in trouble, he'd know it, being connected and all.

His sharp eyes took in the details of the forest. He spotted the glowing life forces of squirrels, birds, raccoons, and all the forest creatures wherever they were. He also saw the other dimly glowing life forces of the old creatures of the earth. Older than man, who seemed to dwell in the wild places, never letting humans know they were there. He shivered at the thought of them, not liking the look of their auras at all, even though they seemed mostly benign.

He caught a strange scent on the wind and turned toward it, lifting his head to fill his nostrils with the atoms of odor. *Monster.* He hurried down from his perch and galloped through the birch stands, over logs, through the rushes of a swampy place, and broke out into a meadow. Something was standing in the distance. No, it was only a tree. He sniffed around and turned toward the tree again.

And then the tree turned toward *him.*

It stood tall and thin, with branches coming out of its head, high like a crown. Its arms were gangly and spindly, longer and more out of proportion than normal human arms and ended in long branch-like fingers. Its mouth and eyes were like knots or gnarled hollows in the bark. *That shit is scary*, he thought. And then, *How am I going to bite a tree? I could pee on it…*

It raised its knee with difficulty as if pulling its leg from the ground. And as it took another step, it did the same thing, like it took root every time it made a step. That gave Jeff an idea.

He charged forward and landed hard on its trunk/body. It teetered but didn't quite fall. It frowned its barky face and pulled hard to straighten. Jeff ran back as far as he could and charged again. He landed square on it again, and this time it fell over.

If a tree monster falls in the woods and only a werewolf is there, does it crap its pants? Jeff chuckled in his head. That seemed to have done the trick. It flailed on the ground like a turtle on its back. It might even have been starting to take root. He was about to approach and make sure it was down until a patrol could take care of it, when it suddenly erupted into a brilliance of light and stars.

Jeff faltered and flipped his body away, dropping to the ground with a yip. He looked behind him for some wand-wielding Wiccan, but there was no one there. The sparks fizzed and flitted, and the creature suddenly vanished. *What?* He trotted along the meadow, first one way and then the other. He even ventured to the place it had lain. The grass was bent but it was definitely gone. What could that mean?

Oh no. Did it mean…was it because…? His heart gave a lurch and he raised his head, ears twitching as they listened, nose sniffing the air. He galloped up the incline and through the woods. He ran harder and faster than he'd ever run before. He couldn't think, didn't want to. He burst through the dark woods and hit the highway almost ramming into the Interceptor. It skidded to a stop and spun the wrong way round, but he didn't wait. He kept going until he made it to Lyndon Road. Her shop was ahead. He pounded along the asphalt until he arrived to the front door, lit by the waning sun. Morphing as he reached for the door handle, he threw it open and stood naked in the doorway.

"The creatures…"

Doc looked up mournfully. "I've heard reports from all the patrols, from Doug, from Sheriff Ed. All the creatures. They seemed to have… disappeared in a shower of sparks. Every one of them. Even those in the jars. They've vanished."

"Does that mean…"

He nodded. "I think it means…the Booke of the Hidden is closed again or…destroyed."

"Kylie…" Jeff whispered. He threw back his head and howled.

CHAPTER TWENTY-EIGHT

MOVE IT, KYLIE. I just couldn't run as fast, and Erasmus realized it and scooped me up. I hated feeling like a damsel in distress, but I had to consider that this was the most expedient way. And I'd much rather Erasmus held me than Shabiri, who would probably have thrown me over her shoulder in a fireman's carry.

It was the Hound of Hell, Cerberus. He was back, probably egged on by Satan. Maybe these guys could outrun him, maybe they couldn't. I sure wish I had my crossbow. Wait!

"Shabiri, do you still have my spear?"

"Spear? What spear?"

"The Spear of Mortal Pain. You had it last."

"Did I?"

Erasmus gave her a sharp glance. "Dammit, Shabiri! Do you have it or not?"

"Everyone is so touchy." She pulled it out of some miraculous pocket of her tight catsuit and telescoped it out. "And it isn't *your* spear. I'm the one who got it for Dougie. So by rights it's really mine—"

"Either use it," I screamed, "or give it to me and *I'll* use it!"

"It was all 'thank yous' an hour ago and now it's all demands and threats." She flew up in the air, spreading her shoulders like

264

wings. Despite her bitching, she came down over the hound's back and plunged the spear deep.

Cerberus' three heads all howled and stuttered to a stop. The dog whipped its snaky tail around, trying to dislodge the spear, but couldn't quite reach it. Finally, he rolled over, howling more as the spear dug deeper. But after a lot of rolling the spear fell out. Cerberus shook itself, zeroed in on us, and continued to run after.

"That was a good idea while it lasted," I said as Erasmus ran faster. "Where's the damn border to this place?"

"It's not far. Just over that hill." He gestured with his chin to the distant ash-gray hills.

But what he didn't say was that even though we'd turned on the speed, we weren't going to outrun the massive three-headed dog behind us.

"We're just going to have to take a chance and fly," I said.

Erasmus looked at me, then glanced toward Shabiri. She looked back as the dog gained on us. She gave a quick nod, and leapt into the sky, her body widening and flattening into that manta ray shape again. Erasmus did the same. Almost immediately, something large came up over the hills we were heading for, with huge bat wings that reminded me of Baphomet.

"What is that?"

"What we were trying to avoid encountering," he said.

It had a huge lower jaw like a pelican which hung open, waiting to scoop things out of the air.

"Sh-shabiri!" I cried. "The spear!"

"I seem to have left it behind in that infernal dog."

"What?"

"I *can* blast things, you know. So can your boyfriend if he didn't have his hands busy."

"Then you'd better start blasting *that*!"

She wound her arm back, like a pitcher on the mound. A ball of lightning coalesced and shot forward. When it hit the big-jawed creature, the ball exploded. The creature faltered its flapping, even lost a little altitude, but it recovered quickly and headed for us again.

"Shabiri!" I warned.

"I see it very clearly, darling," she said between gritted teeth. She fisted her hands and her whole body began to glow red.

"What's she doing?" I asked Erasmus.

"No idea," was his casual reply, as if a great mouth monster wasn't barreling down on us.

Abruptly, she streaked forward with a huge amount of force and crashed right into the beast vanishing into its bulbous flesh. This time, she managed to knock it out of the sky. They both spiraled downward. I watched in horror and kept looking at Erasmus.

"Aren't you going to do anything?"

"Why?"

"Because she's in danger."

"Is she?"

"Well, I don't know. She just disappeared into that guy's body like it was Jell-O."

The creature flapped weakly but continued to fall, turning on its back. Finally, it splatted spectacularly on the red earth below. We continued flying onward.

"Erasmus!"

He sighed with impatience. "Kylie, this is the Netherworld. Things happen here. And no one mourns."

I couldn't believe it. After all we'd just been through, all that Shabiri helped us do, this is how he acted? *He's a demon, Kylie. This is what you signed up for.*

"We have to go back and see if she's all right?"

His glare was noteworthy. "No, we don't."

"Yes, we do. Erasmus, we don't let our friends down."

His brows were thoroughly furrowed as he continued to glare...until they rose and he threw back his head and laughed.

I hit his chest with my fist. "Erasmus!"

"Shabiri, will you please materialize before she beats me to death?"

There was a pop and Shabiri was suddenly there, flying beside us. "Am I really your bestest friend?" She batted her eyes.

"The two of you! A demon's sense of humor, huh? I'd throw something sharp at the both of you if I could."

"Spirited," she said, "isn't she?"

"Can we fly the rest of the way?" I asked, ignoring them.

"I think we had better," said Shabiri, scanning the plains below. "I'm seeing more of Lord Satan's welcoming party."

I turned to where she was looking. An army of what looked like trolls were marching across the savannas and kicking up a cloud of red dust.

"That...doesn't look good." I held tighter to Erasmus.

He spared them a look too. "No, it doesn't." He and Shabiri exchanged a silent commiseration.

"The faster we can get to the exit point, the better," he said.

He seemed to turn on the speed again, but over his shoulder a swarm of something was following us in the air.

"One measly human can sure cause trouble," I muttered. "I hate to tell you this..."

"I smell them," said Erasmus. "More gargoyles. Unfortunately, they didn't all fall into my trap as expected. They aren't the brightest of creatures."

I stared up at him. "Are we going to make it?"

He looked down at me with a determination I hadn't seen in his eyes before. "If I have anything to say about it, we will."

He poured on the speed. I could see how much of an extra burden it was for him to carry me. I looked down at the dead book crushed between us. For once, I was actually regretting that it didn't have any power. I knew I could have summoned something to keep them back.

What was I thinking? Of course I didn't want the book back. *Get a grip, Kylie.* And then I *did* grip because Erasmus was making all these acrobatic turns.

I looked around. Even more creatures were showing up.

Those dragon raptors. Looked like Satan was pulling out all the stops. Jeesh, what a crybaby. He got *most* of a soul.

"As soon as we pass over those hills, we'll have to descend," yelled Erasmus over the rush of the wind. "Be ready with the book. You won't be able to pass through without it."

And just that moment, I almost dropped it. I clung on to the book with one hand, and Erasmus with the other. His arms tightened around me. "I haven't come all this way to let you fall now."

Scant relief with armies coming after us.

I watched carefully as the ridge passed below us. As soon as we flew over to the darker side, the demons began to descend. The wind blew my hair back, and I gazed down to the rough terrain below. Erasmus and Shabiri landed at a run and as their bodies morphed back to normal, they kept running. I could see the place. I hadn't noticed it when I arrived, but I could tell that this was it—a dark, shimmering gash in the rock face. I could see how beasties and demons could pass through it. Why couldn't I?

I tried to resettle myself and suddenly the book slipped from my bloodless grasp. I had been holding it so tight I hadn't noticed when my grip had gone numb. "Oh shit! Erasmus! The book!"

He looked back, about to spin around when Shabiri dove after it, scooping it from the dirt. She came up beside us. "And to think I wanted this old thing."

"For Doug," supplied Erasmus.

Shabiri and I exchanged a loaded look.

"That's right, darling. For Doug."

Poor, clueless Erasmus.

We made it to the deep bruise in the hillside. "Give Kylie the book, Shabiri."

"Hmm," she said, looking it over. "It can't do what it did before, but like you said, it *is* still a key."

"Shabiri," he growled.

She looked at me then. "You offered anything if I would help."

"Shabiri." I was so disheartened. I thought she'd changed. Even a little. "I can't get back without it."

"And once you go back, it will cease to be a key. But there are some in this world who would pay a handsome price to crossover. There are demons who can't, you know."

Erasmus was full-on growling now. "Shabiri! Give me the damn book or I'll take it!"

She swiveled and held it away from him. "I'd like to see you try."

"Please, Shabiri," I said. "I know I promised you. I'll find something else."

She looked me up and down with a sneer. Had it all been an act? Everything she said, every secret she spilled?

A bark and a growl. Cerberus stood on the top of the hill and howled when he saw us. And then he started to trot downward.

"Shit," said Shabiri. "You know, this just isn't fun anymore." She shoved the book into my hands. I stood there, immobilized. "Well?" she said, frustration and maybe something else I couldn't identify written on her face. "Go! I'll hold it off."

"But…" I watched as the angry three-headed beast barreled toward us. "You can blast him, right?"

"He's a hell hound," said Erasmus. "She can't."

"But you can stab him with a spear?"

"And he didn't die, did he?" she snarked. "You can't kill a hell hound. You can only delay it, and I can't use my powers against it. He's Lord Satan's own."

"Come on, Kylie," said Erasmus, grabbing my arm to lead me away toward the shimmering exit.

"Wait. We can't just leave her."

"Beelze's tail! I'm beginning to wonder about all this friendship you keep spouting. It's liable to get us all killed."

"And while you chatter about it," said Shabiri, "the beast closes in. Honestly. Can't someone tell a tale about how brave *I* was for a change?"

A hot lump formed in my throat. "Shabiri…"

"Will you run already? I don't fancy people *watching* me get torn to shreds."

I didn't know what to do. She started to run toward Cerberus to distract him, giving us precious time to jump through the gateway, but I just couldn't leave her.

I started toward her.

"Kylie!" Erasmus yelled with the intensity of all his emotions rolled into one.

I looked back at him. "How can we leave her?"

He glanced toward the gateway, glanced at Shabiri and sighed. "Oh hell." He ran forward ahead of me.

Cerberus was almost on Shabiri. She'd picked up a big branch on her way there with every intention of giving at least one head a smack, when out of the sky, there was a streak of gray. She was suddenly scooped up from the ground. She and her rescuer shot forward back toward the gateway.

Erasmus was right there when they landed. "Focalor!"

"It was such a good story; I had to see how it ended. Are you all going through the gateway?" He looked back as Cerberus galloped forward. "You'd better hurry."

"Thank you, old friend," said Erasmus, patting his shoulder.

"Thanks, Focalor," said Shabiri. "But you absolutely spoiled my heroic ending."

"Oh, well. I can always tell it as if you'd died. It would still make a good tale."

"Beware, Focalor," said Erasmus, tugging me toward the shimmering gate. "There is an army of trolls and several gargoyles heading this way."

"I shall be gone before they arrive. As for this beast…" He flew up and began haranguing Cerberus just above the snapping jaws. He put a hand to his mouth and shouted to us, "Get going!"

"Will he be all right?" I asked.

Erasmus tugged me hard toward the shimmer without another word. I held the book tight to my chest and closed my eyes. When we passed through, it was worse than the first time.

As if thousands more tiny ants stinging and biting me and tearing apart my every molecule. My skin, my nerves were on fire, burning down to my muscle and bones. I screamed and screamed until I was being shaken and someone was yelling at me.

"I slapped her the last time to make her stop," I heard vaguely.

"Kylie! Kylie, you're safe! You're home." It was Erasmus' voice and I opened my eyes. "Oh my God." It was the cold woods of Maine by moonlight, near Hansen Mills, where the ley lines crossed. I somehow didn't believe we could ever get back.

"We did it." I hugged him and kissed him. Then I turned to Shabiri. She looked startled and backed away from me, but I managed to grab her anyway and hug her tight. "Thank you, Shabiri. You are the second bravest person I know."

Stiffly she accepted my embrace but looked all kinds of relieved when I let her go. "The *second* bravest? Can't I be the first?"

"Nope. Sorry. That title belongs to Erasmus." I gave him a warm, contented smile.

We took one step down from the precarious rock ledge and were almost run over by a herd of deer.

"What are *they* running from?" I wondered aloud. But then I looked up.

Baphomet was strafing the woods and setting them on fire.

CHAPTER TWENTY-NINE

I LOOKED DOWN at the book. I had nothing. I didn't have the power of the book, I didn't have the Spear of Mortal Pain, and I didn't even have my chthonic crossbow. I turned to Erasmus. "Take me back to my place."

He clutched my arms and the dark coldness of transportation gripped me until all three of us appeared, rather dramatically, in the middle of my shop…surrounded by my astonished coven, the Ordo, and some new recruits.

Everyone froze, mouths hung open, eyes wide.

"Hi, everyone. Did you miss me?"

"Kylie!" screamed Jolene and launched herself into my arms. I embraced her with one arm, still holding the book.

"It's okay. I'm back."

She sobbed on me, and then Nick put an arm around the two of us, and then Seraphina came up and did the same. I looked past them to Doc. He had tears in his eyes and was shaking his head. "I'll be gosh-darned," he kept saying.

I shuffled forward, loosening my coven hug, to gaze at Doc. Even Jolene stepped back, wiping her eyes.

"How in tarnation did you ever do it?" he said, voice shaky.

And then Seraphina looked to Erasmus. Before he could

escape, she grabbed him into a hug and kissed his cheek, leaving a big purple blob of lipstick there. When she let him go, he hung back, trying to disappear into the shadows, but the auxiliary Wiccans wouldn't let him, all vying with each other to shake his hand.

He looked absolutely miserable and I couldn't stop smiling.

When I turned my head, I saw Ed. He was blinking away tears. I offered him a warm smile. But when he noticed Shabiri, his whole demeanor changed. He stalked right up to her, took her in his arms, and kissed her. She struggled for only a moment before succumbing. Maybe she'd be getting over Erasmus in no time.

"How the hell did you do it, babygirl?" Jeff embraced me, and I couldn't help but inhale a whiff of what smelled like...wet dog.

"As always, I had a lot of help."

Doc was stepping forward to take my hands. "But how *did* you do it, Kylie? Last we saw of you and Mister—dang it, I'm calling you 'Erasmus' from now on, young man."

"I am hardly young or a man," he said from the shadows. He had managed to shake off his admirers.

"I don't care. I never should have let you talk me into doing that spell for you. I'm so sorry."

He seemed puzzled by Doc's remorse. "Don't be. It was the means by which we bargained with Lord Satan."

"I don't understand."

"Look, we'll give you all the explanations you want later," I said urgently, "but Baphomet is on his way and he's setting the forests around Hansen Mills on fire."

The auxiliary Wiccans burst into murmuring. I knew some of them were from there.

"And we'll deal with him when he comes," said the last voice I wanted to hear.

I whirled. Ruth Russell...wearing cargo fatigues, a trooper sweater, and sporting a...sword?

"You've had quite an adventure," she said, hand on the hilt of the sword, hanging in its scabbard on her belt.

I turned to anyone who would listen. "What the hell is *she* doing here?"

"Mrs. Russell is okay," said Jolene. "You should have seen her use that sword on a lindworm. It was very Bayonetta."

"Since when?" I said, glaring at *Bayonetta*.

"Since she showed up expecting to be the Chosen Host," said Doc. "Kylie, don't you remember? No one could recall your grandfather ever having lived here. And the Stranges had been wiped out of the memory of even people who looked at the archives. Your grandpa had used a very powerful forget-me spell."

Seraphina stepped in. "And she didn't know who you were. Only that odd things were happening around you. It wasn't until you reminded her of your grandfather that she remembered she even knew Robert Strange."

"So what?" I couldn't believe everyone was falling all over themselves to defend her. "What about all the stuff she supposedly knew about? What about Dan Parker?"

"Yes," said Ruth. "What *about* Dan Parker?"

"He's dead. And you killed him in a summoning ritual."

"No, she didn't."

I turned. I couldn't believe Jeff of all people was saying this to me. "Oh yeah? And what do *you* know about it?"

"When I wolfed, I didn't get a sense of evil from her. Because believe me, when I'm wolfed, I can tell something's off."

Well damn. That was a whole lot of corroboration. I turned to Ruth. "Okay. I guess I'm wrong. I'm sorry."

"I'm sorry too. I thought a lot of bad things about you until I figured out who you were."

We seemed stuck and just stared at one another. Until I put my hand out to shake. She took it. "All fair and square...cos?"

She winced a little. "Don't call me that." Old habits die hard, Ruth.

"Okay then," I said, trying to put aside my own prejudices.

"If it wasn't Ruth, then who was it? Someone paid the Ordo to start summoning and someone ritually killed Dan Parker to summon a demon assassin to get me."

No one could offer any suggestions.

"A lot of folks in town aren't fans of you," offered Ed, who still had his arm around Shabiri. And she didn't seem to mind one bit.

"Yeah, but if they don't like witchcraft, I don't think they'd indulge in their own summoning. Doug, how much cash did they send you?"

"A lot. Ten thousand bucks."

"Whoa. So someone with money. Ruth, among your cadre of friends…"

"There is absolutely no one I suspect. No one even remotely interested in the occult that I can tell. No one side-stepping the mandala on my porch. Except for your Mr. Dark there."

Erasmus coolly acknowledged her with a nod.

"Haven't we got bigger fish to fry?" asked Nick. "Isn't Baphomet on his way?"

"Yeah. And the book…" I dropped it onto the table with a slam. "…is dead. Its last act was to get me out of the Netherworld. I'm not a Chosen Host anymore, Erasmus isn't tied to it, and Baphomet can't get it. Oh! What about the rift or vortex-thingy? We have to close that—" I made a rush to the door, but Doc stopped me.

"Already taken care of. It's done."

"Oh. You've been busy."

He smiled with pride. I glanced to where the auxiliary Wiccans were huddled together. Mostly the teenagers who had stood by Jolene and Nick. Some I recognized from when they defended by shop from Baphomet. There was about a dozen of them. "So then, Baphomet is looking for something that doesn't exist anymore. Do you think he knows that?"

Something slammed hard to my roof, making the rafters shake. "I thought there were wards."

"Oh no," said Doc. "Jolene, get out the scryer."

The auxiliary Wiccans stepped aside for Jolene. She grabbed her Hello Kitty skull bag and took out the stick with the crystal attached. She shoved it into my face. But nothing happened. She pushed it toward Doc, toward Nick, toward Seraphina…only a faint glow. The magic wasn't gone, but it had returned to whatever level it had been before. The book had enhanced the magic while it was alive; there was nothing but their own skills to rely on now.

"What about our enchanted bullets?" asked Ed.

His what now?

Doc pursed his lips in thought. "Now that, I don't know. We infused magic into an inanimate object. I believe it would still work. But…I'm not sure. And as for the wards, they *should* hold. The house, too, is an inanimate object."

Ed got out his gun. "Well, no time like the present to find out."

George took out his weapon as well and Nick hurried forward to grab his arm. "Be careful, okay?"

"I'll do my best. Citizen." He smiled, mustache and all. I took that to be some kind of game they played. Made a note not to ask.

There was something I was missing. The book was alive once and now was an inanimate object. And things, not people, could retain magic. "Is the chthonic crossbow still here?"

I was shocked when I heard it coming toward me, and I didn't have those Chosen Host skills anymore to catch it. The auxiliary Wiccans dove out of the way when it cleared the staircase. I chickened out at the last minute when it got near and ducked. It smashed into some teapots on a shelf and clattered to the floor. Sheepishly, I went to retrieve it. "Sorry, old buddy," I said as I gingerly picked it up. I blinked for a mere fraction of a second and it had armed itself. "Okay, you're still working. But I doubt this will kill a god."

Ruth unsheathed her sword and it glowed.

"Cool," I said. "A magical object?"

"It's called the 'Answerer.' A legendary Irish sword. It might slay a god."

"Isn't it amazing what you can get on the internet these days?"

She gave me a searing look.

Just for old time's sake—and maybe to shove it in Baphy's face—I grabbed the book and tucked it under my arm.

I turned to the teens, who had decidedly confused looks on their faces. "You guys, just…hang here. Stay safe." I looked to Ed, George, and Ruth and gave the go ahead.

We four…no, make that six with Erasmus and Shabiri…no, now eight because Jeff and Nick had wolfed—walked outside to meet our doom. Wouldn't it be a stupid trick of fate if I had survived the Netherworld only to die here in Moody Bog? I didn't want to think about it. I didn't want it to happen to any of us.

The sky was bright from the fires in the distance where Hansen Mills used to be. I hoped there would be a chance to rebuild it. I know Ed and George should have been over there, but they sensed, as did we all, that this was more important. We had to subdue Baphomet somehow or there would never be any peace in Moody Bog or anywhere else. I guessed this was the final showdown. Gee, I kind of hoped it would have been with Satan…and there again, a sentence I never thought I'd say.

Something cleared the trees. Something gigantic. It blocked the moonlight for a moment before he landed, goat feet and all, on good-old, now scarred Lyndon Road.

I shivered. I had forgotten to put on a coat. I'd left mine in the Netherworld. But with the book under my arm and the crossbow tucked at my side, I stepped forward.

"Kylie Strange," he said in that imperious voice. "I—"

"Honestly, blah, blah, blah! Did you go to the villain school of villainy talk? What's with all the speeches? I know you want the book, I know you want to be worshipped, I know you want your fellow gods and goddess to take over my world. Anything else?"

He scowled. "Yes. I want your head."

"You want an awful lot. But hey. Here's something for you." I tossed the book toward him and it landed on the asphalt beneath him.

Bless his little goat eyes. They lit up. Reaching down for it, he grasped it in his clawed hands and lifted it up in triumph. He used a claw to open the book and frowned. "What's wrong with it?"

"No more power. It got all used up. I'm the last Chosen Host there will ever be."

He tossed the book back at me. I stepped out of the way just in time as it landed.

"You lie! Nothing can destroy the book!"

"Satan can. I took it to him and he destroyed it for me."

"Lord Satan?" He took a step back. "*He* destroyed it? How can this be?"

"Because I asked him pretty please."

"What did you give him in return?"

"A year's supply of beef jerky. No! What do you think, goat head? A soul."

"But…you live."

"Not *my* soul. *His* soul." I pointed to Erasmus.

"He is a demon. He has no soul."

"Well he doesn't *now*. He was human for a little bit. And then we bargained with his soul."

"But…he's a demon! You lie!"

"No. He was human and I waited till he was just about out of soul and then I gave him his amulet back."

Ed gasped. He was staring at me with rounded eyes.

Baphomet was still puzzled and appeared uncomfortable as he took another step back. "You…*tricked* Lord Satan?"

"Yeah, and lived." I raised the crossbow. "So…what do you think I can do to you?"

His weird goat eyes scanned my posse: two demons, two werewolves, two cops, one sword wielding witch, and one *former* Chosen Host. Maybe the odds were against him this time.

But as he measured us, his eyes narrowed. "There is no magic in you. You cannot defeat me."

"But we *are* gonna try." I fired. My aim wasn't that bad, even without the Chosen Host skills. It hit him dead center. He cried out with that goat/cow sound, but no light emanated from him. It slowly began to occur to me that there was nowhere for him to go. The rift was closed and so was the book. Unless he operated like a demon—and I was pretty sure he didn't because he had to be summoned—he was trapped here. That wasn't good for us.

I cast a glance at Ruth. She was ready with that gleaming sword. It was weird seeing her in anything but her self-important skirt/jacket combos, but even in her combat fatigues, she still wore that damned necklace like a badge of honor or something. She must have thought of me like I thought of her; reckless, stuck-up, dangerous—

Hold on a second.

"Ruth, what's the inscription in that locket again?"

"What? At a time like this?"

"What did I tell you it said?"

She puffed a breath, keeping half an eye on Baphomet. "'*Within the hurasu gates, the enemies of man shall fast remain.*'"

I motioned with my crossbow—that had armed again— toward Baphomet. "He looks like an enemy of man to me."

"But what does it mean?"

"Doc said that 'hurasu' is Babylonian for 'gold'. The locket is gold. The *locket* is the *hurasu* gate!"

She was still staring at me as if I'd lost my mind. And yeah, that was a possibility these days. I knelt, grabbed the book, and thrust it toward her necklace. When they connected, the little secret slot opened. The book still worked.

And then the sky lit up with fire all around us. At first, I thought it was the forest, ablaze thanks to Baphy. But the fire came from around Baphomet himself.

He was more than puzzled now. He was terrified. He swiveled his big goat head all around, looking at the strange magical fire shooting up around him. "What's happening? What are you doing?"

The fire encircled him and then converged, encasing him in flames. But it didn't seem to be consuming him, or hurting him. But it definitely trapped him.

Ruth's locket was rising up on its chain as if it were in zero gravity. Rising up toward Baphomet.

The flames were like a cage and he began to struggle. "No! NO!" The flames started to shrink and took Baphomet with them. He shrank and shrank until he and the fire were the size of a single candle flame. And then, all of a sudden, that flame shot toward the locket, entered it, and slammed the little slider shut.

The necklace fell to Ruth's chest while we all looked around astonished.

"Did that just happen?" asked Nick, morphing back in to a guy. A *naked* guy.

Slowly, everyone converged on Ruth, even the extra Wiccans, warily coming out the door. She quickly whipped the necklace off her neck and held it out, staring at it. "It doesn't feel any heavier," she said quietly.

Doc was suddenly beside her, and so was the rest of the coven. "By Godfrey," he whispered. "May I?" He reached for the locket and Ruth was happy to give it to him. He examined it from all angles. "I think he is well and truly in there. For good. Unless this touches the Booke of the Hidden again."

I tossed the book against my door as Doc turned the necklace, catching glints of moonlight on it. "It's a prison now."

"Can it be returned to the Netherworld?" I asked.

Erasmus shook his head. "No. Because of the presence of the god, it cannot be taken through."

"Then…what do we do with it?" asked Jolene.

I shrugged. "I'd drop it in the middle of the ocean."

Erasmus took the necklace from Doc. "Is that the consensus?" He looked to each face.

"I'm planning on burning the book," I said. "So anything that will keep him imprisoned is fine with me."

Erasmus studied it, brows gnarled over his eyes. "*I* was imprisoned by the book."

"But your intent wasn't evil," I said before anyone could say anything. But they all still looked at me doubtfully. "It wasn't! Yeah, he eats souls but that wasn't his fault." I turned back to Erasmus. "You only knew this life. Baphomet had his chance and he didn't take it."

He glanced at me. It seemed as if my opinion was the only one that mattered. But I wanted to make certain that it was the right choice, so I turned to Doc. "Well? Should it go to the bottom of the ocean?"

Doc nodded gravely. "This isn't a decision we make lightly. This is an intelligent being, but he won't live *with* us. His only desire is to control. For the sake of my species, I say yes."

Erasmus smiled grimly. "I shall return momentarily." He vanished, and seconds later he was back, soaking wet. He whipped his hair back, sending a shower of sea water all over Jeff who had also morphed back into a naked man. "I had to make certain it wouldn't float or be found by adventurers," said Erasmus. "I placed it in the bottom in a great underwater canyon."

"Do you mean…the Mariana Trench?" I asked.

He shrugged. Steam puffed off of him and his leather duster. "Has it a name, now?"

"In the *Pacific* Ocean?"

"Do you think there are limitations to my transport?"

That was another heady thing to think about.

"Well, that's that!" said Doc.

A car pulled up and we all stepped back. Jeff and Nick excused themselves, running between the teen Wiccans, and ducked inside the shop, no doubt searching for their clothes. When the headlights switched off, Reverend Howard climbed out.

"What a relief! You all look like you're all right."

"It was touch and go there," I admitted, looking to my comrades, "but we're fine."

"And Mrs. Russell. What an…unusual outfit you've got on."

"Do you like it? I'm thinking of wearing it more often."

He took measure of her—and the sword in its scabbard—before facing the rest of us. "I saw this strange light over here and I worried some of our more reckless citizens were causing a ruckus."

Ed holstered his gun and adjusted his belt. George followed suit. "We took care of those troublemakers earlier," he said in his best officious voice.

"No one got hurt, I hope. It's been a crazy few days here, I don't mind saying. I've got a lot of questions." He walked around us, nodding to each coven member, to the teens. And then he spotted the book in the doorway. He bent down to pick it up. "Booke of the Hidden? What's this?"

"It's the seat of all our troubles," I said.

He opened the cover, and I was relieved not to feel any sense of ownership or jealousy. It was dead to me, just like it was supposed to be.

"It's blank," he said, thoughtfully. "How does it work?"

I scoffed. "What do you mean?"

"How do you make it work?"

"It doesn't, thank goodness."

"But, uh, how can my Lord Baphomet use it, then, if it doesn't work anymore?"

CHAPTER THIRTY

I DON'T THINK anyone moved. We just stood there with dumb expressions on our faces.

Reverend Howard turned toward Shabiri. "Let me guess. I bet you're the demon our Ordo friends summoned."

"And who the hell are you?" she said, hand at her hip.

"Me? Oh, I'm the quiet and trusted pastor of the local church. Just diligently giving my sermons every Sunday to the slack-jawed hicks in this dirty, little town. For eight years I've been preaching to them to love thy neighbor, and do you know what I discovered after eight years? Not a thing I do makes one bit of difference. Not one single thing."

Doc, as flabbergasted as the rest of us, was amazingly able to speak. "But…Howard. Your kindness and gentle words never failed to—"

"Oh shut up, Fred," said the pastor. "You're the biggest hypocrite in this village."

"I beg your pardon!"

"All that down-home advice and nodding your head sagely… and what did *you* do? You *left* the church. You left it for all this banal oil and herb pagan 'faith'…." He gave the last word air quotes. "But you know what? *I* delved deeper. I found out what you couldn't. I discovered ancient writings about the gods, about Baphomet and how to summon demons. I became a pretty darned good mage myself. *Better* than pretty darned good."

Doug looked him up and down with disgust. "*You* sent us that money."

"I saw how you and your biker gang toyed with the occult, saw you stumbling around. As a matter of fact, your logo gave me the idea to summon Baphomet. I figured I'd get *you* rubes to summon him in case things went south…like they had."

"Where did you get $10,000?"

"Why do you think the church roof still leaks? It's called embezzlement, idiot."

"Howard…" said Doc incredulously.

"Didn't I tell you to shut up, Fred?" The Reverend waved his hand, and Doc took several steps back, putting a hand to his throat, his mouth. He couldn't seem to open it, couldn't speak.

"What did you do to him?" I demanded.

He turned sharply to me and from the look on his face, I took a step back. "And you! You were supposed to be dead. I summoned Andras to kill you. What happened to *him*?"

Ed took out his gun. "You killed Dan Parker."

"Of *course,* I did! And put that sigil in the church hall closet," he said to me. "What a sorry sonofabitch Dan was. Believe me, wasting money on his salary was more of a crime than I ever committed. What a pathetic use of humanity. Well, he finally proved himself useful in the end. He never saw it coming. It was a good summoning. Messy, though."

"I can't believe this," said Seraphina.

He turned to her with a sneer. "Believe it. I am so sick of this stupid village and Hansen Mills. Hansen Mills! What did they ever do besides produce drunks and juvenile delinquents? I ministered to every *one* of their damn families, and all of my suggestions and counseling fell on dumb, meth-addled ears."

This was insane. "But…why summon Baphomet?" I asked. "He was killing everyone."

"Precisely! And when I offer him the one thing he craves, he'll shower me with all that I desire. Except..." He still had the book in his hands and looked at it. "You killed it. He really wanted this."

"Yeah," I said. "And you know what? Old Baphy is also out of commission. He's gone. Dead and gone."

He stared at the book and then up at me. "You're lying."

"Nope. He's gone. He's never coming back. Everything you did was an utter waste."

"Enough of this," said Ed. He grabbed his handcuffs from his belt. "You're under arrest for the murder of Dan Parker and conspiracy to murder Kylie Strange."

Howard didn't even turn toward him when he waved his hand. Ed froze, couldn't move at all.

"Hey!" said Shabiri. "I was getting to like him. What did you do?"

"Something I should have done to everyone in this town from day one. Did I forget to mention I was a *mage*?"

Doc still couldn't utter a sound and Ed was frozen.

But Howard went on, venting. "So no book of power and no Baphomet, eh? That puts a damper on my plans. But no matter. I can summon another god. Maybe a bigger, better one."

Erasmus stepped forward. "You cannot be allowed to summon more gods and demons."

Howard chuckled. "Right. And why should I listen to you, Mr. *Dark*, as if that's a real name." He waved his hand at Erasmus and he froze.

I gave a cry and lunged toward him.

But he hadn't frozen. He was just very still, until he moved even closer to Howard. "I'm hungry," he growled.

Howard scoffed. "So go get a burger. And why didn't you freeze?" He waved his hand again, but Erasmus didn't oblige. He directed his glance at me.

"Kylie...I'm hungry."

Erasmus was hungry. And I knew what he meant. "Erasmus,"

I said breathlessly, "I…I don't think—"

Jeff suddenly morphed into a werewolf again and leaped forward, teeth bared…only for Howard to wave his hand freezing *him*. Jeff fell to the ground with a hard crunch.

The teens cringed in a group by the door. Jolene hunkered with them.

"Boy, you people are getting more tiresome by the second. It took me a while to research what it was Kylie had there. How the hell did *you* kill the book?"

I was getting scared. At least Erasmus wasn't affected, but how long could he hold out? "I don't care to share that intel with *you*."

"Really? I can freeze your friends one by one." He swept his glance over the teens and they shrunk back. The girl Jessica Marie began to cry. He turned from them and set his glare on Seraphina. "Like this." He waved his hand and Seraphina froze. "And then leave them outside until the snow drifts up around their necks and watch them die. We could do that…or you can tell me what I want to know."

I looked at the frightened faces of my friends, saw George getting ready to do something heroic and maybe get killed. Saw Nick getting ready to do the same thing. I was horrified that this man, someone that *everyone* in this village trusted, was a hidden evil mastermind who had murdered and would continue to do so if not stopped.

I glanced at Erasmus. There wasn't any choice. "If you're hungry…" I took a deep breath and gritted my teeth. "Then…*eat.*"

He smiled and kept on smiling wider and wider until his smile was wider than his ears, and his teeth, like a shark's, suddenly layered one over the other. He turned to Reverend Howard.

"I'm hungry," he growled with a different voice I had never heard before, and this time, Howard was finally taken aback by the demon's repulsive appearance. Howard frantically waved his hand, yet nothing happened. He backed away but Erasmus kept coming.

"What's he doing? What is he talking about? How come he's not freezing?"

I said nothing. I was horrified that I had given him permission. It would be on my head…as so many other deaths in this village were.

Howard backed against the wall of my shop, trying all sorts of spells and enchantments on the demon, but nothing worked. Erasmus stalked right up to him, opened his now enormous mouth, and covered Howard's entire face.

I couldn't look away. Even with the stifled screams coming from Howard and the terror of his stiffened body. The air around them shimmered. Erasmus fed—his awful, terrifying feast—and Howard slowly fell lax, as if all his energy was seeping out of him. It wasn't like what the succubus had done to that bicyclist up at Falcon's Point. It was something different, something perhaps more horrific. Howard looked much the same, but there was no life left in him. His eyes…his eyes were like a dead fish; blank, open, nothing. When Erasmus released him, he fell back against my shop and slithered to the ground, a husk.

Erasmus closed his eyes and breathed deeply. "I've been hungry for 300 years." He belched and thumped his chest. "Pardon me. I've never had parson before."

He had planned to do that to me as he had done to every Chosen Host who had ever lived.

When he looked at me, he realized that same thing and had the grace to look ashamed. He also had the sense to give me space.

Everyone who had been frozen came back to life. Doc could speak again.

One of the teens began to scream, and it was Jolene who calmed her down.

"Oh goddess," Doc whispered, standing over the stiff body of what had been Reverend Howard Cleveland. "How could we have not known?"

"I was close to him," said Ruth, shaken. "And I never knew."

"We all thought it was you," I said, teeth chattering from cold and from the horrors I had been a witness to. One too many, I thought.

"I may have been an old sour puss," she said, "but I was never evil." Gently, she put her arm around me and I turned in to her. I couldn't seem to stand up anymore and I couldn't speak. Instead, I sobbed. She embraced me and let me cry. It had all been too much. Far, far too much.

Ed looked down at his gun and slipped it back in its holster.

"Let's go inside," said Doc. "Kylie needs to warm herself by the fire."

* * *

WE ALL GATHERED in my shop. I was bundled in a quilt next to the fire on a wooden chair. The fire helped, but my core was cold. It would be a long time till I could forget all the sights I'd seen. Especially Erasmus. That's what he would have done to me. If he hadn't fallen in love with me, that's what I would have been; a gray, shriveled husk. How was it possible to face him again?

Jolene looked around to everyone. "It's done, isn't it? It's all done. No more book, no more Baphomet…and no more Reverend Howard."

"Don't say his name," I said. I was still angry and horrified. I didn't know which was worse. After all, I had given Erasmus permission…

Shabiri seemed to be clinging to Ed, always touching him in some way, either hanging on him, or a hand clutching his sleeve. Maybe she was just beginning to realize what she had and how easily it could have been lost.

I lifted my eyes and searched in the shadows for Erasmus, but he was staying away.

Doc was sitting deep into one of my wingbacks, squeezing his lower lip in thought. Finally, he raised his head. "We have one more important thing to do. We've got to make a decision about these villages. Are we going to let the memory of what transpired linger…or are we going to do our best to eradicate all memories of the last month?"

Jeff paced. "I don't know that it's up to us to make that decision. Seems a little…I don't know. God-like?"

Seraphina had a smudge of soot on her cheek. It didn't look right on her normally flawless appearance. "It's not god-like, Jeff. It's maybe the kindest thing we can do."

"I think we gotta do it," said Jolene. "There's too many unpredictable emotions out there now."

"But how do we explain it?" asked Nick. "The deaths, the destruction?"

"We can always come up with something," said Ed.

"What about…" Nick licked his lips, darting a glance at me. "What about Reverend Howard? How will we explain his disappearance?"

Ed shuffled, looking at his feet. "He said he embezzled the church's books. We'll let it be known that he likely skipped town. I don't think we need to include him among the dead."

"But…" I looked from Ed to George. "What will you do with the…the…?"

"Don't worry, Kylie. We'll take care of it."

Oh God. I dropped my face in my hands. Now Ed was not only going to be faking documents, but dumping a body. Down some old mine shaft or something. And that was my fault, too.

I wiped my face. I was going to have to learn how to deal with this, or there wasn't going to be much left of me.

We sat is silence for a time, until one of the auxiliary Wiccans, Emma, spoke. "I don't want to forget. I like Wicca. I like the magic, even if it won't be quite the same. But…" She sniffed, remarkably holding it together. "My mom, and a lot of her friends…I'm pretty sure they don't want to remember. Some people in town…they saw some really bad things."

Doc appraised her for a long moment. "Then how about this.

Those that don't want to forget can stay in this shop. And those that want to, can stay where they are, outside it, at home."

Everyone seemed to nod and softly agree. Some of the teen Wiccans got up and quietly left. I sure didn't blame them. I thought about it myself. But upon looking around, I was glad to see the Wiccans and the Ordo standing fast. Ruth did too, as well as Ed and George. Many more left.

"Then it's just us," I said. "What do you propose, Doc?"

"Well, your grandpa did a helluva forget-me spell. But I think it had help from the ley lines crossing at his place. Shabiri…"

She looked up. She had a finger hooked with Ed's.

"If you take us to the place where the ley lines cross in Hansen Mills, I think it will be powerful enough to work for this whole dang area."

"Yes," she said. "I should think so. I'll help."

My, my. How times had changed.

The Wiccans set about preparing a big charm pouch. It took a surprisingly short time to create and when it was done, Seraphina asked, "Who's going to take it there?"

"I will," said Doc. "They'll forget there ever were demons and creatures in these villages. They'll forget there ever was a Booke of the Hidden." He gazed at me for a long moment, almost asking me if I wanted to forget too. And I did. I did want to forget. But then…how could I? And what about Erasmus?

"They won't remember the destruction," Doc went on, eyes sweeping past me, "only that we had a devastating forest fire. And they'll only remember the dead as getting in the way of it. Will that suffice?" He looked toward Ed.

Ed and George silently conferred and nodded their heads. I knew they had a lot of details to fake in many coroner's reports.

"All right, then. Shabiri, if you will?" He didn't mention Erasmus' conspicuous absence.

One more auxiliary Wiccan—Jessica Marie—started sobbing, and hurried out the door, running home.

"Is everyone sure, now?" Doc looked around one last time.

Only four auxiliary Wiccans had remained, some of the few that had joined us that first day. "Then let's go, Shabiri."

She took Doc by the arm and they vanished.

I got up and went to the window, clutching the quilt around me. If Erasmus wasn't here, would *he* forget? I worried for only a second. He was probably here, only invisible.

I wondered if we'd know the moment it happened. Would the landscape look different? Would the animals forget? We all waited in tense silence and then were startled when the two returned with a pop.

"Well, that is a most interesting way to travel," said Doc, pleased again with demon transport. "It's all done."

"How do we know it worked?" I asked.

"Well, let's find out." He got out his phone, punched in someone's number, and put it on speaker.

"Moody Bog Hardware," said the voice of Barry Johnson.

"Hi, Barry, this is Doc Boone. How are things going over there?"

"Well, with this forest fire we've been busy beavers, I can tell you. You must be up to your ears in injuries."

"We're doing okay. Everything else all right?"

"It's fair. It was a quiet Halloween, wasn't it?"

"The quietest I can remember. But then again, what with the fires, I know folks didn't let kids go out this year."

"Yeah, that was a shame. Maybe they can put on a post-Halloween shindig for the kids up at the church hall…oh. But that got damaged by the fire, too. Well, maybe the school, then."

"May-*be*. You take care, Barry."

"You, too, Doc."

He clicked it off and glanced at us. "Well, that seems to have done it."

We all sighed in relief.

"There'll be more coordinating to do," said Ed. "It's got to look like a forest fire. All the fire fighters around here should have had their memories adjusted as well. That will make it easier." He swung his Smokey Bear hat up to his head. "Come on, George."

George walked up to Nick, kissed him, and fixed his own Smokey Bear hat. "I'll see you later, Nicky."

"Go get 'em, deputy," said Nick with a weary smile.

They left, and soon the others were gathering their things. "Well, Kylie," said Doc. "It's been one crazy adventure."

"Yeah," was all I could manage.

"Listen, young lady, if there is ever a time you need to talk, you know I'm available. Night or day. You understand?"

I nodded. I suppose he was the best person to play psychiatrist. "I'll be okay."

"You've done more than any human being has ever done, has ever *had* to do. And we're grateful and we won't forget it. Don't think for one moment that it wasn't important and didn't make a difference."

"I know. I just feel…a little guilty, too."

"I think that's quite natural to a moral person. And as I said, you can talk that out with me any time you'd like. I'd, uh, like it if the coven could still meet here, unless you think it's best we don't. We'd understand perfectly if you'd rather we didn't."

"Oh, no. I think I'd really like you all to be here. I think of it as *your* home as much as mine these days. You all are the closest thing to family I've got."

Doc reddened. The others seemed embarrassed too, but in a good way. "Well, that's fine," said Doc. "Doug, you and yours are welcome to join our coven."

Doug glanced at his own posse. "Thanks. I think we'd like that. If it's okay with Kylie."

"There's no way I'd refuse any of you. You don't know how grateful I am for all your help. Really."

Doug patted my shoulder and so did Bob as he passed by. Charise was ducking away, not looking at me, until she stopped, turned, and suddenly hugged me. "I'm sorry," she whispered to my ear and then just as quickly scurried out.

Everyone waved their good-byes. My shop was emptying and

soon there was no one there but me. It was quiet in the shop for the first time in a long while. The crackling of the fire seemed loud and so did the silence.

I turned and there was the book on the table. I hugged the quilt. "What am I going to do with you?"

"You can burn it now," said a dark voice from the shadows.

"Were you there all this time?" I didn't look in his direction, but instead touched the brass lock on the cover of the book.

"Yes." He emerged from the shadows. "I was afraid…you wouldn't love me anymore, seeing what I really was."

My heart broke a little at the pain in his voice. "You idiot demon. Of course I still love you." I dropped the quilt on the chair and approached him. He looked miserable. "It does kind of scare me when…when your mouth…" I took a finger and without touching him, drew a line from his mouth to his ear. "When your mouth gets really wide with all those extra teeth. Is that how you really look…or is this?"

"Both. Both are a part of me. I cannot change that."

"Can you show me, then. I want to see it. Up close."

He had the look of someone caught in a trap. He clearly didn't want to do it now. "Are you certain?"

"Show me." If I couldn't love this or at least understand it in some way, how could I claim to love him?

He stepped back from me. His eyes, always intense, narrowed, and suddenly his face morphed in that sickening way and his mouth widened and widened with all those teeth. God, it was terrifying. I stared, trying to look at it as if studying it like a scientist, with impartiality. But of course, I had seen what he could do with it.

I couldn't help but turn away.

"Kylie," he said softly.

When I turned back, I knew he was probably normal again… and he was. I swallowed. "That's quite a trick."

"It isn't a trick. I am what I am. A demon of the Nether-world, capable of transforming. Capable of…death."

I looked at him, really looked. Yes, he was handsome this way, but in his eyes was such pain. I think he'd finally figured out who he was after all these centuries, finally discovered how trapped he was by *what* he was, and maybe he wasn't happy about it. He was a man without a country. Or worse. Without a future.

I stepped closer again. "I didn't know I was capable of death, and yet I was."

"But you—"

"No, Erasmus. Now is the time for truth. I never thought I was capable of killing. But I killed. Wherever it is those creatures go and in whatever state, I killed them. And not only because I had to. After a while, it was because…I *wanted* to. I wanted them gone. I wanted my friends safe. Now, I wasn't born that way, the way you were, but I learned by necessity. That doesn't make me better than you."

He looked like a kicked puppy. I wanted to make it all better for him.

"You can't change. Of course you can't. And I guess I don't want you to. I get that this *is* you. And I get that this is me now. If I can get used to myself, then I sure as hell can get used to your two natures. Because…all in all, I love *you*. Nothing's going to change that either."

"You do?"

"Yes." I grabbed him and slipped my arms around him, holding him close. His arms quickly encircled me desperately, engulfing me with smokiness and warmth. It was good to feel him again. And I was looking right at his amulet. The gem eyes glowed red.

Gently I withdrew and walked to the fireplace, hugging my arms and keeping myself warm. "So now you're really free. Free from the book. Free from the Powers That Be. You never have to go into that stasis thing again."

He rested his hands behind his back and rocked on his heels thoughtfully. "Yes. It is rather mind-boggling."

"I expect you'll want to travel, see things, go places you could never go before. You're not tied to any one place. You can even go to other worlds with no one telling you what to do or giving you a deadline. I won't hold you back."

"But…" He blinked at me, puzzled. "Why would I ever leave *you*? Oh. I see. My presence can only serve as a reminder of your horrific experiences. Even as you say you…you love me…perhaps it's best I leave so that you can heal."

I turned to him. "Why are you such an idiot?"

"Why do you insist on insulting me? I am trying to do the right thing and I'm not sure what that is!"

"So am I! I'm trying to tell you that you aren't even tied to *me*. So if you wanted to go…*needed* to go…I'd understand."

"But I *am* held here. By you. I don't want to go anywhere without you."

I shook my head, wiping away my tears. Two natures or not, I could never doubt his love for me. "That was the nicest thing anyone's ever said to me," I said quietly. "Okay then. Come here."

"Why?" he said petulantly, folding his arms in front of his chest and clamping them there. "So you can continue to insult me?"

"For the rest of my life."

"You—what?"

"Erasmus." I crept closer to him, taking baby steps so I wouldn't frighten him off. In many ways, he was very much like a child. When I reached him, I laid a gentle hand on his tightly wound arms until they loosened. "You stood by me, even when it was against your very nature. You protected me. You loved me. You tried to sacrifice yourself for me. I'm not going to give you up *now*."

"Oh. But I thought—"

"Like I said. Come here."

The book was in the way, between us. He looked down at it before kneeling to pick it up. "What shall we do with this?"

I shrugged but couldn't avoid flicking a glance at the fire. He nodded, gave the book one more once-over, and tossed it into the flames. It sat there on the firewood in the grate for a second or two and then it began to smolder. I thought it might light up into different colors and smoke, but it had no power left. It was an empty shell.

The leather and parchment soon became engulfed and we both watched it flame, pieces of it curling away, until it was a bright fire, casting light far into the room.

When he turned, he only had eyes for me. He moved in carefully, taking me in his arms with tentative gentleness, as if still asking permission. But when I melted into him, he must have finally figured it out. He kissed me, moving his head to kiss me deeper, taste me. He drew away only a little to speak softly to my lips, kissing me in between his words. "You and I…" *kiss* "…will be together for a long time." Another kiss.

I lifted my face so his lips could kiss my eyebrows, my lids. "Well…as long as a human life, anyway." I was interrupted with more kisses to my mouth. His hands moved over me and I pressed myself against him. "I hope that old ladies can turn you on," I said dreamily, feeling his lips, even a little of his teeth at my temple. "I will be one someday, you know. Wrinkled and gray-haired like Doc."

He nuzzled my lips, then pressed a gentle kiss to the side of my mouth. "Oh, not for a very long time." He pushed a strand of hair out of my face, and gave me that tender look that melted me inside, before he moved on to my neck, sucking on the flesh there and causing tingles over my body.

"Probably sooner than you think," I sighed.

"Probably not," he said to my clavicle. "You see, a human traveling to the Netherworld. It changed you. You will likely live an unusually long life."

I suddenly pushed him back and stared. "What do you mean? How long?"

"Oh, I should think one or two…" He drew me back in and kissed my opened lips "…hundred years. Or so."

"*What?*"

He sighed and though I had pulled back, he wouldn't let me go. His fingers still moved along my hips. "You are changed. You will age slowly. Very slowly."

"Wow. I had no idea. That might be a little…wow." I looked around the shop. "We had better make a damned good go of this, then. We'll need the money."

He drew me in and nuzzled my forehead. "Does that bother you? That you will age more slowly than your friends?"

"I don't know. I guess…maybe I don't quite believe it."

We kissed languidly, like we had all the time in the world. It sounded like we did. But I couldn't help asking, pulling my mouth only inches away enough to talk. "Erasmus, I've been wondering. What about that piece of soul you retained?"

"Gone," he said, still placing pecking kisses to my lips. "As a demon, I don't have a soul."

"Are you sure?"

"Don't worry. I am *all* demon." He ground against me.

I gave up and slid completely into his arms. I reached up and dug my fingers into his hair and tugged, lowering his head so he could kiss me properly, growling deep in his chest. I became suddenly aware that he had transported us to my bedroom.

I smiled and he kissed me, teeth and all. "Are you trying to tell me something?"

It was his turn to smile, rather wickedly I thought. "You once promised me we would break this bed with lovemaking."

I held him tighter. I couldn't relinquish my grin. "I do like to keep my promises."

He might have used a little magic or it was just a good sturdy bed, because for the whole night and part of the next day, we tried our damnedest.

Author's Afterword

THANK YOU SO MUCH for reading this series! It's been a while since I've had so much fun writing characters and their wacky plot. I appreciate all of you for going along for the ride. I hope you enjoyed it as much as I have. Did you know that they will all be audiobooks? Go look for those! But before you go, I hope you sign up for my Booke of the Hidden newsletter so you will have the latest news concerning more paranormal series, including some spin-offs from *this* series.

If you liked this book, please review it. Head on over to BOOKEoftheHIDDEN.com for all sorts of info on any upcoming series, excerpts, my appearances in the real world as well as the virtual.

Remember to keep it spooky. Happy reading!

ACKNOWLEDGMENTS

I'D LIKE TO take the opportunity to thank those who made this series possible. To my agents Joshua Bilmes and Lisa Rodgers, thanks for your patience and for taking the series in hand, gently guiding it forward. Thanks also to Patrick Disselhorst of JABberwocky for doing the heavy lifting of dealing with my whining about the formatting and cover design. And thanks to my stalwart editor Lydia Youngman for being the biggest fangirl ever! Thanks also to the readers who showed up and stuck with it. And very special thanks, as always, goes to my long-suffering husband Craig, who believes in everything I do.

About the Author

Jeri Westerson is the author of the Crispin Guest Medieval Mystery and the Booke of the Hidden series. Her books were finalists for several major mystery awards, including the Agatha, the Shamus, and the Macavity. She lives in Menifee, California.

For more from Jeri, visit BOOKEoftheHIDDEN.com.

Jeri Westerson's **Crispin Guest** *series is available in eBook and Print editions from JABberwocky and Severn House*

FOR NEWS ABOUT JABBERWOCKY BOOKS AND AUTHORS

Sign up for our newsletter*: http://eepurl.com/b84tDz
visit our website: awfulagent.com/ebooks
or follow us on twitter: @awfulagent

THANKS FOR READING!

*We will never sell or give away your email address, nor use it for nefarious purposes. Newsletter sent out quarterly.

Made in the
USA
Monee, IL

15031691R00180